CW00350111

CRIMEWAVE ELEVEN : GHOSTS
CONTENTS

ISSN 1463 1350 ✦ ISBN 978-0-9553683-4-9 ✦ Copyright © 2010 *Crimewave* on behalf of all contributors ✦ Published in the UK by TTA Press, 5 Martins Lane, Witcham, Ely, Cambs CB6 2LB ✦ Further information, discussion forum, online subscriptions and back issues on ttapress.com ✦ Listen to our free biweekly podcast *Transmissions From Beyond* (transmissionsfrombeyond.com) ✦ Subscribe to *Crimewave*: four issues for just £26 UK • £30 EUROPE • £34 ROW, by cheque payable to TTA Press or credit/debit card and sent to the above address or online at the website ✦ Thanks to Peter Tennant for his expert proofreading ✦ Cover art by Ben Baldwin (benbaldwin.co.uk) ✦ Edited and typeset in Warnock Pro by Andy Cox ✦ Printed in the UK by MPG Biddles

DAVE HOING
PLAINVIEW

PART ONE: THE SHOE STORE

Friday, November 28, 1975

The owner of the shop, a local eccentric named Kohlsrud, had liver spots on his hands and nicotine stains on his fingernails. He held the shoehorn in his right hand and cupped it over Leslie's lower calf before slowly sliding the metal down to her heel. His wrist brushed against the smooth and supple contours of her leg. As he guided her foot into the loafer she noticed several scabs on the top of his head. What little hair he had was wiry and longish and white.

"This is a Famolare?" she teased. She knew that the few brands of new shoes Kohlsrud carried were definitely on the low end, but she liked giving the old pervert a hard time. Anyway, anybody could see the sole on this loafer was a poor imitation of Famolare's distinctive wavy pattern.

"Miss," Kohlsrud said, looking up over large black framed glasses, "if you have to ask, then what does it matter?"

He was kneeling right in front of her. Leslie had on a short skirt and unconsciously drew her knees together. "I've got a dance tonight," she said. "I want the best."

Kohlsrud hmphed and pointed toward the door. "New York's that way. Drive east for about two days. When you see the ocean, turn left."

The air was thick with the smells of leather, cardboard, mold, and old floor wax, with subtler hints of rubber and grease. In addition to selling and repairing shoes, Kohlsrud tinkered with bicycles, kind of a running joke in Plainview, an odd combination of shoe and bike fix-it shop.

The front half was reserved for shoes. Rickety wooden shelves were stuffed with boxes of them, some new, most in various states of repair. Kohlsrud had a hammer in his belt, tacks in his front pocket, and holes in his sleeves. "I sell good, sturdy footwear here," he said. "Last you a lot longer than those fancy name brands. Get up, let's see how it fits."

He gently squeezed her foot as she stood, resting his palm against her ankle. Whatever soap or cologne he used smelled like preservative. "Little tight," Leslie said.

"They're made to stretch," he said. "Stick your big toe up." She did, and he used his index finger and thumb to trace its outline through the shoe. He wore a wedding ring, which never ceased to amaze her. His wife was dead now, but whatever possessed her to marry him in the first place? "Perfect," he said. "You want these, then?"

"But they're not Famolares," she pouted.

Kohlsrud rose effortlessly. Despite his frail appearance, he moved with assurance and power. Repairing bikes must keep his muscles strong. He smiled, or leered, or scowled, it was hard to tell. His teeth were stained with nicotine, too. "What do you expect for seven ninety-five?"

Monday, December 1, 1975

"It's spring, and the goat-footed balloonMan whistles far and wee."

Jenny Tanner waited for her classmates to applaud, but they didn't, so she returned to her seat and pretended to dig through her notes. Ms Van Syoc, the English prof, required her students to read the poems out loud before handing in their written analyses. Jenny hated speaking in front of people. She had agreed to type up the entire paper if her assigned partner would do the reading. Unfortunately, her partner, Leslie Frischel, didn't bother to show this morning. Which was typical. Seemed like Jenny's partners never did and she was stuck doing everything.

"Listen to Cummings' wonderful flow of language," Van Syoc said to the class. "But what does the poem *mean*? Who is this mysterious balloonMan?"

No one raised a hand.

Jesus, Jenny thought, *who cares? I ever used grammar and punctuation like that, Van Syoc would give me a big fat F.*

Hills Community College – in a part of the state flat as an old wood floor – was the high school after high school where people sent their kids who were too lazy to get a job and too stupid or poor for a real university. Jenny wasn't lazy or stupid, but the Tanners were not among the town's elite. It was Hills or a lifetime of waitressing at Mom's Diner. Or worse.

Whistles far.

The clock's minute hand clicked one notch closer to dismissal. Jenny looked out the window. The sky was bleak. A cold front out west was about to deliver the season's first snowstorm. This morning a few flakes moistened the glass, but by tonight the whole town would be buried under a foot of snow. The Thanksgiving weekend had been so nice, temperatures in the fifties and a lot of sun. Now this. It was as if the second the calendar flipped to December the weather flipped, too.

The clock ticked and ticked and ticked. "Most critics," Van Syoc said, "interpret the balloonMan to be Pan, the god of nature but also of lust. What do you think this means in the context of *in Just-*?"

Outside, traffic was fairly heavy, people out buying last-minute items before the storm hit. Several cars Jenny recognized passed by: the Alexanders' black 1974 Cheyenne, its pickup bed packed with sacks of groceries from the A&P, lumber, and a snow blower, the Ballwegs' green Impala, their little boy's face pressed against the back window, the Finches' beat-up tan Biscayne, looking, as always, like it had been the loser in a demolition derby. One of the town's four police cars cruised by, probably Chief Grossman out on patrol, keeping the streets of Plainview safe.

And wee.

Jenny smiled. She liked driving fast, and had gotten to ride with Grossman several times because of it, her license in his pocket.

Thursday, December 4, 1975
The girls walked to Hills through piles of snow already blackened by boots and tires and hardened to ice by subzero temps. Hills had no dormitories because almost every student who attended it was from Plainview and lived at home.

The storm had been preceded by freezing rain, which was a horror to navigate but beautiful in the barren trees, an intricate latticework of white crystals in bright sunshine and glittery sheen in the moonlight.

This morning the sky was the color of weak tea, casting a brown pall over the town. Oblivious to cold and gloom, the girls giggled about last weekend's romantic escapades. Their powdery breath flowed between them like sagging power lines. There weren't many eligible men their age in Plainview, other than the outsider riffraff that descended on the town on weekends. The lucky few local boys had, as their parents would say, a full dance card. Sooner or later most of the girls dated them, which was fine, because then they could compare notes or invent petty jealousies.

They came to an intersection and stopped as Kohlsrud approached on his bicycle. The old man was bundled up in a hat with ear flaps and a wool coat and boots he probably bought at the army surplus store. He was struggling mightily to maintain his balance on the ice.

Since his wife died a few years back he had lived alone in a tiny house on the west side of Plainview. Every day, regardless of weather, he pedaled his Sears three-speed into town, crossed the bridge over the Marengo River, and went to work at his shop at the east end of Main just before it narrowed into a gravel road. The shop had once been a laundromat, but that went out of business in the mid-sixties when Lohe's Bar and Grill next door hired go-go dancers and renamed itself Gents. The 'performers' washed their clothes there, which drove out the decent folk. Rumor had it that Kohlsrud liked 'em young and sleazy, so the dancers didn't bother him, even (or especially) when they dropped the go-go pretense and just started stripping. He bought and refurbished the laundromat in 1970. People overlooked his oddball reputation because he was good at fixing shoes, bikes, and whatever other broken things they brought him. The few brands of new shoes he sold were even cheaper than the Pamida's up in Lake Center.

The stoplight turned red. When Kohlsrud tried to brake his front tire caught in a rut, spewing him over the handlebars onto the sidewalk in front of the girls. His glasses went flying and the bike clattered down on top of him.

"Goddammit," he said. In the frigid air the word was a physical presence, a puff of dusty frost that briefly obscured his face from them.

The girls didn't laugh, but they didn't offer to help him up, either.

Kohlsrud fumbled for his glasses, then rose and glared at them through snowy lenses, his nostrils snorting smoke like an angry cartoon bull. Straddling the bike, he snarled, "No, I'll be fine."

As he wobbled toward the bridge, two of the girls looked at each other and said simultaneously, "That guy creeps me out."

Friday, December 5, 1975
The Frischel farm was a bland little parcel of land eight miles north of

Plainview. Not much to look at in the summer, in the winter it was positively desolate. Most farm yards had rows of poplars or spruce on the north and west side of the house to act as a windbreak, but the Frischels had lost theirs to some tree rot a few years back and had never replanted.

There was nothing left to protect their home and outbuildings from the wicked Alberta clippers that blew through nearly every week between December and March.

Chief Alvin Grossman turned his Crown Vic into their gravel driveway, which was packed with ice. If he hadn't already put chains on his tires, the wind would have pushed him into one of the drifts that lined both sides. He inched toward the house, the chains going *thackety-thackety-thack*.

Grossman stopped behind an old green Rambler. *What the hell?* he thought. That was Matt Stigler's car. What was he doing here? Matt was pastor of the Saint Andrew's Lutheran Church. Grossman didn't much like the Frischels, but Matt did. Matt liked everybody.

Grossman got out and looked over a vast ocean of snow, ripples of white that stretched to the edge of the world. Christ, to everyone else Plainview *was* the edge of the world – that, or the hole into which the world's shit drained.

Stigler came to the Fritchels' doorway as Grossman approached.

"Matt," he said.

"Al."

"What's this about?"

"Come in."

Helen and Tom Frischel were seated at the dining room table, an extender placed in the middle to make it longer. Places were set with four cups of coffee. They nodded a greeting at Grossman as he wiped his feet on the welcome mat. They didn't like him much, either.

"So," he said.

"Please, sit down," Stigler said, taking Grossman's coat and hanging it on the rack beside the door.

"Sugar?" Helen said. "Cream?"

Grossman wrapped both hands around the cup. He didn't drink coffee, but its heat felt nice. "I'm fine," he said. "What's the emergency?"

"We haven't seen Leslie in a week," Tom said.

"Your oldest? I thought she was living with your mother in town, Helen."

"Mom hasn't seen her, either," Helen said. "We're worried."

"She's probably just staying with friends."

Tom looked at him like he was an idiot. "Yeah, we thought of that, Chief. Nothing."

"Any reason she'd take off? Boyfriend?"

"None that we know of."

"Doesn't she work at Gents?" Grossman said.

"She's a *waitress*," Helen and Tom said together.

"Just making an observation. Lot of long-hairs hang around that place on weekends, and I've seen some of the Gents girls with them after hours."

Tom slowly turned his cup around and around, watching the dark liquid swirl. "What're you saying, Chief? Leslie isn't a quote unquote Gents girl."

"Maybe she took a liking to one of the hippies."

"Even if she did," Helen said, "she wouldn't run away. She wouldn't miss school. She wouldn't not call."

"How are things between you?" Grossman said. "I hear there's a reason she moved into town."

"That's none of your business," Tom said.

"Ever think maybe she doesn't want to be found?"

"Al," Stigler said, "*they* want her found."

"I can ask around, but if she left on her own, what can I do? She's nineteen. I can't force her to come home."

"Would you be saying this if it was the mayor's daughter?" Helen said.

"The mayor's daughter doesn't associate with that crowd."

Tom slammed his fist on the table. Coffee splashed out of his cup onto the place mat. "Jesus Christ," he said. "It's Vicky Kajeski all over again."

"Calm down, Tom," Stigler said.

"That's not even the same thing," Grossman said.

"How the hell do you know it's not the same thing?" Tom said.

"Because it isn't. Vicky was a minor. Leslie's not."

"Vicky was *raped* and *murdered*," Helen said.

"And you didn't investigate her, either," Tom said.

Grossman stood up. "It wasn't my case, and you know it. It's not where the victim lives, it's where the body's found. DCI handled that one. A trucker probably picked her up hitchhiking."

"*Probably*," Tom said. "You never caught him."

"He wasn't mine to catch, goddamn it!"

"Al, shhh," Stigler said. "They're just saying he could still be out there."

"Leslie hitchhikes sometimes," Helen said, her face gray as drywall. Stigler was holding her hand.

Grossman sighed. The woman was honestly frightened for her daughter. But hell, what did she expect? Any girl who worked in a place like Gents...well. "I'll make some calls," he said.

Sunday, December 7, 1975

Jenny sat in the loft with the choir and looked down on the congregation. She came to church every week because she always had. She rarely paid attention to Pastor Matt's sermons, but she trusted that whatever he said, every word was true. She knew there was a God because, well, there just was.

Jenny liked wearing the black choral robe, and she especially liked the singing. Her voice was never good enough to join chorus in high school, but the Lord was apparently more tone deaf, or more forgiving, than Mrs McKowen.

Below, Pastor Matt was preaching from First Corinthians about love. Even Jenny had memorized that old stand-by. *Love is not proud,* doodah, doodah. As he delivered his sermon she watched the faces of the people he was trying to reach. Sitting apart from their families, the two Mikes (all the girls just called them Mike One and Mike Two) were acting appropriately pious in their plaid suit coats and black ties. She knew better. What they wanted on their dates had nothing to do with love. Often as not they got what they *did* want, pressed into the sticky confines of their fathers' vehicles. In cold and rain it was Mr Bonner's Buick, heater blasting and eight track cranking; in warmth and starlight, a tarp in the bed of Mr Alexander's Chevy pickup. Jenny wondered if guys compared breast size the way girls compared...

Oh, to have such thoughts in church!

Moving up the aisles was like rising through Plainview's social strata, a hierarchy imposed not by the church but by the town itself. In the very back sat the poor farmers like her folks, the Tanners, and the Ballwegs and Andersons and Finches. The Frischels were there with four of their five daughters. Naturally Leslie wouldn't come. That little ditz skipped church like she did school... *and the goat-footed balloonMan whistles far and wee.* Jenny still hadn't forgiven her for that.

The teachers and merchants occupied the middle rows, the Van Syocs and Wellses and McKowens, the Neumans and Reysts. Chief Grossman and his wife Emily had weaseled their way that far forward, although as a low-paid public servant Grossman belonged farther back with the other cops and volunteer firemen. Harley Weissenfluh, owner of the feed and farm implement store, was having a hard time staying awake. Every time his head nodded his wife Shirley poked him in the ribs. Bill and Stella Lohe, owners of Gents, were also in this group, obviously seeing no conflict between the holiness of worship and the vileness of exploiting young female flesh.

Old Man Kohlsrud would probably fit here if he ever attended church, but he didn't, not ever, even when his wife was alive. Unlike every other business in town except the Holiday Station, Gents, and Mom's Diner, his shoe and bicycle shop was open on Sunday.

The lawyers and doctors and politicians took the front two rows. Jenny recognized Doc Murphy and Mayor Philips in their pews, of course, but the rest moved in circles her circles never touched. She knew faces and she knew names, but not which went with which.

Suits and dresses, black shoes and platforms. Such a peaceful scene in such a placid little town. But what murky secrets festered in the dark places beneath the surface? Look at them. Look at them. Maybe that one was overly fond of his secretary. Maybe *that* one liked boys. She liked leather. *She* was sleeping with him, who was sleeping with *her*, who was sleeping with *everybody*. He was skimming money from his children's trust fund, *he* was skimming money from the church...

Only God knew, and He wasn't telling.

Jenny hid her smile behind a fake cough. The world was just so *mud-luscious* when, from her high perch, she could allow her imagination to root about in her neighbors' filth.

Pastor Matt seemed to fix his eyes on the Frischels. He cued the organist, and signaled for all to rise. After the hymn and the announcements he had a special prayer request.

Wednesday, December 10, 1975

The way Old Man Kohlsrud eyed Suzy's pregnancy gave her the heebie-jeebies. She brought out his food just as Chief Grossman sat down opposite him in the booth. Grossman's belly could barely squeeze in, but at least he was clean. Kohlsrud...well, he needed to stand a little closer to the water when he showered. An aftershave that didn't smell like formaldehyde would be nice, too.

"I'd rather eat alone," Kohlsrud said over a mouthful of mashed potatoes.

"I'd rather let you," the Chief said.

Every booth was equipped with a miniature jukebox. Grossman put a quarter in and punched the buttons for Creedence Clearwater's 'Suzie Q,' which he always did for Suzy, and his usual Johnny Cash songs, 'I Walk the Line' and 'Ring of Fire.'

"What'd I do this time?" Kohlsrud said.

"You know Leslie Frischel?"

"Should I?"

"She told a friend she was heading to your shop on Friday the twenty-eighth."

"Stripper?"

"No, but she works there. Nineteen, pretty, long brown hair parted in the middle."

Oh Suzie Q, John Fogerty sang. *Baby I love you, Suzie Q.*

"That narrows it down to every girl in town." Kohlsrud guzzled half a cup of coffee and nodded toward Suzy. "Like her."

"Except Leslie wasn't expecting. Far as I know."

"I'm supposed to remember that far back? What about her?"

"She went missing that weekend."

Suzy cleared her throat. "Can I get you anything?"

"Hot chocolate," Grossman said.

"One bill or two?"

Kohlsrud looked hopefully at Grossman, who stared back stone-faced. "Two," they both said.

Suzy's friends had been talking about the missing girl. *Remember Vicky Kajeski*, they said. She wanted to hear more of the men's conversation, but there was a couple with kids in A-4. "I'll be right back with your cocoa," she said, tearing Kohlsrud's bill from her pad and placing it on the table.

"So how's this missing girl my problem?" Kohlsrud said to Grossman.

Friday, December 12, 1975
It was only a week till the end of the fall term at Hills. Finals started on Monday.

Jenny should be writing her paper on the Reconstruction, but instead sat in the student union, reading *The Plainview Weekly Herald*. The big story on the front page was that the Farm Expo was coming to the hippodrome in nearby Ridgemont in January. All the latest farm equipment would be on display. Harley Weissenfluh was quoted in the story, saying how now was the time to buy. If farmers waited until spring the prices would skyrocket. Mayor Philips expressed the hope that the Expo would bring overflow visitors from Ridgemont into Plainview.

Also on the front page was a photograph of the Christmas decorations lining Main Street and a silly map charting Santa's route from the North Pole to Plainview.

Sports occupied page two, with previews of the upcoming high school basketball and wrestling seasons. Prospects for the Plainview cagers were good, as four of five starters returned from last year's 12-7 squad. (Jenny never understood why basketball players were called cagers.) However, the outlook wasn't as bright for the wrestlers. They could only fill eight of the twelve weight classifications, which meant they'd have to forfeit four matches every meet. Jenny didn't see the attraction of boys grappling with boys, and while she liked the tight little shorts the basketball players wore, those bulging wrestling singlets were just gross.

Page three was filled with Christmas ads. Molly Lutz came by just as Jenny circled a lava lamp from Pamida.

"Really?" she said, looking over her friend's shoulder.

"For my parents," Jenny said. "They're into that psychedelic stuff."

"Mine would freak out," Molly said.

"I can't afford it anyway."

"Look on page four," Molly said.

The last page, beneath the fold, had a small article in which the Frischel family pleaded for their daughter to come home.

Jenny closed the paper. "What was she thinking?" she said. "How's she going to pass her classes now?"

"How's anyone," Molly said, "with this hanging over our heads?"

Tuesday, December 16, 1975

Chief Grossman was in his office playing finger football. The balls were pieces of paper folded into small triangles like Minutemen hats. He flicked them across his desk's polished surface, trying to get them to perch over the far edge without falling off. When he succeeded he awarded himself a touchdown. For the extra point he stood a triangular ball on its point and used his middle finger to 'kick' it over a stapler that served as the goalposts.

"Fourteen zero," he exclaimed as his latest shot sailed directly over the stapler.

The other officer on duty, Jim Engel, looked up from his crossword at the front counter of the station. "You always play with yourself?"

"*By* myself," Grossman said. "Till I get some competition. Wanna try?"

The telephone rang.

Engel indicated the crossword. "I like real challenges," he said as he picked up the phone. After listening for a moment he rolled his eyes. "Oh, hi, Mrs Frischel." He glanced at Grossman, who shook his head. "He's not here," Engel said. "No, I don't know when. Can I take a message?"

Even from across the room Grossman could hear Helen's agitation, if not her actual words. Engel made a jerk-off motion with his fist. "He's doing his best, ma'am. We all are. But those hippies hang around Gents like flies on shit, pardon my French. We're trying to track them down, but they're not local. The ones we have corralled deny even knowing your daughter."

Grossman got up to collect his misses from the floor. *Get rid of her*, he mouthed.

Engel shrugged helplessly.

"No, ma'am, we don't *know* that for sure, but you can't know she didn't – "

Engel held the phone away from his ear while Helen shouted at him. When she took a breath, he said, "Okay. Please. This isn't helping. Now, listen – "

A longer pause.

"We've talked to him. Repeatedly. Says he doesn't know anything about it, doesn't remember her being in the shop that day."

Pause.

"We are *aware* of that. So is he, now. He found the receipt. But if it was a routine sale, he wouldn't have any reason to remember her. We can't arrest people on suspicion, Mrs Frischel. We're not even sure a crime has been – "

Engel looked at the phone curiously, then replaced it on its cradle. "She hung up on me."

Grossman flicked another football. It slid to the edge of his desk and quivered but didn't fall. "Touchdown," he said.

"She's pretty upset."

"Wouldn't you be? But the kid ran off with one of those long hairs, bet money on it." He missed the extra point.

"You need a new kicker," Engel said.

"I'm still up twenty zip."

Thursday, December 18, 1975

Kohlsrud locked up the shop early, something he rarely did. Business was slow – slow, hell, it was nonexistent. Nobody was coming in. He didn't expect bike business this time of year, but apparently no other appliance or gadget or toy had broken, nobody's kids needed shoes, nothing. Kohlsrud squinted up into the cold sun. It was like he'd grown a third eye or come down with leprosy or something. He swung his leg over his bike and pedaled toward the bridge.

Well, screw 'em. Screw 'em all.

Saturday, December 20, 1975

It was one in the morning, and a nasty wind whistled out of the north-west, chasing intermittent clouds across the constellations.

Jenny, Molly, and the two Mikes were paired up in the seventy-one LeSabre belonging to Mike One's father. An eight-track was blaring – not by accident – Zeppelin's 'Whole Lotta Love' while Molly wrestled with Mike One in the front seat and Jenny contended with Mike Two in the back. They were parked next to the office of Neuman's Chevrolet dealership. A car didn't look out of place there, even if it was a Buick, and the building blocked the lot lights, throwing shadows over the LeSabre and making its exhaust fumes less obvious.

"*Gonna give you my love, ah*," Mike One sang along with Robert Plant. "*Gonna give you every inch of my love.*"

"Jesus," Molly laughed, "how many hands do you have?"

"Many as I need, baby."

Jenny scrunched against the door, trying to fend off Mike Two. The window handle dug into her ribs and the frosty glass froze the back of her head. "Stop it!" she said. Usually she was a good sport, but not tonight.

"What's wrong?" he said.

"Leslie Frischel."

Mike Two looked at her as if she were crazy. "Like hell. You don't even like her."

"So?"

"So if you didn't want to be here tonight, why didn't you just say so?"

In the front seat Molly and Mike One were noisily unconcerned about Leslie Frischel.

Mike Two smiled. "I have an idea. Let's pretend you're buying shoes, I'm Old Man Kohlsrud, and my hand is a shoehorn." He caressed Jenny's thigh. "Isn't this how he helps girls try them on?"

Jenny slapped his hand away. "You think it's funny?" she shouted. "You think it's *funny*?"

Mike One diverted his attention from Molly long enough to look over his shoulder and say, "Knock it off, will ya?"

Thursday, December 25, 1975

Most Christmases the traditional Frischel noon meal, held at Grandma Lehr's house in town, was a lavish affair of roast turkey, yams with gravy, jellied cranberry, and hot steaming rolls fresh from the oven, followed by pumpkin pie. This year Helen and Grandma didn't have the heart to cook, which was just as well, because nobody had the heart to eat.

But they were determined to celebrate the season. They should at least try.

The seven of them sat in a circle on the floor in Grandma's living room, the Christmas tree lit up, its silver streamers gleaming and bright star shining. Neatly wrapped and bowed presents spilled out from under the pine needles. An album of music from the *Rudolph* cartoon played on the phonograph. Burl Ives was singing 'Holly Jolly Christmas.'

"Come on," Tom said with false cheer. "Who wants to be Santa Claus?"

Every year one of the girls was chosen to distribute the gifts among her sisters and parents and Grandma. Once all the packages had been received, the family opened them one at a time, youngest to oldest. That way everybody got to enjoy the squeals of happiness or, sometimes, pouts of disappointment. Ever since Lindsey had turned three, she had always been the first to volunteer. Tonight she just curled up in her Snoopy pajamas and sucked her thumb.

Tom looked at Leigh, at Lara, at Lisa. All sat expressionless. He looked at Helen. She wouldn't meet his gaze.

"I'll be Santa," Grandma Lehr said. She moved to the rocking chair beside the tree. The first package was marked Lisa. She slid the box across the hardwood floor toward the girl, who left it lie where it came to rest. Next was Lara and then Lisa again. "Tom, this is for you, from Helen. Oh. Here's one for..." Grandma's voice softened to a whisper. "We'll just set hers aside for when she comes home."

"Set mine aside, too," Leigh said.

"Me, too," Lara said.

"Yeah," Lisa said.

Lindsey continued to suck her thumb.

"Where's your Christmas spirit," Tom pleaded, his own voice flat and lifeless.

"It's no use," Helen said.

Thursday, December 25, 1975

Jenny had a paper due for her Civil War class. Christmas festivities were over for her family, and it was time to hit the books. The whole Leslie Frischel thing had upset her, and she sort of blew off her finals. Since a lot of students were having trouble coping, Professor Wells had offered an extension to anyone who requested one, as long as the assignments were in by the start of the spring term. That was a week and a half away.

Jenny opened her book. Reconstruction. Ugh.

Thursday, December 25, 1975

Matt Stigler hung up his vestments and locked the Sacristy door. The service had been sparsely attended, but that was normal. Most people stayed home to celebrate with their families. Later today Matt would be doing the same with his own wife and kids, and this year his brother and nephews were visiting. It would be good to see them again.

But he had one stop to make first. He donned his winter coat and went out to start the Rambler. The Frischels would be at Leona Lehr's house. On this day, this day of Christ's birth, that poor family was in a place of unimaginable darkness. It was never easy to face people's fear and grief, never easy, but any discomfort Matt felt was nothing compared to the emotions gripping the Frischels. If ever anyone needed the Light of the Lord, it was them.

He put the car in gear and pulled out onto a deserted Main Street, rehearsing what he might say, wondering what prayer could possibly bring comfort to a family whose daughter and sister didn't come home for Christmas.

Thursday, December 25, 1975

The lights and TV were off, a fire popped in the hearth, and Christmas music played softly on the radio. Al Grossman snuggled on the love seat with his wife Emily. They sipped their traditional bubbly and enjoyed the moment.

"Do you ever wish we had kids?" Emily said for the millionth time in their marriage.

"Shhh," Grossman said, kissing her on the forehead. "I just thank the Lord I have you, Emmy."

She leaned her head against his shoulder and patted him on the tummy. "Smooth talking devil," she said.

Thursday, December 25, 1975

Kohlsrud sat on a stool next to the stage, drinking a Schlitz and watching a pretty young thing strut her stuff. The room was dark except for the red strobe lights over the dancers. Kohlsrud puffed on a Camel. The strobes pulsed in the smoke, and the girls moved like staccato bursts of substance through a fiery and ephemeral mist.

It was Christmas night, but Gents was business as usual. Gents was always open, and lonely men always came to drink, to smoke, to ogle the girls and invent conquests that never happened. Christmas didn't change that. Christmas enhanced that. Christmas reminded them of family and happier times, of what they once had and were, and now didn't and weren't.

Kohlsrud looked around. The place wasn't packed, but the hippies were here, of course, along with a fair number of Plainview's upstanding citizens, most of whom crouched in booths away from the strobes. These were the same men who wrote angry editorials to the *Herald* decrying Gents as a den of sin, a cesspool blackening the image of the town and everyone in it.

On most nights the bar blasted twenty-year-old country music through ten-year-old speakers, but in honor of the holiday the girls were gyrating their hips to 'O Holy Night' and 'Silver Bells' and 'I Caught Mommy Kissing Santa Claus'.

The stripper dancing in front of Kohlsrud bent over, shook her tassels in his face, and blew him a kiss. *You don't have anywhere else to go tonight, either*, he thought. Eleven o'clock, time for bed. He stood up and saluted the girl with his beer bottle. "To my Mary," he said.

Friday, December 26, 1975

A few minutes before dawn Chief Grossman got a frantic call from Harley Weissenfluh, demanding they meet at his house out in the country. Grossman had been in bed, warm, Emily at his side. He'd given himself the day off.

"Couldn't this wait for a decent hour?" he grumbled to Harley.

"You need to get over here *now*," Harley said, and disconnected.

Furious, Grossman dressed and stumbled with unzipped coat and untied boots into a clear but frigid morning. He always kept the Vic plugged into a heater in the winter, but the damn car still didn't want to start. A few minutes of persistence and profanity coaxed it to life. Harley was waiting for him outside when he pulled into his driveway. The man's face was bright red, and he looked like he was going to puke.

"This had goddamned well better be important," Grossman said.

"Follow me," Harley said. He had a flashlight in his hand. "Before you ask, I didn't see anyone."

"Jesus, Harley, just *tell* me."

Behind Harley's house was nothing but acres and acres of flat farm fields under foot-tall drifts, now burnished orange by the rising sun. An ice-packed drainage ditch paralleled the driveway before peeling off into a field and emptying into a cement culvert some fifty yards in. "I was asleep when I heard a car pull in my driveway. Nobody's got any business being on my property this time of day." Harley was practically running, difficult for the overweight Grossman to manage on dry, warm surfaces, let alone ice.

"You're gonna kill us both," Grossman said, gasping in the cold and heavy air. "It must be fifteen below."

Harley slowed half a step. "Keep up, dammit! So after five minutes the car leaves and I think, *What the hell?* I get my twelve gauge and come out. I see these tire tracks." He pointed down at the snow. The tracks had a wide wheel base, probably a pickup with chains on. "I followed them back into the field."

"Some stupid kids looking for a place to screw. So what? Happens all the time."

"Really?" Harley said. They walked in the ruts left by the car until they came to the culvert. "He got out here. Look at the footprints."

The prints were a size or two smaller than Grossman's, elevens maybe, made by someone wearing galoshes. "And?" he said.

"And *this*," Harvey said, kneeling in front of the culvert's opening.

Grossman bent down for a better look. It was dark, and Harley shined his flashlight inside. "Oh, Christ," Grossman said. "Oh, son of a bitch. Oh, sweet Jesus."

Friday, December 26, 1975

Helen and Lisa were doing breakfast dishes at the kitchen sink when they saw Grossman's squad car turn into the driveway. When it came to a stop both the Chief and Pastor Matt got out. The men looked at each other and exhaled long powdery breaths.

"Get your father," Helen said. "Then go to your room."

"What's wrong?"

"Please, honey, now."

Lisa left calling, "Daddy, Daddy!"

Helen, unable to support her own weight any more, slumped to the floor. Tom rushed into the kitchen just as the knock came to the door.

"Don't answer it," Helen pleaded, already in tears.

Monday, December 29, 1975

"Can't tell if she was raped or not," Doc Murphy said to Grossman. They were seated in Doc's office, breathing medicinal fumes. "I took swabs just in case, but even if there is semen it's probably too degraded to type."

"Cause of death?" Grossman said.

"Hyoid bone's broke." Doc lit up a Marlboro. "So, strangulation."

"How long she been dead?"

"Shortly after she was taken, I'd guess. If she was outside, the cold would affect decomp, but by the looks of her..."

Grossman rubbed the back of his neck. "She disappeared a month ago, Doc. The bastard just dumped her on Friday. Where the hell'd he keep her all this time?"

Murphy shook his head. "The Frischels identify her?"

"Looking like that? No, I wouldn't let them. Stigler did it."

"Nineteen years old. Christ. Anything on the tire tracks?"

"Truck of some kind. We took pictures, but he had chains on, so we couldn't make out the tread."

Doc blew out a mouthful of smoke, coughed. "Who did this, Al?"

"TV people from Lake Center asked me that, too."

"And?"

"I have some ideas," Grossman said. But he didn't, not even one.

Friday, November 28, 1975

"Little tight," Leslie said.

"They're made to stretch," Kohlsrud said. "Stick your big toe up." Leslie did, and he used his index finger and thumb to trace its outline through the shoe. He wore a wedding ring, which never ceased to amaze her. His wife was dead now, but whatever possessed her to marry him in the first place? "Perfect," he said. "You want these, then?"

"But they're not Famolares," she pouted.

Kohlsrud rose effortlessly. Despite his frail appearance, he moved with assurance and power. Repairing bikes must keep his muscles strong. He smiled, or leered, or scowled, it was hard to tell. His teeth were stained with nicotine, too. "What do you expect for seven ninety-five?"

"I guess they're okay," she said, taking off the loafer and replacing it with her old shoe. She handed him a five and two ones, then rummaged through her purse for change.

"Forget it," Kohlsrud said. He bagged the shoes for her, wrote up a receipt, and gave the carbon to her. "Now get out of here."

"Thanks," Leslie said, and pushed open the door to a warm and sunny November afternoon. Now that her business with creepy old Kohlsrud was done, she could look forward to the rest of the weekend. Mr Lohe had given her the night off so she could attend a Thanksgiving dance. She bounced down the street, smiling and carefree, a southerly breeze in her hair. One more stop for a new blouse at Annie's, and she'd be set.

Dozens of pre-Christmas shoppers were out taking advantage of the nice weather, but Leslie was alone as she crossed the bridge over the Marengo River. A shiny black Chevy pickup pulled up next to her. The window rolled down and the clean-cut driver said, "Looking for a ride, beautiful?"

Leslie's face lit up. "Oh, hi!" she said. "You waxed your dad's truck."

"Hop in," he said.

NINA ALLAN
WILKOLAK

Kip knew the man was the monster as soon as he saw him. He was coming out of the convenience store attached to the garage at the bottom end of Lee High Road, his shopping in an old Tesco bag. Kip uncapped the Nikon and took his picture; the click of the shutter release sounded loud to him, even above the noise of the passing traffic. Kip lowered the camera, suddenly afraid the man might turn and see him, but that didn't happen. Instead, the man crossed the garage forecourt, ignoring the cars parked at the pumps and heading off up the road in the direction of Lewisham. He was of medium height, but skinny, with gangling limbs and a jutting Adam's apple and reminded Kip of Tom Courtenay in *The Loneliness of the Long Distance Runner*. He wore tatty old Levis, and an army surplus jacket that was too big for him around the shoulders. He seemed lost in thought, cocooned in it, shut off from his surroundings, from Kip, from everything.

Kip raised the Nikon again and took half a dozen more shots in quick succession. Later, at home in his room, he downloaded the images to his hard drive, storing them in a file he labelled MONSTER. A fortnight ago an eight-year-old girl from Marischal Road had gone missing on her way home from school. The girl's name was Rebecca Riding. Her body was discovered a week later in a disused mobile home on the Isle of Sheppey. She had been raped and then suffocated. The police issued a photo fit of a man they wanted to question, a man with thinning hair and a scrawny build, teachery little wire-framed glasses. The police said he was probably in his early forties, and living in the Lewisham area. Kip thought the man in the photo fit looked like a school nerd gone bad. He also looked exactly like the bloke he had seen coming out of the garage on Lee High Road. Kip remembered the man's walk, slightly knock-kneed, the Tesco bag bumping against his thigh as he moved along.

The tabloids had already dubbed him the Manor Park Monster.

Kip selected one of the photos and printed it out, the best one, showing the man's face in profile like the double agent in a spy movie. It was the kind of photo you could imagine flashing up on the TV news, or on the front page of the next day's papers. Rebecca Riding had been all over the news, always the same photo, a blonde kid with a demon smile and one of her top front teeth missing. Rebecca Riding had gone missing just before the start of the holidays and at school her name quickly became that summer's catchphrase: *what do you get if you cross Rebecca Riding with a rubber glove? What did Rebecca Riding's dad say when the cops asked him why his trousers were at the cleaner's?* The jokes were disgusting but you couldn't help laughing at them. One dork had laughed so hard Kip thought he was going to piss himself. Kip didn't want to think about the murder. It was the photograph of the murderer that interested him, some loser with a plastic carrier bag crossing the street. The image might seem ordinary but Kip knew it wasn't, that the very act of framing the man in his viewfinder and then choosing to release the shutter made the picture significant. The main point of a photograph was to invite you to *look*, to concentrate on the world around you a little harder. The photographer recreated the world in the way he saw it and in this, Kip supposed, he was the master of his universe. A guy who worked for the *Star* and who had once come to the school to give a talk on photojournalism said that all photographers were grubby-handed alchemists, pier end magicians, words that stuck in Kip's mind like splinters of glass. Now that he had the photograph in front of him Kip found he didn't really care whether the man was the monster or not. The point seemed to be that he *could* be. He could just as easily be a hero. If you mounted a photo on a nice ground and gave it an interesting title then anybody could be anything.

He shut down his computer and went downstairs. The television was on in the back room, his mother slumped at the end of the sofa watching *The Weakest Link*. She was folding and unfolding a tea towel, one of the souvenirs she had brought back from their holiday in Tenby three years before. It had the Welsh dragon on it, in red.

"Your father won't be home for supper," she said. "He has work to finish."

"OK," Kip said. He sat down beside her, his eyes on the screen, careful not to look at her directly. This was a game they played together all the time now. She would tell him his father was working late at the site, and he would pretend to believe her and not care less. He would ignore the bunched, grasping look of her hands, her puffy eyes, and concentrate on Anne Robinson torturing a bank clerk from Cleethorpes over the identity of the currency in Argentina.

The thing he was not supposed to know but had known for six months was that his father was having an affair, that on at least three evenings a week Andrzej Kiplas would knock off work early and drive over to Streatham, where he would spend an unspecified number of hours with a woman named Grace Hemingway. Kip didn't know who she was or how his father had met her. Sometimes he imagined her as one of the peroxide Pirelli blondes on the calendar in the site portakabin; at other times he saw her as a mousy little librarian with a flat full of dusty books, like the women in films by Wajda or Kieslowski.

Andy Kiplas sometimes didn't return until ten, eleven o'clock at night. On the nights when this happened, Kip would slope off to his room as soon as he heard his father's key in the lock. There would be a short interval without much happening, then his mother would start crying or his father shouting or both. This usually went on for about an hour. Then it would all go quiet, and later he would hear the headboard banging against the wall in his parents' bedroom.

Andy Kiplas was almost fifty, but his body was still lean and hard from his work on the site. Kip's mother Lynn was like an overblown rose. When she smiled and if the lighting was right she could still be beautiful, her heaviness transformed into a pink softness that put him in mind of strawberries, candyfloss, September sunsets. But when she was unhappy she turned pallid as lard.

Kip itched to photograph her. With her inflamed eyelids and the ragged cloth in her hands she looked like a war victim, one of the refugee women in the immigrant camps outside Calais. Sometimes on evenings like this Kip would stay downstairs and play cards with her, or backgammon. At some point during the game Lynn would get up from her seat and pour them both a vodka, a double *Zubrowka* straight from the freezer. The fumes rose up in a smoky cloud as she unscrewed the cap.

"One little nip can't hurt you," she would say. She had been saying that since he was thirteen. "Don't you go telling your teachers." She would laugh then, a raucous, ribald sound, the same laugh she used with her friends on the phone and that Kip loved to hear. She would knock back her vodka in one, and two bright tears would appear, squeezing like liquid crystal from the corners of her eyes.

They sparkled there, jewel-bright, on the rims of her cheeks. Kip wondered what he would do if she cried for real. No matter how much he loved her he still hated her need of him, the way her fingers twisted together when she told him the pointless lies about his father.

The only thing to do was pretend not to notice. Once the truth was out in the open it would be impossible for either of them to put it back.

They ate supper off a tray, watching the news.

"I'm going out later," Kip said.

"Where to?" Lynn said. She glanced up from her plate. Her food was still mostly untouched. "I don't want you roaming the streets half the night, not with that man on the loose."

"I'm only going to Sonia's. I won't be late."

"Well, make sure you catch the bus coming home." She took her plate through to the kitchen and Kip heard her scraping her supper into the waste bin. It was the first time she had mentioned the monster, at least to him. He thought it was probably her way of trying to stop him from going out and leaving her by herself.

"I don't know," Sonia said. "It could be him, I suppose." She held the photograph in both hands, tilting it against the light. "They all look the same though, those photo fits. Just think how awful it would be for this man if you got it wrong."

They were sitting on the grass behind the garage in Sonia's garden. Sonia's hair was drawn back off her face in a ponytail. Loose strands glimmered at the nape of her neck like copper wire.

"I suppose," Kip said. There was a number you could ring, a police hotline. On the way over to Sonia's Kip had tried to imagine what would happen if he called it and told the cop at the other end that he had seen the monster. They would ask for his name and address, that would be the first thing, and later on they would make him hand over the photograph. He supposed the photograph was evidence of a kind, evidence that linked him with the monster. The idea was disturbing, not so much because the link existed as because it might become known. Sonia's uncertainty about the photograph was a relief because it seemed to free him from the obligation of having to do anything.

He leaned in over her shoulder, pretending to look at the photo but in reality just wanting to get closer to her. She smelled of the coarse-grained pine soap the Vardens had in their upstairs bathroom. He imagined her at the sink, her bare feet on the coconut matting. The Vardens' house was like that, all polished wood and cream-coloured walls. Sonia went to Forest Hill Girls' School. Sonia's father Timothy had a good job in the City.

"I really like this photo though," Sonia was saying. "Can I keep it?"

"Course you can," Kip said. "What are you going to do with it?"

"Nothing." She laughed. "I just like it, that's all. He looks lonely, don't you think? The kind of man who's always alone." She was still studying the picture, as if she had come upon it by chance in a magazine and was trying to decide whether she should cut it out or not. The way she looked at the photograph made him feel strange, weightless, as in the moments before an orgasm. There was part of himself that wished he had not shown it to her, that felt convinced it was dangerous. And yet the idea that she would want to keep something he had made, that she could like it that much, made his insides hurt.

He began to count the freckles on the back of her neck, concentrating hard to stop himself getting an erection. The freckles were red, like her hair, the glinting vermilion of the jagged patches of rust on the disused water tank around the back of the school toilets.

He'd had sex with Sonia twice, once up in Oxleas Woods, and once in her bedroom, when her parents were out for the day at some barbecue or other. The thought of being with her in her parents' house had made him almost sick with excitement, but it turned out not to be such a good idea. Every time a car went by on the street outside he thought it was the Vardens, returning home early. The time in the woods had been better. Sonia held his cock, clasping it in her fist and moving her hand cautiously up and down, as if she was afraid she might hurt him. He came too soon of course, but at least he managed to get inside her. He thought it would be embarrassing afterwards, trying to think of things to say, but it had been fine. Better than fine, in fact. They put their clothes back on and lay in the grass, watching planes soar in low overhead on their approach to Heathrow and talking about TV shows they had liked when they were younger. By the end of the afternoon he felt comfortable around Sonia in a way that went far beyond just wanting to fuck her.

He couldn't imagine what had driven the monster to fuck an eight-year-old. Almost the best part of sex with Sonia was knowing that she wanted it too, and that she liked him enough to want to spend time with him afterwards.

Rebecca Riding would have been rigid with fear, or else screaming and thrashing about like an autistic kid he had seen once, having a panic attack in a supermarket.

The rape was something he was ashamed to think about, as if thinking about it somehow made him a part of what had happened. Had the monster killed the girl in the end because he wanted to cover his tracks, or because he could no longer stand the sound of her screaming? To erase what he had done, like pulling the wings off a fly and then crushing it beneath your thumb to put it out of its misery.

A crime like the monster's was so bad it had its own thumbprint, its own identity. If Kip thought about it hard enough he could feel it beginning to infect his imagination, cell by cell, like mildew creeping and spreading on a damp wall.

His stomach turned over at the thought, the same way it did when you went to pour milk in your tea and found it had gone off. He remembered seeing some kids once, larking around on a building site, using a broken off branch to fish a dead rat out of a rain puddle. They had flicked the rat up in the air, then run away screaming as it plopped down again in the water. The memories repelled him and yet they persisted. You couldn't not watch them playing with the rat, couldn't not smell the curdled milk in its plastic container, even though it would make your guts heave and you knew that perfectly well before you started.

So long as you weren't forced to drink the milk or pick up the rat in your bare hands it was OK. It was interesting even. The rat he remembered especially, because he had been back to the building site later to photograph it.

He leaned forward and kissed Sonia's neck. A strand of her loose hair tickled his lips, and a wisp of his own breath came back at him, rebounding off her skin in a puff of warm air.

She turned in his arms and kissed him. Her saliva tasted faintly of orange juice.

"I'll have to go in, in a minute. I'm supposed to be writing an essay on nuclear power."

"That's OK," Kip said. "I'll text you later." He stood up from the grass. He wondered when he would next get to have sex with her again, then wondered if that was how it was for his father with Grace Hemingway. The idea of his father thinking about sex unsettled him even more than the thought of the rat.

"Thanks for the photo," said Sonia. "I'll buy a clip frame for it tomorrow."

"Be careful," Kip said, and then wondered what the hell he was on about. It was just a stupid photograph, nothing to be careful of there. He hurried away, leaving via the side gate without turning back, not wanting her to see that he was blushing.

He caught the bus from outside the old Capitol cinema on the London Road. He climbed up to the top deck, where he sat alone apart from a gaunt and elderly black man reading the *Metro*. It was just about beginning to get dark. Kip looked out at the amethyst sky, the latticework of interlinked streets, shop fronts and garage forecourts, the chequered fabric of gardens and railway lines. He saw London as a labyrinth, with no way out. Even if you fled to the edge, to the boundary posts at Morden or Edgware, there would still be more roads, more alleyways, more cemeteries. *It was the kingdom of the Manor Park Monster.* Kip wondered where in his kingdom the monster was hiding at that moment.

The streetlights were coming on all over town, and soon it would be dark for real. He got off the bus opposite the garage. Lee High Road smelled of diesel fumes and dying hydrangeas. When he got home he discovered his father had arrived there before him. The back door was standing open into the garden. Lynn and Andy Kiplas sat together at the kitchen table with their elbows touching. Lynn was laughing, small creases at the corners of her eyes. Kip looked at his father, not speaking. Andy Kiplas glanced quickly away, then asked Kip if he would like a beer.

Kip saw the monster again three days later in Manor Park Gardens. Some people thought that this was where Rebecca Riding had gone missing, but it wasn't so. Manor Park Gardens was a landscaped park with a lake and ornamental waterfowl, popular with families and joggers. As a kidnapping site it was close to useless. Kip reckoned the only time you could get yourself kidnapped from the gardens would be first thing in the morning before it got busy, but even then there were the groundsmen and the dog walkers, commuters using the park as a cut-through to Lee station.

Rebecca Riding had been abducted at around three-thirty in the afternoon, not from Manor Park Gardens but from Manor Park. Manor Park was a rough triangle of land sandwiched between Weardale Road and Manor Lane, hemmed in on one side by a swampy and narrow section of the River Quaggy. Sometimes you would see rubbish floating in the water and once there had been a child's tricycle but Kip liked Manor Park because it was quiet, the tall terraces of Manor Lane backing directly on to the tussocky grass and stands of nettles like the last, abandoned houses in a zombie movie. Kip liked to photograph these houses, even though someone in one of the flats there had once leaned out of the window and called him a peeping Tom.

This was the first time he had been back to Manor Park since Rebecca Riding's abduction. He had wondered if the place was still being treated as a crime scene but if there had ever been police tape or anything else of that kind it was gone now. To Kip the park seemed unnaturally quiet, *expectant*, but he knew he was probably imagining it. He took some photos of the park railings and the children's play area, hoping that no one would see him doing it and wishing he knew exactly where the abduction had taken place. He knew his interest in the monster was growing. He disliked this feeling, distrusted it, but was unable to let it go. He would have liked to discuss it with Sonia but was afraid she might start to think he was weird, one of the lonely serial killer types who bought true crime magazines and hung around Cromwell Road and the corner of the modern housing estate that had once been Rillington Place. The day after he gave her the photograph of the monster, Sonia told him an obscure theory some crime writer had concocted about how a famous English painter was really Jack the Ripper. The theory was connected with art though, so it seemed it was all right to talk about it.

The monster was not connected with anything. He was just a monster.

Kip came out on to Manor Lane and crossed quickly into Manor Park Gardens. The sky was a high, dense blue, the sun dripped white light on the water. People sprawled on their backs in the grass, reading paperback thrillers. Kip knew he was invisible here. It was even OK to take pictures. He took a few shots of the fountain, a Dalmatian dog, some kid on a skateboard, but he knew already that the photos would not be much good. The park was not his thing. He preferred the tatty shop fronts and crumbling facades of the terraces on Lee High Road. He turned to go, walking across the grass in the direction of the park exit on Old Road. Then he saw the monster, sitting on one of the benches facing the lake.

He stopped where he was, raising the Nikon cautiously as if he was afraid the man might take flight then fired off seven, eight shots, using the zoom lens to capture him in profile. As he lined up the final frame the man turned his head slightly, giving Kip a better view of his face. Seeing him again Kip thought he looked less like the photo fit, less like a cornered rat and more like a ruined accountant who had just been fired. It was definitely him, though. Kip recognised him by his jacket. He appeared to be watching the ducks, plump mallards, a male and three females, dipping in and out of their limber reflections in a way that made the real ducks look blockish and unnatural as decoys. Kip wandered slowly in his direction, pretending to look at the lake. There were three children on the wooden landing stage, throwing bread crusts from a plastic bag. A horde of ducks surged towards them across the water. Kip slipped the Nikon back into its case and sat down on the bench. He watched the children, who had started to argue over who was in charge of the bread, and smoothed the leather case of the Nikon with the tips of his fingers. The park was full of people – onlookers, witnesses – and yet he could not escape the thought that he had put himself at risk somehow by coming here.

He turned to glance at the man beside him. He tried to make the glance seem casual, but was aware even as he did so that the movement was too rigid, too snatched to appear anything but unnatural, the inept glance of a spy who was new to the job. The monster was staring right at him. His eyes were grey, the colour of tap water with a single drop of black ink dispersed in it. His expression was perfectly calm.

"Hello," he said. "I've seen you before, I'm sure. You're the boy with the camera."

Kip seemed to feel two worlds colliding, the world he saw through the lens of the Nikon spinning and crashing through the wall of reality like a wrecking ball through the shell of a condemned tower block. He noted the monster's clean, almost polished-looking nails, the small scar at the corner of his mouth that made it look as if someone had cut him there once with a razor blade. The idea that he was the watched instead of the watcher was enormous and fundamental and somehow awful.

He felt the air go out of his lungs, as if the world had expanded outwards, crushing his chest. Oddly enough it was the same feeling he'd had the first time he saw Sonia's naked breasts.

"I'm going to be a photographer," he said at last. "That's why I have the camera."

He saw the man's lips twitch, and Kip waited for him to laugh at him, or else demand to see the photographs he had taken. That was what people did, if they were interested at all that was, and then Kip would either have to refuse or hand over the Nikon, let the man see the multiple images of himself that were now locked inside the camera's memory, that final close up, the sunlight flashing off his glasses and into the water.

Instead of asking to look at the pictures the monster smiled, his ridged and slightly yellowed incisors clearly visible.

"I thought as much," he said. "I recognised the signs, you see." He leaned back on the bench, his arms locked across his chest, his skinny wrists snaking out from the sleeves of his army jacket. Kip could not tell if the man was trying to patronise him in some way or if they were having a proper conversation.

"What do you mean?" he said. "The signs?"

"I mean I was the same at your age. Things were different then of course, none of this digital rubbish. I had a Minolta SR-7 and it weighed a ton. I didn't give a damn about that though. I took it everywhere with me. I got so used to the weight of it around my neck I felt wrong without it. Have you ever used film? A film camera I mean, rather than digital?"

Kip shook his head. It was a subject that embarrassed him, because his reactions were based on feelings and not experience. He knew that some people were obsessed with film, some of the younger photographers even were obsessed with it, and with something they called the *tangibility of the image*. Kip thought it was a load of crap. He liked to think of the Nikon as an extension of the eye, an optical application, the closest thing to actual seeing that there was. He loved the *cleanness* of digital, its lack of pretension. The idea of film, with its cumbersome processes, the unnecessary delay between the act of taking and the act of seeing, was something he hated.

He might have known the monster would be a film user. Everything about him suggested it, even his clothes.

"Are you a photographer then?" Kip said. "Do you work for the magazines?"

"I used to be. Not for the magazines though. I did other stuff."

"What kind of stuff? Would I know your work?"

"You wouldn't know my work at all. I worked for the police, as a forensic photographer. My work, as you like to call it, has the curious distinction of never having been seen outside a courtroom."

"You mean you used to go and photograph crime scenes, things like that?"

The monster nodded. "It's not as glamorous as it sounds though, believe me. You see these American cop shows and think it's all about being rushed to the scene of some murder or other. Actually it's about having to get out of bed at two in the morning to take pictures of a sales rep who's managed to get his legs crushed in a motorway collision. It wasn't exactly the career I imagined for myself. Actually I got into it by mistake."

"By mistake?"

"It's a long story."

"Why did you give it up?"

"That's a long story, too. But my dad died last year, left me a bit of money. Not a fortune, but enough to give me some breathing space. You never know, I might even treat myself to a new camera." He sighed and stretched out his arms, cracking his knuckles in a way Kip found nauseating. "You should keep at it," he said. He got up from the bench. "You might even have what it takes."

Kip stared up at him, not moving. He hated the way most adults had of making you feel like a moron, almost as if they resented you for their own failures. It occurred to him that it might all be bullshit anyway, that the monster was trying to lure him with the talk of his defunct Minolta the way he had lured Rebecca Riding with sweets or *Jackie* magazine. Even here he was out of date; most perverts these days used the internet. He wondered why he hadn't used some of his father's money to update his wardrobe.

There was a restlessness that hung from him, baggy and shapeless as his ill-fitting jacket. Kip felt certain he was the killer, as he had felt certain when he first saw the man coming out of the garage. Instead of being afraid he felt a tense, nervous pleasure, knowing that he was ahead of him again, the watcher now instead of the watched.

"I'm Edwin Kiplas," he said suddenly. "Everybody calls me Kip."

"Dennis Croft," said the monster. "I'm sure we'll see each other around."

Croft held out his hand and Kip took it. Croft's hand was dry and rather small, but he had a strong grip, the wiry fingers grasping his own as if he meant to try and stop him getting away. Kip thought of Rebecca Riding and felt a tremor go through him. Then Croft was gone, striding along the tarmac path that skirted the lake then cutting across the grass towards the Manor Park library. Kip watched him merge with the other walkers, become one of them. In less than a minute he was out of sight.

Kip waited ten minutes and then followed him. As he came out of Old Road on to Lee High Road he looked both ways along the street, half convinced that Croft would be lying in wait for him, but there was no sign of him. He wondered what Croft had meant when he said he was sure they would see each other again. His words seemed to hang in the air, like a threat or a curse.

After supper he went to his room and browsed the internet for information about forensic photography. There was a careers website that told him most forensic photographers were non-professionals, police officers with only the most rudimentary training in the use of a camera. Of the others, those who had actually set out to become photographers in the first place, most worked for specialist agencies. Kip supposed that Croft had been employed by one of these agencies; he couldn't imagine him as a cop, of any description. He was too evasive, too much of a loner. You could say he had loner written all over him, that he was a loner archetype.

The agency guys were pretty well paid, because like doctors they were always on call. The careers website listed this as one of the job's main disadvantages, but Kip found he liked the idea. He thought a job that was that unpredictable would be difficult to become bored with. One of the agencies, a firm called Trulite Legal, had posted a series of photos of an office block gutted by fire. The photographer was named as Andrew Watson and the crime was a suspected arson. Kip liked the light in the photos, the strange dead whiteness that made the burned out windows look like portholes into outer space. Most of all he liked the way the pictures showed what was there and didn't tamper with it.

When he Googled Dennis Croft there were no relevant finds.

At a little after eleven-thirty he heard his mother coming upstairs. It was only then that he realised his father had still not come home. His computer whirred, fanning itself in the darkness. He could sense Lynn outside his door, listening to see if he was still awake. After a moment she sighed and moved away. A floorboard creaked. Kip jumped off his bed and went to open the door. His mother was standing right outside. She gazed at him stolidly, her expression caught midway between surprise and despair.

"You should be in bed," she said. "I thought you were asleep already."

"Where's Dad?" said Kip. The question hovered in the air between them, bobbing weakly like a deflating balloon. The hall light glowed a dull orange, reminding Kip of the light in the Midwestern motel rooms Stephen Shore liked to photograph. Kip stared at Lynn Kiplas in her quilted dressing gown and felt envious of Shore's talent, the way he had of making the most casual Polaroid snapshot look like the opening of a murder mystery. Kip had always hated Lynn's dressing gown, which was made of horrible fake mauve satin and reminded him of some naff sitcom set in an old people's home.

She had clearly been crying. Kip didn't know what he wanted most: to hug her or to slap her face. He became suddenly aware that he was dressed only in his underpants, that he was more or less naked in front of her.

"He's at Toke's," Lynn said. Lyonel Toklin was his father's business partner. "They've been playing cards and drinking, you know what those two are like once they get started. Anyway, he's not fit to drive." Her words sounded stilted, a speech she had prepared beforehand. Kip couldn't decide whether her lying was a sign of courage or idiocy. He took a step towards her, meaning to put his arms around her, but she flinched away as if afraid he might hit her.

"Go to bed now," she said. "And make sure that computer's switched off." She moved away towards the end of the landing. Kip watched her go into the bedroom then closed his own door with a bang. He picked his jeans off the floor and fished his mobile out of the pocket then brought up his father's number and depressed the call button. The call went straight to voicemail, which Kip knew meant precisely nothing. Andy Kiplas didn't like mobiles. He kept his phone on during work hours because it would hurt the business not to but as soon as he was finished for the day he switched it off. For the first time Kip saw this behaviour as thoughtless and selfish.

Andy's pet name for Lynn was the Gipsy Moth.

Kip realised he hadn't called Sonia that day or even messaged her. He supposed that made him as bad as his father. He felt a sudden, almost urgent need to speak to her, not about his father or monster but about Andrew Watson's photos of the burnt-out office block, how the pictures looked to him, like stills from a documentary about hell.

Still, it was too late to call. He sent a text message instead, *sleep well* and the letter *K* and then an *x*. He did not expect a reply, but a moment later his phone buzzed and there was a text from Sonia, the word *goodnight* accompanied by the little red heart graphic she sometimes used to sign off her messages.

The thought that she was awake and thinking of him made him start to get hard. Right after the second time they had sex he had jokingly asked Sonia what she wore in bed at night, and she had laughed, and said that when the nights were muggy like this she didn't normally wear anything except a pair of knickers.

He put his phone on to charge. He thought of the picture he had given Sonia, the photograph of the monster that she said she was going to mount in a clip frame. The idea of Croft on Sonia's writing desk or bookshelf looking down at Sonia's naked body made him feel queasy, and once again he found himself wishing he had never given her the photograph in the first place.

Two days later Rebecca Riding was on *Crimewatch*. They showed the same photo again, Rebecca Riding in her red school jumper and with the gap between her teeth, and then they staged a reconstruction of what they called her *last known movements*. A small girl wearing a red cardigan came out of the school gates on Manor Lane and trotted along Northbrook Road towards Manor Park. Just before she crossed to the park side she stopped to talk to another girl, a child actress playing the part of Rebecca Riding's friend Tanya Baker. The actress playing Tanya said she had to go home and change out of her school clothes but that she'd meet Rebecca in the park by the swings in ten minutes' time.

Then there was an interview with the parents of the real Tanya Baker. They looked dazed and spoke slowly, like people who had narrowly avoided being involved in a major road accident. After the interview with Tanya's parents they showed the photo fit of the monster again and repeated the number of the police hotline. Any information at all, they said, might turn out to be of vital importance in the search for the killer. Kip thought the word *killer* sounded worse even than the word *mur-*

derer. Murder always sounded rather grand, something planned out in advance and with at least the semblance of reason to back it up. Killing was just an action, simple as that. A killer was brutal and thoughtless and probably stupid.

With Dennis Croft it was hard to tell where the murderer left off and the killer began.

"Just think of it," said Lynn Kiplas. "Those poor people."

"I'm going out," Kip said. He left the room quickly, before his mother had a chance to ask where he was going. As he unlatched the front gate he saw his father walking towards him up the road.

"Where are you off to, then?" said Andy Kiplas. "Anywhere exciting?"

"Just out." His father looked clean and smelled fresh, as if he had recently stepped out of the shower. His plaid shirt had been recently ironed. He spoke jauntily, with a kind of mock casualness, and Kip thought of the Toklins' dog, which always expected to be made a fuss of even when it had stolen the Sunday joint right off the table. He tried to imagine how it would be if his father left home, meeting him at the site and going off for supper somewhere, to Pashka's Kitchen in Brockley perhaps, where they would eat potato latkes with apple sauce and his father would tell him in blow-by-blow detail about his latest building project.

He thought he could cope with that. It was going to end up like that anyway when he went to college. But the thought of his mother alone at home made him feel trapped and scared.

He thought of packing his bags and leaving, just him and the Nikon, then realised he would never escape this shit, not even if he went to Australia.

For Christ's sake, Dad, he thought. *It's your problem. Leave me out of it.*

"Fancy a couple of rounds of Harris later?" his father said. Harris was a variant of rummy, something he and Toke had invented. The game was named after Bomber Harris, though the reasons for this had vanished into the past.

"OK Dad, maybe. I'm not sure what time I'll be back though." He stepped carefully around his father and went off up the street.

"I'll save you a beer, then," Andy Kiplas called after him. Kip didn't answer. He felt for the Nikon around his neck then realised he had come out without it. Not that it mattered much. It was now almost dark, with just a narrow strand of pink chafing the horizon. Kip did not know where he was going exactly, only that he had needed to get out of the house. He decided to walk as far as the Lewisham clock tower and then turn back. Lee High Road was quieter now. The traffic was always lighter after the rush hour, and there were occasional moments of complete hiatus. Kip loved the houses on Lee High Road because they were always interesting to photograph. Most of them were pretty run down, tottering decrepit terraces constructed from the dirty-looking yellowish brick his father said was called London stock. They reminded him of the Polish war widows in Pashka's, with their camphor-smelling clothes and their vanished hero husbands, their double rows of pearls hidden beneath their moth eaten cardigans. There were still bomb sites along Lee High Road but not as many now as there had been. Mostly they had been built on. The Lewisham end of Lee High Road had suffered most but even that was being done up. It was all hairdressers and cafes now. Kip fingered the loose change in his pocket, wondering if he had enough for a burger or a sausage sandwich. Men and girls slid by in loud gaggles, pushing aside the darkness with their laughter, the glare from the bars and the streetlamps pooling in orange lightslicks on their garish clothes. Kip liked being on the streets at night. There was a restlessness in people, the sense that anything might happen at any time. He wished he had brought the Nikon. He stopped outside a kebab shop, drawn by the scents of sweet garlic and coriander. The yellow glow from the lighted window spilled out across the grubby pavement in a radiant trapezium, a distorted yellow shadow of the window glass. There were three men up at the counter. They all had their backs to him but one of them seemed vaguely familiar and as Kip studied his worn-out jacket and tatty Levis he realised with a sudden start that it was Dennis Croft. His gut twisted in a mild spasm, and sweat broke out on his palms.

Distantly, as if it were something he was watching on a movie screen, he saw Croft turn towards the window and beckon him inside.

"Can I stand you a kebab?" Croft said. "They're always good here."

What the heck? Kip thought. *I was about to buy one anyway*. He found it difficult to explain to himself why he had obeyed Croft's summons, only that he was hungry, and that he wanted to see what would happen. Also, he resented the idea that Croft could make him afraid, that he might start avoiding places just because Croft happened to be there. He stood at Croft's side at the counter, leaning against the angled glass and staring up at the television mounted on the wall behind. The reception was bad, and the sizzling of meat on the grill made the soundtrack all but inaudible. Kip gazed without much interest at the striking tube workers, the visiting president he had seen already on the early news. When the picture of the monster appeared it seemed to come out of the blue, although if he had thought about it more carefully he would have realised it was coming. It had been on the early news also, only he had forgotten. If he had remembered he could have done something, turned away from the screen at the crucial moment. He could have watched the traffic outside until the news had finished. It would have been easy.

Now that Croft was there to compare it with, he realised the photo fit was not all that good. The glasses were the wrong shape, and they made the monster's face look squarer than it actually was. Also the real Croft's cheekbones were more pronounced, the eyebrows thinner and less un-kempt-looking. He saw that Croft too was staring at the picture. He ex-perienced a sinking feeling, the kind of sick resignation he remembered from all the times he had been handed the results of an exam he already knew he had failed, the dismal knowledge of having been *found out*. The silence between them seemed to deepen and increase, spreading through the air like some poisonous gas. After what seemed like a long time Croft turned to him, smiling the ratty little half smile Kip remem-bered from when he had asked him about the Nikon.

"Weird likeness, isn't it?" he said. "I keep expecting them to come and arrest me."

The fry cook was wrapping their kebabs in greaseproof paper, fold-ing it quickly and expertly, the finished parcels like tiny papooses. Croft tore the paper aside almost immediately and bit straight into the middle of his kebab. Kip watched, amazed, wondering how he was able to do that without burning himself. Croft nodded briskly as if in approval and started towards the door. His mouth was smeared with grease, the thin lips glistening. The shop was full now, there were half a dozen people in the queue behind them. The darkness of the street outside seemed deeper and more complete, though Kip knew it was most likely just the contrast with the bright lights inside the kebab shop.

"Your food OK?" Croft said.

Kip nodded. They were walking side by side in the direction of the clock tower. The seconds were passing quickly, and Kip knew he had to say something, that to say nothing would be dangerous, almost as revealing as coming right out and accusing Croft of being the killer. He took a small bite of his kebab. The meat was charred on the outside, pink and tender within. It tasted as delicious as it smelled.

"They all look the same though, these photo fits, don't they? They could be anyone."

"I know you've been following me," Croft said suddenly. The tone of his voice had changed. There was something mean in it, a glistening menace that made Kip think of tensile steel: tripwires, garrottes. He turned to face Kip, forcing him back against one of the shop fronts. "You were taking pictures of me in the park the other day." He spoke in a harsh whisper, leaning in close, and Kip could smell the garlic on his breath. He stared at Kip fixedly, as if he would have liked to grab hold of him, strike him maybe, as if the effort of not doing so was placing him under a strain. Kip supposed he did not want to draw attention to himself, although no one passing by on the pavement was taking any notice of them and Kip realised they probably thought the monster was his father.

"I take photographs of people all the time. It doesn't mean anything. I don't know what you're talking about." His words came out in a rush, slipping over each other like coins spilling from a beggar's torn pocket. Kip replayed them in his mind more slowly, looking for loopholes. So far as he could tell there weren't any. He decided that so long as he stuck to his story he would be safe.

"Those pictures don't look like you anyway," he added. "It's the glasses, that's all." He looked Croft straight in the eye and thought about his father, the way he would come in from seeing Grace Hemingway and ask what was for supper, and his mother would tell him goulash and Kip would play along with her because he knew his world would explode into pieces if he didn't.

The point was to stick to your story. The murderers in the cop films all knew that and so did his father. It was more a matter of nerve than a matter of fact.

Croft took a step backwards, his face relaxing. Kip laughed to signal that everything was all right between them, and after a couple of seconds Croft laughed too. Kip took more bites from his kebab, still seeing in his mind's eye Croft as he had been moments earlier: the hard line of his mouth, the hollow cheeks, pale in the lamplight, the agitated posture, like that of a beast of prey about to spring.

He had seemed for those few minutes to become something else. At first it was rats Kip thought of, the way a cornered rat could kill a dog if it was desperate enough, or so he had heard. But then he found himself thinking of his Polish grandmother Dasha, and a story she used to tell him when he was younger that she called *The Wolf in Sheep's Clothing*. The story was about a monster that could change its shape at will to blend in with its surroundings. There was a special word she had for it too: *wilkolek*, or maybe *wilkolak*, the Polish word for werewolf. He had forgotten all about it until now.

It came to him that murderers, perhaps child murderers especially, were the ultimate shape shifters. You could bump against one in the crowd, on the station platform, in a supermarket and never suspect for a moment that what you were seeing was not an ordinary person but a *wilkolak*. It was only at certain moments that they revealed themselves for what they were. On a darkened street outside a kebab shop, for example. In the nylon-curtained back bedroom of a caravan on the Isle of Sheppey.

He did not believe in werewolves of course, not any more. But he knew the creature he had glimpsed in Croft's eyes was capable of anything.

It was important not to let Croft see that he knew that. It was his certainty over this – a cold feeling, but steady and clear, like the knowledge of his father's affair with Grace Hemingway – that kept him from panic, from simply dropping his kebab on the pavement and running away. He asked himself what he would do, what he would say to Croft now if Croft were not a monster but a human being.

I would talk to him about the murder, he thought. *I would want to find out what he thought.* This answer, the right answer, seemed to light up his mind like one of the illuminated boxes on *The Weakest Link*. He knew also that it had to be now, right away, while the subject still lay open between them. If he returned to the matter later it would just look weird.

"It makes you think though, doesn't it?" he said. "That guy really is still out there somewhere."

Croft swallowed the last of his kebab then used the greaseproof paper to wipe his fingers. "There are always men like that," he said. "It doesn't matter how many you catch, there will always be more." He crushed the paper between his hands and dumped it into a waste bin at the side of the road. "Do you suppose he's really all that different from you?"

Kip shuddered inside his skin, the kind of quick involuntary movement he sometimes experienced just before falling asleep. It was as if Croft had read his mind, yet the way he had twisted his thoughts, turning them back on themselves so they pointed at him instead of Croft, filled him with outrage.

"You can't tell me that a guy who does stuff like that is normal?"

"What's normal?" Croft said, smiling. "Everyone has a side of themselves they don't want other people to see."

"But this is different. This sicko killed someone. He murdered a little girl."

"Soldiers kill little girls every day. You don't see many of them getting arrested for murder." Croft was staring at him intently, in a way that made Kip feel uncomfortable. The look was back, the fixed, crazy *wilkolak* look, not as bad as before but enough to remind Kip of what it had been like to glimpse that side of him, the side he didn't want other people to see. It occurred to him suddenly that it was his job that had made him that way, his work as a forensic photographer, that the sight of the dead and dying had unhinged him somehow, the way it had with soldiers in Vietnam. Kip had gone through a phase of watching 'Nam films, although he had grown tired of them in the end because they only ever seemed to show one side of the story. Nonetheless they might help explain Croft.

For people like the 'Nam vets killing was just another fact of life; they stopped being able tell what was normal and what was not.

"Did you ever have to photograph a murder? A proper murder I mean, with blood and everything?" Kip's heart pounded with a strange excitement. He was surprised and ashamed at how much he wanted to know the answer to his question. *Perhaps he's right*, Kip thought. *There's a monster in all of us.*

"Plenty of times," Croft said. "Do you want to see the pictures?" He moved a step closer, so close that Kip imagined he could feel the heat from his body, even though he knew it was just the night air he could feel, the warm night air mingled with the sharp scent of diesel. For the first time he felt really afraid. He knew there was nothing innocent about Croft's question, that it was indecent somehow, as if he was asking Kip if he wanted to go to a porn film with him, and the worst thing about it was that he *wanted* Kip to know this, he wanted to make him complicit.

Kip realised he hated Croft, that he loathed him in the way he loathed dog turds, or butter beans, with a vertiginous, sliding repulsion that grew out of instinct and not out of reason. Yet still he could not look away. It was the same as with the dead rat, the spoiled milk. It was not just because Croft knew how to use a camera that Kip felt drawn to him; he was drawn to Croft because Croft had seen terrible things.

"That would be great," he said. "I've been looking at some forensic stuff online actually. I was thinking I might want to get into it. Once I've finished college, I mean."

"Are you sure about that?" Croft said. "Most of it's pretty dull."

Kip shook his head. "Not for me. I like the idea of it. I like the idea of never knowing what's coming next."

Croft laughed. "That's one way of putting it, I suppose. Mind your back." He drew a ballpoint pen from his jacket pocket, and a small scrap of paper. When Kip examined the paper later he discovered it was a receipt from the DIY store at the bottom end of Lee High Road, that Croft had bought two tins of white emulsion and a bottle of turps. Croft placed a hand on Kip's shoulder, bending him forward and resting the paper on his back just below the left shoulder blade. Kip could feel the biro moving over the paper, the pressure of Croft's hand firm and even and slyly insistent. Kip fixed his eyes on the pavement. The flagstones were filthy. The whole of Lee High Road was like that, but it couldn't help it. Most of the dirt was caused by traffic fumes.

"All done," Croft said, and Kip straightened up. Croft handed him the paper, which Kip saw now had an address written on it, and a mobile telephone number. "I'm busy over the weekend, but you can come on Tuesday afternoon if you like. We can have a chat and I can show you some photos. Don't forget to bring your camera." He slipped the biro back in his pocket. "See you, then."

He walked off without looking round, heading back the way they had come. Kip took a few steps after him, thinking that he could trail Croft, see where he went, then realised he didn't need to because he had Croft's address already on the scrap of paper. It occurred to him that he could go to the police now, that he could tell them everything. He could have Dennis Croft arrested within the hour.

He knew almost at once that he wouldn't do it. If he went to the police he would be forced to explain himself, to tell them why he had Croft's address, why he suspected Croft of being the killer in the first place. He would also have to tell them who else knew, and that meant Sonia. He imagined a cop car drawing up outside the Vardens' house, Timothy

Varden demanding to know what the hell Kip thought he was doing getting his daughter mixed up with a paedophile. It would be like telling his father he knew about Grace Hemingway, tearing his world apart in all the wrong places.

He also had the feeling that when the police went to arrest him, Croft would no longer be there. It was a feeling he couldn't explain but that he trusted completely, a deep itch, the same feeling he had sometimes during a game of Harris, when he knew the person sitting opposite had the ace of spades.

Still further back in his mind he was nagged by the sense that none of these things explained his refusal to act, that the real truth was that he didn't want Croft arrested just yet, because he was keen to get a look at his photographs.

All he knew for certain was that he wanted to talk to Sonia. He turned left into Brandram Road, walking until he was out of earshot of the main traffic. He keyed Sonia's number, convinced that she would not answer, that she was out with friends, or that she had left her phone in her bag and wouldn't hear it ringing. She answered on the third ring.

"Hey," she said. She sounded happy, and he seemed to catch a trace of her scent, the fresh, tangy scent of the pine soap she used with something else running beneath it, the dense musky smell that came from her armpits and between her legs. He wondered what she had been doing when he called.

"Hey Son," he said. "You OK?"

"I'm fine. What's the matter, Eddie? You sound weird."

His dad called him Ed, his friends called him Kip, his teachers all called him Kiplas. Only his mother and Sonia called him Eddie. He had hoped that hearing Sonia's voice would make things better somehow, would get rid of all his crazy thoughts about werewolves and Dennis Croft being a murderer but instead it was just making things worse. He couldn't get rid of the idea that she was in danger. He wished there was a way of keeping her safe without having to tell her anything. If he told her she might think that he was insane.

"Have you still got that photo?" he said. His mouth felt dry and he swallowed. There was a back-taste of onion and charcoal.

"What photo? The one of the guy outside the garage."

He nodded, forgetting for a moment that she couldn't see him. "Yes," he said. "Did you keep it?"

"What do you think? You know I love your stuff. What's going on?"

He felt a surge of happiness, that she should treat him like a *real artist*, then fought to suppress it. "It's just that, well, I think I saw the guy again, that's all."

"What d'you mean, you saw him again? How long ago?"

"The other day, in Manor Park Gardens. And then this evening, up by the clock tower. I think it was him, anyway. He was too far away for me to see him properly."

The phone went quiet, and for long awful seconds Kip felt certain she knew he was lying, that he was telling her only a small part of the truth. He pressed the phone hard to his ear, but all he could hear was his own breathing. When Sonia spoke again the sound was unnaturally loud.

"Can I tell you something, Eddie? Promise you won't laugh?"

"Course I won't, Son. Just tell me, all right?" He wondered if she was about to dump him, although it didn't sound like that from her voice. *If you touch her I'll kill you*, he thought. *You rat-faced bastard.*

"He reminds me of someone. The guy."

"Someone you know, you mean?"

"Not really." She hesitated. "I think I saw him in a dream once. Only he wasn't really a man, he was some kind of monster. He could kill people, just by looking at them. I had problems sleeping after that, for a while. My mum thought it was all to do with my periods starting." She giggled, a light, tight sound that was not really like her. "It was ages ago now. I'd forgotten all about it until I saw the photo."

"A monster?" He could hear his voice rising in pitch, and he knew he sounded as if he was about to explode with laughter, only it wasn't that, it was the opposite. He felt like breaking down and telling her everything.

"Yes. You promised you wouldn't laugh."

"I'm not. So you reckon the guy in the photo is the guy from your dream?"

"Of course not. How could he be? They look the same, that's all. Something about the cheekbones. And those glasses."

"Like a rat."

"That's a strange way of describing it but I know what you mean." She paused. "I put the photo away in a drawer. Do you mind?"

"Of course I don't mind. I wish you'd chuck it out, get rid of it."

"I'm not binning your work over a stupid dream I had five years ago. The guy in the picture is just some guy, anyway, he's no one. I was just a bit freaked, that's all."

"You'll keep the photo in the drawer though, won't you?"

"If that's what you want. Are you sure everything's OK?"

"Everything's fine. Do you want me to come over tomorrow?"

Tomorrow was Saturday. Croft had said he would be busy over the weekend. Busy with what, exactly? Kip found he didn't want to think about it.

"You'd better, or I might kill you. We can go to the woods, if you want."

Kip guessed what she meant, and felt himself blushing. "I'll bring my camera," he said absently. He remembered how she had looked the last time, afterwards, the yellow leaves in her red hair. If you could capture a moment like that then you were some kind of genius.

"Go home now," said Sonia. "It's getting late."

"How did you know I was out?"

"I can hear the road, silly."

"You're magic, Son," he said, and ended the call. On Lee High Road the buses sailed by like pirate ships, and from the gardens in Brandram Road there came a faint scent of honeysuckle. He realised it was night, real night, the bottomless tract of hours between dusk and morning. In his grandmother's stories this had always been the time of the *wilkolak*.

He met Sonia off the 122 bus at the bottom end of Lee High Road, then they walked up Lee Park to Blackheath Village, where they caught the number 89 to Shooter's Hill. Sonia had made a picnic, cheese sandwiches and flapjacks and orange juice. She had also brought a canvas holdall with a blanket in it. They spread the blanket under some trees and had sex again. It was better than the last time, different somehow, as if both of them had grown older overnight.

Neither of them mentioned the monster. Sonia talked about what might happen when they went away to college, and Kip supposed her need to make plans might have scared some people but it didn't worry him. He found he liked it. He closed his eyes and drifted. A sweet breeze played with the leaves, and Kip found himself thinking that they were safe here, that Croft wouldn't come to the forest, he was a city rat.

He was awakened by Sonia kissing him. She kissed him full on the mouth, pressing her lips carefully against his as if she meant to leave an imprint there, the way girls did with soldiers' handkerchiefs in the old war movies.

"I want you to know that whatever happened today was real," she said. "That all of this really happened." Her top half was still naked. Her hair trailed in the grass, like runners of flame about to start a brush fire.

"What do you mean?" Kip said. "What do you think's going to happen?"

"Nothing," Sonia said. "I'm just saying."

He took some photos of her, just head shots. Her eyes were closed, her eyelashes cast spiderleg shadows on the curves of her cheeks.

Kip knew that someone would have had to photograph Rebecca Riding, that if he was serious about forensic photography he might soon be having to photograph dead girls all the time.

When he arrived home that evening he found his parents were going to dinner at the Toklins'. His mother had put on a dress Kip knew his father liked to see her in: cream-coloured silk cut low at the front and covered in large pink roses. She seemed nervously excited, as if she and Andy had only just met, and her nervousness made her beautiful. She was perched on the edge of the sofa, painting her nails with gold varnish and watching the news.

"Where's dad?" Kip said.

"At the off licence I hope. He's supposed to be buying a bottle of that Bulgarian Merlot Toke likes. Be quiet for a moment, Eddie, I want to listen."

"What's the big deal?"

"It looks like they've caught that maniac."

Kip stared at the television. The photo fit of the monster was filling the screen. A man had been arrested and charged with the rape and murder of Rebecca Riding. The man's name was Steven Jepsom and he was from Brownhill Road, Catford.

"Thank God for that," Lynn said. "Good riddance to bad rubbish."

"We don't know it's him yet," said Kip. "Not until he's been convicted."

He wished they would show a picture of Jepsom but Kip guessed it was illegal to put someone's photo all over the news while there was still a chance they were innocent. He knew he should feel relieved but he somehow didn't. He wanted to know if Jepsom looked like Croft. It occurred to him that Steven Jepsom might be Dennis Croft's real name.

His mother glanced at him, her lips tightening.

"Aren't you pleased? At least it's some comfort for the family, knowing he's behind bars at last."

"I'm just saying," Kip said. "I hope they got the right bloke, that's all."

Lynn frowned, and looked as if she was about to say something else, but at that moment Andy Kiplas returned from the off licence. He had the bottle of wine under one arm, wrapped in a sheet of green tissue paper. The ends of the paper had been twisted into a fan shape.

"Hurry up," Andy said. "I've got us a taxi."

Lynn's cheeks coloured to match the roses on her dress. "A taxi? What's all this in aid of?"

Kip's father was standing holding the door open like a butler in a television murder mystery. As Lynn got up from the sofa he bowed and began humming a tune from one of the opera CDs he sometimes listened to in the car. His mother laughed, and a look passed between her and his father that made Kip feel stupid and in the way, as if all his worrying about his mother had been for nothing. He wished they would keep their business to themselves.

He waited for them to leave, then turned off the television. He fetched the Nikon from his room and began to photograph the back room and the hallway, pretending that the house was the scene of a crime. He did a series of close ups of the glass tumbler his mother had been drinking from. The tumbler was still half full of tonic water, and there was a fingerprint clearly visible near the brim. Lynn had changed her mind about her shoes at the last minute, and one of the discarded ones, a high-heeled pink sandal, lay on its side in the doorway. If you looked at things a certain way the dirty glass and the fallen shoe looked suspicious, as if someone had left the room in a terrible hurry.

He became so absorbed in the details that there were moments when he forgot he was in his own home. Eventually he laid the camera aside on the sofa and went through to the kitchen. There was potato salad in the fridge, some Polish salami, the remains of his parents' lunch. He piled it into a bowl and was about to put it all in the microwave when his phone rang. It was Sonia. He picked up at once.

"Did you hear?" she said. "They got him."

"Yes," Kip said. "I saw it on the news earlier."

"Do you reckon it's him? The guy in the photo I mean?"

"I doubt it. I'd forgotten all about him, really." He was caught off guard by a memory of her, leaning against a tree as she pulled on her jeans. Her back was long, with a very slight curvature of the spine. There were exercises she was meant to do to stop it getting stiff but she was always forgetting. The skin over her vertebrae was taut and pearly white, the row of smooth bumps reminding him always of a saying of his mother's: *rare as hens' teeth, they are.* Quite suddenly the last thing he wanted to talk about was Dennis Croft.

"Can you call me back on the landline?" Sonia said. "They're showing *Donnie Darko* on Channel 4 in a moment. We could sit and watch it together, if you like?"

"What about your parents?" Kip said.

"They're out. With some people from Deutsche Bank. They won't be back for hours."

He finished microwaving the food then took the hall phone upstairs to his room. He dialled Sonia's home number and she picked up almost before it had a chance to ring. Half way through the film Kip got undressed and lay down on his bed, clutching the phone between his neck and his shoulder to stop it slipping.

"You're taking your clothes off," said Sonia. "I can hear you doing it."

"I am not."

"Liar!"

"Shut up, I'm missing the film."

He closed his eyes and thought of Sonia lying on top of him. The fact that she was both far away and close made him feel breathless with excitement. He began to rub himself, focussing on the sound of her breathing and trying not to make any noise.

"Kip?" she said some time later. "You OK?"

"You're rare as hens' teeth, you are." A single tear ran diagonally across his face. "Watch the film."

When the film was over they said goodnight and ended the call. Kip pulled up the duvet and lay in the dark, watching the television with the sound turned down. Eventually he fell asleep. He woke briefly just after two. There was a light on downstairs and the sound of voices. For a moment Kip felt frightened. He remembered the dirty tumbler and the discarded shoe and thought something awful had happened. Then he realised it was just his parents coming home from the Toklins'. They spoke in loud whispers like miscreant school kids. He could tell from the way they were moving that they were both drunk.

He began to drift off again almost at once. His father was humming the Toreador Song out of *Carmen*. His mother stumbled against the box of newspapers in the hall, swore loudly and then stifled a laugh.

The box shouldn't even have been there. His father was supposed to take it out on Fridays for recycling.

Just before he fell asleep, Kip decided he would not go to Croft's house on the Tuesday, after all.

Croft's house was on Belmont Hill, the Lewisham end, one of a long Victorian terrace, the tall, gabled houses running away down the steep gradient like toppling dominoes. Kip photographed the house from both sides of the road, wondering if Croft was watching him from behind the curtains. He doubted it. He had already made up his mind on the way over that Croft would not be in when he called, that the address on the piece of paper was not even his. He told himself the only reason he was going there was to prove the whole thing was a fake. He pressed the bell, trying to work out what he would say if the door was opened by a complete stranger, a large woman in a flowered bathrobe say, or an old man in a saggy green cardigan with the elbows worn through.

Excuse me, but does Mr Gaumont live here? I promised my uncle I'd change his library books for him.

Kip liked the sound of Mr Gaumont. The idea of him was so convincing that when the door opened and Croft appeared Kip had to think who he was. It seemed for a moment that Croft was the fantasy, not Gaumont, old Gaumont who was so harmless and so plausible. It crossed his mind that Croft had done away with Gaumont, just as he had done away with Rebecca Riding.

"Hi there," Croft said. "Come in."

He took a step back from the door. As Kip entered the house it occurred to him that nobody in the world knew where he was. He found himself wishing he had left a note in his room, or that he had texted Sonia. He wondered how often bad things happened to people because they were afraid of looking stupid, and supposed it was often, more often than you might think, anyway.

"Excuse the mess," Croft said. "This was my dad's place. He left it in a bit of a state. It's taking me a while to get things straight."

There were some black bin bags at the foot of the stairs but other than that there was no mess that Kip could see. The hallway of the house was dark, made darker by the varnished wood panelling and dull red carpet. There was a smell of mothballs and furniture polish, reminding him of the Toklins' house, which was owned by Lyonel Toklin's ninety-year-old mother, Violet. Lynn Kiplas always joked that Violet Toklin was so stingy she hadn't had the place decorated since Victoria was on the throne, and Kip felt half-inclined to believe her. Croft led the way through to a room at the back, home to an enormous buttonback sofa and a boiler on a tiled hearth protected by a square metal cage. There were piles of books everywhere. Kip noticed a stack of *Photography Now* and some issues of another magazine that he knew you could only get on subscription from America.

"Can I get you anything?" Croft said. "A drink maybe?"

Kip shook his head, then asked for a glass of water. It seemed safer to ask for something than nothing at all. He perched himself on the edge of the sofa and fiddled with the strap of the Nikon. He was desperate to photograph this room, with its stacks of old magazines and blacked floorboards, the sofa itself, leathery and vast as a beached whale. *Leviathan*, he thought, savouring the sound of it, a word that seemed to open its jaws and admit the world.

Croft disappeared into the kitchen, returning a few moments later with two glasses on a tray and two cans of Coke. He sat down next to Kip on the sofa, placing the tray on a low stool that stood close by.

"You can have water instead if that's what you want," he said. "But I thought you might like one of these. They're straight from the fridge."

"No, this is great," Kip said. "Thanks." He popped the seal on the can and poured the frothing liquid into the glass. He thought how typical it was of Croft, that he would drink Coke from a glass instead of straight from the can. It went with his old Minolta, his Oxfam clothes, and the thought that he could still predict Croft this way, that he could read him, made Kip feel calmer. He had come here of his own free will, after all. If he wanted to he could just get up and leave.

"Well?" Croft said. He took a sip of his Coke then wiped his mouth with the back of his hand. "Did you bring anything to show me?"

"You can have a look at these if you want. They're my most recent." Kip hesitated. "I didn't print them out. I don't think they're good enough." He handed Croft the Nikon. He had cleared its memory of everything except the pictures he had taken on the Saturday night, the mock scene-of-crime photos of his own living room. He wondered if Croft would have any difficulty operating the camera but he handled it as if he had been using digital cameras for years, and Kip supposed he probably had. He wondered if all the spouting about film was just guff, a pose that Croft had affected to impress him.

Croft scrolled quickly through the series of images and then worked his way backwards more slowly, taking time to examine each frame.

"These are good," he said. "Interesting. Did you take them at home?"

Kip nodded. "I was trying to look at the room in a different way, as if there'd been a murder there or something. It made me wonder what things might be important, you know, if you were photographing a real crime scene. I never thought about working for the police before but I think I might like it. It's interesting."

"Do you think you'd be able to handle seeing the bad stuff?"

Kip looked down at his hands. "It'd be my job to handle it, wouldn't it? I'd have to get used to it."

"Well, that's something you'd have to find out for yourself." Croft put his glass down on the floor and stood up. He leaned over, resting a hand briefly on Kip's shoulder and reaching behind the sofa. He drew out a large portfolio, black leather with a long brass zip. The zip gleamed in the black like a row of bared teeth. "I've got some shots here you can look at. Some of them are quite strong. I'd probably get into trouble actually, if anyone knew I'd been showing you these without your parents' permission." He caught Kip's eye and winked, though whether to show he was joking or trying to involve Kip in his guilt Kip didn't know. Croft retook his seat on the couch, so close beside him now that Kip could feel his warmth through his jeans, Croft's leg resting against his own with a slight outward pressure. Croft smelled of the house, as if his clothes were not quite fresh. Kip unzipped the portfolio. It was crammed with images, photographic prints mainly though there were some newspaper clippings and photocopies, everything jumbled together like an insane montage. On top of the pile lay an enlarged shot of what had once been someone's living room, only now it was mostly reduced to a heap of ash. On the picture's right hand margin stood a humped black thing about the size of a wheelie bin which Kip guessed had probably been an armchair. In front of this object was a single plate-sized patch of carpet that had somehow escaped being burned. Its colours were still bright, an interlocking pattern of blue and red diamonds. Kip thought there was something naked about the colours, something horrible. Underneath the photo of the burned-out living room there was a picture of a bicycle wheel, bent almost in half by the force of some impact. Its spokes jutted in all directions like shattered ribs.

"The lad on that bike was fifteen," Croft said. "He died at the scene." He pulled another picture from the stack, seeming to do it at random though Kip found time to wonder later if it had all been planned. The photograph, an enlarged detail, showed a pair of hands bound at the wrists with a coil of barbed wire. The thumbnails were caked with blood, so thick in places that Kip thought at first it was mud. There were long vertical gashes around the wrist bones, showing clearly how the wire had been dragged into place before it was tied.

Kip could not tell if the hands belonged to a man or a woman though the crooked, rather ugly shape of the top thumb joint gave him the feeling it was probably a man. The photograph was horrible, yet it was also beautiful, immortal somehow, like a still from a documentary about the First World War. It was clear as life, with the kind of singing exactitude people meant when they talked about photographic clarity even when most photographs taken by ordinary people, Kip knew, were not clear at all. Most amateur shots were blurred or badly composed, off kilter in some way. The photograph of the bound hands was so true to life it leaked its atmosphere all over the room, the drizzle-grey of a cold morning in November when a man had died in pain with his face in the mud.

"This guy turned up on a building site in Charlton," Croft said. "He was dead when they found him. I took these pictures while we were waiting for the ambulance."

"Did they catch the killers?"

Croft nodded. "It was a gang crime. Seven men were arrested. Two of them got long prison sentences."

"And your photos helped to get them put away?"

"Maybe. Probably. But that's never the thing you think about, at least not until later. At the time all you care about is the picture, about getting it right. I hardly gave that poor guy a thought while I was taking these shots, he was just a subject. I despise myself for that, but it doesn't change anything. But you already know all this, Kip, you're an intelligent boy. If what you wanted was to help catch murderers you'd become a detective inspector, not a photographer."

Kip stared down at the photograph. He knew that what Croft said was true, truer even than Croft realised. If Kip's interest lay in solving crimes he would have reported Croft to the police a fortnight ago. Instead he had taken pictures of him, and now he was here in Croft's house, talking with him about photography. He did not care if Croft was the monster, only that he was here to have this conversation. He was glad the police had arrested Steven Jepsom instead of him. He wondered if Croft would help him with his college application.

"Can I use your loo?" Kip said suddenly. It was not just that he needed the toilet, although the can of Coke had filled his bladder to bursting. Mostly it was that he wanted to get away from Croft for a couple of minutes. Being with Croft was exhausting. He was also curious to see the upstairs of Croft's house.

"It's the first door upstairs, to your right," Croft said. "We could go for a curry later, if you like."

"That'd be good," Kip said. He got up from the couch. He tried to smile at Croft, but the smile seemed to slide from his face at the last moment. He made his way back down the hall. He noticed that the door to the understairs cupboard had a bolt on it, wondered briefly why that was and then supposed that the basement floor was where Croft kept his darkroom. He went upstairs, stepping over the bin bags, which looked to be full of old clothes. There were four doors on the upper landing. Kip opened one at random and found Croft's bedroom, the bed unmade, a crumpled T-shirt strewn across the floor. The room next door was piled high with old furniture.

The bathroom, when he found it, was at least clean. The window was open, letting in the outside air. There was a faint smell of disinfectant.

He used the toilet and then washed his hands. He thought he would tell Croft that he had decided against the curry, that he should go home, that he had schoolwork to do, something or anything, he did not know why. He turned to go back downstairs, glancing as he did so into the one room he had not yet entered, a narrow room at the back, a spare bedroom most likely, or the bedroom that had belonged to Croft's dead father. There was a wooden bedstead, the mattress stripped to its striped cover, stained with age, the shallow depression towards the centre where the old man had lain. Kip wondered if he had died there. He felt instinctively for the Nikon, then realised he had left it downstairs. He pulled the door to, wondering if Croft might give him permission to photograph the room anyway, whether it would be rude or strange to ask.

He noticed there were some photographs propped by the skirting board, enlargements mounted on cardboard and protected by cellophane. They did not look like forensic shots. Kip bent to look at them, curious. He remembered how Croft had talked of using some of his father's money to buy a new camera. He wondered what kind of photography Croft was into, now that he was no longer working for the police.

There were six photographs, and they were all of Rebecca Riding. Two were in colour. Kip recognised her red jumper from the *Crimewatch* reconstruction, the fair hair hitched up on one side by a hair slide in the shape of a butterfly.

The rest of the pictures were in black-and-white, four miraculous, pristine prints that revealed the child for what she was: the only girl in the world at that moment, and Dennis Croft her only audience. In the final shot she looked straight at the camera, her gappy teeth bared in a sweet, shy smile that seemed to suggest she knew she was being looked at, but didn't mind.

She did not seem in the least afraid. Kip felt a rush of nausea, and then of cold, as if he were going down with a virus. The girl was so *there* in the photographs it was impossible to accept that she was no longer alive.

He turned the pictures around to face the wall then went back into the bathroom. He leaned over the toilet bowl, wanting to be sick, but the only thing that came was a kind of dry gagging. He ran water into the basin, turning both taps on full to make the maximum noise. Then he flushed the toilet again. He knew he had to go back downstairs, that his life might now depend on him being able to act as if nothing had happened.

He crossed the landing to the head of the stairs. He stared down into the hallway, at the front door with its stained glass fanlight, the delicate leaded panes arranged in a design he believed was called *fleur de lys*. The door was probably not locked, Kip could not remember Croft locking it. The idea that he might have done was crazy of course, but all Kip could think of was the image that had come to him before: worlds colliding, a wrecking ball spinning on its chain as it crashed through the wall of the known universe.

He heard footsteps at the end of the hall. A moment later Croft's voice came rising towards him up the stairs.

"You OK up there?" Croft said. "I want to show you the darkroom. Dad's cellar was part of the reason I moved back in here permanently."

Kip stayed where we was, paralysed by the sound of his own breathing. He knew that what he did in the next few seconds would decide everything.

CHRISTOPHER FOWLER
THE CONSPIRATORS

At the next table of the hotel restaurant, three waiters took their places beside the diners, and with a synchronised flourish raised the silver covers on their salvers. A fourth appeared, bearing a tray containing a quartet of tiny copper pots. Each waiter took a handle and proceeded to pour the sauces from the pots onto the salvers from a height of not less than eighteen inches. They might have been tipping jewels into coffers.

Court and Lassiter barely bothered to break off their conversation and look up at the display. They knew that these ostentatious rituals were the hotel's way of justifying the risible menu prices to tourists.

The waiters finished serving and tiptoed away, leaving the diners to warble and coo over their miniscule meals, some kind of cubed chicken in cream. The restaurant was steel, glass and black crystal, with the occasional tortured twist of green bamboo providing natural colour. It was as hushed as a funeral parlour. Everyone seemed to be whispering.

Sean Lassiter had ordered a steak, medium rare, the only item on the menu that looked like meat. He had eaten it as if he was in an American diner, using only a fork. The steaks were so tender you could do that here. "When was the last time you knew exactly what you wanted?" he asked Court, raising his whisky tumbler and studying his former business partner through the diamond-cut lattice.

Oliver Court's palms were dry, but he still pressed them against his thighs. Lassiter had once been his mentor, and was the only man in the world who could make him uncomfortable with a simple question.

"Come on, Oliver, I saw the look in your eyes the first day I met you. Nowadays I can't read your eyes, because you're wearing coloured contacts. I remember, you were so hungry and envious I thought you might actually start taking notes during our meal. I see that look a lot, but it's not usually so obvious. When members of my staff get that anxious, it usually means they're frightened of failure and they're scared of being found out. Well, I can't blame anyone for wanting to make the best of themselves. But you were prepared to leave behind an awful lot in order to be a success."

It was a gentle rebuke, but a rebuke nonetheless. Lassiter was old school; his compliments were backhanded and his criticisms were constructive. He knew the difference between perspicacity and merely being rude. For a businessman who had been on the road for the past forty years, he was immaculately groomed. His hair was sleek and white, his tan subtle, his suit quietly extravagant.

He's heard something about me, thought Court, shifting carefully on his chromium chair, which was too low. The central column of the table prevented him from stretching out his long legs.

"Have you got where you wanted to be?"

Court did not trust himself to tell the truth. From here he could see out through the curvilinear glass of the restaurant. In front of the hotel, trucks drove back and forth along the spotlit spit of land that projected into the blackness of the Persian Gulf. The Indian workers went around the clock in shifts, building ever further out into the sea.

They had kept the conversation light while they ate. Families, schools, colleagues, holidays, topics suitable for food. The serious part required a clear table and strong drinks.

There was only one other drinker at the bar, a nylon-haired brunette with long legs, a tiny waist and perfectly circular breasts, like a character from a video game. The décolletage of her tight black dress was cut to the aureoles of her nipples. Lassiter assumed she kept herself more carefully covered beyond the confines of the hotel. They were in the Middle East, after all. Seamed stockings, high heels, a brassiere that must have presented an engineering challenge, she was about twenty three years old and blatantly selling herself. He wondered what the young Arabic barman thought of her.

Court caught him thoughtfully studying the call-girl's legs. "How long have you known me, Sean?" he asked, buying time.

"Long enough to see where you're going." Lassiter smiled. He'd had his teeth bleached. They shone peppermint white in the black light from the bar, and made him look like a game show host. He noticed Court following his eyes to the girl. "It's just an honest question."

In truth, Lassiter had been disappointed by his apprentice. Court needed the approval of others, and as a consequence, his ambitions were displayed for all to see. He never took advice, so why was he here? Somewhere deep inside Lassiter an alarm bell rang.

Court knew he could not be completely honest, because there was too much at stake. "I think I've been pretty successful," he answered carefully. "There's still a way to go. That's why I value your advice."

Lassiter looked almost relieved. Perhaps he didn't want to have an argument with his former pupil. "Your division is doing very nicely, Oliver. You're about to expand it, you wouldn't be human if you didn't feel a little nervous. From what I hear, my directors will back you, but in these uncertain times you'll need to detail your long-term plans. Just don't be too eager. The English don't trust people who are anxious to please. It puts them off. They want negotiations to be tricky enough for their colleagues to see how hard they work."

"I can't remember a time when I didn't look up to you," said Court, catching the waitress's eye and sewing the air with his right hand, the universal sign for *check, please.* "You've always been my – "

"Don't say mentor, Oliver, it makes me feel positively ancient."

"I was going to say friend. I feel I can tell you anything and I'll always get a straight answer."

"So long as it works both ways."

"You don't have to ask that. I was still just a property agent when you gave me a job. Now I run the whole of the US division. I'd appreciate it if you could cast an eye over my proposals, just to get your feedback." Despite the difference in their ages, they were now almost evenly matched in terms of their careers within the company. Lassiter still gave the hotel chain class and respectability. Many considered Court to be an upstart, but he had made North America profitable again by building flashy boutique hotels aimed at kids with money.

Lassiter smiled at his glass, twisting it. "It would be my pleasure, you know that." Court was offering to show him his plans ahead of the directors' meeting? He'd want something in return, but what, and how badly?

Lassiter looked around at the empty bar, the midnight blue carpet, the silver walls, the glittering star-points in the ceiling. He wondered if this was what Heaven looked like, without a bill at the end of the evening.

"Excuse me for a moment." Court rose from his chair and went to say something to the girl. After the exchange, she followed him back to join the table. "This is my friend Sean Lassiter," he said, introducing her.

"Hi, I'm Vienna." She tossed her hair back in a movement designed to help her avoid bothering with eye contact. She was American, he supposed, or had been taught English by one. "Look at this place. The Jews and Arabs agree so completely on soft furnishings, you'd think they could work everything else out from that." She had as much confidence as either of them, but Court knew that if they ignored her, she would drop out of the conversation. She was a professional. She had brought her own drink with her.

"Mr Lassiter here owns the hotel."

That wiped the smile from her face. "Is that true?" she asked, lowering her glass. Court could tell she was racking her brains to recall the name.

"Well, I'm the managing director of the consortium that owns it," said Lassiter, managing to make the role sound unimportant.

"He's being modest," said Court, "he owns the entire chain."

If Vienna was impressed, she was too smart to show it. Her deal was with the Maître d'. She only cared about her direct contacts. "Is it owned by the Americans?"

"No, it's mainly Indian and Russian money."

"They charge non-guests an entrance fee just to look around the lobby of this hotel," she said, "but I guess you know that."

"I don't suppose that affects you." It seemed that, having made the effort to talk to the girl, Lassiter was happier talking to Court. "You're not staying at the Burj Al-Arab, Oliver?"

"Even I can't justify that kind of expense. Besides, loyalty dictates that I stay here. I suppose you've got a suite."

"Penthouse sea-facing corner, but not the royal suite," said Lassiter. "That's reserved for heads of state."

"I heard quite a few of the rooms are empty." The Middle East was part of Lassiter's domain.

"It's not just here. There's been a lot of over-construction. Look out of the window along the coastline. Everyone's been affected by the bad publicity lately, those stories of raw sewage being pumped into the sea, but it doesn't stop them from building."

"You're not worried enough to reduce the cost of a room yet," Court added. "So, do we get to see your view?"

He wants to bring the girl, Lassiter thought in some surprise, *how will this work out?* "Sure, if you want."

Court paid without checking the total and stood up, placing his hand in the valley of Vienna's back. This small gesture was enough to seal the deal. She showed no reaction as she rose and left with them, the light from the neon bar-sign casting a crimson stripe across her neck that appeared to sever it.

"At these prices I thought you'd have your own elevator," Court needled gently.

"Only the royal apartment has that. For security purposes." Lassiter stabbed at the illuminated gold lift button. "We need to invent something better than first class. The whole concept of privilege has become debased."

"I read somewhere that you need to earn six million per annum to live like a millionaire these days," said Vienna.

Court watched his boss against the dark golden glass of the elevator. Lassiter had started to put on the kind of weight he would never be able to shift. His new suit was already becoming too tight. He was in his mid-sixties but showed no desire to stop working or even slow down. *Sharks drown if they stop swimming,* Court thought. *The only way he'll stop is if he dies. I'm surprised Elizabeth still puts up with it.*

He wondered if Lassiter went around telling people how he'd given Court a start in the hotel business. Mentors had a habit of doing that.

"Welcome to my world," said Lassiter without an obvious hint of irony as he held open the door for Vienna. The suite displayed all the accoutrements of wealth without any of the concomitant taste. A curved bar was lined with gold-leaf piping that rose to enclose a range of vintage whisky bottles presented on sheets of underlit crimson glass like items of baroque jewellery.

"Want to try the whisky?"

"I'm staying with vodka."

Vienna watched until her own drink had been poured, then went to the bathroom.

"She's very beautiful," Lassiter conceded.

"She doesn't have to be here if she doesn't want to," said Court. "She's with your hotel, which presumably means she has quality control."

Lassiter walked to the glass wall and looked down to the beach. Spotlights picked out the tall wavering palms that had been transported fully grown and impatiently planted into the unfinished esplanade. The crystal blackness reflected every glittering pinpoint in the apartment, creating a second starscape above the sea. There was no natural sound in the suite, only the faint but steady hiss of cold ionised air pumped up through the ventilation system, and the settling chink of perfectly cubed ice on glass.

"Allow me," said Court, pouring a heavy measure of Scotch. "It's a nice view. Although I don't like to look at the sea. I'd prefer to be surrounded by buildings. City boy at heart."

Lassiter accepted the proffered drink and downed it in one. He had been drinking hard all evening. The New Business Model Seminar was so stultifying that everyone had been pushing their upper alcohol limits for the past three days, and there was still another day to go.

"Did you learn anything at all today?" Lassiter asked. "Spare me all those speakers from the Far East with their strangled English and aching politeness. Did you actually get anything out of it?"

"No, but I didn't expect to."

They studied the view. Lassiter pressed his chilled tumbler against his forehead. "Look at it. There's no-one out there and nothing to see. You could be in Monte Carlo, Geneva or Madrid. That's the beauty of our European hotels, Oliver. Whichever one you use, there you are, home and safe again. Sometimes I wake up and have no idea where I am. And it doesn't matter."

"How's the seminar working out for you?"

"I'll go home four days nearer to my death with a sun-reddened face and a portfolio full of brochures my PA will eventually tip into the bin."

"It's not like you to be a cynic," Court observed. "I remember when you first saw potential in me, the things you taught me, all that practical advice and optimism for the future."

"I'm afraid my hopes atrophied somewhat when our so-called first-world society decided to hand over the reins of financial responsibility to a bunch of cowboy bankers." He drained his glass, the ice clinking against his white teeth. "I'm old enough to remember when selling was a challenge. These days I feel like a nurse spoon-feeding paralysed patients. Christ, I want to start smoking again, but these rooms are alarmed. Pour me another, will you?"

Court headed back to the bar. He picked up a matchbook, crested and labelled ROYAL PERSIAN HOTEL, DUBAI and slipped it into his pocket.

"How come there are no cameras in the corridors?" he wondered aloud.

"The Arabs are like the Swiss when it comes to issues of privacy. The rich need to treat each other in an adult manner because there are so many dirty secrets to keep tucked away."

Court was not familiar with this reflective side of Lassiter. The man who had elevated as many careers as he had destroyed was going soft. Men became vulnerable to strange fancies when they felt their sexual powers waning.

"The most powerful religious leaders emerge from desert states, have you noticed?" Lassiter mused. "Whereas political leaders nurture their theories in cities. One thinks of Pol Pot's agrarian revolution being discussed in smoky Parisian cafes. In my darkest nightmares I imagine a new business model, one where morals and decent behaviour are considered detrimental, where only grabbing the next million in the next hour commands any respect at all. And at some point – I'm not sure when – my nightmare became real. This is what we do, Oliver, and we all collude in the process. The definition of a conspiracy is the combination of any number of people in a surreptitious agreement to commit a secret, unlawful, evil and wrongful act. Think about what we do and ask yourself if you really want to join the next level."

He's lost it, thought Oliver. *The great Sean Lassiter is stepping out of the ring to watch sunsets and talk hippy-dippy shit. This is too good to be true.*

"You've made your money, Sean. If you feel like this, why don't you just sell up?"

Lassiter regarded him from beneath hooded eyelids. "There's no-one I trust enough. You want to know if that includes you. I groomed you, I knew what would happen. Give someone the benefit of your experience for long enough, and it stands to reason they'll eventually try to buy the company out from under you. I never held your success against you, Oliver."

"That's because your own success always remained greater. It's easy to be magnanimous when you're at the top. What if I really wanted to buy the company now?"

There it is, thought Lassiter, *the real purpose of dinner.* "I wondered when you would finally ask."

"You don't think I'd look after the staff."

"My people? I replace them like batteries." Lassiter looked toward the bathroom door. The girl seemed to be taking a long time.

"Then why not sell to me?" Court walked over to the balcony and unlocked the doors, rolling them silently back. The cool night air was a relief after the chemically conditioned atmosphere. "Hey, we can smoke out here. Doors and windows you can open forty floors up, they'd never allow this at home." He laughed, patting his pockets.

With one last glance back at the bathroom, Lassiter joined him on the balcony. He leaned over the edge and looked down. "You're right, there's hardly a light on in the entire building. We should be renegotiating the prices of the suites. Europe holds too many festivals and seminars at this time of the year. Half the salesmen in America leave home in March and don't get back until their houseplants are dead."

"Your profits are down, and I've heard the next quarter will be even worse."

"Maybe we did expand Europe too quickly. When a wolf is sick, the others decide what to do; whether you live or die depends on how important you are to the pack. You think we're going lame, one of the pack lagging behind?" He sighed wearily. "Are you going to bite me on the leg and drag me into the bushes? Why not, it's what I would have done."

The only sign of life came from the headlights of the gravel trucks swerving past each other in the distance, like tin toys on a track. Their thin bright beams shone into total blackness. Back along the coastline, a line of steel towers glowed through the sea-mist like a phantom stockade.

Court realised that to get an answer he would have to give one. "You asked me. What do I want?" he repeated. "I want to reach the top of my profession."

"That's not a desire, it's an instinct, like releasing air from a diving tank." Given the amount he had drunk, he surprised himself with the analogy. It was true; his career was as lonely and claustrophobic as being under the sea.

"All right. Then I desire respect."

Lassiter turned to study him. "Surely you have that already. Don't you?" From the way he said it, Lassiter made it clear that Court had yet to earn it from his teacher.

"I suppose so. In that case, I don't know. That's the answer to your question; I really don't know."

"Fair enough. I suppose that's more honest than saying you want our hotels to be the finest in the world. You're still only in your thirties – "

"Thirty four."

"You have time on your side. Now I suppose you want an answer to your question." Lassiter lit the proffered cigar and drew hard on it. "I can't sell you the company, Oliver."

"Why not?"

"It would be too obvious."

"What do you mean?"

"It's what you want. I can always tell what you're going to do next. You're positively metronomic in your habits. I can see inside your head, which means that from a business point of view I can always out-think you. And if I can, others will. That's not good."

"It's because I learned everything from you. You'll always be the one person who knows exactly what I think. You'll always outguess me."

The ocean air should have started sobering him up, but it was having the opposite effect. Lassiter struggled to understand what Court was saying to him. The air was completely still, and there was no sound. Even the distant trucks moved past each other in silence. If his wife was here he knew she would appreciate the beauty of the night, but she was asleep in London. It was late and he was still wearing his business suit, and polished black shoes that pinched.

"You know the story of the Caliph of Jaipur?" asked Court, draining his glass and setting it down on the balcony table. "He hired the finest painter in the land to create a fresco of heavenly angels for the walls of his harem. When it was finished, he asked the artisan if it really was the best fresco in all the kingdom. The painter told him that there was no finer artwork to be found beneath the horizons, nor would there ever be again until someone else could afford his services. So the Sultan had him beheaded."

Lassiter looked at him blearily. Only the whites of Court's eyes showed in the jet night, and then they were gone. A streak of silver sparkled in the ocean like a flash of static electricity, the signature of the moon. He felt tired and looked for a place to sit, but Court was crouching beside him. When he rose, he was holding Lassiter's right ankle. Court stood taller and taller, rising higher and higher, until Lassiter realised he could no longer remain upright. "You're not drunk," he said absurdly.

"I don't drink whisky." Court raised his old friend's ankle higher, until pain shot through Lassiter's thigh muscles.

"Vodka – "

"Because it looks like water. Sure you don't want to sell?"

"Over my dead body."

Court shrugged his shoulders. "That was the general idea." With both his hands clasped beneath Lassiter's foot Court leaned suddenly back, like a Scotsman tossing a caber, raising his arms smartly so that Lassiter lost his battle with gravity and found himself cleanly lifted into the air, over the wall of the balcony. His mouth opened in shock, but only the smallest sound emerged. His fingers grasped at the air beyond the low rail, too late, and he tumbled silently down, past the empty dark floors. The first part of the fall seemed to last forever, as if he was wheeling through the night in slow motion, like a firework that had failed to ignite, or a spaceman with a cut cord.

But then he hit his head on the concrete lip of the thirtieth balcony, and this sent him spinning madly out of orbit. His head turned from white to black, leaving a matching stain on the building wall. His leg hit another ledge, his arm another, his head again, his arm, his leg, until there was hardly a bone in his body left unbroken – and that was long before he hit the ground.

Court stepped back into the room. "You might want to come out now," he called. "We're alone." He heard running water stop.

The bathroom door was padded crimson with gold studs. It opened cautiously. Vienna emerged with her makeup refreshed, like a meticulously restored painting. She took in the suite, three glasses, one occupant less, an open balcony door, and decided to say nothing. Had she an inkling of what had just happened? Her face was a mask. Court's decision to act had been spontaneous. He knew she could not have seen anything, and Lassiter had made no noise. He doubted that she cared anyway. It was not her job to care. She worked in a service industry.

"My colleague had to leave. Thanks for coming up," said Court, feeling inside his jacket. He unclipped her handbag and dropped in a roll of banknotes. "Maybe we'll see each other again."

"I'd like that." Vienna's smile was unreadable. She turned and walked to the door, seemingly aware of exactly how many steps it would take. "You know where to find me."

And she was gone.

Court closed the window and rinsed the glasses, placing them back on the bar shelf. He had left no other mark in the suite. Letting himself out, he padded along the corridor and caught the elevator to his own room. He had paid the girl too much, but would not have been able to get Lassiter back to his suite without her. Everyone knew that even though the old man loved his wife, he still needed to prove himself with the ladies.

He would heed his mentor's advice and not suggest the buyout immediately; that would be crass. There were plenty of other preparations he could be making while the company came to terms with Lassiter's death. It would be interesting to see how long they could keep it out of the news.

Before the last day of the conference began, he took a stroll outside. The sky was a painful deep blue, sharper than knives. The pavements had been hosed down, and were already nearly dry. He circled the hotel but found no sign of any disturbance. Shielding his eyes, he squinted up at the balconies, trying to spot where Lassiter had hit the building, but realised that he was standing beneath the ledges, and would not be able to see anything.

The day dragged past in parades of PowerPoint bar charts, each more candy-coloured than the last, as if their radiance could make up for their dullness. At lunchtime he saw two men who looked like plainclothes police. They were standing motionless in the reception area, in mirror shades and shiny blue suits. By the time afternoon tea was served, even Lassiter's reservation had disappeared from the records. Clearly, the hotel's reputation was more important than its founder's demise. *The things we create outgrow us*, thought Court, shutting down his laptop. *One day you own the company, the next even your PA can't remember you. I thought there would be repercussions. I guess Sean was right. It's all part of the new business model.*

Two weeks later, Court found himself at Domodedovo Airport in Moscow. He always seemed to be holding meetings in departure lounges. In the business class bar he had bumped into an old English friend, a nervy, sticklike redhead called Amanda, and had invited her to join him. Watching snow fall on airfields from behind picture windows always had a calming effect on him. Amanda was a seasoned executive with half a dozen personal communication devices in her briefcase and no hint of a private life. She told him she was going to try internet dating when she finally settled in one city long enough to do so.

"I was wondering what you thought about Sean Lassiter," she said, slowly emptying another miniature bottle of Tanqueray into her glass. "There's a rumour going around that Elizabeth was about to leave him."

Court had no idea. Suddenly the lack of publicity surrounding his death made sense. "I heard something to that effect," he said.

"They hadn't been sleeping together for years," she told him knowledgeably. "I was reading an article in The Economist about the similarities between successful businessmen and serial killers. They share the same lack of compassion, the same selfishness and determination to succeed. They exploit the flaws of their opponents, and lose their ability to judge on moral grounds."

For a crazy moment he wondered if she had heard another, darker rumour, but decided it was impossible. The buyout had only been discussed with a handful of board members. It would not be made public until after it was successful.

"I guess you're going on to St Petersburg," she said. "Where are you staying?"

"The Grand Sovetskaya. How about you?"

"Oh, nothing so fancy. That was one of Sean's personal favourites, wasn't it?"

"Well, it's part of the chain."

"I slept with him, you know. Our flights were cancelled and we were stuck at the Espacio Rojo Hotel in Barcelona. I was really sorry to hear he died. Or was it the Severine in Paris? They have this fabulous spa treatment where they wrap you in oil-soaked gauze and place hot stones down your spine."

He listened without hearing. The image of the old man pumping away on top of poor bony Amanda while whispering sales figures in her ears was best left behind in the departure lounge.

The Grand Sovetskaya was an unashamedly old-world hotel in the French style, with green copper gables and crouching gargoyles. In the domed reception area hung a crystal chandelier the size of a skip. The rooms were filled with dark wooden dressers, sideboards and wardrobes, and were locked with huge brass keys. There were twenty one floors of corridors that smelled of furniture polish and boiled cabbage, all identical and gently curved, like those of an ocean liner. Thick floral carpets and heavily lined drapes deadened all sound.

Best of all was the bar, a paradise for the serious drinker. The shelves were stacked with dozens of flavoured vodkas and an immense range of mysterious liquors, vaguely medicinal in appearance. Court suspected that the elderly hatchet-faced bar staff had arrived with the first guests. Heavy marble ashtrays lined the counter. This was clearly no place for lightweights.

Court was there to conclude the discreet negotiations with Lassiter's board, but if anyone asked, he was attending a forum staged by the Opportunities In New Business Development Commission. Discretion was second nature to him. He spent most of his life in hotels as quiet as libraries where the patrons were defined by the depth of their expense accounts. Lighting a cigar, he thought about Lassiter turning over and over in the warm night air, a tiny flailing puppet whose existence had been erased almost before he hit the concrete. How many Indian workers had been employed to scrub the blood from the stones before another harsh dawn flooded the hotel with sunlight? Had the manager posted Lassiter's luggage back to his grieving wife? Had Elizabeth pored over the spreadsheets, graphs and overlays, hopelessly looking for answers?

He felt no guilt. Lassiter's downward spiral had begun before Dubai. Court had saved him the incremental degradation a man feels when he realises the company he has founded no longer needs or desires his advice. He waved aside the blue haze of cigar smoke and studied Vienna. She was seated in a red leather horseshoe between two short bald oligarchs. When she saw him looking, she momentarily forgot what she was saying. Her eyes lingered a moment too long.

Clearly, she was good at her job if she was travelling to international clients. For a second it crossed his mind that they might make an interesting team, but he knew that the best call-girls stayed at the peak of their trade by giving nothing of themselves to others. Even so...

It would have been unprofessional to send her any kind of message while she was working, so he smoked and waited, and treated himself to a golden *Comte de Lauvia* 1982 Armanac. The Russians here were loud and unsophisticated, but Vienna never appeared bored. After an hour they were clearly drunk. Court had no idea what she said to them, but they suddenly fell into a sombre mood and rose together, bidding her good night.

She came to him with her shoes in one hand, and he realised how much they added to her height. "However long your evening has been," she told him, taking a sip of his brandy, "I promise you mine was longer." She licked her lips appreciatively and allowed her head to fall back against the red leather seat. "Mm. Can I get one of those?"

The waiter appeared without asking, delivered and departed. She seemed content to drink and drift without making small talk. She wore another low-cut black dress, and a single strand of pearls. Her perfume had faded enough to allow a natural womanly odour, faint but arousing, to rise from her peach-coloured skin.

He relit his cigar and watched her, wondering how much she remembered of their last meeting. The bar was almost empty. It was a quarter past two in the morning. "How long are you staying here?" he asked.

"Two nights. I'm entertaining those guys."

"They must be important."

"To someone. Not to me. It's a job."

"They left without you."

"I sent them away." She took the cigar from his fingers and smoked it for a minute.

"I'm here for – "

"I don't want to know why you're here." She studied the glowing tip of the cigar. "I'm sure you get tired of talking shop. I do."

"So, Vienna, what would you rather do?"

She turned her eyes to his. Her pupils were violet, the lashes long and black. "Shall I tell you what I would really like to do?"

He gave no response, but waited with a small catch in his breath.

"I would like to fall asleep in a great big soft bed with my head on your chest."

"We can do that." Then he remembered. "Wait, they screwed up my reservation. I have two singles. We can push them together."

"Thanks, but no thanks."

"Well, where are you staying?"

She held up the key. It was the first time he had seen a genuine smile on her lips. "I have the royal suite."

Now he was impressed. "How did you get that?"

"How do you think?"

They made their way to the twenty first floor. As they followed the curve of the passage, Vienna entwined her fingers in his. *I don't have to tell this woman anything,* he thought, *she and I are the same kind.*

When she unlocked the door at the end of the corridor and turned on the lights, he was disappointed to see that except for an extra pair of curtains covering the end wall, the room was almost identical to his. It was unbearably hot. He removed his suit jacket, threw it on the couch and loosened his tie.

"Make me a drink," she told him, "I'll be back." She headed for the bathroom. Something made him uncomfortable. He heard the bathroom door shut, then silence. He poured two whiskies at the wet bar and thought for a moment. It was exactly what she had done in Dubai.

No, it wasn't.

She had waited until she had seen her own drink poured. Call-girls always did that, just to be careful.

She wasn't going to drink anything. Then why had she asked him to make her a drink?

"Vienna?" He knocked on the bathroom door, but there was silence beyond. He placed his ear against the wood and listened. Nothing.

The room was spectacularly hot. Vienna was obviously missing Dubai. There didn't seem to be a thermostat anywhere. Then he remembered; his was in the bathroom. "Vienna," he called, "turn the heat down, will you?"

The floor tipped, just a little, but enough for him to realise what had happened. He headed back to the bar and examined his drained whisky tumbler. There was some kind of white residue in the bottom of it. Sweat was starting to pour between his shoulder blades. The front of his shirt was darkening around his armpits and in the middle of his chest.

The carpet seemed to be pulling away beneath his feet. He needed cold air, fast. He reached the end window and pulled back the curtains, but there was just more wall behind them.

The big French windows were in the same place as the ones in his room. He lurched across to them and tried the right handle. It turned easily. He pulled the glass door toward him and a blast of subzero air filled the room. It was snowing hard. Almost instantly he began to sober up. He tried to think.

Stepping onto the balcony, he breathed in the stinging winter air, filling his lungs with ice. Fat white flakes settled on his eyelids, in his ears. His head was clearing fast but his reactions were still slow.

Too slow to stop the door from being shut behind him. Vienna was standing beyond the glass. She studied him blankly, as if watching an animal at the zoo. Her right arm was raised, her hand against the wall. She was pressing something. She wiggled the fingers of her left hand slightly, waving goodbye.

The steel shutter that fitted tightly over the windows was swiftly closing. He tried to seize its edge with his fingers, to push it back up, but it was so cold that the flesh of his fingertips, still wet from his whisky glass, stuck to the metal, pulling him down.

And then it was shut. He tore his fingers free, leaving behind four small scarlet patches of skin. The sweat on his back was already turning to ice. He hammered on the steel shutter, but was shocked by its thickness. It barely rattled. Old French-style hotels always sported European shutters. He moved around the edges of the metre-wide balcony. A sheer drop down, no lights on anywhere. The rooms on either side had bricked-up windows.

The bitter wind had risen to a howl. He was in his shirtsleeves, and knew he had but a short time to live. He had been drinking all evening; his blood was thin. He fell to the floor of the balcony and pushed himself into the wall, but the ice and snow still blew through the balustrade, settling over him.

His first instinct was to assume he had been subjected to a woman's revenge. Then he remembered she was merely an employee.

He tried to laugh when he understood what had happened, but the saliva was freezing in his mouth. Even his eyes were becoming hard to move. He fancied he could hear the ice forming beneath his skin. Tiny crackles like rustling cellophane filled his ears.

Looking out into the night beyond the balcony, the darkness was sprinkled with swirling white flakes that looked like stars. He could have been anywhere in the world.

They'll leave the shutters down for twenty four hours, he thought, *just to be absolutely sure. Vienna will be back on a Dubai beach by then.*

His mind was growing numb. He remembered something from a history book he had once read. When the Persian matriarchs wanted to rid themselves of the most treacherous family members, they locked them away in sumptuous apartments and left them to die. From a business point of view, it made perfect sense to do so. He should have put forward the idea as part of his new business model, but, just as Lassiter had warned, someone else had thought of it first.

He found himself laughing as the freezing snow-laden winds whirled about him, and then he could no longer close his mouth.

MIKAL TRIMM
WHO'S GONNA MISS YOU WHEN YOU'RE GONE?

The trailer sat at the end of an unpaved stretch of hard-packed red sand and crushed oyster shells. Desmond Fells drove slowly through the gulf-spat detritus that served as dirt in the Florida panhandle, taking home the groceries in his parent's ancient International Harvester station wagon. The shocks screamed in protest as he hit another hole in the road. Something clinked ominously against the hatch.

No breakage, please no breakage. A jar of pickles had shattered in the wagon last month, and the smell of vinegar still fouled the air. Mama had not been happy.

"I live on my Social Security, Desie. You know how much that is? Not a whole helluva lot. I don't have welfare, like those trash-folk down the street."

That would be the Sowells. They lived in an old shack of tarpaper and rotting timber about a mile up the road from his mother's decrepit Fleetwood. She felt an innate superiority to the Sowells. Her home was made of *metal*, dammit. She railed against the trash in the Sowells' yard and the abandoned Chevy on blocks in their driveway, even as the floor of her mobile home rusted out beneath her.

I hear you, Mama. I'm a good boy. I'll always be your good, good boy.

Desmond decided he wouldn't tell her about the little blond boy.

"You gettin' out now, son. Free as a bird. Tell me you ain't gonna do nothin' like that again, hear me?"

Desmond, a week from sixteen, nodded and nodded and cried and cried...

And Mama was there to take him away from the Formell County Juvenile Detention Center, standing beside her damned old Harvester station wagon. She just nodded and nodded.

But she didn't shed a tear.

The boy slumped down the road, carrying an old gunny-sack across his back. Desmond could tell he'd been walking a while – the sack was covered with damp sand, like the kid had dragged it for a while before shouldering it once more.

Sack probably weighs more than he does. Wonder what's in it?

Desmond slowed the wagon and drove up closer to the boy. *Ain't seen him around. Wonder who his folks are?*

"Hey! Hey, kid!" Desmond pulled up in front of the boy, reached over and opened the passenger door. "Where you goin'? That bag looks heavy, need a ride?" His heart pounded. He could feel the sweat on his face, beads dripping down his sideburns. Still hot in September, but not hot enough for this downpour. Not near hot enough.

The kid dropped the sack, shrugged the stiffness out of his shoulders, and gave Desmond the once-over.

The boy looked twelve years old, or maybe a big eleven, blond hair waving like straw in the light breeze, jeans tattered and faded to near-white, T-shirt more hole than cotton. Reminded Desmond of that kid back in fifth grade, what was his name...

"Yeah, mister, guess I wouldn't mind a ride. Ain't far to go. That okay?"

Desmond motioned the kid in. "Sure it's okay! We're all neighbors round here, right?"

The boy nodded, struggling to pull the sack into the car behind him. Desmond thought about getting out and helping, but instead he watched the sweat glistening on the boy's forehead, watched his young muscles working beneath his smooth skin.

Once the boy got settled in his seat and closed the door, Desmond put the wagon in gear and took off slowly, trying not to kick up too much sand from the unpaved road.

"You live around these parts? I don't remember seeing you before."

The boy arranged his sack between his legs, sat back in the seat. "We been around for a while now."

Desmond brought the Harvester up to about twenty, taking his eyes off the road now and then to risk a furtive glance at the boy. Desmond noticed the fine hair on the boy's forearms, shifting in the hot breeze from the windows. He saw the thick long lashes, almost girlish, hiding the boy's eyes. *Handsome boy. Bet he don't even know it.*

"My name's Desmond, Desmond Fells, but most folks call me Desie." *Well, Mama does, anyway.* "What's your name?"

The boy reached out a hand to shake, well-mannered. "Joshua, sir. My people call me Joss, though."

Desmond shook, nervous about taking a hand off the wheel. He took his foot off the gas while he did it, and the car came close to a stop before he finished. "Good to meet you, Joss." Foot to pedal, and the Harvester crept back up to twenty, shuddering with the effort. "So, what's in the sack?"

Joshua stared at him, hard enough so Desmond could feel the heat of his eyes. "Just...stuff. For my kinfolk. We all got jobs to do."

Desmond nodded, still feeling the boy's eyes on his face. Sweat rolled down his forehead, broke in tiny rivulets across his eyebrows. "Sure, sure. We all got to help out the family. Right?"

He felt Joshua turn away. "Yessir. Long as there's nothing wrong with it."

Desmond was about to ask Joshua what he meant, but the boy pointed off into the woods and gestured. "We need to stop here. My kinfolk live out there."

Desmond slammed the brakes, heard the groceries in back shifting, bottles clinking together. *Oh, no, no, hell no!* and by the time he quit worrying about broken jars and smashed eggs, Joshua was out of the car, already making his way into the woods. The sack didn't look as heavy now – Joshua had it slung over one shoulder.

Without thinking, Desmond called out. "Why ain't you in school? School started last month, right?"

Joshua turned, right before he disappeared into the treeline. "Little late for school now, Desmond. Least for us."

Then he faded into the woods, and Desmond was left sitting in his mama's wagon, sticky with sweat and filled with wrongful thoughts.

He only noticed the scrapbook lying on the floorboard of the passenger seat when he finally got home. He grabbed it and, looking to make sure Mama couldn't see him, hid it under the trailer, tucking it well back through a hole in the skirting.

"That you, Desie-roo?" Mama sat in her rocker on the back porch, her bones creaking with the chair's runners. Desmond rustled through the grocery sacks, finding no evidence of damage, and whistled a sigh of relief.

"Got the groceries, Mama. Didn't have no trouble." Why'd he say that? Made it sound like something happened, but he was covering it up. "At the grocery store, I mean."

"Your voice sounds funny." He heard the creak of Mama's rocker as she lifted her broad fanny out, the click of her cane, the wounded shriek of the back screen door. "You break something?"

"No!" Desmond reached for the bag with the eggs, found them whole, carried it in first. "Everything's fine, Mama!"

She stood in the kitchen, leaning on her cane, and it amazed him again how quickly she could move, arthritis be damned. "No need to yell, son. Now put that down before you spill it all over the floor."

Desmond kept his mouth shut, bringing in the groceries while Mama put them away. He heard the erratic hiss of Daddy's oxygen from the living room as he slowly lost the fight against emphysema. The TV blared out the noon news to the backbeat of Daddy's exaggerated breaths. It sounded like he was hissing at the newscasters, disgusted with their performance.

Desmond finished carrying in the groceries, waited until Mama put them away where she could find them, even if no one else could figure out her system, and then relaxed. *No breakage, no spills, no problems. I'm safe.*

"Took you too long to get home. What were you doing?" Mama locked a fat liver-spotted claw on his arm, squeezed.

"I...I wasn't doing nothing, Mama. I just drove real slow, like you told me. Don't want no more pickle-juice in the car, right?" Did she see me? Did she jump out of her rocker and look around the corner of the trailer when I couldn't see her? *Did she see me?*

Mama dropped his arm, nodding. "Good. That's what I keep trying to tell you, Desie. You ain't in no hurry, son – you got plenty of time. Just keep your eyes on the road and your foot off the gas. You young'uns like to speed, and there ain't no sense in it. You're thirty-six years old now, Desie, time you started acting like it."

She wandered away finally, leaving Desmond to rub the circulation back into his arm and try not to breathe too hard.

Thirty-six years old. Yeah, Mama, I guess I know that.

Later that evening, when he and Mama got Daddy squared away in bed and Mama finally dropped off reading her Harlequin romance book, Desmond crept out of the trailer and retrieved the scrapbook.

It smelled of decay. Dampness, the scent of brackish water, the elusive dry-skin funk of Florida's red sand. The pages of the scrapbook turned easily, though, and the contents – yellowed and curling with age sometimes – still held together without crumbling.

And the contents themselves...

What is this? Desmond turned the pages carefully, trying to make sense of the fragments of words and images he found. Little scraps of newspaper clippings scattered through the pages, not full articles, just a line or two at most: *...won the third grade spelling bee at Seminole Elementary... wanted to be a doctor or an astronaut... worked for this paper on weekends, selling subscriptions and delivering the Sunday edition... was due to be inducted into the Webelo branch of the Cub Scouts in June...*

And placed randomly around the clippings, pictures of young boys. Sometimes grainy pictures taken from the newspapers themselves, and sometimes just hasty sketches, little more than line drawings. Enough to suggest a brow line, maybe, or a thick head of hair, or in one case a ragged scar down the side of a boy's face.

Stop looking. This isn't yours. It belongs to a family, to that boy's family, probably. You need to give it back to him, Desie, you got to find him and give it back. More things glued to the pages, little pieces of cloth or hair, a lost tooth wrapped in cellophane, a Cub Scout badge, tattered and faded.

What would Mama say if she caught you with this?

And Desmond felt the night-sweats start up again, just like when he was a kid. He wiped his hands against the sheets, his palms sticky and damp, and closed the scrapbook up, making sure not to bend the pages. *Got to give it back. Shouldn't even touch it.* That's *what Mama would say.*

Desmond noticed something black sticking out from the cracked binding of the scrapbook. He winnowed it out carefully, surprised at the cold touch of plastic when everything else felt so warm. Cloth, and paper like Mama's romance novels, but more interesting. More stories to tell.

Desmond sniffed the plastic, rubbed it between his fingers. Something about the lack of scent, the thickness and texture... *Garbage bag.* Mama never needed them around here – they burned all their trash in a fire pit behind the trailer – but Desmond had worked for a lawn service for a while, and they used these things constantly. He even knew this was a good product, just by the thickness of the ply. *You could stuff five trees' worth of leaves in something like this. Surprised it tore at all.*

Didn't matter. No need to think – Daddy always said he wasn't much good at it anyway.

Tomorrow, I find that boy, and I give it back. That's all there is to it.

He crept back out of the house to hide it again, listening for Mama while absently stroking the book like a kitten the whole time.

The nightmare came back.

He'd had it, on and off, since he'd come back home with Mama twenty years ago, but never like this. Strong enough to drag him under and hold him there, struggling, unable to surface. Underwater, in water, surrounded by water...

...and images, words, feelings, swirls and eddies, clippings of memories like in that book, the book, no it's not here no that's up there and Daddy shouting something, mad, his face hovering over the waves like a bursting red sun saying what the what the what the hell and other faces, white ghosts burning under His gaze –

– and Desmond swimming-not-moving, engulfed (the Gulf) and choking, something holding him down shaking him like a rat bringing him up, all? none? all at once? And that damn voice again, waterlogged and heavy with tidal power what the hell what the hell –

– and some kid what's-his-name never even liked him much too old for me to be hanging around Mama said but there he is and he's grinning grinning and blue crabs crawl out of his mouth clicking their claws against his big white teeth and he says he says –

– c'mon Desmond ain't you never been skinny-dippin'? and that bad boy that bad bad boy comes flying out of the water and his pecker is big as a gar and it has teeth like one and the boy's holding it in his hand like he's reeling it in and he says dang Des ain't you ever even touched yours? –

– and Desmond feels the weight of the water and the voice of the Sun

God hammers them both under and Desmond does something, he does something –

Nightmare. Blood. Sharks, or just one. Red sun bursting, wave and wave and wave again slapping him beating him driving him under under under...

Desmond woke to the creak of his mother's rocking chair on the back porch. First light, and she was already up, waiting to tell her boy what to do that day.

Desmond saw a deep red stain on his pillow, wiped pink foam from his mouth, and felt a deep throbbing pain hiding behind his clenched teeth.

He spat something out, a tiny piece of gristle clotted with blood. Dimly, still trying to pull himself out of the black depths of nightmare, he realized he'd chewed the tip of his tongue off in his sleep.

Desmond showered, letting the weak pulse of the water rinse his mouth again, again, until the pink traces of blood finally stopped coloring the flow. He scrubbed his chin, found spots of dried blood on his shoulders and chest, scrubbed them away as well with a desperation that left his skin an angry red. *If she notices, I'll tell her it's just sunburn.* He finished his shower quickly, being careful around his personal parts. Mama didn't want him to spend any more time than necessary down there.

Dressed and nervous, he forced himself to meet Mama on the back porch. His tongue ached, and it felt swollen, so thick in his mouth that he didn't know if he could even talk. Mama's rocker creaked monotonously, covering the sound of the screen door opening. She stared out at the backyard, not even noticing him when he came right up beside her. The morning light glinted off her face – Desmond could make out the wetness in her eyes, the silver snail-tracks of tears running down her cheeks.

"Mama?" The word sounded muffled, like speaking through cotton-balls.

"I saw a boy." Mama's voice sounded even stranger than his own – distant, speaking to someone else far away. Desmond still couldn't tell if she'd noticed him or not. "He was back there," and she gestured vaguely, "walking through the brush, and he looked at me."

Desmond held his breath, thinking of the boy with blond hair, and the scrapbook under the trailer. "What – what'd he look like, Mama?"

Mama stopped rocking, leaned forward in her chair as if trying to get closer to the ghost of the child's passing. "He's out there, the little bastard. He's out there waiting for me to close my eyes." She relaxed suddenly, her bulk settling back so quickly in the rocker that Desmond thought it would tip over. "Doesn't matter. They'll never catch me out. I don't sleep no more."

Desmond felt a numbness creeping through him. Mama never acted like this. Her eyes looked cloudy, her hands fluttered in her lap like trapped moths, her breath hitched in and out like Daddy's did before the oxygen tanks. Desmond reached out a hand, wanting to comfort her, stroke her shoulder or pat her hair down or –

She slapped his hand away, her eyes darting to his face, clear and vicious again. Desmond wondered if he'd imagined them ever being any other way. "Where's your Pa?"

"In bed, Mama. He don't wake up this early, so I didn't check on him yet."

"Go do it!" Mama moved to get out of her chair, and Desmond scurried out of her reach before she had to make the effort.

Daddy's room stank of sweat and stale air. Desmond heard the tortured hiss of Daddy's breathing harmonizing with the constant hum of the oxygen tank. Daddy didn't move, just lay tangled in his yellowed sheets, his face distorted behind the loose plastic tent he slept under. Desmond couldn't help but think of Daddy as he was ten years back, before the emphysema took him down. He'd been a driver for Southern Foods, going out for days at a time on a route that took him all over Florida and into parts of Alabama and Georgia. Big truck, big man behind the wheel. Daddy looked like he could barely fit in the cab, all muscle and shoulders and cracker-barrel chest. Now he'd shriveled away to become little more than a pale-skinned skeleton.

Desmond sniffed for the ammonia tang of urine, gave thanks when he couldn't smell it. Daddy pissed the bed sometimes, and Desmond had to change the sheets when it happened. Mama took care of Daddy's underwear, though, and she cleaned Daddy up and bathed him when he needed it. All Desmond had to do was help Daddy to the bathroom and into the tub, and Mama did the rest.

Desmond turned to leave the room, but something didn't look right, or maybe it just didn't *feel* right. He made a quiet circuit of the room, making sure Daddy still slept, the windows were sealed, the window shades blocked out the light so the room stayed dark. He almost left again before he smelled something different. Hard to sniff out anything new over the general stink of the room, but this was concentrated in one place, near Daddy's dresser. Desmond looked closer, his eyes adjusted now to the darkness. Daddy's watch, his wallet, his wedding ring all laid out. Daddy's clothes for the day, hanging from the mirror behind the dresser, ready. The dresser drawers...

Desmond bent down, noticed one of the drawers partially open. The smell came out of it, faint but distinctive. Desmond pulled the drawer out further, wincing when the old warped wood squeaked.

Daddy's underwear and socks. Graying underwear stacked neatly on one side, socks lined up in rows on the other, thanks to Mama. Desmond went to close the drawer, saw something roll around, pale-brown on off-white. Bending closer, the smell stronger, he found a handful of items scattered across his father's underwear. He took one, felt it, smelled it, knowing what it was before he could even see it clearly. Then he gathered the others, making sure he found them all while trying his damnedest not to wake up Daddy.

Once he'd made it out of the room and closed the door softly behind him, he opened his hand. The smell of burnt tobacco wafted up.

Cigarette butts. Half a dozen, all Marlboro. Daddy's brand, back when he could smoke.

Desmond flushed the butts down the toilet and washed his hands three times before he could get the smell off them. God forbid Mama smelled tobacco on him, she'd think he smoked himself, instead of Daddy.

But Daddy hadn't smoked in ten years.

Too much to think about. Desmond let it go, made himself forget. He was good at that.

When he finally went back out to Mama, he found her sleeping in her rocking chair.

"You said you never slept, Mama." Desmond didn't whisper. Mama didn't stir.

Off in the distance, something moved. Just a flash of motion in the corner of his eye. Desmond couldn't tell what it was, but he thought he saw a flash of gold, like the sun brushing against pale blond hair.

Leaving Mama in her chair and Daddy in his bed, Desmond took the scrapbook and the Harvester and went looking for Joshua.

Where did he get out?

Desmond searched the dirt road, using the gas and brake pedals without regard to the age of the wagon. Every tree looked the same, every deer-path looked like it might be right. He couldn't remember any landmarks. Joshua left the car in a hurry, and Desmond didn't think to check out the surroundings – the Panhandle was the Panhandle, and in the backwoods, everything looked alike.

Desmond parked the car, shut off the engine, and picked up the scrapbook. Pocketing the keys, he walked through a thin cover of underbrush and made his way into the woods. After a few minutes of pushing away nooses of Spanish moss and fighting off yellow-jackets, he found a small clearing, no more than five feet across. A little boy, maybe eight years old, stood dancing erratically, his hands messing around near his personal parts. Desmond turned away, not sure what he was seeing or even wanting to find out. He stumbled over a fallen branch, caught himself before falling, and swore to himself softly.

"Hey, mister."

Desmond pretended he hadn't heard, took another step.

"Mister! I need some help. Could you help me? It's real important!"

"I don't think... I can't..."

The boy snatched at the front of his pants, squeezing. "My zipper's stuck, mister! I gotta pee real bad, and I can't get my pants open, and it hurts! I'm like to bust!"

He just needs his zipper opened. Not a big deal, it's happened to you before, you know what it's like, go on and help the kid, Desie. You ain't doing nothing wrong. Desmond walked toward the boy, nodding his head over and over like he was coming up on a frightened dog, *just here to help, calm down boy, just want to help you with your britches, that's all.* He took in the kid's mussed-up hair, black and thick, maybe some Seminole in him, watched the way the boy kept a firm hold on his personals – holding back the flood, Desmond could almost feel the pressure himself – and he got close, knelt slowly, and reached out his hands. "Can't do nothing if you're gonna keep grabbing yourself like that."

The boy nodded, tears glinting in his eyes, and let his hand fall away. Desmond reached out to grab the waist of the boy's pants, saw a piece of the boy's underwear sticking out from the zipper. "Yeah, you got yourself in some kind of fix there, pardner." He hated the words as soon as they came out – hated the way his voice trembled, the way 'pardner' sounded sneaky and false, instead of comforting like he'd meant it.

"I'm 'bout to go," the boy whispered, and Desmond worked quick, pulling the waistband of the boy's pants out, working the zipper at the same time. "You grab hold of your underpants and pull them up tight, okay?" He didn't look up at the boy, but a small hand came down and did what he said. "I might rip your undies a little. Sorry." Desmond pulled at the zipper, moving it up and down a little at a time. It gave up the caught fabric grudgingly, clutching the cotton firmly in its teeth. Desmond felt the sweats start up again, pouring down his forehead, soaking his shirt, and his hands trembled so bad he lost the zipper.

"Geez, kid, sorry sorry sorry, I'm doing this fast as I can." Back to the zipper, trying to keep his hands arched and away from the boy's personals, the pressure of urine outlining the boy's *thingy* tight against his pants. "Lord, kid, this is stuck real good, sorry," and Desmond's arms glistened, the thick hair plastered down into near invisibility, "almost got it, hold it in, pal," and he saw his father's face, the angry red sun from his dream floating in his vision, mouthing silent curses. Desmond jerked in response, his muscles clenching with adrenaline. He gave the whole mess one strong hard tug and the zipper came free, but the force of Desmond's final attempt pulled the boy's pants and underpants down around his knees.

Desmond shouted and fell back, pushing himself away from the boy as quickly as his off-balance position allowed. *Sorry sorry sorry* and he couldn't tell if he was thinking it or saying it.

The boy just stood there, pants slowly falling down to his ankles, tears running freely. "You're not going to touch me, are you?"

"What?" Desmond felt dizzy, and his stomach clenched in a tight knot. Hot bile rose in his throat. *God, kid, just pee, alright?*

"You're not going to – " the boy's voice cracked, and a thin stream of snot dripped from one side of his nose " – not going to *hurt* me, are you?"

Desmond slumped forward, wanting to retch, wanting to scream, wanting the boy to just go away go away go away. "I ain't going to do nothing to you, son. I just wanted to *help* you! I just wanted – "

And the bile burned his throat and his stomach turned against him, and Desmond Fells closed his eyes and retched until he had nothing left in him. His tongue burned and bled, and he barely noticed the pain.

When the dry heaves finally passed, the boy was gone. Desmond lay on his back, vomit-smeared and sweat-soaked, staring at the bright light shining through the treetops and wondering what time it was. *Gotta get the car back, Mama will have a fit if she finds out.* He finally rolled over, so weak that he wasn't sure he could even stand, much less walk back to the car.

The scrapbook lay a foot away, face-open on the patchy grass beside him. He pulled it to him, not even remembering when he'd dropped it, praying he hadn't hurled all over its pages. He went to close it, hesitated when he saw the boy's face.

Blurred, faded on the old newsprint, but there in front of him – no doubt in his mind – was the face of the boy with the stuck zipper. It stared at him, eyes blazing from the yellowed clipping, and Desmond could almost see the tears forming, dripping down its cheeks, smearing the cheap ink across the page. Desmond read the small paragraph below the picture. 'Jaime...' and someone had scratched out a sentence or so, leaving a ragged tear in the clipping '...enjoys archery and astronomy, and he is active in his church youth group. Any – ' and the rest of the paragraph had been torn out from that point.

"Don't mind Jaime. He's always been a little nervous."

Desmond jumped back from the scrapbook, sure for a moment that the picture had been talking to him. Then a shadow fell over the pages, and he looked up to see Joshua standing beside him. "I didn't do nothing. I swear to God I didn't hurt him."

Joshua nodded. "I know. You're not the kind of guy who'd go hurting kids, are ya, Desmond?"

The nightmare flashed through Desmond's mind – water, that other boy, blood – and he shook his head to clear the images. "I don't – not sure..."

"Why you hauling that thing around, Desmond? It weighs a ton." Joshua's foot nudged the scrapbook, flipping the pages away from Jaime's face.

Desmond struggled to keep up with the shift in subjects. "It's not that heavy."

Joshua looked straight into Desmond's eyes. Desmond saw something flash across the boy's face, rage or regret. "To me it's heavier than the whole world, sometimes." He turned and started walking away, leaving Desmond crouched by the book.

"Hey! I wanna give this back to you! You left it in my car!" Desmond grabbed the scrapbook and got to his feet, brushing dirt off his pants as he rose.

Joshua turned back. "It ain't mine, Desmond. One of my kin found it out back of your place – I figured it must belong to you." Then he smiled and disappeared into the woods.

"It ain't mine! I never saw it before!"

But Joshua, if he heard, didn't answer.

When Desmond drove up to the trailer, he could hear Mama yelling something inside. Sure she must be yelling at him, he stuffed the scrapbook way back underneath the bench seat and hurried inside.

Daddy stood in the living room, his oxygen tank laboring even more than usual. Mama shut up as soon as Desmond came inside, but he'd caught something about 'boys' before she'd realized he was home.

She'd been yelling at Daddy.

With the tirade broken, Daddy collapsed back into his recliner, still fighting for each breath. Mama stood looking at Desmond now, her hands clutched in great arthritic knots. Desmond could feel the pain in his own knuckles until she finally relaxed her fists enough to let her fingers go back into their familiar semi-clawed positions.

"Where you been, son? I had to get your Daddy out of bed all by myself. You know my back ain't cut out for that kind of strain."

Desmond, expecting her to turn her ire on him, was surprised at her tone – quiet, almost defeated. *Heck, she's exhausted. You shoulda been here to help.* "Sorry, Mama. I – I went out looking for that boy who's been messing around in our backyard."

Mama limped into the kitchen and started making Desmond a breakfast plate. "You don't worry 'bout that child. That's – it's not your business, Desie. You just get something to eat and don't pay no nevermind to all that. Be my good boy, Desie-roo."

Desmond sat down to eat. Mama poured him some milk, then wandered out to the back porch.

After a minute, he heard the steady creaking of her rocker.

The boys came out that night.

Desmond had spent the day waiting for Mama to act normally – cussing at him for some imagined fault, or nagging him to get some work done around the place, anything – but she drifted through the day as if he didn't exist, unless it was mealtime, or time for Daddy's bath.

He almost forgot about the scrapbook. They'd put Daddy to bed, and Desmond was already in his underwear and about to go to sleep himself when he remembered. He put his pants back on and listened at the bedroom door for Mama, but he couldn't hear her shuffling around out there. When he opened the door, he heard the faint creak of her rocker, and he slipped out front as quietly as he could, making his way by moonlight to the Harvester.

The driver's side door squealed like there was a cat caught in its hinges. He heard Mama's voice from the back porch. "Who's out there? You boys go to Hell, you hear me? Go straight to Hell!" Desmond grabbed the scrapbook, pulling up on the door as he closed it so it wouldn't squeak again.

As he made his way back to the trailer, he caught a quick glimpse of blond hair, and the shadowy figure of a boy running past.

"Joss!" Desmond realized he'd shouted the name only after the fact, and he held his breath, knowing Mama must've heard. But she still cussed from her rocking chair out back, oblivious.

A whisper, then, from around the side of the trailer. "C'mon, Desmond. Don't you wanna know where I found that?"

Desmond looked down at the scrapbook, almost forgotten in his hands. *Do I? Do I really want to know?* He stood rooted as deeply as the magnolia trees in the front yard.

Again the whisper. "What's a matter, Desie? 'Fraid your Mama might find out?"

Hell with it. Desmond tucked the scrapbook under his arm and headed where he'd seen Joshua; not running, but keeping to a fast walk, at least.

He rounded the back end of the trailer, almost collided with the propane tank, then followed the shadow of Joshua into the backyard. He glanced in Mama's direction, but she was still shouting curses from her rocker, her attention locked onto the treeline.

Desmond glanced that way himself. It was hard to make out anything in the darkness. The back porch light made a half-hearted attempt to illuminate the yard, but years of accumulated dirt and bug guts had turned the light fixture into an effective baffle for the bulb it encased. Mama sat in a dim semi-circle of yellow light, yelling at shadows within the shadows.

"Desmond." A whisper to his left, then a bird-whistle farther out, away from the weak porch light. Desmond hesitated, not sure if he could make himself go into that darkness. Daddy may not have put much money into their home, but he'd made damn sure to invest in land.

"Don't want everybody breathin' down our necks," Daddy'd always said. "Don't need no strangers tendin' to our bizyness." That's how Daddy said it. *Bizyness.* When Desmond first saw the word 'business' in spelling lessons at school, he didn't even recognize it. It had nothing to do with Daddy's word.

Desmond didn't remember how many acres they owned, but the nearest neighbors were pretty much a mile in any direction. He'd never even gone out past the backyard tree line as a kid – things got swampy back there, and Daddy had scared him with stories of moccasin nests and poisonous centipedes and lizards, and God-knows-what-all back there since Desmond was old enough to get the fear.

Joshua's voice called to him again, *Desmond?*, fading away in the distance, and Desmond found himself following it, skirting Mama's blotch of light and heading into the trees, through them.

Past them.

A tiny creek meandered through the woods and petered away in the thick underbrush, keeping the ground soggy even during the driest heat spells. They'd had a lot of rain out this way recently, what with all the hurricane activity in the Gulf, and Desmond couldn't make out where the thin strips of dry land ended and the murk began.

"I can't go no farther than this." He wasn't sure if he spoke to Joshua, out there in the darkness, or just to himself.

"Yes you can, Desmond. You *have* to." And there stood Joshua, so close to Desmond that he could feel the boy's breath on his arm. "Take my hand, and I'll lead you."

Desmond clutched the scrapbook tight against his chest with one arm. The other dangled uselessly at his side. He couldn't move it, couldn't even imagine he'd ever be able to move it again, until Joshua's hand slid into his own. He grasped it by reflex, surprised at how small the boy's hand felt, how cold. He waited for the sweats to come on again, clenched his stomach in preparation for a wave of nausea and anxiety. Nothing. Just a small boy's cold hand in his, and Daddy's swamp before him.

Joshua tugged. Desmond, defenseless as a blind man, followed.

They wove their way through the marshy ground, Desmond stumbling now and then but never falling. He lost track of time and distance, measuring his progress by the number of stars becoming visible in the night sky. He wanted to search for the Dippers – the only two constellations he knew by sight – but whenever he took his eyes away from Joshua he tended to trip or wander too far to the left or right. Finally, he just looked for the reflections of the stars in the pools of stagnant water around him.

Joss stopped Desmond, finally, merely by letting go of his arm. Desmond stood still, his arm once again dangling limp, as if the batteries that made him work had been removed.

"This is the place. Be careful walking around – you gotta watch what you step on."

Desmond looked around himself, trying to make out his surroundings in the starlight. The ground looked black to him, nothing but pitch, but as he strained his vision, he could make out areas that seemed even darker – a series of depressions in the earth. *Just like little sinkholes.* Desmond knew about sinkholes, everybody who lived in Florida for any length of time did. Streets disappeared in them, houses sometimes. People got swallowed up, every now and then.

"I don't want to be out here, Joss. Can I go home now? Please?" Desmond heard his own voice sounding like a scared child's. But he didn't care. He *was* scared, and if he sounded like a baby, who cared? "Really, Joss, I wanna go back home, if that's all right."

Joss reached out and touched Desmond's hand, the one holding the scrapbook. "We all want to go home, Desmond. But you gotta see something first." Joss bent over what Desmond could just make out to be a hole in the ground, recently dug up. The boy looked up at him, tears gleaming like tiny stars on his cheeks. "I'm sorry, Desmond. I'm really, really sorry. But it's time to grow up now."

Joss pulled something free of the earth, thrust it in Desmond's free hand, then turned and walked away. "I'll be near, Desmond. When you need me, I'll be close by."

Then Joss joined the darkness, just another shadow in a night full of them.

Desmond felt the thing in his hand, slick and unnatural. He wanted to drop it and just run away; instead, he knelt and gently laid the scrapbook down beside him. Now, with both hands at his disposal, he examined the thing with his fingertips, and realized that he'd found a piece of it attached to the scrapbook.

He held a heavy-duty garbage bag – black, he knew, just like that scrap of it he'd found earlier. There was weight still dragging it down, more than could be explained by the muddy clots of dirt that fell, even now, around his feet. Finding the neck, he opened it up. A whiff of stale air, a strange metallic smell along with it…

"I can't see." Desmond barely whispered the words. He stood there, the blackness inside the bag threatening to suck him in. "It's too dark, Joss – I can't see what's in it."

Joss whispered back. "We'll give you some light, Desmond. Just look."

A pale, wavering glow surrounded Desmond, as if a thousand fireflies circled his head. He wanted to look up, see where the light came from, but some deeper instinct told him to keep his head down. *Just look in the bag. It's what they want. Look, and then you can go home.*

There were clothes, jeans and a heavy denim shirt, both stained with something dark and colorless in the uncertain light. Work-boots as well – thick-soled and dirty, stained and well-used. Digging past these, Desmond saw a glint of metal, and the glint became a crescent, and the crescent became…

Daddy's showing him the knife, saying "It's a Gerber, boy, best knife made," and Desmond's wondering why they named a knife after baby food, while Daddy runs the edge up his forearm, shaving hairs off like they weren't even attached

…the crescent became the tooth of a shark, a Great White bigger than a whale…

"Call it my shark's tooth, boy, 'cause it bites in and don't let go, ever"

…and Desmond reached for the tooth/knife, and his hand brushed against other things – small, dried things, like the deer jerky Mama used to make when Daddy was still able to hunt…

and there he is, Desmond in the water, all of twelve years old? yes, twelve, he knows it because sometimes he still feels twelve, like he'd just stopped growing then, no matter his size. He's in the water, the Gulf, he'd walked there from his house like he did every day in summer, but this time

…not jerky, no, these things were too small, too fragile – he felt one crumble in his hand, leaving a dry, silky residue on his fingers…

this time he's a shark, Daddy's great Tooth strapped to his leg in its waterproof sheath, and he feels like a predator, slipping through the bay water silently, holding his breath and hugging the bottom, hunting rays or flounder or whatever comes within his range

...and Desmond closed his eyes, prayed for the glow to go away now, he didn't want it anymore, because he knew what those things were in the bag, he'd seen what was in his hand before he'd crushed it in reflex – the poor shriveled thing, the dried sack of flesh with its pea-hard contents still in it...

and suddenly someone puts a foot on Desmond's back, holding him under the water, and Desmond isn't the predator anymore, he's prey. He can't move, pinned to the sandy bottom, his lungs swelling in his chest, ready to burst

...nonononono not just from Desmond's lips but from many, a lone, sad ululation echoed by a pack of others, and Desmond tried to stop it but he had no control, the sounds and the images were stronger than he was...

and then he's up, pulled from the bottom by the gaff of an arm. An older boy – "One of them damn Sowell kids, Desie, you stay away from them," Mama told him and told and told, but this wasn't some Sowell kid, sorry Mama, just some big dumb older boy – picks him half out of the water, laughing at Desmond and helping him stand at the same time. "Damn, I just caught me one big ol' fish, didn't I?" Desmond can't answer, his lungs too busy learning what air is again. The boy's shorts are slung around his neck, and Desmond focuses on them while the lights quit swirling around in his eyes and his heart quits beating in his ears

...without thinking, Desmond grabbed the knife, blade toward his palm, and squeezed. Still sharp, the blade bit into his flesh, deep, and as Desmond held it tighter, still deeper. But the pain could not stop memory...

the boy stands there, water lapping around his thighs, and Desmond can only stare at the boy's nakedness, his eyes wide with fright. "C'mon, kid, ain't you never been skinny-dippin'?" he says and Desmond shakes his head no, watching as the boy strokes himself idly with one hand, his other still holding Desmond's arm. He notices Desmond's expression, brays with laughter. "Dang, kid, ain't you ever even touched yours? 'Fraid it might fall off?" And Desmond sees

...and then the pain stopped, and Desmond felt a hand on his shoulder and a voice saying, "You're almost there, Desmond, just a little more pain and you're done, I promise, *we* promise," and Desmond dropped the knife back into the bag, felt the blood dripping freely from his hand,

and wondered how much more pain anyone could take…

Daddy, Desmond sees Daddy's face, blocking out the yellow sun with his own blood-red face. "What the hell are you doing, boy, what the hell?" *and Desmond isn't in the water with that bad bad boy now, no, he's at home in his bedroom, earlier that morning, afraid of his own body, touching himself with no idea what this strange swelling meant, or why it hurt so much but still felt good, and Daddy grabs him, throws him across his bed, grabs him* there, *and twists. Desmond screams, and Daddy, panting for breath, his eyes glazed, reaches for his belt, realizes he isn't wearing it, and shouts out for Mama.* "Faye, bring me my knife, I gotta do some cutting, woman, bring it in here!" *and Mama runs in, sees what's happening, and starts screaming herself,* "No, no, not this one, Donnie, it's your* son, *baby, you promised me, you* swore, *baby, leave my boy alone, oh God leave Desie be!" and Daddy breathes harder, snot flying out his nose, his lips flecked with foam, and he pulls once, hard, and Desie almost faints at the pain.* "Not again, boy. Don't ever let me catch you again," *and Daddy's gone, out the trailer and into his rig. Desmond hears the motor kick in, rumbling and farting exhaust, and Mama just stares at him, shaking her head.* "Go away for a while, Desie, just go out somewhere and don't come back 'til dinner, you hear me?"

"…almost done, Desmond, you're just about there…"

and Desmond goes to the bay, a safe familiar place, but before he goes he grabs Daddy's knife off his dresser, why? who knows why, but he does it, to feel safer, *to feel* in control, *that's why sharks have teeth, and now this boy, this big bad boy is hurting Desmond with his stupid voice and his nasty thing – his* dick, *dammit, just pointing at Desmond like some pale poisonous eel and Desmond grabs Daddy's knife from its sheath and he*

"…almost there, Desmond, you're almost…"

cuts, he slices out with the knife and he cuts and cuts and cuts, trying to make the bad boy and his nasty stupid bloody eel just go away, and the boy slogs through the water, bleeding and bleating, screaming without words, and Desmond just stands still in the bay, the bloody water washing around his chest, cleaning the knife blade for him, and then finally, finally, he walks home.

Desmond raised his head, eyes blinking. The images of blade and blood still threatened to bring him back into his world of hurt, but the glow around him served as some kind of anchor, keeping the dark edges of his memory dull and distant.

Joss, his hand still on Desmond's shoulder, smiled at him. "Hey, you did it."

Desmond felt dizzy, his vision lost in the warm light around him. Everything looked larger, magnified in his blurred sight. The glow around him peaked, then softened to something approaching the faint starlight he'd been guided by earlier.

Joss stood there before him, a strange smile on his face – half happiness, half sorrow – and Desmond realized that Joss had somehow grown to his own height, his eyes meeting Desmond's on an equal level. "Hey, Desmond. Hey, hey, Des. Welcome to the family."

And Desmond looked around him at the gathered fireflies, the muted stars. The other boys.

"Hi, Des. I'm Jaime. Sorry 'bout last time, okay?" Desmond reached out a hand, stunned, not knowing what to do or what to say. The firefly/star/boy pointed down, and Desmond saw the scrapbook, still lying there at his feet. The pages turned, but Desmond couldn't feel a breeze.

Then the pages lay still, and Desmond saw Jaime's clipping again. It glowed, brighter, brighter, Desmond feeling like he looked into the bright-hot center of a fire, then the clipping faded, curled, and disappeared. The scrapbook page lay blank but for the ashes covering it.

Jaime bent over, breathed, and the ashes were gone, swept away across the strange depressions in the swampy ground.

Jaime walked away, but another took his place. "Derek," he said, and the pages turned again, and flash, ashes, just like how it happened with Jaime. Then Derek walked away, fading, like Jaime did, back into the glowing masses.

"Jeremy." "Ryan." "Buddy." "Chris." "Julio." "Brandon." They were all about Desmond's height, and he suddenly realized that Joss hadn't gotten bigger. Desmond was a kid again, he knew, not how or why but dammit there he was, eleven or twelve or so, just like these other boys. They looked him in the eyes as they passed by, some a little taller, some shorter, but all of them just like Desmond – young, and scared, and innocent. And on and on they came, pages turning, clippings burning, and Desmond stood there, seeing their faces, black and white in the dim moonlight and black and white in the scrapbook, but while the pictures disappeared the boys didn't. They filed by and went back to the field they'd come from, waiting.

Joss came again, last in line. "You're a good guy, Des. We could've been friends, maybe. I think so, anyway." Desmond felt his knees tremble, and he wanted to cry, but he didn't want to look like a baby again, so he just looked away from Joss' smiling, shining face.

He saw the other boys sinking slowly into the ground, their lights dimming, dimming.

"Des." Desmond wouldn't look at Joss again. "Hey, Des. There's something else in the bag. You need to look closer." Joss' voice was moving away, slowly, along with his light. The scrapbook pages didn't turn for him. Desmond wanted to flip the pages himself, releasing Joss somehow, but instead he found himself digging at the bottom of the garbage sack, pushing past all of the frail, crumbling relics of his father's work. *Don't want nobody in our bizyness, right, boy?* And Desmond knew what his daddy's bizyness was now, didn't he, he knew the business of the bizyness, and Desmond almost screamed when he touched something cold and hard sticking out of something crisp and dry, almost squealed like a damned old baby...

No. Be a grown-up, Desmond. For once in your life.

He pulled the thing out of the bag. An old, dried-out pack of Marlboros, half-gone. Sticking out of the plastic sleeve, a tarnished Zippo lighter. Desmond could see, even in Joss' fading light, the stylized monogram on the lid: MLF. Morris Luther Fell, Daddy's name. His initials, anyway, not that Desmond needed the hint.

But it wasn't a hint, was it? No, no, and Desmond could see the next few minutes of his life clearly, just a quick flash like he was glowing from the inside, just like those lost boys buried in his backyard, and he dropped the garbage bag, took up the almost-empty scrapbook, and headed for home.

Mama sat on the porch, her rocker squeaking back and forth, constant motion held in the memory of her thighs, her knees, her feet. Desmond watched her for a long while, noticing the way the dim porch light played across her wrinkles, her thinning grey hair. Her head lay tilted across the back of her chair, mouth open not with threats but snores. Moths circled her head like tiny vultures.

Desmond leaned forward, not wanting to wake her, and placed the scrapbook on her lap.

Mama's eyes snapped open, and she screamed out another curse before she saw Desmond standing there. "Damn you, boy, you scared me half to death! I ought to take a switch to you right now." And Desmond saw the fear in her eyes as she looked up at him, her Desie all grown up now – *not a twelve-year-old anymore, Mama, don't call me boy* – and he pushed her back down into her rocker, not gently, picked up the scrapbook from where it had fallen when she stood, and handed it to her.

"Why, Mama?" He wanted to say so much more, but enough, enough.

Mama tried to push the book off her lap. Desmond stopped her. Mama cried. Desmond let her.

Finally, she straightened up, her tears gone as quickly as they'd started. She didn't pay any attention to the weight in her lap, dismissing it as easily as if it were a clod of dirt, a pile of dirty laundry. "Someone had to remember them."

"What are you talking about?"

"*This*," and Mama prodded the scrapbook. "Your Daddy never remembered what he'd done, afterwards. He'd come home from a long haul, just be sweet as could be, and never say a word. I'd go out to his cab later, once he'd had a few beers, gone to sleep, and there'd be another one, bagged up and tucked behind his seat. Then I'd drag them away – I was stronger then, Desie, not like now – and I'd take care of things. Come back and clean up what needed cleaning. And I'd find newspapers from where he'd been, scattered around in the cab, and I'd find pictures of the boys, sometimes I kept little souvenirs from what they were wearing, sometimes a lock of hair..." Desmond watched as Mama slowly pulled the scrapbook off her lap and hugged it to her chest, not even noticing what she was doing. Her eyes, wet again, sparkled like shattered glass. "And all the time I kept thanking God that it wasn't my baby this time, it wasn't my little Desie."

Desmond felt an overwhelming urge to throw up. He swallowed by reflex, over and over, until he thought he could talk without spewing his insides across the porch. "Why didn't you – Mama, why didn't you ever call the police? Why didn't you let somebody know?" *Why, why, why*, and Desmond knew he'd never get answers, not for all the questions in his head.

Mama snorted. "What were they going to do, son, cure him? You think the cops are doctors, that the Sheriff was just gonna come down here and give your daddy a shot and say 'all better now'? Hell with that, son. We're family. Family takes care of their own."

Not like them damn Sowells, Desmond thought. *We're better than they are, right Mama?*

Desmond turned away, headed for the back door, leaving Mama clutching the near-empty scrapbook to her chest.

"Desie? Where you going, baby?"

"Just saying goodnight to Daddy."

"He's sick, Desie, okay? You remember that. He's a good man, but he's just sick, that's all."

"Yes, ma'am." *Faye, bring me my knife!* "He's just sick. I know, Mama." Then Desmond opened the back door and walked inside, not wanting to talk to Mama anymore.

Not ever.

Daddy lay sleeping in his oxygen tent. Desmond heard the rough hiss of air coming from the tank, filling the room but still not loud enough to cover Daddy's labored breathing.

Desmond walked over to his father's bed, pulled away one wall of his oxygen tent, and leaned down. "Daddy," he said, shaking the bed. Nothing but the hint of a snore, and legs shifting under the sheets.

"Dad. Wake up." Louder, Desmond raising his voice to his father for the first time in his life. He grabbed the mattress and shook it, his father's body tossing around as if at sea.

Finally, the old man woke up. He croaked something out, and Desmond recognized it through the phlegm and faint breath. *Why?*

Desmond couldn't answer that. Instead, he pulled the cigarettes and lighter from his pants pocket. He thought of Joss, telling him they could've been friends. He breathed in, deeply, felt dizzy and clean, all at once.

"Just found something you lost, Daddy."

His father looked up at him, and Desmond saw nothing in the man's eyes – no fear or sorrow or regret, just a blank, guiltless stare. Didn't matter, really. Desmond was done with him, done with him and Mama and nightmares and anything else trapped in this damned trailer.

Desmond left the old stale cigarettes and the lighter on Daddy's lap, turned, and walked away, closing the bedroom door behind him. Even with the door shut, he could still hear the hissing of the oxygen tank, a thousand rattlesnakes trapped in a small rotting box.

Can we still be friends, Joss?

Desmond didn't hear Joss answer, but he felt a little warmth in his chest, his belly. Like something glowing there, deep inside.

Desmond walked out the front door of the trailer, paused by the Harvester. He went so far as to open the door, ready to drive away from Mama and Daddy until the gas ran out or the old relic died, whichever came first. But he could smell them in it, the old smells of Daddy's cigarettes and Mama's cheap perfume, and he couldn't get in, couldn't even manage to sit in the seat anymore. *Too much breakage.* Digging in his pockets, he found the car keys and threw them on the driver's seat, then turned and walked down the red sand path away from home. He thought he heard Mama's voice calling after him, but it might've been the crickets, it might've been the wind through the magnolia leaves.

The explosion knocked him off his feet, sent pieces of trailer-made shrapnel through his back, and wrapped him in a sheath of hell-heat and hungry flames. As he tumbled across the rough surface of the road, he just wondered whether Daddy or Mama had flicked the lighter...

"Hey, Mister."

Desmond felt pain. He wasn't even sure if he was awake, didn't *want* to be awake because the pain would be worse then, he knew it.

"Mister, you okay?"

"Joss?" He might've said it, might have just thought it, but the pain was getting worse, oh yes indeed it was, so Desmond figured he must be waking up, whether he wanted to or not.

"You look hurt real bad. I'm gonna run home and call the cops, okay? You be alright 'til they get here?"

"No." Desmond opened his eyes, his eyelashes coming unstuck from each other with the effort. The kid standing next to him wasn't Joss, no way – dark hair and eyes, tan skin that probably came from some Seminole or Choctaw in his blood. *Maybe he's one of them damned Sowells*, and Desmond wanted to laugh, but he was afraid what it might do to the tight, burned skin on his face. "I mean, it ain't that bad, I just... just need some help getting up."

An arm reached toward him. Eyes burning, Desmond could just make out the dark hair on the boy's forearm, glimmering in the early morning sunlight.

We could've been friends, Joss. We really could've.

Desmond grabbed the kid's hand and pulled himself up.

And the pain wasn't that bad at all.

RICHARD BUTNER
HOLDERHAVEN

In 1911, Nerissa and Jorn Holder move into Holderhaven.

In 1966, Nerissa Holder dies, having outlived her husband, both sons, and a son-in-law.

In 1983, Holderhaven opens as a country house museum.

In 2003, Rudy needs a summer job. His friend at college, Bill Mills, says he can pull some strings. Bill does not need a summer job. Bill's family is not quite as wealthy as the Holders had been, but they are rich enough. Bill's father is Ol' Dick Mills. Dick Mills' house does not have a name. It is much smaller than Holderhaven, but it still has a tennis court, a swimming pool, and a separate climate-controlled warehouse for his collection of vintage Jaguar convertibles. Ol' Dick Mills knows everyone in the county. Everyone who matters, at least. He places a call to Harriet Diamond, supervisor of operations at the Holderhaven House Museum.

Holderhaven has four floors, including a basement. Sixty-four rooms. The first and second floors are open to the public, as long as the public stays behind the velvet ropes and doesn't try to touch the leather-topped parquetry desk in Mrs Holder's den, or the tapestries hanging on the balcony walls of the central hall. The board plans to open the basement to the public soon. The top floor, originally for storage, is occupied by the museum staff. Harriet Diamond has an office. Mary Holder Hodgson has an office on the top floor too, with access to the roof walk, but she is rarely around. Rudy gets to stay in a bedroom on the top floor for the summer. The bedroom had been the majordomo's originally. In the 1960s it had been renovated as a teenager's hideout. As far as amenities are concerned, it is not much different from Rudy's dorm room.

Rudy is not particularly qualified to work in the house. He is studying math, not architectural preservation. The museum employs specialists to conserve the artwork, to clean the tapestries, to preserve the library books, to ensure that the flowers outside match the photographs of the gardens from the 1920s. That has been the great project of the museum: to send the house back in time. To erase the renovations and redecorations done by the family over the course of the 20th century. To make the house suitable for population by flappers, bootleggers, and gentlemen in straw boater hats. Mary Holder Hodgson has decided that the 1920s would be good for business. Competition in the house museum market is stiff. Everyone is second place to the Biltmore House. Everyone is trying harder. For a time, Mary Holder Hodgson pushes to come out with Holderhaven branded wine. But grapes had never been grown on the estate, and the board nixes this plan. Plans to re-create the 1920s continue.

Rudy is given keys and alarm codes. For the first weeks of the summer, he and Bill Mills spend their off hours together. Bill Mills is an avid moviegoer. Bill is looking forward to the next *Matrix* movie.

In 1974, Harriet Diamond is a Black Panther. She wears a black beret, a shiny black leather jacket, dark sunglasses, and a stern expression as she delivers breakfasts to hungry schoolchildren. In addition to holding a Black Panther ID card, she also holds a membership card to the Women's Auxiliary to the White Knights of the Ku Klux Klan. She and all her fellow Panthers sent in fake photos to a PO Box address they saw on a flier stapled to a telephone pole. They all received Klan cards. There was no membership fee.

"Know your enemy," Harriet said. Sending off for the Klan cards was her idea.

In 2003, a black and white photograph of herself and the other Panthers sits on Harriet Diamond's desk. Rudy steals glances between the photo and Ms Diamond, trying to interpolate the path between the two endpoints. He wonders if Ms Diamond feels conflicted as an African-American about working in a place like Holderhaven. He never asks her about this, though. In Harriet Diamond's wallet, she still carries her Panther and her Klan membership cards. They are creased and torn now. Realistically old, unlike Holderhaven, which is constantly policed for any sign of decay.

Harriet Diamond is not surprised that Rudy's knowledge of upkeep and repair is not quite as expansive as Ol' Dick Mills implied it would be when he got Rudy the job. Rudy painted houses the previous summer.

"Rudy, what do you know about carpentry?"

"Not much, Ms Diamond."

"What do you know about plastering?"

"Not much, Ms Diamond."

"What do you know about, oh, swimming pool filtration?"

"Not much, Ms Diamond, but I'm a quick study."

"What do you know about secret passages?"

In 1910, Nerissa Holder works with architect Irving Gill on the house plans. She supervises every aspect of planning and construction. Mr Gill wants an asymmetrical design, with only one wing. Mrs Holder asks for two wings off the grand central hall. The primary building material will be rough granite stones, with a clay tile roof. She asks Mr Gill to design matching structures in miniature for the separate servants' quarters and for a playhouse for the children she plans to begin producing. And she asks for a secret passage. No one but Mr Holder is to know about the secret passage. She works closely with Mr Gill to ensure this. After the house is built, she burns the blueprints in the fireplace in the great hall. She adds them to the fire one page at a time, ensuring that each is completely consumed, leaving no trace.

In 1911, the secret passage exists. It begins in Mrs Holder's closet in the master bedroom. Clothes hang to either side. Pressing on the back wall panel at doorknob height pops a magnetic catch so that the entire panel swings open. There is no landing; the spiral staircase begins immediately, down a shaft barely wider than a chimney. The interior is black and featureless, and there is no source of light inside. Any traveler in the secret passage would navigate by feel. The staircase leads all the way to the basement, bypassing the first floor. The basement is a floor of amusements: a party room with large granite fireplace, a billiards room, a one-lane bowling alley, an indoor swimming pool, an elaborate bar with mirrored walls. The secret passage exit is disguised as one of the mirrored panels behind the bar.

In 2003, there are no plans to put the secret passage on the public tour. Instead, it is to be fixed up for the wealthiest donors. A bonus for them. They are also going to get to use the bowling alley and swimming pool in the basement on special occasions. Harriet Diamond gives Rudy the task, for most of June, of fixing up the secret passage.

The secret passage is not the only unusual feature of the house. There is a safe in the master bedroom, behind a painting of a fox hunt. The painting is now hinged to the wall to make it easier for the docents to swing it away dramatically as they tell schoolchildren the tale of Mr Holder's money. There is an impressive collection of taxidermed animals in the library. Because of the harsh chemicals used – arsenic and mercury – they have been encased in plastic. Mr Holder had been a keen naturalist, and his love of nature is another paragraph in the script that the docents memorize.

When asked, Mary Holder Hodgson says she is not sure why there is a secret passage. Because the passage is not going to be placed on the public tour, there is no need to "interpret" it. When Harriet reveals the existence of the passage to Rudy, he asks her why it exists.

"Rich people," she says, lowering her head to gaze at him over the top of her reading glasses. This is the only answer she gives.

Tours continue through the summer, so Rudy cannot leave the upper entrance open as he works. He places a fan at the lower entrance, trying to pull out the hot still air. He wears a mask, which makes breathing more difficult. First he sands the rust off the metal stairs, beneath a worklight tethered to a long orange extension cord. He starts at the top, wielding sandpaper and steel wool, dripping sweat, trying not to make too much noise. The docents are used to seeing workers painting a hallway or trimming the hedges, but Rudy wants to keep the secret passage a secret.

He has been sanding for a week when he makes the discovery. Swinging the light around, he notices scratches in the wall. About halfway up the climb, someone had carved a word. The letters are blockish and clumsy, all capitals. Perhaps this word was carved in the dark. The word is LIZZA. Following that name are tally marks, two sets of five plus four more.

Rudy tells Harriet Diamond many things, but he does not yet tell her about his discovery in the secret passage.

The history of Holderhaven is available in a coffee table book. It is also spelled out on a series of kiosks in the tour entrance area, which Harriet refers to as the emergency room. It's the converted garage. Behind velvet ropes sits a 1930 Rolls, not actually one that belonged to the Holders. The original car was totaled in the wreck that killed Crosby Holder, the eldest son, in 1932. The garage is where you buy your ticket and where, if you want more than the docents will tell you, you can learn about the history of the Holder estate. Rudy cursorily read the kiosks when he first started working at Holderhaven. Harriet asked him to check them for typos. She seemed pleased rather than annoyed when he found and fixed two: Pennslvania and capitol instead of capital. Now he returns to the kiosks, looking for mention of anyone named Lizza. He finds none, not even an Elizabeth. Not one on the family tree chart. Not one in the endless paragraphs on Mrs Holder's various projects: her unsuccessful attempt to cultivate tulips, her more successful dairy operation, the school she founded to instruct the servants. No mention of a Lizza in the descriptions of the famous personages who stopped by Holderhaven to play croquet or to dance the Charleston. These personages included Charles Lindbergh and Calvin Coolidge.

Bill Mills calls up Rudy, wanting to go to a movie and then out to Jay's, his favorite bar. Rudy begs off, says he is feeling ill. He stays up late working on Harriet's computer, looking up more genealogy, looking up the names of Lindbergh's wife. Her name was Anne, not Lizza. Coolidge's wife's name was Grace.

Finally he gives up and goes back to the secret passage with a flashlight. He pores over the walls looking for any other marks. For anything at all, but finds nothing. No hidden chamber. Just the inscription.

It is against the rules, but that night Rudy steps past the velvet rope and sleeps on the Holders' bed, with the door to the secret passage left open. There is no pillow on the bed. There is no pillow on any bed in the restored rooms of Holderhaven. Mrs Holder believed that it was healthier to sleep without a pillow, to preserve the youthful straightness of the spine. Rudy does not have any revelatory dreams.

In 1899, Holderhaven does not exist. Mr William Bagge, sheep farmer, owns a small tract that will form the heart of the 1,066-acre Holder estate. Mr Bagge's daughter is born. After Mr Bagge's death, his wife and daughter will go to work for the Holders. His daughter's name is Elizabeth, but she is called Lizza.

In 2003, Rudy and Harriet are having a conversation.

"What do you think the secret passage was for?" Rudy asks.

"Jorn Holder was a strange man. Maybe to make it easier to run down and get a nightcap from the bar? We know he liked to take over from the bartender and mix drinks. Maybe he liked to appear suddenly behind the bar at parties."

"Seems like a pretty useless trick to go to so much trouble."

Harriet is moving numbers around in a spreadsheet as she talks.

"He couldn't swim, either, but that didn't stop him from building a pool. And I hear he was lousy at bowling, too. How's the bowling alley coming?"

Rudy shrugs and winces. In addition to the secret passage, he is tasked with repainting the bowling alley. The restoration consultant, a big man named James, has chosen a color called Peach Surprise that is the closest match to the original paint. The bowling alley, though small, is airy and temperate compared to the secret passage. Rudy has inspected all of its nooks and crevices for markings or bits of papers and found nothing. He has not actually started painting it yet.

"Speaking of tricks, pick a card," Harriet says. She proffers a deck to Rudy.

"Do I get to inspect the deck first?" he asks.

"No, you don't get to inspect the deck. What, don't you trust me?"

"All right, Harriet, I trust you."

He pulls a card from the set fanned out before him. He tries to pull it from a non-obvious place in the deck. Not the middle. Not either end. Not halfway between the middle and the end. The card is the Jack of diamonds.

"Don't show me the card," Harriet says.

"Is this a comment on me?" Rudy asks. "Because if it is, I don't get it."

"I don't know what you're talking about. Put the card back in the deck."

He slides the card in, again to a place that he thinks is the least likely. Harriet raps the top of the deck sharply, then carefully flips over the top card.

"Is this your card?"

The card is the nine of clubs. Rudy really wants the trick to work, but he doesn't want to lie. So instead he just waits. She repeats the question.

"No, Harriet. It's close, though!"

Harriet scrunches her brow.

"Not your card, huh? Damn. All right, sort through the deck and find it for me."

She hands him the pack, which he flips over and begins sifting through. To Rudy it looks like a standard deck of cards. He can't find the Jack of diamonds, though, even though he'd just put it back in there.

"Hang on, hang on, I'm feeling something," Harriet says. "Stand up."

He stands up.

"Put your hand in your left trouser pocket."

He puts his hand in. There is the usual junk: assorted change, a little pocket pen, his lucky paper clip. There is also a playing card. Rudy pulls the card out slowly, and as he does he unconsciously takes a step back from Harriet. The card is the Jack of diamonds.

"Pretty good, huh?"

"Damn good, Harriet."

In 1912, Crosby is born, the first of Jorn and Nerissa's three children. Immediately after the birth, Jorn Holder commissions a painting and a statue. The painting is a portrait of a prepubescent girl, clad only in a diaphanous white dress. She clutches a spray of white flowers and has a pixie grin on her face. She has sharp cheekbones and a snub nose. The painting hangs over the mantel in his office. The statue is bronze, placed in the terraced garden, in the center of a circular slate walkway surrounded by rhododendron and azalea. The terraced garden is on the north side of the east wing, visible from the master suite and from Mr Holder's office. The statue is of the same young girl. She is nude, facing toward the house, her arms spread to display the bounty of the garden and grounds. Mr Holder calls her 'Lady Liberty'.

In 2003, Rudy continues his investigations. He is surrounded by objects, rooms full of them. He is surrounded by texts. Books in the library. Paperwork in Harriet's office. Mary Holder Hodgson's office is always locked, but he imagines she has some records too. It turns out that most of the surviving records from Holderhaven are now kept in a vault at the university. Not available to the public. Someone is doing a dissertation, but she is out of town for the summer. Rudy sends the doctoral student an email, but gets no response.

Rudy imagines all these objects, all this text, laid out in a giant matrix. He is slowly picking his way through each cell in the matrix. He looks in the big maintenance building that's hidden at the end of a paved pathway in the woods. It's a modern structure, built after Holderhaven's transformation into museum. The gardeners' tools and machinery are kept there. There is also furniture from the now deprecated mid-century era of Holderhaven. Rudy carefully inspects the jumble of bent plywood chairs and steel and fiberglass tables, but he finds no graffiti, no spoor of the mysterious Lizza. He looks in the playhouse and the servants' quarters too, but finds nothing of interest.

Rudy takes the keys to these buildings back to Harriet's office, to replace them on their labeled hooks. He plops down in Harriet's chair, spins to face the shelf on the far wall. There is a series of boxes, labeled with years starting with 1923. He starts to pull the earliest one off the shelf.

"You don't want to touch that one," Harriet says, from the doorway. "That's what they call a valuable collector's item. Those have nothing to do with the house. It's my complete set of back issues of The Linking Ring. I'm reading through them on my lunch breaks."

Rudy raises his eyebrows, not comprehending.

"The magazine of IBM, the International Brotherhood of Magicians. They don't have an International Sisterhood, so I make do."

"I'm sorry, I wasn't trying to snoop through your stuff."

Rudy gets up and moves to the chair on the other side of the desk. Harriet takes up her position behind the desk.

"How's the bowling alley coming?" Harriet asks.

"Uh, it's taking longer than expected."

"Has to be done by the party, which is next Friday. What are you looking for in the maintenance shed, anyway?"

Rudy hesitates.

"And don't lie."

So he doesn't. He tells her about the inscription in the secret passage. He offers to take her to see it, but she declines.

"I believe you. I don't need to see it."

Harriet tells him that the name Lizza does not ring a bell with her.

Not the name of any family members. Not the name of any of the servants that she can recall. Harriet pulls her copy of the coffee table book from the shelf. She points out the photograph on page 27: 'Crosby, the governess Mags, Alvis, unidentified women and Jorn at Holderhaven, circa 1915.' Three-year-old Crosby is wearing a suit that matches his father's. They stand at either end of the group of women. One of the women is holding Crosby's younger brother, Alvis, in her arms. On top of the hill in the distance sits Holderhaven. The women all wear white dresses. Six women are unidentified; any of them could be Lizza. Mags wears her hair in a bun perched on the top of her head. Her hand rests on young Crosby's shoulder.

"There are a lot of unidentified people who passed through these hallowed halls," she says. So many names, especially servants' names, are practically lost to history. Possibly recorded on census rolls, probably never engraved on a tombstone, just a dimly remembered story to their descendents. At any given time, especially in the early days of Holderhaven, there would have been cooks, laundresses, gardeners, maids, nurses. Someone to set the pins in the bowling alley. A chauffeur, whose name does survive, as does the name of the majordomo: Arthur Doyle.

"No relation to Sherlock Holmes," Harriet says. "Trust me."

"We could just ask Ms Hodgson," Rudy says. "Maybe she knows some lore that didn't get set down in the book."

"Mary Holder Hodgson can tell you a whole other book's worth of family history. If you want to talk about the ill-fated attempt to bottle and sell salad dressing made on the estate during the Depression, she can tell you all about it. If you want to know all about her uncle Alvis's pet monkey that he kept in a cage next to the swimming pool, she can reel off a list of all the furniture and objets d'art that it broke or ruined every time it escaped during its two-year tenure in the house. If you want to talk about Nerissa Holder's fondness for tomato pudding and lamb sandwiches at her Whist Club luncheons, she will recite the entire menu and then teach you to play Whist. Which is a boring damn game, by the way. But she didn't even know about the secret passage's existence – it had been sealed shut for decades when the restoration architects' discovered it while they were drawing up plans. I doubt she wants to know that some girl's name is scratched on the wall in there next to some tally marks.

"Also, she always keeps her office locked. And she's the only one with the key."

In 1965, two magicians visit Hattie Diamond's fourth grade class. She and nine of her classmates pose for a photograph with them. The magicians, both of them white men, wear bow ties and plaid tuxedos. This photograph is published in the September issue of The Linking Ring, just above a joke about spades.

In 1916, Jorn Holder dies. The cause of death printed in the Daily Lookout is a combination of gastritis and exhaustion. Nerissa has the painting of the young girl removed from Jorn's office and the nude statue removed from the terraced garden. Alone one night soon after, she burns the painting in the fireplace in the great hall. Later she will donate the statue to be melted down for the war effort. She has a large marble obelisk constructed and put in the place of the statue, a cenotaph for Jorn, whose remains were sent back to the old Holder family cemetery in Pennsylvania. Almost nine months after Jorn's death, on Christmas Day, Nerissa bears their final child, a girl, Noelle.

The secret passage is not the only way to traverse the floors of Holderhaven. There is an elevator, but it is locked shut, deemed unsafe and too expensive to repair. There is a dumbwaiter, too, merely broken. And of course there are stairs; narrow ones to get up to the top floor where Harriet works and Rudy lives, grand ones on either side of the central fireplace to ascend from the first floor to the second, less grand ones to descend to the basement. Rudy wonders if the elevator holds any secrets, or the dumbwaiter. The dumbwaiter compartment itself is stuck between floors. He manages to pry open the doors and finds nothing but a black chimney, a secret passage in miniature. No scratches, no hidden messages. He crawls up as far as he can, which is not far, searching with a flashlight and finding nothing.

Holderhaven has its own ghost story. Everyone who works there, including Harriet, knows the story. The ghost in the story is Mrs Holder. A portrait of her hangs over the fireplace in the great hall. In the portrait, Nerissa Holder is thirty-one years old. A little brass lamp illuminates the portrait, night and day. The story is, if the lamp is shut off at night, Mrs Holder's ghost will emerge from the portrait.

Rudy hears this story from Harriet, but assumes it is merely to keep him in his room at night, instead of wandering about in the dark house pretending to be an early 20th century aristocrat. Going beyond the velvet ropes, sitting in the chairs that are never to be sat in again.

Rudy decides to ask Mrs Holder herself about Lizza. He waits until midnight, goes downstairs and positions one of the dining room chairs in front of the portrait. He flicks off the light switch next to the mantel and takes a seat. And waits. In the portrait, Mrs Holder is kindly and radiant. She looks like Rudy's high school world history teacher, Ms Raney. The same knowing smile, the same piercing green eyes. Rudy has seen actual photographs of Mrs Holder and the portrait is a vast improvement. His eyes adjust to the darkness. It's a full moon outside but it remains extremely dim in the grand hall. On the third floor, the windows are normal glass, but on the public floors, the windows have been coated to keep out the damaging rays of the sun. Mrs Holder does not emerge from the painting. Her mouth does not even move. Rudy conjures up a mental image of Mrs Holder talking to him, but in reality the thin painted smile does not vibrate in the least. Mrs Holder says nothing. Rudy keeps waiting. It takes time to prove a hypothesis, he thinks, wondering if hypothesis is the right word. Rudy is also falling asleep.

He thinks about leaving his mark in Holderhaven, just as Lizza did. Not scratched into the wall of the secret passage, though. Something even sneakier. Maybe written in permanent marker on the bottom of one of the circular stair treads. Who would ever look there? RUDY and his signature doodle, a hyperbolic spiral. Permanent, or as permanent as anything in the house, living on unseen until the house collapsed or burned or until someone decided to repaint the bottom of the treads on the circular stairway. When would that ever happen?

He is jarred awake by a noise, or possibly just a dream of a noise. He focuses on Mrs Holder but she is as flat and lifeless as ever. The noise had not come from the painting. The noise had come from inside the secret passage.

Rudy flips the light switch back on, replaces the dining room chair, and slips upstairs to the master bedroom. He pushes the panel in the back of the closet and it pops open. He leans into the passage.

"Mrs Holder? Nerissa Holder?"

And then, after a moment: "Lizza?"

He is met with silence. He goes and gets a flashlight from his room, walks down the stairs and back up, but he finds nothing amiss. On his way back up the steps, he stops at the marks. Checks them with the flashlight – no change. He reaches out and touches the wall, brushing his palm over the scratchings. The marks are warm.

"Lizza?"

He turns and sits on the steps, flicking the flashlight off. He hears no more noises, though, and after a time he goes up to his room and to bed.

Downtown one Saturday at the end of June, the annual Summersplosion is happening, and Harriet is one of the entertainers. Rudy catches the bus to see her perform. She does sets on the side stage at noon, three, and six. In between she roams the crowd, doing close-up magic. She wears a gold robe with embroidered stars, and a turban with a large ruby brooch. Rudy gets there in time to see the finale of her three o'clock set. It's a card trick. The audience volunteer, a middle-aged white man in khaki shorts, discovers that the card he chose from the deck and signed with a permanent marker has vanished from a locked box and reappeared underneath his baseball cap. The crowd goes wild.

Rudy buys a hot dog and a plastic cup of beer from a tent set up by the local microbrewery. Across the square, a reggae band on the main stage has started up a song about a shantytown. Rudy walks along looking at the craft booths as he polishes off the hot dog and the beer. Pottery, beads, beads made from pottery, pottery featuring beads. He turns the corner and sees Harriet working the crowd. She has a brass urn in one hand. With the other hand she is discovering gold coins on the person of a young girl holding a helium balloon. The girl is extremely ticklish; she cackles as Harriet plucks coins from her armpits, from behind her ears, from out of her shoes. Endlessly they appear, and endlessly Harriet tosses them into her urn, which makes a loud clinking sound each time. Finally Harriet goes to work on the father of the girl with the balloon. Harriet is a lot bolder here than she is at Holderhaven. She displays an empty hand, then reaches around behind the man to pull a gold coin from his butt. The girl with the balloon spasms with laughter. Harriet tosses the coin into her bucket, clink, bows, and moves on.

Rudy walks up to her before she can find another victim.

"Great show, Harriet," he says. She is squinting at him, not responding to the compliment.

"What is that?" she asks. Her arm shoots out near his head, to pluck something from behind his ear. She holds it up between them. It's a key.

"Look what you had behind your ear. Didn't your mother tell you to wash back there? Looks like the key to Mary Holder Hodgson's office to me. Maybe you better hang on to it."

She presses the key into his hand.

"No, Harriet, I – "

"You take the key, do what you need to do. If I got caught snooping in there, it'd cost me my job. Magic pays well by the hour but it's not enough to pay the bills."

"Thanks, Harriet."

"For what?" she says loudly, then she pulls a gold coin out of his nose and drops it in her bucket.

Rudy pockets the key and takes the next bus back to Holderhaven.

The sun is still out when Rudy unlocks Mary Holder Hodgson's office and slips inside. He is immediately confounded. The office is much emptier than he'd expected. The desk is bare except for a computer monitor and an inbox. Unlike Harriet's computer, Mary's is password-protected. He tries a few passwords, but none of them work: Holderhaven, Hodgson, Nerissa, passage. He types in Lizza, feeling sure that it's the one, but when he hits the Enter key the same ACCESS DENIED message appears. He flips through the papers in the inbox, but nothing looks promising. They are mostly current magazines and newspapers, or clippings related to the Holderhaven House Museum. Nothing that looks old or archival. The desk is unlocked but contains mostly cosmetics. One drawer contains only skin creams.

The walls are covered in framed photographs: Mary Holder Hodgson shaking Ol' Dick Mills' hand as he offers her a check and mugs for the camera, Mary Holder Hodgson showing Nancy Reagan around the great hall, pointing at the fake medieval tapestries. There is a locked cabinet next to the desk. For all Rudy knows, there might be another safe hidden behind one of the framed photos. So he checks behind each one, finding only bare walls.

An unabridged dictionary and a large, leather-bound Bible sit on top of the locked cabinet. Rudy flips open the Bible. It opens to a section in the center for a family tree, but this has not been filled in. Pressed between the pages is a small stack of old, fading photographs. He sorts through them. None look promising. Color snapshots from the 1950s and 1960s, children sledding, children hunting for Easter eggs on the grounds. An old black and white photo of the portico, with curvy edges. He checks the backs of the photographs for writing, finds none.

The photograph of the house feels thicker than the rest, because it's actually two photographs stuck together. Rudy carefully pries the photographs apart with his thumbnail.

In the photograph, Jorn Holder stands next to a statue of a girl in the terraced garden. Her nude torso touches his clothed torso. She has her arms outstretched, and his arm is draped over her shoulders. Jorn is smiling.

For a moment, Rudy can't breathe. He commits the photograph to memory, and replaces it and the other pictures in the Bible.

The door to the roof walk is not locked. Rudy walks out and up the steps to the flat tile spine of the roof. Most of the 1,066 acres of the Holder estate have been sold off long ago, but he squints and tries to imagine the surrounding countryside covered in green woods and pastures instead of parking lots and strip malls, lined with dirt paths instead of asphalt roads. The sun goes down and he says goodbye to the day.

The next weekend is the annual reception for the patrons of the house. This year they celebrate the imminent opening, thanks to their donations, of the bowling alley, the swimming pool, the bar and the party room, the same rooms that Rudy and the conservators have been trying to put in order. The patrons love doing things that ordinary visitors are not allowed to do. The frisson of going beyond the velvet rope is their reward for donating the hundreds of thousands of dollars that it takes to keep the place running.

Harriet asks Rudy if he is going to attend.

"I'm invited? I don't have to work the reception?"

"No. Mary Holder Hodgson suggested that you might be able to assist the caterers, but I talked her out of that."

"Thanks, Harriet," Rudy says.

"You might even get to meet some folks who really were in the Klan," she adds, as if that is a bonus.

The party invitations suggest that attendees dress up in the style of the 1920s. Bill Mills loans Rudy an ivory linen suit. Bill goes in a top hat and tails, as if he'd walked out of a Monopoly set. Rudy scrounges up some spectator shoes at a thrift store, but he cannot find a straw boater hat. Bill's suit is a little too big for him.

Ol' Dick Mills is a platinum patron of Holderhaven. Platinum is $10,000 a year and up. Platinum members are listed in the brochure, on a plaque in the entry hall, and in the back of the coffee table book. As it turns out, the platinum members, most of the patrons in fact, are not interested in dressing up in the style of the 1920s. There are a few people who make an attempt. The men are all would-be gangsters, in black shirts and white ties. The women are all would-be molls, in short dresses and shiny headbands.

Harriet wears her mentalist outfit, an embroidered wrap dress and turban with a large fake ruby affixed to the front. Harriet's husband, Harvey Roseboro, does not attend. Harvey never attends functions at Holderhaven.

The croquet lawn is lit up, and there are tents and tables set up on the south lawn. Most patrons circulate through the party room to take a cursory glance at the restoration before retiring to the tables outdoors to smoke and talk. Waiters circulate with trays of champagne, trays of foie gras on toast. Rudy politely turns down the champagne. Instead he orders a Maiden's Prayer, an authentic Prohibition-era cocktail, at the bar. He looked up the recipe earlier in the day, from the Savoy Hotel Cocktail Book in the house library. Gin, Cointreau, lemon juice, orange juice. The bartender is happy to make something that's not yet another bourbon and ginger ale. Twelve-year-old bourbon, bottle after bottle, drowning in a sea of ginger ale, sucked down by the platinum members who don't like champagne because it gives them gas. Ol' Dick Mills, he prefers single-malt Scotch doused with Coke.

Bill Mills is drinking both champagne and beer. He and Harriet and Rudy stand together, making small talk. Ol' Dick Mills has long since retreated to a table outside where he can smoke with his cronies.

"Hey, do a trick," Bill says to Harriet.

"I am doing a trick. I'm reading your mind," she says, then she asks Rudy to get her another glass of that Austrian rosé.

Rudy goes, and Bill decides it's time to go to the bathroom.

"The seal is broken!" he announces, for the benefit of anyone who cannot read his mind.

The bathroom in the basement is still not renovated. There are portable toilets set up outside, twice as big as the type used by construction workers. They are hooked up to running water. An attendant sits next to them in a folding chair, supervising a stack of cotton towels.

Rudy returns with Harriet's wine, and Bill re-enters the party room from the hall. They both notice the young woman at the same time. Ella is standing by the hearth, next to the restored mural. Ella is extremely short. Ella has had the most success dressing in the style of the 1920s. She wears a loose slim dress, gray with a white collar, and a single long strand of pearls. Most importantly, she wears a cloche hat. Like Rudy and Bill, she is significantly younger than any of the other attendees at the reception, except for the waiters and bartender, and the waiters and bartender are all male.

After a few more minutes of conversation, Harriet says to Rudy: "Why don't you stop staring, and just go talk to her."

Rudy walks over to Ella. She's still scrutinizing the mural.

"It was just restored," he says. "We can't identify everyone, though."

The mural is of a party scene, caricatures of the Holder family and their close friends. Painted in the 1920s, when Mrs Holder was courted by many men but deigned to marry none of them, it was covered with geometric wallpaper in the 1950s, when Mrs Holder declared that looking at a mural with so many dead people in it was exhausting.

"Well, that's clearly Jean Lilly, the polo player," she says, pointing to a tall man with a big nose and mustache carrying a polo mallet over his shoulder. "My grandfather told me about him."

"Your grandfather knew the Holders?"

"Yes. His father was their attorney."

Ella has a pronounced gap between her top two front teeth. Rudy finds it fascinating, but tries not to stare.

They continue to talk about the people in the mural before moving on to talking about themselves. Ella is leaving the next day for Geneva, to get an early start on her JYA: Junior Year Abroad.

Bill Mills walks up with two glasses of champagne and tries to hand one to Ella.

"I never touch the stuff," she says. "I'm more of a scotch woman."

"Go get the lady some scotch," Bill says to Rudy. "The good kind."

Rudy does not budge. Ella suggests that they all walk to the bar to peruse the scotch selection.

"Rudy's the houseboy here, he should get your scotch," Bill notes.

They go to the bar and Ella chooses her scotch.

"Neat," she says to the bartender.

"Neato!" the bartender replies.

Bill offers to give her a ride in his convertible after she finishes her drink. As he says this, he slugs back a half glass of champagne in one gulp. Ella says that she does not ride with strange men in convertibles.

"I'm not a strange man, I'm Bill Mills. Son of Ol' Dick Mills."

Ella laughs.

Rudy and Ella attempt to continue their conversation. Bill continues to talk about his car and about what a nice night it is and how great the stars look and the wind feels when you're driving in your convertible at night.

"You're in no condition to drive," Ella says.

"She's right," Rudy adds, although he remembers more than one occasion when he rode in a car driven by a drunken and insistent Bill.

Bill is unaccustomed to so much disapproval, so he goes off to find more alcohol. Ella and Rudy step outside. They pass the tent and the croquet lawn, wandering through the gardens around the house. They walk slowly and look up to confirm at least part of Bill's assertion: the stars do look beautiful.

Rudy learns that Ella attends Smith College. She will return directly to Smith after her European jaunt. She likes Smith, but complains about the lack of boys. In addition to Geneva, she plans to spend time in Prague and Berlin. She's majoring in Environmental Science and Policy, but is considering law school.

Rudy reciprocates, talking about university, and about his summer with Holderhaven and Harriet Diamond. They pass through the pergola and into the terraced garden. Bill Mills is there. In the interim he has had four more glasses of champagne, and he has misplaced his top hat. He is urinating on the marble obelisk.

"Ella Minnow Pee!" he observes loudly, when he realizes who it is that has happened upon him. He zips up and wipes his hands on his pants.

Ella seems tolerant of Bill Mills, so Rudy follows her lead. The three of them sit together on a bench in the terraced garden. Inside Rudy is imagining fighting with Bill. Fencing with him. Throwing down his glove to defend the lady's honor. He took fencing to fulfill his physical education requirement, but he wasn't very good at it. Bill keeps staring at Ella's chest, even though the flapper dress is neither revealing nor form-fitting.

"Are you a shy boy, Bill Mills?" Ella asks. "Because it doesn't seem you like to make eye contact."

"Are those things real?" Bill asks. "I thought flatters had flap chests. I mean – "

"Are you saying I have a flappy chest?"

Ella twists from side to side, sending the strand of pearls swinging. She and Rudy both laugh, but Rudy is worried that this will only antagonize Bill. Bill is already nodding off, though, and he does not respond.

Rudy leans in and whispers to Ella.

"I know where we can go," he says. "I want to show you something."

They go inside, slip behind the now-empty bar. Rudy clicks the mirrored panel open and then stands aside and says, "Watch your step."

She climbs up and he follows. Halfway up he tells her to stop.

"Give me your hand," he says.

"Don't try anything stupid," she says. "Or you will be filled with regret as you go tumbling down these stairs. Also pain."

"Not stupid," he says.

She gives him her hand and he traces the outline of the inscription in the secret passage.

They ascend to the master bedroom and plunk down on the floor, on the safe side of the velvet rope. Rudy removes the linen jacket, and she kicks off her heels.

"I found a photograph last week. I think it has something to do with those marks. That marker that Bill was peeing on? Didn't used to be there. It used to be a statue of an extremely young, extremely naked girl."

"Yes, that was her," Ella says, staring at the bricked-up fireplace. "And now I guess we know that her name was Lizza. I'd always heard her referred to as 'that poor girl', never a name. It's interesting that she was a cutter – she just cut the house instead of herself. My roommate freshman year was a cutter."

"Wait, back up," Rudy says, his mind on fire. "You know who left those marks in the passage?"

"I've got a pretty good idea. Hello? My great-grandfather? Attorney to the family?"

"I have a lot of questions to ask you," Rudy says. So he does. He offers to swear himself to secrecy, if she'll just tell him everything she knows about Lizza. Ella laughs.

"I don't care about secrecy," she says. "Tell Harriet Diamond. Tell Bill Mills. Don't bother telling Mary Holder Hodgson, because I'm sure she knows some version of the story, unless she's in complete denial.

"Jorn Holder had always liked little girls, ever since he'd been a little boy. Nerissa Holder had mistaken his lack of ardor for gentlemanliness when they were courting, but clearly this became a problem after they were married. So instead of trying to dampen Jorn's passion, she merely redirected it for her own ends. Allowed him to molest his favorite servant girl, as long as he – I hope this doesn't offend your delicate sensibilities – made the deposit with Nerissa. Of course as time went on he got bolder. Thus, the statue of the nude girl in the garden. When the secret passage was discovered when they were restoring the house as a museum, well, anyone who knew the story could figure out what it had been used for.

"So this went on, Lizza acting as the catalyst for Nerissa to generate children. Then Jorn dies, under mysterious circumstances."

"Lizza killed him!" Rudy says.

"I have no idea. I suppose it's possible. The story I heard was that Nerissa killed him, because he'd gone insane and actually thought he could marry the girl. Maybe he really died of gastritis and exhaustion? My great-grandfather never saw the body. That was his story, as my dad told it to me one night when he'd had too many martinis: that Nerissa killed Jorn, and then had the servant girl and her mother paid off and sent far away. Clearly when Jorn dies, it's right around the time of conception of the last child, Noelle. Nerissa then has the secret passage sealed off and begins the task of raising her brood. Anyway, that's quite a discovery you've made there. The fourteen marks...do you think she was fourteen when her semi-conjugal visits ended? Do you think there were only fourteen of them? That can't be."

"No. I wonder if any of the platinum level patrons will notice them."

"Hope not. You can bet that Mary Holder Hodgson will have them covered up if she notices them."

"Can I ask you another question?" Rudy says. "It has nothing to do with Jorn Holder, Capitalist Pedophile."

"The answer is no," Ella says. "Because I'm leaving for Europe tomorrow."

"That's not the question. The question is, why didn't you get braces?"

"Oh. I did have braces, when I was a kid. My teeth started moving again."

"Is the answer to that other question still no?" Rudy asks.

"Come here," Ella says.

Later she gives Rudy a printed card with her email address, and he scrawls his on the back of one of her cards. Ella leaves at midnight, as workers are packing up the chairs and tables and tents.

Bill Mills wakes up on the concrete bench, alone. He makes his way to his car only to find that the car keys are no longer in his pocket. He is briefly furious before he passes out again in the back seat.

In 1916, Lizza Bagge prepares for another night. She leaves the house where the other servants live, telling her mother that Mrs Holder has once again asked her to clean the mirrors behind the bar. Mrs Holder feels that this is a job best done at night. Lizza takes the wooden cleaning box and carries it up the hill, entering the house through the door to the swimming pool. The lights remain on in the pool area; the still water glows green. She walks down the hall, past the bowling alley and billiards room, into the party room and then back behind the bar. She sets the wooden box down on the floor. She removes her belt and her white dress and stands, wearing only her slip, examining herself in the mirrored panel. She will turn seventeen soon, but she still has the same face and the same slim build she has had all of her teenage years. Sharp cheekbones, bobbed nose. You'll fill out, just you wait, her mother often says to her.

She opens the cabinet next to the icebox, moves items aside as she looks for one particular implement. There, behind the punch bowl and a stack of Bakelite ashtrays, she finds it. She looks back to see if anyone can see her, then she pops open the door in the mirror. She steps in and up, pulling the panel closed behind her. Then she's climbing the stairs, ice pick in hand.

Later, she will go swimming.

CHERYL WOOD RUGGIERO
ELEVEN ELEVEN

Of course the old man should never have sold Alsie the gun. She was twelve years old today. She had no ID. But she had often hung around in the pawn shop when it was really cold outside, and the old man had let her stay because he was a kind man, even if he did take all kinds of bad things in for pawn and never asked where they came from.

Alsie picked her moment when he started shouting over his shoulder toward the back curtain, arguing with his wife who was dead. He wouldn't even know who Alsie was, wouldn't remember it.

She had a magic number of dollars: $11.11. It was not enough for the gun, of course, but it was a magical number. She'd found coins on the sidewalk; she'd dragged a lady's suitcase up the stairs of a private rowhouse hotel and been given a dollar; she'd minded the newsstand for Mr Benford all week and been allowed to keep ten per cent of whatever was paid for magazines and papers and cigarettes and little packets of aspirin while he was away for his lunch. Last week she was paid a dollar for sweeping the sidewalk in front of the Limin Boutique – too bad Madame Limin's assistant came back the next day.

So today, which was Alsie's twelfth birthday, she had exactly $11.11. How often do numbers stand in line like that? It was her birthday, and she had magical money, and she should buy herself a magical present. So she hung around in the pawn shop until the old man started arguing with his wife, and then Alsie pointed to the gun in the locked glass case and offered him $11.11, and he never even stopped arguing with his wife – just took the money and handed over the gun.

She knew that later, when he would come back from this argument with his dead wife, he wouldn't know where the gun had gone. He would shrug and go make himself some tea. She'd seen that happen before, like the time he sold a gold necklace out of that case for $30 to a mean-faced woman with inch-long golden fingernails. He was arguing with his wife the whole time. The next day, Alsie came back in to get warm and heard him wondering out loud about the necklace. Alsie said she saw him sell it for $30 and put the cash in a coffee can on the shelf behind the register. He looked in the can, and there was the money. He shrugged and made them both a cup of tea.

Alsie didn't know why she wanted the gun. She didn't have any bullets for it or any idea where to get any. She didn't know how to open it or load it. But when she saw the little pistol, about as long as her hand, with its small six-bullet cylinder and its crosshatched handle, all dark steely gray, it just seemed to her that she should have it. She could have bought a lot of hot dogs from the cart with $11.11. Mittens or socks. Or a lot of coffee with cream and sugar. Or a brown military blanket that smelled of old mothballs. A pack of lawn-size trash bags – lots of things can be done with trash bags, the good three-layer kind. Trash bag plus blanket equals rainproof sleeping bag. A lot of things she needed, she could have bought. But she bought the gun.

She put it in the itchy, red-striped wool bag woven in Chile that a street vendor gave her for watching the stuff he had laid out on a blanket for an hour one afternoon. She wore the bag on its long strap under her jacket and sweater, across her chest that didn't have any breasts yet. She thought she really ought to start having breasts soon. On the other hand, since she had no breasts and cut her hair short with a pocketknife and wore jeans with holes in the seat and a red baseball cap, most people thought she was a boy, and that was probably a good thing.

Nobody ever asked for her name. Nobody ever asked why she was not in school, not even the cops she sometimes could not avoid.

That was another reason Alsie knew there was magic about her: Nobody asked. Nobody saw a girl sleeping in the church tool shed, or sometimes under a pew, or in the low crown of that big old willow in the park, or in a shipping box behind the boutique. Nobody looked twice at her if they found her washing her face in a public restroom. Nobody at a diner told her she was too young to drink coffee. She had thought for a time that she must be invisible. But the hot dog vendor took her money and handed her a hot dog, and Mr Benford's customers took magazines and aspirin from her and handed her money. So she wasn't invisible. She was magical.

And now she had a magical gun.

The other magical thing about herself was that she didn't have anything to remember before her eleventh birthday, which she didn't remember either except that she knew it *was* her birthday when she noticed where she was that day, inside a church with a round window made of colored glass and statues of men with wings and swords. In the year since then, she had read a lot of books at the library, and in all of them, the eleventh birthday was when your magic started, so she figured that's when her real life started, and whatever happened before that didn't matter and didn't need to be remembered. That was another reason why she knew that $11.11 was a magical number.

She had been alone in the church on that eleventh birthday. There were no old women wearing headscarves and praying with beads, no custodian waxing the pews, no priest in the confessional box. She had sometimes wondered how she knew what those things were or that there should have been a priest and a custodian and old people praying. She figured that it was important for her to remember useful things like that, just not her own pre-magical non-history.

No parents were with her that day, so she assumed that she didn't have any, which ordinary people have, which was more proof that Alsie was un-ordinary.

With the gun feeling pleasantly solid over her belly button under her sweater and jacket, Alsie went to the newsstand. Mr Benford pushed open the hinged part of the counter, stepped out, and held the barrier open for her to slide into his place. He watched her take out the box of change and said "Twenty-eight fourteen." That was the amount of money in the box, in coins and bills. There was a notebook for her to write down each transaction: what each customer bought and how much the customer gave her, which she put in a big jar, how much change she took out of the box to give back to the customer. He'd reckon it all up when he got back and give her ten per cent of the intake-minus-change. He went off humming to himself.

That was good – when he went off humming, he stayed gone longer. When he came back humming, he smelled like perfume and face powder, and Alsie's half of the intake-minus-change was a lot more than when he went off frowning and came back pretty soon smelling like coffee and fried potatoes.

The Post: bills in the jar, coins out of the box. The Times and News-week: money in the jar, exact change. Salem Lights, Cosmopolitan, and two packets of aspirin: big bill in the jar, bills and coins out of the box. Mints: coins in, pennies out.

A man was taking a long time deciding which paper he wanted. He read the front page of one, then the other. Alsie figured he wasn't going to buy at all, just read for free. About half the time when she glanced up at him, he was watching her. She thought maybe he was going to try to steal the jar or the box when she wasn't looking. He was tall and had long arms in his black coat. He could reach over the counter and grab the box or the jar off the bench.

He didn't reach, though. Just kept reading and looking at her. "What's your name, kid?"

The magic was going strange. He had asked for her name. She knew better than to give it, though. Names have power. Her T-shirt, hidden under her sweater same as the gun, had a name on it, in an arch just below the left shoulder. St Vincent de Paul. There was a coat of arms below it showing a pair of griffons, magical creatures, holding up a shield with a cross on it. It was from a boys' school across the city. She'd found the T-shirt in the park. If the name was on her shirt, then it belonged to her. It was her name.

"Vincent."

The man looked at her and frowned, tipping his head to one side. "Vincent. Huh." He tipped his head the other way. "Sure. Well, Vincent, I'll take a Post."

Five-dollar bill in, bills and coins out. He walked away.

"Sir!"

He turned back.

"You didn't take your paper."

He stepped back to the counter and looked at the white burn scar on her hand holding the paper out to him, long enough for her hand to start shaking – it was a heavy paper.

Alsie felt the magic tremble. She saw Mr Benford coming back, and he seemed to tremble, too. He was frowning. He smelled of coffee and tobacco smoke. The money he gave her seemed to tremble in his hand, and in her pocket.

Alsie patted the magic gun under her jacket. It did not tremble. She walked past the church and then crossed the street to the park and tried the water fountain. It wasn't working again. Frozen maybe. She heard a snap that she knew was someone closing a cell phone, not far behind her. She turned and saw the man who'd bought the paper. He had a hat with a brim, pulled down so it shaded his eyes, but it left his ears red in the cold. His breath smoked against the black of his coat.

A woman entered the park and walked up beside the man. She was pretty, in a hard kind of way. Her hair was very blonde and wavy, which would have seemed friendly, but she had very red lipstick and very black mascara, and her skin was powdery pale. She wore a red coat that fitted very close to her body. She had black gloves and a black handbag over one arm, black boots, and a black fur hat. Her red mouth moved, but Alsie didn't hear her words.

What Alsie heard was a gunshot. It had been echoing in her head for a year but she hadn't known what it was until now. Its echo made the magic that stopped people from asking her name. It made Alsie see her eleventh birthday again, see her father press his big foot on the water fountain pedal that didn't work then either, see her mother push wavy blonde hair back under her black fur hat as she sent Alsie off with the driver to get a bag of peanuts from the snack trailer around the corner. It made her hear the gun pop, turn, and see the little gun in her mother's black-gloved hand, see the flash from the muzzle as it popped again, see her father fall to the ground by the fountain that didn't work, see the man in the black coat take the little gun from her mother's hand and put it in his pocket, see her mother's mouth move, unable to hear her mother call her name called because all she could hear was the gunshot – not loud, just a pop.

Just a pop from the little gun in her own hand that she didn't re-member getting out from the itchy bag under her sweater. She saw her mother in her red coat and black gloves fall and then try to sit up. She saw the man in the black coat kneel and press her down, but her mother grasped her stomach and drew her legs up as she rolled onto her side. The man got his phone out. Alsie stepped close to him and put the little gun into his pocket. He stared at her while his mouth worked at the phone. She walked past his eyes.

She noticed where she was. It was a church with a round window made of colored glass and statues of men with swords and wings. She was alone in the church – no priest or people praying. No mother or father was with her, so maybe she didn't have any. She did know that it was her twelfth birthday. And she knew that she used to be magical, but the magic was gone, now that the elevens were over. She was twelve, and her real life was starting.

She heard sirens outside, and she stepped out into the dark entrance hall. She walked toward the doors. She opened them just a crack – the wind was picking up and it was cold. Across the street at the entrance to the park, she saw medics rolling a woman on a gurney. A man in a black coat walked beside her head, holding up a bag of clear fluid, and a plastic tube carried that fluid down to somewhere under the shiny blue blanket tucked around the woman under black straps.

The woman had blonde hair, wavy, in a friendly way. The shoulders of a red coat showed above the blue blanket. The woman turned her head toward the church, and her dark eyes seemed to be searching for something.

The medics pushed the gurney into the ambulance, took the fluid bag, climbed in, and shut the doors. The man turned to talk to the police. He kept both hands shoved deep in his coat pockets and stood hunched a little, as if he were cold. She closed the church doors. She was not curious about the woman and the man or what might have happened. She didn't know anything about it.

She heard the siren of the ambulance going away. She saw a glow at one side of the entrance hall. There was a tall window of colored glass that formed a picture of a woman with stars around her head, her hands stretched down as if she was asking people to reach up and hold them. The image of light filled Alsie's eyes and made almost everything else in that corner very dim, but she went toward it and saw a glow from a fat candle in a low glass jar, and that some long splinters of wood stuck up from a black iron pot filled with sand. Beside the candle, Alsie could barely see a black wrought iron rack with rows of small candles in short red glasses.

She knelt and found a padded bench below her knees – she had known it would be there, but she wasn't sure how. She lit a splinter from the fat candle and then lit the first small candle in the first row. It made the red glass glow. She blew out the splinter and pushed it tip-down into the sand. Even with her candle lit, it was still dark in this corner of the dark stone floor, between dark wood walls. The woman with the starry crown looked sweet and still, though the light from her still dazzled

Alsie's eyes and shadowed everything else.

Alsie could feel that she had money in her pocket, though she didn't know where it had come from. She took out all the coins and held them up to the glass light – a nickel and seven pennies. Twelve cents. A good number for today. If she were still magical, she would think it was a magical number because today was her twelfth birthday, but it was just a good un-magical number. Alsie thought she ought to leave a gift for the woman with the starry crown. The woman was only glass, but Alsie knew the money would help someone who reached up to take the glass woman's hands. She knew there was a box somewhere nearby with a cross-shaped slot in the lid for money, but she just bent down and quietly put the coins on the floor.

Before she could straighten up, the doors opened. The tall man in the black coat strode in. He peered left and right as if looking for someone, then, as the doorway's light closed off, he went forward into the great church with the round window and the statues.

If she were still magical, Alsie would believe it was the magic that kept the man from seeing her. But today she knew it was the light from the glass woman and the shadows that the light made in his eyes. The man came back out and hurried through the doors and was gone.

After her candle had burned down to hold a lovely pond of clear wax reflecting the little flame, Alsie said "Thank you" to the woman with the starry crown, even if she was only glass, and slipped out the great doors into the wind.

ILSA J. BICK
WHERE THE BODIES ARE

You are most likely to be murdered the day you are born.
— **Black, M.: 'Introduction' in** *Medea and Beyond: Psychoanalytic*
Perspectives on Mothers Who Kill, **eds Black, M. & Schwermer, U.**
(New York: Psychoanalytic Studies Press, 1995)

There'd been snow the night before, heavy and wet, another twelve, thirteen-inch dump added to the two feet already on the cemetery. Gulls screamed against a pewter sky, and the keen tang of crushed aluminum promised more snow on the way. Blades of an icy wind off Lake Michigan hacked Miriam's cheeks, cutting tears.

An engine grumbled to her left. Blinking against salt-sting, Miriam watched as a mud-spattered flatbed skidded off thick slush before passing through a gate that was never locked. The truck was Stan's, the Hebrew cemetery's gravedigger-slash-maintenance-guy – and Miriam thought, with all apologies to Queen: *And another one bites the dust.*

Miriam always knew when one of Hart's Jews died because of Stan. Jewish law mandated that, with rare exceptions, burial must take place within twenty-four hours. Stan and his partner, Ronnie, got to work just as soon as they got wind, especially in winter when they had to fire up the propane heaters to thaw out the ground before going to work with their shovels. (In the biz since 1962, Ronnie was a purist. Stan once told Miriam he was just waiting for his mom to kick off already so he could inaugurate a turbo backhoe on her grave and triple his business. Stan had visions of corporate expansion.)

Stan's familiar profile – spongy bulbous nose, several chins – hunched over the steering wheel. Ronnie huddled in a robin's-egg blue parka on the passenger's seat, a watch cap snugged to the angle of a lantern jaw: a look that accentuated a beaky nose that would give a vulture pause. The only movement in the cab was the jiggle of Stan's most prized possession: a Brett Favre bobblehead, signed by the Great Man Himself.

The Hart Hebrew Cemetery was four or five acres, and nowhere near capacity. (There just weren't that many Jews left to plant.) The land was steam roller flat: a featureless rectangle studded with graves and a single whitewashed, tumbledown mausoleum – a *genizah* – in which the remaining Jews solemnly deposited their worn-out siddurs and scrolls and anything else inscribed with God's name that, by law, couldn't be destroyed.

The graves were arranged in tiers four wide by twenty-seven long. Most were no-nonsense gray granite rectangles that, with the new snow, looked like teeth rotting from the root up. Some were embellished with oval bronze plaques, verdigris with age, the kind with a cover you could lift to see an enamel portrait of whoever lay beneath the ground. Her personal favorites were a clutch of twenty-seven markers shaped into white marble tablets written entirely in Hebrew she could neither read nor understand.

Unlike many other cemeteries, there were no trees actually within the grounds, although trimmed cedars hemmed the graveyard on three sides out of the four. The lone exception was an enormous errant willow at the far right corner, four stories high with an umbrella of branches wide around as a circus tent. Miriam loved that willow, knew it intimately, had spent hours clambering its branches when she was a girl. In the dead of winter, of course, the yellowish branches were completely bare. Get close enough and they chattered in the frigid breeze with a sound like the knocking of bones. In summers past, she could stand beneath that verdant bell jar and not a soul would know she was there. The willow was hers: special and private. Safe.

Miriam wasn't particularly morbid – or Jewish, for that matter – and she wasn't one of those sicko graveyard junkies. Just kept an eye on the place. Easy, considering her office was right across the street. She knew who was where and what was up with every body in that cemetery, and she visited the girl – Sarah Abramowitz – every day. Sarah had been two years old when she died in 1918 in the flu pandemic, and lay alone. Miriam was Sarah's only visitor and had been for the last twenty years.

As it happened, Miriam knew a lot of Jews, not just those left in Hart. Most were other analysts she saw at the annual meeting in New

York. (When you were an analyst, especially one of a certain age, you couldn't help it. Freud hadn't called psychoanalysis 'the Jewish science' for nothing.) No one would ever believe that Wisconsin was a hotbed of Jewish activity, but Hart crouched on Lake Michigan a ten minute drive down the coast from Sheboygan. After New York, Sheboygan had been a major debarkation port for Eastern European Jews fleeing the pogroms of the 1880s. Hart once supported a population upwards of seven hundred Jews – not as many as Sheboygan, which had boasted a thousand and acquired the nickname 'Little Jerusalem', but close.

Those days were long gone, the immigrants' children having trickled away, dooming the remaining Jewish population to death by slow and inevitable attrition. In winter, the synagogue was lucky to get a minyan, for heaven's sake, and she should know. Miriam went every Saturday morning, which was the only service the shul kept up these days because old people didn't like venturing out on Friday nights. She'd gotten up close and personal with every Jew: knew everyone by name, sympathized about their ailments, was privy to their histories and petty rivalries. (Her supervisor once said she could get information from a stone.) Morris, the synagogue president, used to joke that she qualified for honorary Jewish status, or something. A nice man. Pity he'd died three months ago: four rows over, two up, third grave from the left. No headstone yet, of course. His replacement, Saul, was an ass they wouldn't suffer long. The last hospitalization, she'd peeked at his chart. Cirrhosis (Saul was a bit of a shiker, his nose always in the Kiddush wine), congestive heart failure... Miriam gave him until April.

She watched as the truck rolled past the Weintraubs, the Steiners, Reggie and Rose Schroeder, the Fetzers, and Johnny Katz and then ease past the site the Roths had purchased, what? Seventy years ago? Fannie was the sole survivor, had outlasted Harold by six years and was ninety-four if she was a day. Miriam would've laid odds that Fannie wouldn't make it past the holidays, but she was a tough old bird...

She mentally riffled through the folks planted out that way against a list of likely suspects, which included just about every Jew left in town. About fifty at last count, and all except Victor Samuels, a spring chicken at seventy-two, lived in one form of assisted living or other. Miriam figured it was just a matter of time before every last Jew was planted, every available slot in the old cemetery filled.

And the day that happened? Miriam would take a vacation, a very long one. Somewhere warm. Fiji was good.

The truck's brakes squealed as Stan rolled to a stop. Stan's right fist was glued to his head. Cell phone? Giving directions, she thought.

Perhaps four minutes later, a black limousine carefully negotiated the turn onto the cemetery drive and churned after Stan's Toyota. The limo's windows were heavily tinted. She couldn't tell who was in the back seat, and from this far away there was no way to get a look at the license plates, but Miriam smelled money. Chicago, maybe. As the limo nosed behind Stan's truck, the Toyota started up again, the tires spinning on compacted ice beneath the fresh-fallen snow and sending up twin white roosters' tails that spattered the limo's grill.

Pushing up now from the girl's grave, her knees crackling, Miriam watched as Stan hung a right, not the left that she expected, and she thought: *Hunh*. As far as she knew everyone in town who'd claimed a spot out that way was, well, in residence.

The truck's brakes squalled again; Stan killed the engine, and he and his mother pushed out of the Toyota as the limo eased to a stop. The driver – a lanky guy in a brass-buttoned uniform and perky hat – hopped out and trotted round to open the right rear passenger door. A leggy woman, dressed entirely in black, reached out to take the driver's white-gloved hand and unfolded from the back seat in a swirl of black fur that fell to mid calf.

The man had already pushed from the limo by the time the driver finished handing out the woman. The man was lean, with a shock of silver hair nicely set off by a black double-breasted overcoat with a back vent. Ralph Lauren, or Oxxford. Polo. No Gander's for these people, and they carried themselves in that entitled, impatient, you-yokels-are-complete-hicks way she associated with New Yorkers.

Okay, that was interesting. The only person with New York connections out there was Sadie Brandt, and she'd died in 1995. She and Paul had no children, though Miriam thought there might be a sister. So maybe the sister...

Her cell brrred against her hip, making her heart jump. Tugging the cell from the pocket of her parka, she checked the winking display then flipped open the cell. "Yes, Courtney."

"Sorry to bother you, Doc, but the ER just called. They got a college kid they think you ought to see."

"Ah." Stan and the man in black were talking, and Stan was gesturing, shaking his head. Arguing? "Don't I have a full afternoon?"

"Not anymore," said Courtney, and then she told Miriam why.

As Miriam listened, her stomach twisted, and when Courtney paused for breath, she said, "Tell the ER fifteen minutes."

"Okay." Pause. "So who died now?"

Miriam glanced left through chain-link to the converted Victorian right across the street. Courtney was Wisconsin-lean – which meant she was round as a raspberry – and Miriam recognized her at the office's bay window right away. When she saw Miriam look over, Courtney waved, and Miriam said into her cell, "Has anyone ever told you that you have an unhealthy obsession with the dead?"

"Look who's talking," Courtney said, and then her tone turned serious. "Go, Doc. I don't think that baby has much time."

We must face the fact that any profile we have of women who kill their newborns only reflect those women who were caught.
— **Auerbach, G.: 'Neonaticide: Risk Analysis and Demographics', in Black & Schwermer, *Ibid***

"We know she had a baby," the OB – Meckels – said. Stocky as a fire-plug, Meckels had pellet-gray eyes tiny as BBs behind Lennon specs. "Uterus is enlarged and she came in bleeding like stink from a couple tears in the perineum. Retained placenta. Cleaned her out, sutured her up. Damn lucky she's not septic. Blood tests came back, and blood don't lie. That *kid* had a *kid*. So." He snapped the file shut. "Where the hell's the baby?"

"What about her car?" Miriam asked. They stood behind a high counter at the nurses' station. The ER was busy but not frenetic: a motley collection of fretful children with their exhausted mothers; an old guy complaining of chest pain after shoveling his drive; an MVA in the trauma bay (a burly, blood-stained college kid in a neck brace and ripped cargo pants who kept shouting that he wanted to use his cell to call his parents, and to hell with the regulations). "Car would be logical. You can drive somewhere, park, stay relatively warm."

"First thing I thought of," said Meckels. "Got one of the techs to go take a look because she wouldn't give us her keys. Car's clean...well, as clean as a kid's car usually is. Car trash, you know, couple McDonald's wrappers, backpack, crap like that. Tech said there're couple bloody towels on the driver's side, and her jeans were soaked, but there's nothing else in the car that we can see."

"How long?"

"Since she gave birth?" Meckels excavated a nearly-empty box of Krispy Kremes, extracted a glazed cruller, took a bite, chewed, swallowed, said, "Given the size of the uterus, probably no more than six, seven hours. Ask about the baby, though, and she clams up, gives you the thousand-yard stare, you know what I'm saying? These kids..." Meckels folded the remaining Krispy Kreme into his mouth until his cheeks bulged like a chipmunk's, and said, around doughnut, "She wouldn't talk to the social worker, or Child Protective Services. Social worker put in a call to the police about ten seconds after that kid showed up. They're on their way. But the baby's running out of time...if it's still alive."

"What about her parents?"

"Dunno." Meckels sucked glaze from his fingers. "*I* haven't talked to them. They're out of state... Ohio, I think. I don't know if the kid's given her permission either. I mean, she's eighteen..."

"What about the roommate? What about a boyfriend? Has she said who the father is?"

"Haven't spoken to the roommate. As for a boyfriend or the father... can't get a thing out of her, but I sure as hell don't think we're talking Immaculate Conception here." When she didn't smile, he continued, "Look, what do you want from me? This isn't really in my job description. That's why we got CPS and social workers." Miriam could tell he wanted to add: *And shrinks like you.* But Meckels said: "I've done my job. We've called the police, we've called CPS, I got the social worker down here, and for your information, we *did* call the college and campus security *did* start a search of this kid's room, the dorm..."

She was getting tired of Meckels. "This young woman have a name?"

"Woodward. Emma. You want a middle initial?"

She ignored the sarcasm. "Okay, so what *have* you done in terms of tracking down the baby? Have you spoken to the docs at the college health service? Maybe she saw someone."

"Hey, don't give me this sanctimonious crap. As far as I know, no one knew the kid was pregnant, meaning she hid it real well. There's no baby in the room or the dorm bathrooms, or out back in the dumpster. And for your information, I already thought of the college docs, and they didn't see her. You know, you got all these questions, why don't you talk to the social worker? She's in seven, talking to another family, but I can have her find you when she gets out."

"That'd be good." Miriam felt a headache beginning to thump behind her eyes. "In the meantime, I'll go talk to your patient."

"Fine by me. Any chance we can work a transfer to psychiatry? I really don't want a kid like her on my ward, and I know the nurses aren't gonna like it. We've got a lot of women up there who'd have killed for a chance to raise that baby."

She wanted to laugh in his face. "No. When she's medically clear, then we can talk about a transfer." *If she's not in jail...*

"That could be days."

"Then it'll be days. I'll see her in consultation."

"Great." Meckels was pissed. "How the hell do you feel sympathy for someone like that?"

"Obviously, you don't."

"Damn straight. I know she had a baby and it's probably dead, and we're working on *her*. We'll make sure *she* doesn't bleed to death or die of an infection, but her baby..." The OB's lips thinned to a gash. "Makes me sick. So I don't get it. How can you even talk to her?"

"Well, you know what they say about shrinks: either you're really normal, or it takes one to know..." She trailed off as the ER doors sighed open and two men in street clothes pushed in – and then it was like someone had sucker-punched her in the gut.

Of all the bad timing... She'd been lucky for so long, ever since moving back from New York after her analytic training. With the college, Hart was just large enough so you really didn't have to run into anyone you'd rather avoid. Not that she hadn't known about him: sometimes his picture made the papers, especially after that drug thing the year before. Yet their orbits were so different, no mutual friends and, as the years passed, she'd begun to believe their paths never would intersect. But as soon as Meckels said he'd called the police, she'd thought that maybe, finally, her luck had run out. It was just the way the day felt.

He hadn't changed that much: still a big man but lean and muscled. He towered over his partner, a wisp of a rookie with a buzz cut who was thirty if he was a day. He hadn't spotted her yet and so she had a few precious moments which she took, greedily, her eyes raking his features, so familiar and yet now a bit alien with age: a square open face that was less fleshy than she remembered so the cheekbones cut planes and the dark skin – Ojibwe blood, he'd said – stretched tight over the jaw; big shoulders and heavy arms and hands; raven-black hair touched with silver at the temples; gray-blue eyes so pale they were almost silver.

No ring. So either he never wore his wedding ring, or...

Grant Bonner was still talking to his partner as she erased the distance between them: "...need to get the sheriff's people to – " But then he got a good look, and she saw the moment recognition broke, the way his eyes widened and his jaw unhinged, the emotions that chased across his face.

"Detective Bonner," she said, offering her hand to a man she'd left in her bed twenty years before. "We might have a problem."

A therapist has no obligation to report a past crime revealed in psychotherapy. Ten minutes ago, or ten years – it makes no difference.
— **Schwermer, U.: 'Keeper of the Secrets: The Troubling Analysis of a High-Functioning Child Killer', in Black & Schwermer,** *Ibid*

CPS was treating the incident as child abuse, and that gave the police a lot of latitude. Grant had his partner go with a uniform to crack open Woodward's car while he and Miriam talked in an empty treatment room.

"I still can't..." Grant paused, swallowed hard, looked away. "I wish..."

Miriam never wanted so badly to let go and huddle within the circle of Grant's arms and allow all the hurt and years to fall away. But, no, a woman didn't run out on the love of her life and then keep herself under the radar, successfully, for over two decades without a fair degree of self-discipline. Hugging herself close, she waited.

Finally, his haunted eyes found hers. "Miriam, you've been here all this time. Where? Why did you leave? Why didn't you call me?"

"Grant, I want to answer your questions," she said. "I do. But we don't have time for that. Right now, we've got this woman, and we have to deal with that first. After...we can talk after, okay?"

"Damn it." The small muscles of his jaw worked. "You don't know how much I want to chuck this whole damn thing and just go somewhere we can..."

He didn't finish the thought, but she knew how he felt. But they had to stay on track for the moment – a good thing because that gave her time to make her lies plausible. Because Grant would find it very strange – anyone would – that a woman so intent upon avoiding her former lover would move back to their hometown a few years later and then hide in plain sight. If she thought about it as a psychiatrist – *duh* – she realized that, honestly, writing the book eventually might put her on his radar. On the other hand, the book had been years ago and she'd been very selective in terms of which cases she agreed to consult on. She never worked with local lawyers – not much call, actually; Hart was a pretty quiet place – and most of the cases for which she offered an expert opinion were out-of-state. In a perverse way, her behavior – moving back, the book, consulting – it all was a kind of dare: catch me if you can.

She said, again, "Grant, we've got a problem. A bigger one than you realize."

"You think?" He washed his face with his hands and blew out. "Right… the girl. What do you mean?"

"I mean that the minute I walk into that young woman's room, she becomes my patient in the eyes of the law."

"So?"

"*So* whatever she says is privileged information. If she tells me she's killed that baby, I'm not obligated to tell you a thing. The law's very clear when it comes to information divulged when there's an expectation of privacy."

"Not. Obligated." He said the words as if they were a foreign language, and then his expression went from stunned to flinty. "Not *obligated*? To *her*? Miriam, what if the baby's *alive*?"

"That changes things, of course. I have an affirmative duty to a third party."

"You sound like a lawyer."

"Occupational hazard when you spend a lot of time around them. But what are the chances of the baby being alive, Grant? Honestly. It's ten degrees. The sun's going to set in another hour and then the temperature's going to plummet. Snow's on the way. Besides, many of these women let the baby expire passively… You don't want to know. Now, if she says the baby's alive – that when she left it, it was still breathing – of course, I can tell you and CPS. I'm not bound by confidentiality in that situation. Otherwise…"

"Screw otherwise," Grant said, and put some steel in it. "If she killed that baby…"

"I have no duty to report a past crime, whether that past is ten years or ten minutes ago, Grant."

"I can't believe I'm having this conversation," he marveled. "What about morality, Miriam? What about what's *right* and *decent*? What the hell about *justice*? Oh wait...I forgot. I'm talking to a woman who thinks it's fine to renege on a promise and screw a guy – in more ways than one."

That hurt more than she'd thought it would. She pulled in a deep breath. "Okay, I deserved that and probably a great deal more. Maybe it would be best for me to step away from this case – "

"Oh no," and then he had her by the forearm before she could react. She flinched, but his grip – steely as a vise – only tightened, and then she gasped with sudden pain. He didn't relax his hold. Instead, he pulled her close enough that she felt the hot slant of his breath slash her face. "You don't get to just step away again. That would be easy for you, wouldn't it? One of those things you used to talk about, where you repeat what you do because you can't help it."

"A repetition compulsion," she said. "Grant, you're hurting me."

"Good. Because I'll bet it doesn't hurt half as much as what you did to me, only mine was a knife in the guts. Did you ever think about me, Miriam? Did you ever wonder what my face must've looked like when I woke up and you were gone? No message, no forwarding address, nothing. Just...gone. You even took one of my goddamned suitcases. What, some kind of sick keepsake?"

"Look, I understand you feel betrayed, that you're angry."

"You understand, you think... Very brainiac, Miriam, very...intellectualized, isn't that what you call it? Don't tell me how I feel, or felt. I'm not one of your damned patients. So where did you go, Miriam? Back to New York? Why the hell didn't you just *stay* there? You had to *know* this would happen someday."

"Hart was my home..."

"And mine. I had no choice but to come back. You knew that. So you come back, and you never once pick up the phone?"

Oh, she had, many times. Sometimes she'd even dialed the number, listened to the phone on the other end begin to ring – and then always replaced the handset, knowing she could never go through with it because she would have to account for herself and what she'd done. She couldn't do that.

"Look, I know you want answers," she said doggedly, "and you might even want revenge for how I hurt – "

"Oh shut up," he said, and then before she could react – no, that was a lie, she saw it coming and she let it happen because she wanted it, she hungered for him after all these years – he had a double fistful of her hair and pulled her close and his mouth found hers. Her back stiffened, just a bit, and then her knees went a little wobbly and she felt the yearning – because that never *had* died – firing to life in the pit of her stomach. When he finally pulled back, he didn't let her go, and that was fine, that was all right.

"Miriam." His voice was husky. "Please. Don't – "

Whatever he was going to say was interrupted by a knock, and they barely had time to step back from one another before Hart's partner pushed into the treatment room.

"Oh." The partner looked from Grant to Miriam, then back to Grant. His face settled into a study of neutrality.

"What?" Grant snapped.

"Nothing," said the partner. "And nothing in the car except the towels. Backpack's just got books – psychology and art – and there's a sketchpad and pencils, but that's it. I talked to the social worker and she said the kid's zipped up tight. We're just lucky she hasn't lawyered up."

"That's coming," Grant said darkly and then jerked his head at his partner. "Come on, let's go talk to her before that happens."

"Detective, I don't think you'll get anything," Miriam called after.

"Watch me," Grant said.

These women live a lie for nine months. They give birth alone and in secret, without support or medications or even a warm bed. They are some of the most courageous, determined and willful women with which one can do battle.
— **Black, M.: 'Therapeutic Considerations', in Black & Schwermer,** *Ibid*

Grant didn't get anything. He emerged from Room 3 twenty minutes later, looking thunderous, tossed Miriam a glare and then shouldered past, with his partner in tow. Going to the college, he said.

Room 3 stank, not the vaguely clinical smell of a meat locker but one Miriam remembered from her days as a medical student rotating through surgery: an odor of burned fat and boiled pennies from cautery.

A nurse looked up from fiddling with an IV when Miriam pushed aside the yellow curtain drawn around the gurney. "I'm finished here. If you're staying…?" the nurse asked, hopefully, already moving for the door.

"No problem. If you'll shut the door on your way out?" Miriam waited until she heard the snick of the latch and then looked down at the girl.

She'd seen Emma Woodward's driver's license photo: prom-queen pretty, blonde, intensely blue-eyed, a toothy smile. Probably a cheerleader. Now, against white sheets and in a fan of fluorescent glare, Emma Woodward was drawn and haggard, her skin sallow, her blonde curls lank and dull. Her eyes, sunken and smudged with purple, were closed. Leads snaked from beneath her hospital gown to a cardiac monitor, and the IV pumps chugged, one dispensing saline, the other a fresh bag of blood. A pad and pencil lay on her abdomen.

Miriam said the girl's name twice before Emma cranked open her eyelids. Her blue eyes were a little unfocused – probably from pain meds, Miriam guessed.

"I'm Doctor Black," Miriam said. "I'm a psychiatrist. Doctor Meckels asked me to speak with you."

No response.

"Have you ever seen a psychiatrist before?" After a beat: "Well, let me tell you a couple things, okay? Whatever we say in here is between you and me except if you're going to hurt yourself, or somebody else. Then I have to tell somebody what you say. Otherwise, I don't and won't." When Emma still didn't respond, she continued, "Doctor Meckels said that you're going to need to stay in the hospital a few days. You've lost a lot of blood, and they're concerned about possible infection. They're getting your room ready upstairs. Did you want someone to call your parents?"

Emma said nothing.

"Right." Miriam looked around, found a stool, pulled it over, slid onto the seat. Crossing her legs, she folded her hands over her knees. "Do you understand *why* Doctor Meckels wants me to see you?" When Emma remained silent, Miriam went on: "He says you've given birth and won't tell anyone where the baby is. You need to know that he's called CPS – Child Protective Services – "

"I know." Emma's voice was very soft, a little slurry from meds. "And the police. I met them. I'm in a lot of trouble."

"Yes, you are. You really can't blame them. All they're interested in right now is where the baby is."

A tremor rippled through Emma's face. Her gaze sharpened on Miriam. "There is no baby. There isn't anything."

"You mean, there is no baby anymore?"

"No, I mean, it was never there. But I'll bet that means you think I'm crazy." Emma fingered up the pad, flipped back the cover. "I'll bet *you're* only interested in whether it's dead or not, too."

It. So long as the baby was a thing, the mother had an easier time dismissing the child as unreal, or an annoyance, something to be gotten rid of. "Well, you decided two things about me, if I heard you right: that I think you're crazy, and I'm really only interested in the baby. Now, I'd be lying if I said I didn't care about whether the baby was still alive."

Emma worked the pencil across the paper in studied strokes. "What if it is?"

"Is that what you're telling me? That the baby's alive? Because – "

"I didn't tell you anything."

Miriam rode over her. "Because you and I both know that every second that passes is another moment ticked off your baby's life – if the baby isn't dead already... I'm sorry. Was the baby a boy, or girl?"

She was pressing too hard, she knew, but Grant's urgency was infectious and, yes, damn it, she *did* hope the baby was alive even as her common sense told her the opposite. She knew all about mothers like Emma. She knew exactly how they thought.

Emma drew. The pencil scratched over paper. The cardiac monitor blipped.

Miriam said, "You know, you wouldn't be the first woman not to want a baby, to wish that the baby would just go away. You wouldn't be the first not to tell the father...unless you did."

"I know what you're fishing for. There's no father. I don't have a boyfriend, and I wasn't raped. I'm not here to play around. I'm here to study. My parents are paying good money."

"I don't see how – "

"So I wasn't pregnant," Emma interrupted. "I was never pregnant. I just needed to go on a diet. All that blood in my car...it was a really heavy period. That's why I came in because I couldn't stop bleeding."

"Emma, you had a baby. That's an undeniable medical fact. So, are you saying that you didn't *know* you were pregnant? Ever?" She watched Emma toss around the options, wonder which answer was best, and said, "The police are on their way to your room. That means, they're going to go through your drawers and closets."

A flicker of interest. "So?"

"So, what if they don't find napkins or tampons? What if they don't find birth control pills or a diaphragm? What if they find ace wraps or girdles, or those panties with the special tummy panels? If they find things like that, a lawyer could say you used them to *hide* being pregnant and, of course, *not* having napkins... What girl doesn't? Lawyers are ruthless. So what did you think when your period went away?"

"Nothing." Emma shook her head, returned her attention to whatever she was sketching. "I've never been regular."

"But I'll bet you haven't missed for nine months in a row." She watched Emma think about that. "So when did you figure out you were pregnant?"

Emma's eyes bounced to Miriam then to the pad. "I started gaining weight in...I don't know...July. August."

"Did you talk to your boyfriend about being pregnant? I assume you had one, or did something else...?"

Emma ignored the question. "I gained weight, so I went on a diet. I'll bet that's why my period stopped." Her eyes suddenly lit with inspiration. "That happens when you're anorectic. I know because one of the girls in our high school threw up all the time and didn't eat, and she lost her period. She got this kind of peach fuzz on her face and her teeth started to get all brown and..."

"You need to understand what the police are going to do next. They'll put a guard on you, maybe handcuff you to the bed. If you think they're going to leave you alone, you can forget that."

Emma's airy chattiness evaporated. "What will they charge me with?"

"I don't know. I'm not a detective or attorney. Murder, negligent homicide, manslaughter... Depends."

"But there's no body." Emma's pencil jittered over paper. "They can't charge me if there's no body."

Something dinged in Miriam's brain. She chased after the thought. "Where did you – " Her cell brrred and she made the mistake of looking at the display. Frowned. Tried to regroup but realized she'd lost whatever had been on the tip of her tongue. "Where are your parents? Are they at home? Is that where I'll find them?"

"You don't have my permission to talk to them," Emma said, quickly.

"I don't want you talking to them. They'll kill me, they'll be so disappointed."

"Emma, they're going to find out because this is going to get ugly. Trust me on this."

"No," Emma said, "no, you can't charge – "

"And I don't need your permission either. You've got school insurance *and* – " Her cell started up again: same number. What the hell? She pulled her focus back to Emma. "You're on their health insurance. That means the reasons for your hospitalization will be on the forms the insurance company sends. That's public record. So I'm just going to have the insurance company call them a lot sooner than they would otherwise."

"You can't do that."

"Actually," Miriam said as she pulled open the door, "I can."

"Wait," Emma called – and then bit her lower lip as Miriam paused. "You're a psychiatrist, right? So what if I'm mentally ill?"

Miriam waited.

"If I've got a mental illness…wouldn't that change things?"

"Not necessarily. Depends on the diagnosis." Her cell nagged again. "Look, I'm going to answer this. You think good and hard about the spot you're in while I'm gone." She pulled the door shut before Emma had a chance to respond and flipped open her cell. "Saul?"

"Miriam." Saul Koblensky spoke with a heavy, labored Polish accent that, according to his friends in the shul, hadn't faded at all since his release from Auschwitz decades before. "Your office said you were busy, but…" A long sigh. "I needed to speak with you."

"Sure, but…" A gurney rattled past with a gaggle of chattering techs, and she stuck her pinky into her free ear. "Saul, it's not a very good time. What is it?"

"I am afraid I have some very bad news."

"Oh?" She tried to think what it might be. Her parents were dead. (Thank heavens: arrogant, impatient, exacting, always disappointed with her – she didn't miss them in the slightest.) She had no siblings. Her only living relative was her mother's half-aunt who lived in Arizona and had her own family. So that couldn't be it. (And why would they've called Saul anyway? No one in her family was Jewish.)

She opened her mouth to ask Saul what the problem was when the ER receptionist tapped her on the shoulder. "Sorry, Doc. No cells in the hospital. Regulations."

She remembered the kid in the collar, and nodded. "Saul, I'm going to find a phone and call you right back." They said goodbye, and she closed the phone, got pointed to an empty office. As Miriam punched in Saul's number, her mind sorted through a meager list of possibilities. Maybe the synagogue was finally closing? Then she remembered about Stan and Ronnie, and the couple in black – thought, *New York* – and wondered.

She and Saul exchanged about three seconds' worth of pleasantries before she said, "So, what's up?"

"I received a call this morning. This was about nine o'clock. I know because I had just finished the paper and my second cup of coffee."

"Uh-huh." Saul loved to draw things out. "And?"

"And the call was from New York."

Ah, she'd been right: the couple in black. "Is this about the people at the cemetery?"

"Oh." She thought she heard disappointment. "You saw them?"

"I'm right across the street, Saul. It's hard not to. Who are they?"

"They are relatives of a woman who's requested burial in our cemetery. It's all very unusual..."

"Okay. So...what? I don't see what this has to do with me."

"I was getting to that." Saul sounded peeved. He was a man who liked a good story. "These New York people, they said you knew the woman who died. You were...friends? Yes, from a long time ago. Her name was..." A pause, and Miriam hear paper being unfolded. "Uta...ah...Uta Schwermer?"

The words hit like a hammer-blow. Saul was still talking, but his words thinned to a buzz. The blood drained from her face. Her lips went numb. She felt hollow. The background roar of the ER faded as if someone had drawn the blinds, shuttering out the world. Miriam had to work to make her mouth cooperate. "Uta? *Uta* asked to be buried...?"

"Here, in Hart. I know," Saul said, "it is very strange. I've met her son and daughter-in-law, and they are mystified. She never lived here, but her will was very specific. She also requested that you give the eulogy. Her son said that the two of you wrote a book together?"

"I..." Miriam began, and then cleared her throat. "Yes. Co-editors, actually, ten, fifteen years ago... Saul, they're *sure*?" It was a dumb question and she knew it.

Just as she knew exactly what Uta was doing. Had *done*.

"Absolutely. Of course, we can't refuse and it's not as if we don't have the space. She even specified *where*, in the cemetery, she wanted to be buried."

Miriam didn't have to ask because she knew – oh yes, she knew – but her traitorous lips formed the question anyway: "Where?"

"Under the willow. Stan is unhappy because..." Saul nattered on, but she ceased listening. She thought she now understood what people meant when they said they felt as if the earth had just opened beneath their feet.

She came back as Saul said, "...tomorrow morning, so we don't run into Shabbos. Ten o'clock. I am sorry. I know this will not give you much time to prepare."

No, not much time at all. "Not a problem, Saul." She was surprised how calm she sounded. "It'll be..." She looked up as the receptionist came to hang in the doorway. "Hold on, Saul," she said, and put a hand over the mouthpiece. "Yeah?"

"Detective Bonner's trying to reach you," the receptionist said. "I can pipe it in here, you want."

"You know, it would be a lot more efficient if I could just use my cell."

"No can do, Doc. You know hospital regs."

"Sure. Give me a minute." She returned to Saul, said she'd be happy to give the eulogy, disconnected and replaced the handset. As she waited for the receptionist to transfer Grant's call, she thought about how perfect Uta's timing was. Grant comes back in her life, and so does Uta: a zero-sum gain, and then some.

No, she thought as the desk phone chirped, *more like a net loss*. She picked up. "Grant?"

"She's got your book."

"Pardon?"

"Your book, Miriam, the one you did on child murder? She's got it. I'm looking at it right now. She's read your goddamned book."

And what? Planned how she would act? Or was Emma curious, maybe even desperate to understand why she felt the way she did? "Can you tell what she read? Which parts?"

"How about all of it... Give me a sec." Sound of pages turning and now Miriam heard background noise: muffled voices, dull footsteps, the clap of a door. Grant came back: "Lot of yellow mark-up but the chapters that are marked up most are about criminal penalties...figures...and... hunh..."

"What?"

"Where the Bodies Are?"

Uta's chapter. "'Where the Bodies Are: Proximity as Parapraxis in Neonaticide,'" she finished. "I know the chapter."

"What's it say? In English."

She gave a wan laugh. "In a nutshell, many of these women both want to get rid of the infant and yet paradoxically want to keep the infant close. It's how some of them are caught. They can't bear to have the child, but they can't bear to be far away from it either. It's a Freudian slip, in a way; that's what a parapraxis is: literally, a faulty action, something the unconscious does to give you away. You know, you might want to say one thing, but you end up saying or writing down something else."

"So they want to get rid of the baby but then put it someplace close so they'll always be reminded of it?"

"Right. It's even better if they actually can keep an eye on – " She broke off. Thought: *of course.* Into the phone: "Grant, I got to go." Broke the connection before he could respond, and then made a beeline for Emma's room.

She pushed in without knocking. Emma still had the pad in her hand, and the pencil, but she'd either finished the picture, or lost interest. Miriam allowed herself a moment's pity. She could imagine what the girl was thinking and feeling. Then she squashed that, thought: *Time for one more move, Uta...*

She said, without preamble, "You read my book."

Emma's expression was stolid, her response wary. "That's not a crime."

"No. After all, you're a psychology major."

"That's right. I was thinking of a project..." She toyed with the pencil, tapped it on the pad.

"Right. So if you've read it, you know I'm bound by confidentiality standards. You *know* this. You know I can be sued, maybe lose my license, go to jail if I tell anyone what you say to me because I can't reveal a past crime..."

"Whether ten minutes ago, or ten years." A thin smile touched Emma's lips. "I know. But I didn't commit a crime."

"So you say. Most women I've met have a hard time forgetting, though. It's like their minds get greedy and they eventually slip."

"Return to the scene of the crime?" Emma said melodramatically.

"In a way." She changed tack. "So you're an art minor?"

"Yeah." Emma's eyes slitted. "So?"

"So, nothing. What do you like to draw?"

Shoulder hunch. "Bunch of stuff. I'm not very good."

"Well, I'm no critic," Miriam said, smoothly – and just as smoothly slid the pad from Emma's abdomen. The girl opened her mouth, but Miriam was already flipping. Emma hadn't had the pad for long and there were only four sketches: three of the same lima-bean shaped lake from different angles. Vague ballooning shapes in the background that reminded Miriam of nuclear bombs, and what Miriam thought might be...

"These aren't bad," she said, and then pointed. "Is that a gazebo?"

Emma gave a hesitant nod. "They do concerts there in the fall and spring. It's just off the lake...you know, Lake Michigan. Reacher Park?"

Her heart thumped. "Oh. Gosh, I haven't been there in so long. I wasn't sure... What about those things at the shore? Those aren't sand dunes. You know, they remind me of, you know, atomic bombs."

Emma laughed. "No, they're ice floes. You know, how the ice freezes right at the shore. But, you know, the first time I saw them I thought of mushroom clouds, too."

"Hunh. Well, must be tough drawing that in winter," she said, handing the pad back to Emma who palmed it flat against her chest. "Or do you do that from memory?"

"Oh no, something as complicated as that, you know with the ice and all those weird shapes, you have to go there. You know, get the clouds and sun and shadows and everything and it's quiet, and in the winter, you know, there's never anyone around. This morning, I – " Emma stopped talking.

Miriam said nothing. Her nerves hummed.

Tears pooled in Emma's eyes. "What we say in here is between you and me," she whispered. "What's past is past, no matter if it's ten minutes ago, or ten years."

"Or twenty," Miriam said. "I know."

"That's what you said."

"No, that's actually what Uta said, but same diff," Miriam said as she turned on her heel.

"It's *your* book. What *you said*."

Miriam looked back. Emma was struggling up on her elbows, and for an instant, Miriam allowed herself a twinge of pity.

"I know what I said." She pulled open the door. Thought: *Gazebo. Got to be. It's the only thing out there.* "I lied."

"You can't do that!" Emma shouted. "You'll go to jail, you said so! You won't be able to practice anymore! My parents will *sue* your *ass* – "

The door clapped shut, hacking the girl's words in two.

"Getting my ass sued," Miriam said to no one in particular, "is the least of my problems."

Then she fished out her cell phone and thumbed in Grant's number, and to hell with the regulations.

Yes, the past is past. Still, the outrage is enough to make one long for the future.
   — **Schwermer, U.: 'Keeper of the Secrets', in Black & Schwermer,** *Ibid*

Late afternoon, the light bleeding away and the air turning grainy, the day dissolving... But she still could see well enough to know that Stan and Ronnie had removed a good two, maybe three feet. After all these years, she was pretty good at gauging how the work went, and how far down they'd dug. Not long now...

From her left came the squeal of snow flattened by someone with rather large feet. "Your office said I'd find you here."

Miriam looked up. "Did you find the baby?" When he nodded, her pulse jumped in her throat. "Was it...?"

"Milwaukee's sending up a med-evac," he said, hunkering down beside her. "The docs say, maybe, thirty-seventy. He was out in the cold a long time. He was...so," his voice clogged, "he was so small, just a little thing..."

She covered his hand with hers. "I'm glad you found him, Grant."

"Me, too. I don't get it. Yeah, she was scared, but why not tell her parents, or the boyfriend? Why not give up the baby, or get an abortion?"

"Sometimes," she said, gently, "people just get scared, and they do stupid things we can't understand. But they're so ashamed. The baby's just a thing to be ignored, negated until the last second and then when the baby *does* come, they still can't believe that anyone would understand or love them. They feel backed into a corner, with absolutely no recourse, no choice. All these women know is shame and an awful, crushing dread."

"You make it sound so...lonely. So terrible."

"It is. It's a horrible feeling. It's...it's like death."

They fell silent. From across the cemetery, Miriam heard the rasp of Stan's shovel biting the earth.

Grant cleared his throat then gestured toward the small headstone. "Relative?"

"No." Miriam pushed to her feet. "A little girl. She died way back in the flu pandemic. Her family's gone and no one ever comes by, except me."

"How do you know? Other than the fact that your office is across the street. You can't keep an eye on the place twenty-four-seven."

Oh, you'd be surprised. "Well, there are no stones, except the ones I put there. It's an old Jewish custom, putting a stone on the grave whenever you visit. Just like a stone is supposed to last forever, so does the soul. And memory, I guess. But there's never been anyone to remember this girl that I know of."

"Why do you do it?"

"Seems wrong that a child passed through this world and someone loved her enough to put up the marker, but no one ever visits. I guess it's my way of taking care of her."

"Miriam." Grant put his hands on her shoulders and stepped so close that all she'd have to do was relax and let him fold her into his arms. But she didn't. He said, "Miriam, that's either the strangest thing I've ever heard, or the most touching. I can't figure out which." He paused. "You did good – with Woodward, I mean. You did the right thing. And I'm here for you, you know, in case..."

"Oh, this isn't going to court, Grant. Thanks, though."

"But I mean it, Miriam. The past is past." He pulled her into his arms. "We can start over. We can start from right now."

Of course, they couldn't. This time, though, she didn't resist. Because what the hell. She listened to the slow steady beat of his heart and thought: *One minute, I can have this for one more minute...*

Then she turned her head and glanced right. Beneath the willow, Ronnie had clambered out of the grave to sharpen her spade with the file she always kept in her back pocket. Stan was still going, and she watched as his spade stabbed the earth – and then she saw the moment he hit something he wasn't expecting. Even at a distance, she read first the mild surprise then the bewilderment in the set of his round shoulders. He tipped his bulldog's head to his mother, who now joined him at the graveside and peered in.

She knew what they saw: something vaguely rectangular with brass clasps and a brass nameplate (probably still legible because she'd been so particular with the jeweler). An object that once held clothes but now contained the tatters of a secret buried these last twenty years – and in about two minutes, Stan or Ronnie either would open the valise, or it would disintegrate in their hands...

No matter: it would all amount to the same thing in the end.

Well-played, Uta. Talk about taking secrets to the grave...

Then Miriam cupped Grant's face between her hands and kissed him deeply and thoroughly and for the very last time.

"Grant," she said, "there's something I need to tell you."

CODY GOODFELLOW
NEIGHBORHOOD WATCH

This is a nice neighborhood: the houses upper middle class, postwar modern villa styles, big backyards, meandering drives up and down gentle hills that promise a spectacular view from any window. Quiet. To look at it on paper, you might think it was just another anachronistic suburb long since swallowed up by the city. The city peers over the low roofs and eucalyptus-lined avenues, but nothing bad from outside gets in, nothing but a hushed whisper from the freeway, so far as anyone who lives here knows.

The Jennings house on Capri was on the market less than a month before the current occupant snapped it up and moved in. Houses in a neighborhood like this only change hands when someone dies, and when old Mrs Jennings passed, some relative back east dropped the ball and sold to an out-of-towner.

The alarm is loud, but I can hardly hear it from across the street. Their solid walls and high hedges probably keep the neighbors from hearing anything, and the street is empty when I walk over and ring the doorbell.

I used to sell home security systems. It was a good product for the money, and what I lacked in salesmanship, I more than made up for in my sincere belief in the ideal of a vigilant protector over every house. What turned me off, however, was the human element – no matter how perfect the system might be, the weak link was always bored dispatchers, incompetent security guards, overworked cops, oblivious neighbors.

The door opens and a big man in a tracksuit, a mint of gold chains around his neck, leans out. With the door open, he has to shout to be heard over the alarm. I made it loud, but I didn't wire it to call the police.

"What do you want?" he shouts.

"I'm from the neighborhood watch. Is there a problem? Your alarm is going."

"No shit. Get lost."

"I can turn it off from the control pad right behind you," I shout back.

He looks around, then over his shoulder, lets me in.

I go past him into the atrium, the big Spanish tiles like cobblestones slippery under my oversized boots. He breathes all over me as I punch in a code. The alarm gets louder. "You have to enter your password now," I shout in his ear.

He pushes past me and scratches his big greasy head, then he remembers and punches in a number. He looks down at my hands and sees the remote in my hand, the red light blinking in sync with the pulsing light on the control. He doesn't see what's in my other hand before I blow his right ear out his left with it.

I drag him to the entry hall closet and dump him among the light stands and sand bags and junked computers and monitors. It makes a fearsome racket, but I can barely hear it over the alarm.

I lock all the exterior doors, then shut off the alarm.

From the master bedroom upstairs, I hear music, moaning and groaning, cheers and simian hooting. It occurs to me just then, that there are women present, and I remember to put on the ski mask.

I have lived in this neighborhood my entire life. My parents bought their house here when I was eight, and the neighborhood was new. I was an only child. I delivered papers, ran the school safety patrol, drove the church Meals On Wheels van. My father died when I was sixteen. I went to work to learn a trade, and got married. My wife moved in with us, but my mother succumbed to diabetes and died not too long after. We never had any children. My wife died five years ago. A lonely life, viewed like that, but I have always thought of myself as a man with a very large family.

My neighbors are good people; people who work, raise their children, see them off into the world, and live out their lives in decency and quiet security. I see to it.

I'm the umpire at the softball field that abuts the old Jennings house. The girls' eight-and-under team last year went to the state championships, and would have gone to the nationals if the coach's daughter, Becky Chernow, had not sprained her arm whipping out those vicious sidearm strikes against a team from Bakersfield. The Chernows moved in down the block seven years ago. Becky Chernow walks past the Jennings house every morning to school with her mom. I don't think either of them know what goes on here. Tomorrow, everyone will know, and it pains me that this can't be helped. But a message will be sent, and it will stop.

I go up the stairs, skipping the risers that creak, and sidle down the hallway, looking into each of the four bedrooms, the bathroom and the den where Mr Jennings drafted the initial plans for the big shopping mall downtown. Inky dark in the hallway, splashes of copper light from the streetlamp outside pooling before the open doors.

Each room has been converted into a bordello stall, with a king-sized bed or a mound of chintz and satin pillows. Carts like in a surgical theater parked in each room, loaded with dildos, vibrators, plugs, clips, whips, pills, water pipes, nitrous oxide tanks – everything to make them pliable, the boys and girls who let themselves end up here. Cameras everywhere – their cameras, and mine.

The upstairs office is filled with computers and editing equipment, a wall of monitors showing girls on themselves, on each other, on boys and men, while others tabulate subscriber traffic to the host of websites where this filth spews out. Almost every night, one or more young, dumb, misguided young woman gets steered in here and plied with drugs and drink by one or more sex professionals, and many more have, knowingly or not, webcams in their bedrooms.

I think I recognize a few of the boys and girls on the screens. None of them are eighteen.

From the master bedroom, somebody calls out, probably for the doorman. The door hangs half-open, so I go back there, unscrewing the blown-out silencer off the gun. From here on out, no reason to be quiet.

I recognize the owner first because he's the only one without a camera or a crotch in his face. He sits on the floor beside the enormous round bed, a mirror balanced on his knee and a balloon pinched in one hand. His eyes are glazed, jaw slack, drool drizzling down onto his silk robe.

I know he made hardcore porn and ran swingers' clubs in LA for years, but he crossed the Mob, who bought him out, presented him with a generous golden parachute, and cut the head off his celebrated cock. Banished from the business and the act he lived for, he got the bright idea to move into my neighborhood under an assumed name.

Two young men in T-shirts and nothing else probe the orgy with little digital camcorders. I shoot them first. The bodies on the bed take a few awkward moments to react. Two girls, one wearing strap-on male equipment, shrivel away from a third body whose equipment is real, and shrinking like a snail with salt on it. I shoot him in the solar plexus and he flops back on the bed. The girls jerk upright, then drop to the floor as I wave the gun.

The owner jolts out of his nitrous trance, spilling coke on the shag rug. He looks around, but his vision is still buried too deep in molecular sunburst hallucinations to figure out where the shots are coming from, even after I shoot him in the head.

I got this automatic from a sometime Mafia contract killer. A nice old lady on Helena Place whose five children were all nearing retirement themselves, and she had the bad grace to go on living, spry as thirty. Her oldest hired this killer through his business associates in New York. He took the son's fifty thousand dollars, but he never showed up. The son took it on the chin, and his mother passed away naturally eight months later, and everyone got what they wanted. The police may find the gun tomorrow and trace it, and follow the motel bills and gas station receipts back out of town, but they will never find any trace of the assassin, unless they get very lucky while gutting fish.

The girls sob and hug each other. One of them tries not to scream, but her mouth works, a whispering, babbling litany of improvised prayer. She's not looking at me, but my mouth almost says her name all by itself. Naomi McKinney, just around the corner from me, on Argo Court. Why is it always the cul-de-sac people?

Not a bad girl, at least not when she lived with her parents, but a timid hitter and apathetic outfielder. When they divorced, she went with the mother while the father stayed behind. Broken homes should be everyone's responsibility, but when even the community can't hold it together, the broken bits must be ejected. I never should have let him stay. She brought whatever sickness she contracted outside back here, when she moved back in with her father, last year.

Naomi has friends here, I see her around with local kids all the time. She's dating, or just fucking, Christian Gallo, the varsity backup quarterback at Patrick Henry. I disapproved, but I never thought she would sink so low.

I look at the other girl. A pro, probably from the San Fernando porn circuit or the strip joints downtown. A few minutes ago, she didn't care what these animals did to her, but already the dregs of the Ecstasy, coke and nitrous are draining out of her glassy eyes. She's already prepared for the worst.

"Out the front door, go. Get in your car or walk, there's a pay phone in front of the elementary school down the street." Reaching into my pocket for the remote, I unlock the front door. "I have eyes outside. Don't call the cops, or we'll find you before they will. And don't ever, ever come back to this neighborhood."

The pro picks up an article or two of clothing off the floor as she darts out of the room. Naomi follows her, but I catch her arm and throw her back on the bed.

"I'm sorry, Naomi," I say. "You're going to talk."

"No, I'm... No, I'm not," she keeps saying, but there's no point in arguing. I call them like I see them.

And I see.

I've never believed in hurting women. No matter how debased, I think that in every woman lives the possibility of redemption that is at best a hopeful lie for all men. They are the vessels of all that is most virtuous in humankind, and I don't say that with any illusions about what women's liberation has done. I see how new opportunity has shown women to be as corruptible, as cruel and as violent as men, and that only men's shielding of women from the lower side of life allowed that illusion to survive. This, I think, is the only truly virtuous act to which men can lay claim.

I do not discriminate. I can see.

When the Hurstons moved into the old Sabey place on Camino Way, some people complained, but I could see that they were good, respectable people of color who wanted the same things we all wanted, and slowly, I like to think I helped the rest of the neighborhood see it, too.

When a girl steps up to my plate, I can tell before she fans out a first practice swing whether she will get a hit or not, because I can see in their eyes if they will or won't, can or can't. And where, in the other girl's eyes, I saw a home six and nine states away from here, and getting right with Jesus and away from this business, in this poor girl – in my neighbor – I see sirens and TV reporters and all of this just a movie that she might find herself starring in. Too bad. I honestly wish whoever filled her head with stupid ideas like that were here to face the music with her.

She turns and tries to run, and I shoot her in the side of the head, knocking her back across the naked dead man on the bed, who just then jerks and gets up.

Naked but for his gold chains, he still looks like he's wearing a black angora body sweater; so much hair, more on his ass than on his head, and his manhood, though wilted with blood loss, is still heroically long. Built like an artillery shell, and he seems to have overdosed on tanning pills, because he's so very orange.

He tramples Naomi's corpse, begging, "Don't do this, please don't," but I have to. Two more in the chest, and he sees no bargain will be cut, so he charges me, driving me into the fireplace hearth, and my hands fumbling find no iron poker, no firewood, because the fire is a gas hose feeding feeble jets of flame through an asbestos sculpture of a log, and I look at it for a while as the big orange pornographer strangles me and stabs me in the side three, five, six times. My hand beats up the side of his head with the empty automatic, and blood pumps out of the holes in him and stings my eyes.

I teach kenpō karate at the community center. I'm only a fifth-degree black belt, but after the old instructor left and the program threatened to dissolve, I took over the kids' instruction. Becky Chernow is in my class, a green belt, a real competitor.

I squirm and bridge my hips up into his crotch, reach up and squeeze his scrotal pouch with all the fading strength I can muster. His grip weakens enough so I get my hand up and chop his neck until something vital inside breaks and he flushes all over, orange to red to violet like a setting sun.

I roll him off me. My breathing is shocky. The object he stabbed me with sticks out of my side. A ballpoint pen. I clean up, leaving nothing behind.

I go to the owner, take down his pants and saw off the rest of his penis with a Buck knife. Castration isn't the kind of thing a man spreads around town; this will send the right message, to others who would do this kind of thing here, and to the cops, about where to look.

One of the cheap hatchbacks is gone from the driveway when I step out onto the quiet street and walk back home.

I change and bag my bloody outer clothes as I watch the raw feeds, then cut a rough edit of the action. Nobody called the police. I know because they are all doing what they always do. If anyone heard anything, they would not call the police. They would call me.

I watch them. In every room of almost every house in the neighborhood – ninety-four homes, to be exact – I can see.

A wired, motion-triggered closed-circuit camera built into every sensor gives the kind of intelligent protection a household, a community, really needs.

I was able to use my old company's equipment, and my family's house as a control center. All the old neighbors were eager to sign up, as they knew it would not be some stranger at the other end, but a neighbor they could trust. I think they almost trust me enough that I could tell them about the cameras. Sometimes, when I watch them, I think they know.

I don't expect to find much at this late hour, but I am restless from the act and the anticipation of tomorrow, when it will come to light.

I review the field, and come across several spikes in activity. The Myers boy is one I thought I recognized on the screens at the Jennings house. He delivers groceries for Stump's Market. He's in his bed.

He's watching a video and jacking off with a woman's undergarment. On the screen – God bless digital resolution – a clumsy home video of a middle-aged blonde blowing a big black man while another takes her like a dog on the deck of a yacht. The whore is his mother.

I skip around some more. Myers associates with Gallo, if only because Myers sells him weed. Gallo is true to type, an arrogant second-string quarterback who gluts himself on the worship of his peers in return for a mediocre season fraught with interceptions. Next year, he wants to go to USC. His youngest sister played on Becky Chernow's team. Good eye, lousy arm.

I am not surprised to find him naked and smoking a joint in bed, receiving a blowjob from a cheerleader, though I am taken aback that it is a male one. Gilbert Rudolph – another Myers associate.

My hand itches to grab the phone and hit all the panic buttons, lock all their doors. My neighbors are asleep in their beds, and the whole community is on fire. How long has all of this been going on underneath my nose?

I hope they're smart enough to see tomorrow's news as a message.

My heart rate spikes, and shooting pains transfix my right side. The stab wounds looked shallow, but when I take the broken pen out of my pocket, I get a nasty surprise. It's not a pen, it's an X-Acto knife, with no blade on it. I think I know where the blade is.

I really should go to the hospital. Because of its proximity to San Diego State, Alvarado's emergency room handles all kinds of ridiculous injuries.

But something else nags at me.

I switch over to another house. Becky Chernow lies in her bed on her left side, with one closed fist near her mouth, her thumb almost touching her lips. She only stopped doing it in her sleep a year or two ago, and she'll probably need braces, Coach Chernow told me.

And there is the Coach now, looming into frame and hovering in the girl's doorway in a sweatshirt and boxers. He stands there for a long time, like all parents do, as they ponder the dreams of their children, and make their peace with the inevitability of the future that will someday whisk them off into the world.

But for several months now, Coach Chernow has stood here longer than he should, since his wife got fat and keen on Jesus. He's doing it almost nightly, and every time, he seems to be an inch or two closer to her bedside.

The low resolution won't let me see his eyes, but I can see inside him through the granulated feed. He rocks back and forth like a car stuck in mud, but presently, he's moving, slow as the sun, towards her bed.

I pick up the phone and hit his number.

On the screen, Coach Chernow looks around. Becky stirs and turns over. I switch screens to follow him down the hall to his den. He sits down, takes a deep breath, and answers the phone.

"Coach Chernow?"

"Who is this?"

"It's Rudy, Coach, from the softball league."

"What the heck, Rudy, it's kind of way past our bedtime here..."

I try not to watch him scratch himself, no doubt to keep his erection alive. "Just wanted to let you know there's going to be some rule changes in team selection this year."

"Great, Rudy, great, but I'm sure it can wait."

He's halfway to hanging up, so I have to shout to make myself heard. "Nobody gets to coach their own kids."

He jumps out of his chair. "But that's bullshit!"

"The league's going to spring it on you at the draw tomorrow night, but they're voting it in, in the morning. I'd hate to see you get screwed, not with the little firecracker you've got under your roof. She's really something, isn't she?"

"Well, we're all real proud of her, Rudy, but what do you – just tell me what they're going to try to do..."

"I can't talk to you about it over the phone, Coach, but I've got some papers they gave me to review, before they vote the league rules. You want to see them, you come by my house tomorrow, but keep it under your hat."

Coach Chernow's hand snakes out of his shorts. "I could... If I could... Do you have those...right now?"

"I do, I do," I assure him, and I take out some pills I got at the Jennings house the first time I cased it, reading the bottle's warnings in English and

French: DO NOT TAKE WITH ALCOHOL.

I stifle a cough and wipe blood off on my pants. I should call for an ambulance.

Last season's scrapbook is open on my desk. Pictures of Becky at the plate, on the field, in the bath, the page torn from last season's eight-and-under division championship scorebook. This isn't the kind of thing you can undo, the kind of punishment that fixes anything. I can fix it before it gets broken.

"I was just about to open one of my Dad's old bottles of single malt… You know, toast the start of a new season? I could wait for you, if you come right over… And, Coach?"

"Oh, I'll be right there, just… Yeah?" He already sounds pretty wobbly. It won't take much to get him to write a suicide note.

"Kiss your daughter good night for me, would you?"

"Right, yeah, bye."

I watch him look for his pants and I ask myself, as I often do, lately, why nobody else is willing to fight for this neighborhood.

O'NEIL DE NOUX
K LOVE

odie Kintyre found the suicide note in a clear, plastic sandwich bag in the right front pocket of the jumper's faded jeans. She carefully opened the bag and removed the handwritten note, laying it on the hood of the Humvee that had driven her to the scene. She put her useless portable radio on the note to keep it from flying away in the post-Hurricane Rita gusts that still blew across New Orleans. Behind her the three National Guard MPs, fresh-faced youngsters from Connecticut, stared curiously at her. They'd kept their distance from the body in the center of Bourbon Street.

Their sergeant said, "What is it, Detective?"

"Suicide note," she explained and decided to read it aloud for the eager MPs who'd driven her from the unofficial NOPD Homicide Division Headquarters at Armstrong Airport – two hangars, one for personnel, one used as a temporary morgue since Hurricane Katrina hit less than a month ago.

"'To The Police...'" Jodie's voice echoed off the lacework balconies lining both sides of Bourbon Street "'...send a patrol car to 1010 Dumaine Street, Apartment A. The door is unlocked. Inside is the body of my girlfriend Amanda Dalkey. I warn you. It's gruesome. She's in *pieces*.'"

The printing on the note appeared shaky. Jodie read the rest: "'I gotta give up my life for the one I took.'" The note was signed 'Michael Edward Timkin'. She felt the hair standing on the back of her neck. This couldn't be just a *suicide*. No. 'She's in pieces'?

"Jesus," muttered Jodie as she slipped the note back into the sandwich bag. She readjusted her shoulder rig, balancing her handcuffs and extra magazine under her right arm and her new Glock nine-millimeter beneath her left arm. She'd bought the new weapon two weeks BK. Now, everything was either BK or AK – Before Katrina or After, the dividing line between when New Orleans seemed eternal and now seemed... almost gone.

As Jodie moved back to the body, another gust of hot, damp wind ruffled her blonde hair which hung in a long page-boy. At five-nine Jodie was taller than two of the MPs, even in the black running shoes she wore with the baggy police tactical pants – the ones usually worn by bike cops – and black T-shirt, POLICE stenciled in white across her chest and shoulder blades.

She started her notes with the date and time – *Sat. 9/24/05, 7:06 a.m.* Then she studied the body more carefully as it lay on the street. He was in his twenties, about six-four, in a green muscle shirt, faded jeans, well-worn white tennis shoes, no visible scars or tattoos. She added *Blond hair, blue eyes.*

"We call doz wife-beater shirts," said the sergeant now standing next to Jodie. He had a New Yorker's accent.

"What's your name again?" Jodie didn't look up from her notes.

"Staff Sergeant Michael Montesteri."

"And the other two?"

"PFC Cannina and Specialist Cash." On the way from the airport they'd told her Montesteri and Cannina were Sicilian names. "That's why we sound like da Sopranos."

She didn't bother telling them New Orleans had the largest Sicilian-American population in the country, BK. Her first partner in Homicide was named LaStanza. He sarcastically proclaimed he was so Sicilian it hurt.

"You ever in da military, Ma'am?" the sergeant asked.

Ma'am. The word dug at Jodie. They may call women officers *ma'am* in the army, but at thirty-five the sound of a young man's voice calling her ma'am grated on Jodie.

She looked up at the five story hotel from which the jumper had leapt, L'Hotel Désespoir. A tall, narrow hotel with balconies hanging above Bourbon Street, it was stucco with brick accoutrements.

"Could he 'a been thrown?" said the sergeant. "You know, like maybe he was murdered." He pronounced it *moidered.*

She nodded toward the victim. "He's at least six four, weighs well over two hundred pounds, looks like mostly muscle. Maybe the Hulk could throw him out this far in the street. If he slipped and fell, he'd be on the banquette. He made sure he wouldn't hit anything on the way down. He's a jumper."

"Banquette?"

"Sidewalk. It's French. A long story," she added wearily. She hadn't slept well. Who had since Katrina? She had a room, more like a closet with an army cot, at the far end of the airport hangar. They took turns at the showers, two portable stalls with curtains, ladies first, the men ogling her when she passed, even wrapped in an oversized terry cloth robe and her hair in a towel. Strangers mostly, national guardsmen, cops and firemen from all over the country. Most of what was left of NOPD was housed in two cruise ships on the Mississippi. The Homicide Division, Jodie and a few others, each taking a shift, were at the airport, where they brought out the bodies before shipping them to the big morgue at St Gabriel.

Jodie started to turn back to the body just as a red-headed young man came rushing out of the hotel. "Officer! Officer! We got it on tape."

He stumbled off the banquette and almost ran into Jodie. He wore black dress pants and a white shirt with a gold name tag that read SIM-MONS. ASSISTANT MANAGER.

"We just got our surveillance cameras working again and we got it on tape. The jump."

Jodie turned to the sergeant. "Keep someone out here with the body," she said. "You can come with me."

She turned back to the assistant manager. "OK, Mr Simmons. Show me the tape."

"In my office." Simmons backed up and almost stumbled again on the high banquette. "I made a copy for you."

"Thanks." Jodie followed him with Sgt Montesteri right behind. The lobby smelled of flowers, the floor shined to a BK brilliance. The French Quarter had been spared the flood waters that had inundated eighty per cent of the Crescent City and so far, the levees had held against Rita's fury. Hurrying ahead, Simmons led them through two big offices just past the long front desk to a smaller office with a bank of televisions and video decks.

Simmons slipped a cassette into a VCR, hit a button and stood back. "I edited the parts you'll need." He pointed to a screen as a view of the rooftop came into focus. "The door was blown off in Katrina. We re-placed it, but there's no lock yet, so anyone can get on the roof through the stairwell. The roof's flat, you know."

The jumper walked into view, moved to the edge of the roof and looked down. The video was only in black and white but was quite sharp. The man looked huskier on film.

"He did that twice," said Simmons as the jumper turned and walked out of camera range. A minute later he came back, hurrying this time but stopped short of the edge, moved to it and stood looking down, his arms hanging limp at his sides as gusty wind whipped his short hair. Jodie noted the time on the tape read – 5:42 a.m. The jumper slowly turned and walked the way he'd come. Exactly two minutes later he raced forward and leapt from the roof, his arms waving as if he was trying to fly.

"Wanna see it again?"

Jodie shook her head, stepped forward and hit the eject button. The white label on the tape had the hotel's name, address and the date and time. Jodie asked Simmons to put his initials on it, she added hers and tucked the tape into her carrying bag on the way back out. She thanked him again.

Rain started peppering the street. The sun was shining but dark clouds were moving in. Sgt Montesteri and his men brought out a black body bag, pulled on the same type of rubber gloves as Jodie wore. It took all three men to manhandle the body into the back of the Humvee. Jodie climbed in front and gave the sergeant directions to Dumaine Street.

"You have a flashlight?" she asked as they turned up Dumaine.

1010 Dumaine was a half block from Rampart Street, a two-story wooden building painted light pastel green with a wooden balcony above the banquette. Two doors faced Dumaine, the one on the left had 'A' above the door, which Jodie found unlocked.

"Want us to come in with you?" Sgt Montesteri asked from the driver's seat of the Humvee.

"Wait here." Jodie flipped on the large flashlight and opened the door slowly, calling out, "Police!"

The air inside was stale and smelled ripe. Jodie reached in and flipped the light switch. Nothing. She swung the flashlight's beam to the left to illuminate three shelves, long boards supported by gray cinder blocks. Atop were over a dozen candles, some in glass jars, all unlit. The second shelf had newspapers and paperback books. Clothes, some folded, occupied the bottom shelf. The coffee table was covered with empty brown MRE meal bags, the meals the National Guard had been providing since Katrina, the floor littered with empty beers cans and bottled-water containers.

Two blankets covered what lay on the orange sofa. Jodie moved the flashlight to her left hand, stepped closer, picked up the edge of the nearest blanket and pulled it off. A dozen cockroaches drove her back as they scattered. It took a second for Jodie's eyes to focus on the twisted legs and bare feet. The jeans were dirty and worn, the feet clean and bluish. She touched the left foot and it was cold.

Jodie moved around the coffee table to the other blanket, yanked it off as she stepped back. Only a few roaches this time. The T-shirt on the body was once yellow but was now mostly black from dried blood. The corpse was headless and missing its left hand, both crudely severed by what had to have been a dull knife.

Jodie found the head in a large pot on the kitchen stove. Next to it lay a knife caked in dried blood. The pot was covered with a towel and only two roaches came out when she uncovered it. The hand was in the stove. Neither had been cooked. Jodie turned on a back burner. No gas. She was sure this part of the Quarter had gas and electricity AK, but not this place.

There was a portable Smith Corona typewriter on the small Formica kitchen table with a sheet of white loose-leaf paper in it. In the upper right corner of the page was the number five. A stack of loose-leaf pages, all with typing, lay next to the typewriter. The top page on the stack was numbered four. On the far side of the typewriter were two driver's licenses, the jumper's face on one from Kansas, the face of the head on the stove on a Georgia license. His name was Michael E. Timkin. Her name Amanda B. Dalkey. She was twenty-five.

Jodie dug out the small digital camera from her bag and took pictures of the table and typewriter. She checked the camera to make sure the images of the head in the pot and the hand in the oven were clear before moving back into the living room for more pictures. Stepping outside, she took pictures of the doorway and building, then turned to the MPs and asked for another body bag. The rain had stopped, the sun beaming down on them, but the wind still blew in gusts.

"It's gruesome in there," she warned. "There's a woman's body in three pieces and lots of roaches. We have to get her out of there right away.

Think y'all can keep your breakfasts down?"

The three nodded.

As they carefully stuffed the body into the bag, Jodie watched their determined faces as they worked, their jaws tightly set. She noted the victim was petite, couldn't be more than five-three. Jodie brought out the pot and slipped the head, then the hand, into the bag herself.

"Y'all take the bodies to the airport then come back and get me. I have work to do here."

"But what if the levees break again?" said Sgt Montesteri. "Your radio still doesn't work."

The Corps of Engineers colonel at the airport had warned them the levees might not hold, even with Rita hitting on the far side of the state. Hurricane Rita, another Category Five storm, was bigger than Katrina. Her winds had slammed them at the airport all night.

Jodie said, "I told you. The Quarter didn't flood for Katrina, she won't flood even if the levees break again. Just come right back."

"But if the streets flood..."

Jodie gave the sergeant a weary smile. "You'll find a way."

"Yes, ma'am."

She tried a quick canvass but no one answered any of the doors, even across the narrow street. Most of the ones who'd come back AK had left for Rita.

Jodie went back to the kitchen table for the papers. Bright sunlight streamed though the curtainless window, giving the room a golden hue. She looked around, noticed six empty bottles of Scotch whisky, White Horse brand. Jodie wasn't much of a drinker but she'd never heard of White Horse Scotch. Had to be a cheap label. She sat and reshuffled the pages, having a little trouble with the rubber gloves. She started with page one, reading aloud...

"I always wanted to write a story. Never had anything to write about until now. So I'll start with me sitting at the kitchen table and looking at my girlfriend's head. It's propped in front of me. On top of a pot. I got her eyes closed but I can still feel them looking at me through her eyelids because of what I done.

"Something is very wrong inside me. I can't be human anymore. Not just because of what I done, but because I don't feel sad, not a bit of remorse for the girl I loved. Only emptiness because it's all over for both of us and I did it.

"My name is Michael Edward Timkin, born November 22, 1975 in Junction City, Kansas. My parents are Ray and Bonnie Timkin of 11023 Little Horse Road, Junction City, phone number 316-555-6441. They will be shocked so don't tell them right away what I done. They don't know the demon in me.

"I guess I should start at when I met Amanda. It was the Sunday everyone left town for Katrina, which hit the next day. I was walking down Bourbon Street and she was sitting on the stoop outside the Mucky Duck Bar. She had on a blue dress and showing off her legs to me as I passed. She waved and said, 'Don't you know the world's about to end?'

"I stopped and told her I could see up her dress and she threw back her head and laughed, saying that was the idea. She climbed off the stoop, came right up to me and stood almost touching me and said I was a tall one. I'm six-four and she was five-three. Her blonde hair danced against my chest in the wind, which was coming in short bursts before the storm.

"'If the world's about to end,' I said, 'why you still hanging around?'

"'Let me tell you a secret.' She leaned even closer, her body brushing against me. 'I don't believe the weathermen. They spout doom and gloom every year. I've been here ten years and watched everyone evacuate for hurricane Georges and Ivan and all they did was get stuck in traffic for hours and hours.' She went up on her toes and brushed her lips across mine. 'Nothing can get this city. New Orleans is indestructible.'

"She took my hand and led me to the stoop out front of the Mucky Duck and told me her name. I told her mine and we sat there. For maybe an hour and did nothing.

"It was so quiet it was eerie. I'd only been in the city a week, been crashing with fellas I met at the Black Cat Lounge on Toulouse Street. When they headed out of town they locked me out of the apartment, so I was on the street, walking around, looking at the people rushing to get away. But when I met Amanda, it was like we were the only two people left.

"'Come on,' she said, taking my hand again and leading me into the bar. 'They got the liquor locked up but the beer cooler's still frosty.' She dug us both out a couple Miller Lites and the brew was so cold it chilled my throat, I could barely swallow.

"'Drink up,' she said as she sat up on the bar. 'The electricity'll probably go out tonight.'

"Just before dark the owners of the Mucky Duck came back. They got tired of waiting in traffic and turned around. They said they didn't mind us drinking some of the brews as Amanda was watching the place so it didn't get looted but I could see they wanted us out so we went to Amanda's apartment here on Dumaine Street.

"There really is a calm before the storm but when the storm hit I thought the world was ending. The electricity went out right away and we sat on the sofa, holding hands as things crashed against the walls and the balconies outside. A piece of aluminum siding broke through one of the windows in the living room, but we stuffed an old blanket in it.

"The building began shaking, only a little at first, then more and more as things hit it, sounding like incoming rounds in a war movie. The building moaned and groaned (see, I read Edgar Allan Poe).

"I know about incoming rounds since I was in the army, even went to Iraq in the quartermaster corps. Heard a lot of gunfire but I was such a fuck-up they sent me home early with a general discharge. Couldn't even do the military thing right. Just like when I was at K State. Flunked out. I could blame the drinking, but nobody held me and poured it down my throat. I did it all to myself. I've been drinking for years. Hell, it's the only thing that's kept me going since I killed her. If you look around the kitchen you'll see what I spent our last money on. Scotch.

"With Katrina howling outside, we made love on the sofa after the lights went out and again on her bed before the house started getting too hot. By the next morning it was so hot we had to throw open all the windows and fan ourselves with pieces of cardboard. We sat out on the front stoop drinking more beer as the refrigerator was still cold inside.

"Amanda said we fell in love the night Katrina struck. She called it K Love. She talked a lot. Me, I'm kinda quiet. She kept explaining things to me, labeling things, like calling her apartment the cave, calling daylight the heat, calling nighttime the passion. She was the engine behind our love affair. Me, I went along for the ride, I guess.

"Two cop cars rushed past the day after the hurricane hit and we tried to flag them down. Then Amanda got an idea and we stopped the third one when she stood up and flashed her boobs at them. They told us the city was flooding. Almost immediately we saw people streaming through the Quarter all heading to the Superdome and the Convention Center.

"'Treme's got water,' they called out. 'Water all through the Ninth Ward all the way to Marigny.'

"Amanda explained, telling me Treme was one of the neighborhoods bordering the French Quarter. So was Marigny.

"'Maybe we should leave?' I said.

"'What? Go to some shelter full of smelly people?' She wouldn't have any part of it. 'We'll be OK here. The French Quarter's the highest ground in the city.'

"I wasn't so sure, especially when another cop car came by and the driver told us the levees had collapsed all around town.

"'There's a levee right over there,' I said, pointing down Dumaine Street toward Jackson Square and the levee right across from St Louis Cathedral.

"'That's the river levee,' she told me. 'He's talking about the levees up at Lake Pontchartrain. No hurricane's powerful enough to push the Mississippi River backwards. And the river levees are much bigger.'

"She was right about the river but, as we all learned, the damn lake flooded most of the city. She was also right about the Quarter. We sat out the next two weeks, just her and me in her apartment, living like cave people, going out during daylight hours to track down food and water. Only I didn't have to drag her into our cave to mate, she dragged me, the little hussy.

"After the looters broke into Benoit's Grocery on Rampart, we went and helped ourselves before the food ran out. We found a barbeque pit and started cooking stuff, using branches and boards, old newspapers and books.

"Those were heady days after the storm. We were reduced to basic living, gathering food and water, making love every night when it wasn't too hot. We bathed each other in the courtyard behind the apartment house, standing in the grass, pouring water over each other. Not a lot of water at first because we had to conserve it.

"Then the National Guard starting coming by and Amanda flashed them so they'd come back with the MREs and lots of bottled water.

"Some nights we'd stay up and talk all night. She talked mostly, but she got me to talk about my lousy childhood and the damn army and told me it wasn't me that didn't fit. The world didn't fit me. When she told me about her childhood, I got goosebumps, how her uncles molested her and how she took to hooking for a while.

"Man, she really loved me. More than anyone ever has. But things started going bad when we heard about Rita. I don't know why exactly, but that second big bitch of a storm coming right for Louisiana got to us. We saw it on the TV that was working at the Mucky Duck. In New Orleans, the first things to reopen after Katrina were the barrooms.

"Rita was so big she covered the entire Louisiana coastline and they said she was an even more dangerous Category 5 than Katrina. The locals were taking it bad, yelling at the TV, cursing God, telling us they had roots here and mother nature was yanking them out. I had the shakes and drank to stop them. Amanda cried herself to sleep. She told me Rita could wipe away everything, even K Love.

"I killed Amanda in the middle of the night with Rita's wind screeching outside. She was sleeping on the sofa and I lit a candle and watched her. She kept twitching and I was drunk, but that's no excuse. Her face looked tired and worn out and I was worn out too. I wrapped a T-shirt around her neck and she stirred a little but didn't open her eyes. It was quick.

"I don't know why I cut her up. I kept staring at her skin and the next thing I knew I had a butcher knife and started slicing her wrist.

"She's got to be in a better place now. I'm about to go to a far worse one. We had a love, Amanda and me, a love born of a mass murderer named Katrina. We were doomed from the start with K Love."

That was all he'd written.

Jodie pulled the final sheet from the typewriter and stacked them. She felt a sudden constriction in her throat, took in a deep breath, closed her eyes and shut it out. Hell, she was a homicide detective. Violence was part of her life. She'd seen more than enough of this shit, but this, this love – born of one storm and killed by another – love that produced this insanity – it was something she'd better bury quickly or it would bubble out. Detectives didn't cry.

She got up and found a couple bags, secured the blood-caked knife, the pot where the head had lain and the murder weapon, the knotted T-shirt lying on the floor next to the sofa, shaking out two cockroaches in the process. Stepping outside, she felt a strong burst of heated air against her face. The sun beat down on her as she waited. Not for long, thankfully, as the Humvee turned down Dumaine from Rampart.

"You're going the wrong way down a one-way street," she told the sergeant.

"The Industrial Canal levee broke," he said, eyes bulging. "On the other side, so the lower Ninth Ward's filling up again."

"What about this side?"

"No. The colonel says the levee's holding on this side and the 17th Street Canal levee's holding too."

"Good." Jodie went to the back of the Humvee and one of the men inside unlatched the rear. She put the bags inside and went around to sit in the front passenger seat. She slipped the typed confession into her clipboard. As she buckled her seat belt, the sergeant gunned the Humvee and they headed away from 1010 Dumaine.

"You wanna talk about it?" asked the sergeant.

"Nope."

Tooling back up to Rampart, they hurried to the interstate ramp to get out of town, back into Jefferson Parish and the airport.

"This is one deployment we'll never forget," the sergeant said as they zipped along the elevated expressway past the Superdome with its peeled roof. "I never knew anything about New Orleans besides Mardi Gras and fancy restaurants."

Jodie closed her eyes and wished he'd just shut up.

"You know," he said after a minute. "We been talking about all this. Don't mean no offense, but the only pretty cops we've ever seen were on TV. Until we saw you."

Jodie felt anything but pretty.

"Sergeant," she snapped. "Shut up. That's an order."

"Yes, ma'am."

STEVE RASNIC TEM
LIVING ARRANGEMENT

Monte had never been a good father, in fact he had been pretty lousy by anyone's standards, but after he lost his job and became too ill to work and the arthritis made it so he could hardly move his legs, his daughter pretended otherwise and asked him to come live with her, her young son, and the current boyfriend. "You always took care of me," she said. "Let me do this for you."

That wasn't true, not by a long shot – he'd had shit to do with her upbringing. He'd left all that to her mother and he'd been gone half the time and the half the time he was there he'd made them all miserable including himself.

But he accepted her offer. What else was he supposed to do? He didn't know why she was lying to him, or if she was just lying to herself *about* him. Nor did he particularly care. He had to survive somehow. Or did he? That was one of those questions that got harder to answer every year.

His little corner of her house was a closet of a room at the back, just off the porch and the kitchen. In a fancier house it might have been called the mud room. A battery-powered radio. One box for his toiletries. One box for his miscellaneous. A mail slot of a window let some light in. It was a lot better than he deserved. He actually couldn't remember if he'd hit her when she was a kid, but he probably had. He didn't remember a lot from those days. She could have been a little yippy dog running around for all he could recall of her childhood.

He had a single bed, and she made him strip it and hand her the sheets for the wash. If it had been up to him he'd have let the sheets go yellow, then brown, then replace them. Monte discovered he liked the look, and the smell, of wet sheets flapping in the wind. Old age was full of surprises.

She didn't expect anything from him, or at least that's what she said. He got a small social security check every month which he just signed over to her, leaving it under the peanut butter jar in the pantry. They never talked about it, but those checks got cashed.

He had no use for spending money. He used to drink. About fifteen years ago he stopped, and he couldn't have told you why. One day he just woke up and decided he didn't care to anymore. It might not be permanent – he reserved the right to start up again at any time. Maybe if this living with family thing didn't work out. And he'd been a smoker until recently, quitting cold turkey when he moved in with her. He actually liked the discomfort the craving for it gave him. It kept him focused.

For entertainment he read old paperbacks people threw away, he didn't care which ones. He never turned on the TV. Almost everything on it seemed stupid to him, including the news. When the boy turned on the cartoons and Monte was in the living room, he either left the room or made himself fall asleep. Falling asleep was easy – it was the waking up that was hard.

His daughter had had a lot of boyfriends. He made himself not think about that too much. He was no one to judge, but she had a history of making bad choices. Maybe she learned that from him. It made life pretty hard sometimes. And possibly dangerous. None of his business, but she had a kid to think of.

Pete, the current boyfriend, wasn't there much, either working late, or out hitting the bars, doing the kind of things guys of that age and type usually do. Guys like Pete didn't have much going for them. Monte had been a guy like Pete, pretty much. Monte guessed if he was healthier, he'd still be a guy like Pete. Monte guessed it was a good thing Pete was gone so much. He also guessed Pete was cheating on her. Something about the way Pete was when he came in late, the way he kissed her. And the way Pete talked about how much he'd had to do that day – just a little too eager. Monte recognized that particular performance. Shit, he practically invented it. Most men were terrible liars, transparent as hell. The only way a woman could buy such crap was because she *wanted* to. He figured his daughter was just desperate for the company. If she truly believed Pete's garbage, well then, she was worse off than Monte thought.

Monte could also see that Pete had a dangerous side. He just didn't know *how* dangerous. He watched the two of them together, even when they probably thought he was sleeping. They had arguments, some of them bad. Hearing his daughter cursing and shouting at her man made Monte angry, but he wasn't sure why. It was none of his business. And Pete sure deserved it. But she was aggravating Pete. Things were okay for now – there was a balance going on, but that could end any time. Monte had seen some bad things. But maybe this would be okay.

If they got too loud Monte would just turn up his radio. Everybody had a messy life. She didn't need Monte to defend her – she knew what she was getting into. He'd never met her boy's father, but he didn't need to. Monte reckoned he was the same kind of guy as Pete. One thing Monte knew about women – they stuck with what they knew.

The boy, his grandson, was a quiet boy, and a good boy. Seven years old. A great age, from the little Monte could remember. Monte had had a dog when he was about that age. Monte tried not to say too much to the boy because he was afraid he'd fuck him up. He didn't want to tell the boy it was all downhill from here – maybe it would turn out different for him. Monte didn't believe it would, but sometimes things surprised him.

"Take off those jeans and let me mend them," she said to the boy and the boy did as she asked without saying a word. The three of them were in the living room, Monte pretending to read the paper but he was actually more interested in his daughter's and the boy's conversation. The truth was there was never much interesting in the paper, just people behaving badly and he knew all he wanted to know about that.

The boy wore white Pooh underpants with red trim. His T-shirt had a picture of a honey pot on it. It looked kind of sissy but Monte didn't say anything.

His daughter sewed the tear in the left knee slowly and carefully using small stitches. Monte wondered if she'd learned that from her mother. "It's important that no matter how poor you are you don't go running around wearing torn clothes," his daughter told the boy. "Your grandpa taught me that. He wouldn't let *his* kids run around in torn clothes, no sir." She glanced at Monte then and he nodded at her. She'd made the whole thing up. Monte considered whether she could have learned that from her mother as well.

He thought about the boy – "his grandson" was the way somebody might say it. Somebody might ask him, "Is that your grandson?" and he'd have to say, "Yes." He couldn't say why exactly, but that was a pretty big deal. It surprised him that he could feel that way. But he couldn't stop thinking about the boy. He wondered if that meant he loved the boy. He didn't like thinking about that, it embarrassed him to think about that, but he couldn't help himself. It made him feel weak, but he'd been feeling weak for a very long time now, so maybe it didn't make any difference that he was weak. Weak was still better than dead, most of the time.

"Dad, why don't you tell Brian a goodnight story?"

"A goodnight story?"

"Brian, your grandpa is a great storyteller. When we were little he told us stories every night to help us go to sleep."

Why are you lying like this you stupid bitch? But Monte didn't say anything out loud. Brian walked slowly over to Monte's chair and sat down on the dark blue rug in front of him. The boy gazed up at him, waiting. Monte figured the boy must have heard lots of goodnight stories before and this was the way he'd been taught to listen to them.

Monte said to his daughter, "I don't know any stories."

"Sure you do, Dad. Everybody knows some stories."

The boy, his grandson, was still waiting. Monte frowned down at the boy, not knowing what to do. Monte started clearing his throat because something was there, something was in there bothering him.

Then he just began talking. "A long time back, when I was just a young man." He stopped and spoke to the boy. "I'm not going to say 'Once upon a time.' Is that okay by you?"

The boy said nothing and Monte took that for a yes. "I was older than you, Brian. But I didn't have a wife yet, or kids. I was a *teenager*, I guess." He glanced over at his daughter, who was watching him so seriously he felt embarrassed and angry, so he looked away. "I never thought I'd have kids. I never thought much of anything, past the particular day. I was never a planner." He stopped.

The boy appeared to be listening intently, but Monte knew he'd already screwed up. This was no way to tell a kid's story.

"But I had a serious problem. I guess you could say I had a *giant* problem." Monte felt himself dripping with sweat. But the kid seemed more interested. "There was a giant in my life, tall as a house, wide as a four lane highway. And that giant, he was always getting in my way, hassling me. He never had a good word to say about me, or anybody else. And if you objected to anything he said, you'd get the back of his hand, broad as an elephant's backside, right in your face. Sometimes he'd hit you so hard you'd be flying right into – "

He paused, glanced at his daughter, who was staring at him. He couldn't tell if she approved or disapproved of his story – most likely she didn't much care for it. But she'd asked for it, hadn't she?

"You'd be flying right into Never-Never land. Leastways, I think that's what they called it. Anyway, this went on for some years. Some days the giant would be nice as pie. Apple Pie, I reckon, since that was always my favorite. But most days he was just this big monster of a thing you'd best stay away from. And on the worst days he would chase me around the house and when I got mad about that he'd say I was really in for it. He'd say he had special plans for me that I wasn't going to like at all. Well, I had seen some examples of his special plans, and no sir, they weren't nice things for anybody to have to go through."

Monte looked at his daughter again, thinking *Okay, you wanted me to do this. See what happened?* But he couldn't tell at all what she was thinking, which was really no surprise. He wondered if he'd gone too far, but the boy didn't look scared. The boy seemed very interested.

"That was when I knew I had to do something. I had to do something to protect myself. Of course, killing is a bad thing, an *evil* thing. It's something a person should only do when they *have* to, to protect themselves or the ones they... They love."

Monte stopped, trying to think out the rest of the story. He knew his daughter was watching him closely, but he avoided eye contact.

"But it's okay to kill an evil giant, isn't it? If I remember right, that's what Jack did in *his* story. Well, in *my* story I knew I had to do pretty much the same thing. I was small for my age. A lot like you, Brian. I was a tough little beggar, but I wouldn't say I was strong. There's a difference. No, I wasn't what you would call strong.

"But you don't have to be strong to kill a giant, Brian. You don't even have to be big. You just have to be... *Persistent*, that's the word for what you have to be. That means you have to keep trying. You keep at it and you keep at it until finally that job is done.

"So I was persistent, Brian. That giant drank a lot. I think a lot of giants drink a lot. Giants just have giant appetites, I guess. And one night that giant drank so much he fell fast asleep. And then I saw my chance. I went into the kitchen. I was still in my pajamas. I went into the kitchen and I opened the drawer and I found a giant knife. A giant knife for a giant." Monte tried to laugh but it sounded fake. It sounded high and strangled and not like his regular laugh at all. "And I took that giant knife and I carried it into the giant's bedroom. The giant snored like most giants, so loud it made the walls and floors and my own chest shake. It even made my hands shake.

"Then I climbed up on the giant's bed with the knife and I just kept at it. I kept at it and I kept at it until that giant was dead. End of story."

Monte glanced down at the boy and saw that he was asleep on the floor. And he didn't look worried. If anything it appeared he had a little smile on his face. Monte's daughter went over and picked up the boy and carried him into his bedroom.

When his daughter got back she said, "That was quite a story, Dad."

"I think you must have heard some of that story before. Maybe from your mother."

"Maybe," she replied. "Why did you tell him that story, anyway?" She averted her gaze.

Can't look me in the eye, Monte thought. "Don't do that, honey," he said.

She appeared surprised. Monte tried to remember if he'd ever called her 'honey' before. He didn't think so. He figured that's what surprised her.

"What are you talking about?"

"I think you *know* that's my only story, the only one I have to tell. I think you knew it was my only story when you asked me to tell him one. I think the question should be why you wanted me to tell him that story."

Pete got home during the middle of the night. Monte didn't know what time – he had no watch, or clock of any kind. He just woke up to a bunch of stomping, and cursing, and things getting knocked around, breaking.

He had to use the bathroom bad, but he didn't want to walk out there in the middle of all that. It wasn't like he could do it quick and sneak back into bed. Everything took him a long time to do. He just hoped he wouldn't pee the bed again, or soak these old man pajamas that did a pretty good job of keeping him warm. The last time his daughter didn't say a word – just took the wet sheets out of his hands and went to wash them. It shamed him something terrible, but she could have made it worse and didn't.

But the yelling and the throwing went on another half-hour or more, and Monte was fit to burst. His daughter was crying and he could ignore that, or almost, but he couldn't ignore his bladder. He crawled out of bed as quick as he could, but already he could feel himself leaking a little. So he redoubled his efforts to hold it in, shuffling down the hall toward the bathroom all bent over like he was a hundred years old.

Monte didn't intend to look at anything, just make a bee-line for that bathroom; that is, if the bee was old and arthritic and the slowest bee that still lived. But he was a little confused by the hall, and the shadows, and all the noise. So he found himself peeking into doorways as he passed, trying to remember where the bathroom was, and that's when he saw Pete standing in the living room, his daughter lying on the floor with her mouth bleeding, and little Brian standing on the other side of the room, wedged into the corner, crying, a big red mark tearing down one side of his face.

"Well, if it ain't the man of *leisure!*" Pete called drunkenly. "You best get on with what you were doing, old man!"

Monte's groin buzzed with the pain. But he stopped, thinking about it. Was he just going to go on down to the bathroom and pee? And then what? What could he say when he got back? Or would he just hide out in the bathroom until it was all over? Hell of a thing. He gazed at Brian, who had his hands up over his face now, but still watching with one shocked white eye. Right then the only sound in the room was his daughter's torn breathing.

Monte shuffled a couple of feet into the room, still bent over. To his alarm, he began to cry from the pain.

"Hey, old man, what did I tell you? I pay for the roof over your head – you realize that, don't you? I pay for both of them, too. Why do you think she's here? Because I *pay*! She's a whore and he's just a bastard!"

Monte, still bent over, spit on the floor. "You're not even worth their shit," he said.

Monte didn't see it coming, but he felt the thunder of it. Suddenly he was on the floor, his side and his back on fire from a series of Pete's clumsy but enraged blows. He thought he could feel the blood pooling out under him, then realized he'd pissed himself. He turned his head to the side to avoid the spreading wet stink, which allowed him to watch Pete take a swift kick into his daughter's side as he passed her, on his way to grabbing Brian – hysterical now – by the arm and jerking him into the bedroom. Monte lay perfectly still as the piss spread to his cheek, watching through the open bedroom door as Pete stripped the boy naked and beat on him with a belt. There might have been worse, but he couldn't see it all, so he tried not to think that far. He closed his eyes.

The odd thing was, in the past Monte might have fantasized what he was going to do to Pete later, if he could have. At least he would be figuring out who he could call, who might do the job for next to no money. Monte didn't know men like that anymore, but he knew there were always men like that.

But those fantasies were bullshit. He'd never find anybody. Nobody was going to do anything like that for him anymore. Nobody was taking him seriously about a damn thing.

So he thought about things he *could* do. And Monte thought maybe he could kill the boy. Monte was old and weak but he could still probably kill a seven year old boy. If he was determined enough. If it would save that boy some of the pains seven-year-olds had no business to know, but that Monte knew all about.

Monte woke up the next morning in his bed, naked, feeling like he'd fallen down a rocky mountainside. When he moved he felt a sharp pain near his left shoulder blade, but he discovered that if he held his body a certain way, keeping that shoulder slightly back behind the rest of him, he could sit up and swing his legs around without too much pain. He had a vague memory of picking himself up, like picking up an armful of broken branches, and wandering down the hall, finding his room, fumbling with the light switch, stripping out of his stinking pajamas and boxers, leaving them on the floor just inside the door, as far away from the bed as he could think of. Crawling under the blankets so carefully, thinking that something was going to tear open if he wasn't as careful as he could possibly be.

He didn't think he had turned off his bedroom light. But it was off now, and what appeared to be his cleaned pajamas and boxers lay neatly folded on top of the dresser, along with some towels, a basin of water, wash cloths, giant bar of soap, a big bottle of peroxide.

It took awhile to clean himself up, and he didn't have a mirror, but he wasn't entering any pageants this year, so that would have to do. It took him even longer to get himself dressed, and he wasn't able to struggle into his shirt without some hellacious pain. But he managed. His daughter's message was pretty clear – in this house you took care of your damage before you left your bedroom. Then you put a smile on your face and you walked out the door. Which he did, more or less. What he wore on his face wasn't exactly a smile, but it would have to do.

His daughter was in the kitchen, bent over the sink, palms flat on the counter to either side. "You okay?" he asked.

"Sure." She spoke without turning. "Got to sleep a little late. We all did. Brian's still in bed."

His eyes found the wall clock. It was a Mexican-looking thing: brightly-painted clay rooster with a clock face in the center. It was after ten. "Brian's not going to school? And you're not going in to the restaurant?"

"Brian's feeling a little under the weather. I think we *all* could use a day off, don't you?"

Monte took it wrong at first. *Man of leisure.* Then he realized that wasn't the way she meant it. "Brian okay?"

"Sure. Brian'll be fine. Sit down, Dad. Let me make you some breakfast."

She jammed two pieces of bread into the toaster, broke two eggs on the edge of the skillet and got it sizzling, went searching through the fridge. "No fresh-squeezed OJ, Dad. An orange okay?" Her voice muffled, throaty.

"Sure. It's all great. Should I go say hello to Brian?"

"No, Dad. Just stay here and eat your breakfast."

She had mastered her mother's tone. She hadn't meant it as a suggestion. Monte sat with his elbows on the table, then moved them and folded his hands into his lap, while she dropped the eggs and toast onto a plate, filled a glass full of water, carried it all to the table, the orange balanced in the crook of her elbow.

He watched her as she placed everything on the placemat in front of him. The silverware had already been laid out on a perfectly folded napkin. Her neck had dark purple and green bruises on both sides, strangulation marks, a crust of blood just inside her right nostril.

"That looks bad," he said. "Where is he now?"

"Let's don't talk about it. He's still sleeping it off." She locked eyes with him. She had the look of a stern child, one too old for her years. She sat down across the table from him.

"I'll need a knife for the orange," he said.

"Oh. Sorry." She started to open a kitchen drawer, stopped. She left the kitchen, coming back minutes later with something wrapped in newspaper. She put it down beside his plate. "Happy birthday," she said.

He looked at the package, reluctant to touch it. "What makes you think it's my birthday?" he asked.

"Isn't it?" She seemed suddenly bored, or depressed.

"No. Not unless I forgot."

"It doesn't make any difference, Dad. Do you remember my birthday?"

He thought a few seconds, even though he knew what he was going to have to say. "No. But I remember the day you were born."

"Oh?" Still bored. "What was that like?"

"Scary. I'd never been that close to a baby. Didn't want to pick you up because I was afraid your arms might break off."

"That's stupid, Dad."

Maybe he should have taken offense at this, but he didn't. "Yeah. I was stupid. I just couldn't see the human being in you. If you were talking, maybe, but with you just making those baby sounds, and crying all the time, and needing God-knows-what to keep you alive, I just didn't know what to do with you."

"So you left."

"So I left." He stared at his food. "Sorry."

"Don't say you're sorry, Dad. Just unwrap your package so you can eat your orange."

He examined the newspaper, then tore it away. Inside was a wicked looking thing. "A hunting knife?" It wasn't really a question.

"Now you can cut your orange."

Monte kept thinking that wasn't the right way to use a good hunting knife, and this was a good one, he could tell. It had a polished bone handle, the blade shiny as a new car.

"Something wrong?"

"No, no it's great." He put the orange on the plate. The knife went through it like it wasn't there. Monte felt himself grin involuntarily, then stopped it. What was wrong with him? It was a silly present, he obviously had no use for it, but it excited him just the same.

"Good. Maybe you'll get some use out of it," she said, and got up, grabbed the skillet and a scouring pad, started cleaning up.

Like he'd ever go hunting again, or fishing for that matter. She was a stupid girl. He didn't understand how that could be. His wife had been a smart woman. Maybe she got the stupid from him.

He thought about his daughter's present while he finished his breakfast, and he sat there for a while afterwards thinking about it while she continued to clean the kitchen. He didn't even know what she was cleaning anymore. It all appeared spotless to him. He thought about the boyfriend sleeping in the other room and he thought about his grandson and what he had considered doing to the boy. And he thought about his daughter bringing him here to live with her, saying how he had always taken care of her, when she knew full well he hadn't taken care of her at all. He thought about why in the world she'd want a man like him around when she already had a man too much like him in the other room sleeping it off. He thought about all of these things until he couldn't think anymore.

"Lacey," he said. She turned around, surprised. He knew she was surprised because he'd used her name, and he didn't do that often. "Lacey, I want you to wrap a scarf around your neck and take your son out for some ice cream. He'll feel better once he gets some ice cream in him."

His daughter watched him a few seconds, then she said, "Okay, Dad."

The boy was groggy and-red faced but wasn't unwilling to go. His jacket was too big for him and Monte thought his daughter really ought to do something about some better-fitting clothes. Before they left, his grandson turned to him and waved. "Bye, Grandpa," he said. Monte raised his hand a bit. His daughter rushed the boy out without a backward glance.

Monte didn't know what was going to happen. You get past a certain age and it seems like you never know what's going to happen. He was old, and he was weak, but he could still lie down on top of somebody with a knife in his hand. He slowly made his way down the hall. He might be old but he was a tough old beggar. He was *persistent*. He'd stay at it and stay at it until the job got done.

ALISON J. LITTLEWOOD

4 A.M., WHEN THE WALLS ARE THINNEST

Stumpy Ellis told a lot of stories about how he lost his thumb, and they always seemed to involve violence, and grinding, and eyes. I was the only one who heard the real story, and I never would have told. Stumpy had a temper, and a man with a temper in prison is like a powder keg in a room full of lit matches.

He had a shine in his eyes, Stumpy Ellis: a cold, dangerous kind of shine. It was like seeing a flat, wide sky in there, a grey sky, although the sun was shining in the yard when he stuck out his hand – the one with only half a thumb – and asked if I had a smoke. I looked at those eyes and took a cigarette from my pocket, without seeing what he had to trade. If I'd learned one thing inside, it was when to resist and when to bend.

He muttered around the cig in his mouth, to my back.

"Payment."

I turned and waved his words away: no problem.

"I always pay," he said. "I always pay and I always expect to be paid. Sit down."

I felt stiffness working up my back and into my knuckles, but he sat down himself, so I sat next to him and smelled the burning in his lungs.

"I'll tell you a story," he said. "As payment."

I waited.

He thrust out his hand in front of me, palm down, but I didn't jump. Another thing I learned in prison: it doesn't pay to be jumpy.

"See that?" he said, and I grunted. His left thumb was missing from the first knuckle to the tip, leaving a thick, blunt, flexible mound.

"Want to know how I did that?"

I grunted again.

"There was a guy thought he could cross me," said Stumpy. "We worked together for a while. Building jobs, mainly. I'd get the business in, he'd mobilise the troops. Whoever was hiring us, they paid me, and I paid him. Only this one time, he came to me, he said, 'Ellis, help me out. I need something extra.'"

He glanced at me, so I nodded.

"He took the money and the next time I see him, he's coming out of the jewellers, and he sees me and he turns red-faced. And I knew, you know? You don't fool Stumpy Ellis. Not when it comes to his missus.

"A picture, my missus." He breathed out a long, jagged breath of smoke as he laughed. "Blonde. Tits out here. Legs up here." He stared off into the distance, pulling hard on the cigarette.

"I didn't follow him, didn't need to. Told him I was off to see about a job, something out of town. And then I doubled round and went home. Knew as soon as I got there. Window was open, and this laughing floating out."

I nodded, wondering why he would tell this story, why it didn't bother him what his wife had done.

"She had him on his back when I got there. Her arse stuck up in the air." He sucked noisily on the cigarette. "Know what I mean?"

I nodded.

"Got the shock of her life when I shoved her off the bed. Took half of it with her, and her looking all wide-eyed and surprised, trying to tell me she didn't do nothing, with his blood running down her chin."

He laughed, but I didn't.

"So he was there, practically begging, so I start punching, and she's digging in the cabinet and comes at me with the gun."

I raised my eyebrows.

"My gun. My own gun. Keep it for...special occasions, you know? And she's holding it with her hands shaking everywhere, and screaming, and then she points it in the air, only she's still shaking, and then she squeezes too hard and she fires it. And the only person more surprised than her is me, 'cause half my thumb's gone, and there's blood everywhere. All over the sheets, all over me, and all over the little prick who started it all. And I figure, she's my missus, and what sort of a man hits his missus? So I turns round to him, my old mate, and he's laughing at me. 'See that?' he says, and his voice is high as a girl's. 'See that?' And he keeps looking at me and laughing."

He stubbed out the cigarette, then spread his hand and stared at his thumb. "Put his eye out," he said.

"What?"

"I said I put his eye out." He hooked his thumb and mimed gouging. "Didn't even feel it. My thumb all covered in blood, and half missing, and I didn't even feel it. Seems it wanted it, you see. My thumb knew what it wanted and it took it."

He looked up. "Fucker never looked at my wife again." He spluttered laughter and nudged me in the ribs.

I laughed. It wasn't funny, but I laughed anyway.

He nudged me again. "See him?" He indicated an older man, thin, with white hair. He walked in a wide circle around the yard, his eyes fixed on the ground. "Librarian," Stumpy said and chuckled. "If you want to know anything, ask a librarian. He's the one'll get you out of here."

"What?" I said.

"What, he says. Escape, that's what. That's the man'll show you how. Just climb right out." He gave a dry laugh. "Climb right out."

I waited for him to say something else, but he shook himself.

"Another story," he said, and stood. "You'll have to pay me for that one. You'll have to pay me good." And he walked off without saying anything else, swaggering his way across the yard just as the guard called time.

I knew Stumpy hadn't told me the real story about his thumb, and I didn't care. What he'd said about escape, though; it stuck in my mind, and that was dangerous. Curiosity could get you killed in prison as well as anywhere else.

I didn't approach Stumpy again, but when I got my lunch I saw an empty seat by the librarian, and I took it. If Stumpy knew something, he was a middleman. I didn't deal with middlemen.

I nodded to the white haired man next to me. "Si Jameson," I said to him in a low voice. "Short for Simon." He glanced at me, looked away, and said nothing.

"Hear you're the librarian," I said, but he went on grinding something over and over in his teeth.

"If you want to know anything, ask a – " I began again, but he stood, pushing his chair back so hard it rocked on two legs before slamming down behind him. He picked up his tray and was gone.

It took a moment for the sound of eating to resume, the scrape of cutlery, the low buzz of conversation. I didn't realise Stumpy had sat on the other side of me until I heard his voice.

"He won't give it up, that one," he said. "You can't just introduce yourself to the librarian."

I almost laughed, then remembered the flat metal shine in Stumpy's eyes, and swallowed it down.

"You have to earn it," he said. "It don't come cheap."

"What does he want?"

"Ah," Stumpy said, smiling around a mouthful of sausage and mash. "Not like that. Smokes and money, they won't cut it. You have to do something for him."

"What?" I said, although the real question, the one I was thinking, was 'why?' He was nothing but an old man who spent his days sorting battered paperbacks.

"Nothing you can do for him, not in here. On the outside, though. Once you get out."

Stumpy sat back in his seat and pushed his tray back with a scrape. "Old scores," he said. "You might have noticed, but in here old scores go around and around. They don't break up and they don't fade. Just go round and round in a man's head, never getting any smaller. Looking for payment. And him, he'll never get out. He's a lifer, like you."

"Why doesn't he just climb out?" I said, and smiled.

Stumpy grinned. "He'll never leave, not that one. He likes it here. He's fed, he's watered. Says he'd be happy to stay here forever, only he's scared someone would notice eventually."

I snorted. I guess the shine in Stumpy's eyes didn't seem so dangerous when he wasn't looking straight at me. And I had been wrong to ask, wrong to even think about getting out. Some people shouldn't think about some things, and I was one of them. I'd forgotten that, all for one stir-crazy psycho and an old man – the joke was on me, that's all.

But Stumpy was off again. He waved a hand and the whole table turned to listen. "But anyway," he said. "Did I ever tell you the story of how I lost my thumb?"

There were groans, splutters, and laughter. He began, some story about how he'd had the tip of his thumb removed because it was easier to grind out a man's eye that way, because it was shorter, squatter, stronger. And I knew that this wasn't the real story either, but I also knew something else: if anyone got to hear that story, the real story, it was going to be me.

I didn't say anything, though. I just sat and ate and listened, because prison was like that. You learned when it was time to wait. You did a lot of waiting: I guess you got a feel for it.

I left Stumpy alone after that, but I always had cigarettes in my pocket, so I was ready the next time he put his hand out in the yard and asked me for a smoke.

"Never leave home without them," I said, and passed one over.

"You don't even smoke," he said, "but I'll help you out, don't you worry. You don't even have to pay me." He scraped a match on the ground and lit the cig, shielding it against the breeze, which blew occasional spits of rain in our faces.

I was about to walk away when he gestured towards something. "He's never short," he said.

I turned and saw the librarian sitting on the ground nearby. His knees were drawn up under his chin, his posture that of a younger man. His eyes were a pale, piercing blue.

Then I saw him reach out with one hand and he did something with his fingers. I couldn't quite see what it was: some kind of twist, some kind of flurry, and I lost sight of his hand for a split second. Then it was back and the librarian put a cigarette to his lips. It was lit, and battered looking, half smoked.

"Never lacks for anything, that one," Stumpy said. "Just reaches out and takes it."

I shook my head. I couldn't see how he'd done it, and I didn't know what to say.

"Climb right out," said Stumpy. "That's what he says, only I don't quite have it yet. But one day I will. They'll wake up and I'll be gone." He turned to me, eyes agleam. "I'll show you," he said. "You'll be there. You can listen, anyway, and you'll know I've done it. I'm moving cell."

I raised my eyebrows and he nodded. "Guard owes me a favour. I'm moving tonight."

"What do you mean?" I asked. "About climbing out. You got a plan?"

He shook his head, narrowing his eyes against the smoke of his cigarette. "Don't need a plan," he said. "I've got a book. *His* book." He nodded towards the librarian. "And I made a promise. Got a score to settle."

There was something about the way he looked. "Is it true?" I asked. "Are you going?"

He shook himself. "Everything I tell you is true," he said. "Didn't I tell you how I lost my thumb?" And he was away, waving the stub of his cigarette in the air, his eyes flat and grey and staring off into the distance, focused on nothing I could see. He told me how he'd lost his thumb when he ground it so deep into a man's eye it severed against the skull. The man had been screwing his wife, who was tall and brunette and had tits Stumpy paid a year's salary for.

When Stumpy pulled his thumb out of the man's eye he left the tip behind, protruding from the socket, all the evidence the pigs needed to put him away.

That afternoon I lay on my bunk, staring at the ceiling. I wasn't sharing but had taken the top bunk, so the ceiling was close. I listened to the quiet from below and the noise from the corridor, the banging, half shouts, the footsteps.

I heard when Stumpy moved into the cell next to mine. He was talking to the guards, loud and cheery and familiar. Setting things down, doors sliding and slamming. Then, after it had gone quiet for a while, I heard his voice at my door.

"Come in?" he said.

"Be my guest."

He came in, his walk quiet and steady. His jauntiness had gone. I sat up on the bunk, and when I saw his face, I jumped down. "Smoke?" I offered.

He waved his hand. "Not this time. This one's on the house." He turned and his eyes looked pale, the shine in them absent, leaving them watery and somehow naked.

"I... I thought someone should know," he said. "I'm going, later. Tonight. I thought you should know." He pushed something into my hand. It was a crumpled photograph of a woman. She looked about forty, her hair mousy, her clothes nondescript. She had a good smile and laughter lines around her eyes and no kind of tits at all.

"My wife," he said. "That's my wife." He looked down and I saw that his eyes were full of tears.

"I got her a gardener," he said. "I got her a house and a big garden, and she was always going on about it, so I got her a gardener. But she kept saying how she wanted this gazebo, a love seat she said..." He paused. "A love seat, and I couldn't expect a gardener to build, she said. I was the builder, and she wanted me to do it.

"So I did, I got this – this – gazebo. A stupid word for a stupid thing. It was just a frame that wouldn't even keep the rain off, and a bench. Big enough for two, she said."

I didn't say anything.

"So I started putting it together, only the damn thing wouldn't go straight. And I was nailing one side together when the other one slipped, and it fell, right on my thumb." He looked at his hand.

"Blood everywhere," he said. "And I screamed. She took me to hospital, and they took the end off. But she kept looking at me, like, I dunno..."

I waited.

"She looked at me like I was a little kid who'd wet his pants, you know? All the time. Like I'd let her down. And then later, when we got home – later, after – when they took me away. She looked at me then, too. Like something the dog had shat out on the carpet. She looked.

"The last time I saw her, and she looked at me like that. She never visited me, you know. Never did, not once." His face twisted. "She said she was leaving. I was in the fucking hospital, and she tells me this. She'd been seeing him. Her and the fucking gardener. All the time. Fucking."

I put my hand on his arm, and he looked at it, and shook it off.

"I sorted it," he said. "I sorted him. I had a gun, remember me telling you that? And they took me away and they put me in here. But I'm not staying. I'm going to see her again."

He punched his fist into his palm, over and over. "I can still see her," he said. "The way she looked at me with those eyes. Those eyes."

He sat there for a long time. Finally, he stood and turned to me, although he still wasn't looking at anything, not really.

"You know, people think it's just a bit of your thumb," he said. "But it hurt. It hurt."

He walked out of my cell, then. That was the last time I saw Stumpy Ellis alive.

*

I woke, staring into the dark. I got the feeling something had woken me, but I didn't know what. The night was full of noises. Men muttering to themselves; rasping snores; guards' voices; metal on metal. Prison is never silent, even at night. It was one of the things I missed about the outside – real silence.

Then there was an almighty, shocking bang from the cell next to mine. And a shudder, as though I could feel whatever it was through the walls, the floor, the bunk. The banging noise seemed to hang in the air, echoing.

After that came a wet splatter. Like rain, heavy droplets landing on concrete. It seemed to go on for a long time.

Prison was never quiet at night, but it was quiet then, like never before or since. The texture of the air grew heavy with listening, turning to grey speckles before my eyes.

I was the one who broke the silence.

"Stumpy?" I said. "Stumpy? You there?" and there was nothing, not one sound coming back. Not one.

I slipped down from my bunk and went to the bars, looked out into the corridor. There was a wet gleam on the floor outside Stumpy's cell. I couldn't see any further. But I heard the footsteps of the guards come running. They stopped. Then I heard the splatter of one of them losing their lunch outside Stumpy's cell.

"They say his insides turned to soup," someone said. "As though he'd taken a dive off a building. Everything smashed up."

"They say his skull shattered."

"Every bone in his body, broken, just like that."

"He must have jumped off his bunk, only they say it wasn't high enough to do that kind of damage. Even if he'd hung from the ceiling, it wasn't high enough for that kind of damage."

It was lunchtime, and it was all anyone could talk about, although I said nothing at all. I just kept replaying those sounds in my head, the bang echoing on and on, and the long splatter that came afterward. The thing Stumpy said, over and over: "Climb right out. That's what I'm going to do. Just climb right out." And the way his eyes had shone when he said it.

I kept glancing around, looking for the librarian. But he was nowhere to be seen.

*

It was late before they allowed us back to our cells, and when they did there was a black cloth hanging across Stumpy's bars. It must have been some kind of mess in there if they felt they had to hide it from the likes of us.

I climbed into my bunk and tried not to listen to the silence coming from the next room, but I did, for a long time.

Something woke me later. It was deep night and my head was thick with the confusion of it, night seeping in through my eyes and ears. Then came a distant snore and I remembered where I was. If there was one thing I wanted on the outside, it was to sleep somewhere out of earshot of other men's snores.

I looked into the dark, the walls and the bunk taking shape. I looked at the door of my cell. As I watched, the lock pulled back with a loud metallic clang.

After a time, I resumed breathing. The door was unlocked, but no one came to lock it again. It was just there in the dark, an open door, and no one to stop me walking out. Except of course there were guards at the end of the corridor, more locked doors.

All the same, I slipped down off the bunk and went to the door. I didn't touch it, though, not at first. I put out a hand, saw the thick, open bolt, but didn't touch it. When nothing happened I gave the door a gentle push. It moved easily under my hand, sliding without a sound.

I put my head out into the corridor. I could see a shape further down, a door, more bars, dim light, long shadows. And then I saw the dull mark on the concrete outside Stumpy's cell, a dark stain where the wet gleam had been. I moved out further and saw the curtain hanging across his cell suddenly fall, billowing as it filled with air, finding its way to the floor.

Stumpy's cell was much the same as mine. The same bunk, the same box for a wardrobe. But everything covered in those same dark spatters. The curtain came to rest on the floor, leaving humped whorls and shapes. At first it seemed there was the shape of a body beneath it, but then it settled and was only a curtain.

I looked at the bars and saw that Stumpy's door, too, was open.

I stood and swallowed for a while. Then I went in, trying not to step on that stain in my shoeless feet.

There was stuff all over the floor, and those little number tags the forensics boys put down before they take pictures. It was like seeing two rooms: the one that had been over, investigated, and underneath it, the room where Stumpy lived and slept and shat. Used to, I corrected myself. There was a radio on the floor, and I half expected the little dial to light and some song to creep into the room, under my feet, and that was when the hairs on my arms started to prickle. But it didn't light up, it didn't make a sound. I looked some more. Stumpy's uniform hanging in the box, just like mine. His stuff underneath that, a couple of pictures, a newspaper, a book.

A book.

I picked my way over there, half expecting to hear the door lock behind me, but nothing happened. I just went over there and nothing happened and I picked up the book. The cover was some kind of cloth, rough under my fingers. I ran my hand over it and felt grooves, lettering I couldn't make out. A dark sliver of thread was tucked into the pages. I stroked the cover. A stain had soaked into it and I pulled my hand away. My thumb felt damp, just the tip, and I stared at it.

I turned, and that was when I saw the rope. It hung there in the middle of the room. When I looked straight at it, though, it was gone.

I tilted my head. I could feel those prickles again, but this time they ran all the way down my back, like little hands, unwelcome hands.

I started to edge my way back out of the cell, trying not to step in anything that looked wet. All the time I looked at that space in the middle of the room. Looked up. The ceiling was featureless. There was nothing to hang a rope from. Anyway, it had been low down, as though hanging upward from the floor, just a few of feet of it and then nothing.

As I pieced it together in my mind I thought I saw it again, just for a moment.

My arm pressed up against the cell door and I almost cried out. I tucked the book under my arm and slipped out of Stumpy's cell, down the corridor and back into my room. I tucked the book under the sheets of the bottom bunk and climbed into bed, pulled the sheets over my body, and lay awake, this time trying not to think of the book, somewhere beneath me in the dark.

The book was a joke, it had to be. I turned it over in my hands. There was no stamp inside, nothing to show it belonged to the prison library, no publisher's mark. The first pages were blank. All of them were yellowed and foxed, the edges rough and uneven. Inside the writing was tiny, and it was in script: handwritten, not printed. The ink had faded to a pale brown.

The pages seemed to be full of magic tricks. There were small, hand-drawn diagrams of cards and dice and coins. Coffin shaped boxes and saws. Ropes and knots and means of escaping them. And there, on the page with the fabric bookmark, *The Indian Rope Trick and Secrets Thereof.*

How to make space where there is no space, rope where there is no rope. How to feel with your mind for what you need, and reach out and take it. There was a lot of stuff about dimensions, about how the things you needed were all there, somewhere. Somewhere there was a rope, somewhere, a door. About bending things with your mind, until what's there is also here.

Think of a reason, it said. Think of a reason and the rope will answer. Hold it in your mind as you climb, and the rope will not fail. Hold it in your mind: not the rope itself, or the journey, but the destination.

At the bottom, a note had been added. It was in rough, spiky writing and blue ink, and I could almost picture Stumpy forming the letters, his tongue poking out of his mouth: *Go at 4.00 a.m., when the walls are thinnest.*

I snapped the book closed and stared at the wall of my cell. Smiled and shook my head, as though Stumpy was having one last laugh. *"Did I ever tell you how I lost my thumb?"*

And then I started to dream of it, walking with my back straight, looking people in the eye, a free man. Tasting the air. Just – climbing out. Climbing right on out. And a rope, seen for a moment from the corner of my eye, hanging from nothing in the middle of a cell.

Think of a reason and the rope will answer.

What reason had Stumpy that could be strong enough? All he had was revenge. I saw again the way he talked about his wife, and eyes, and grinding, all the time staring at that thumb of his. His obsession. But it hadn't been strong enough to get him out.

I had no thoughts of revenge. Everyone I hated was already dead. I had no love either, no one waiting. So I tried to think about why. And what came into my mind was a park, a soft, green park, where people sat in the sun. They splotched the grass in twos or threes or fours, talking and laughing, the girls wearing white halter-tops so you could see their shapes beneath. I stood there. I would stand there, and I would turn my face up to the sun, and breathe. Only that.

His insides had turned to soup.

In the cell next to mine was a rope. It hung in the air beneath a blank ceiling.

I looked again at the book and in that second, just in the corner of my eye, it looked as though the tip of my thumb was gone. My left thumb, from the middle knuckle to the nail, leaving only a thick, flexible stump.

I pulled my hand back, dropping the book. I should burn the thing, I thought. Take a match, strike it on the concrete floor, and burn the damn thing right here in my cell. But I didn't strike the match, and I didn't burn it. What I did was slip it back beneath the sheets of the bottom bunk, then sat down, and stared at the wall for a long time.

Some people shouldn't think of some things, I knew that. I was one of those people. Waiting: I was good at waiting.

But somewhere, in the cell next to mine, was a rope. *Go at 4.00 a.m., when the walls are thinnest.* I swallowed.

However stupid the idea of the rope, it was too late. I knew I couldn't let it go, and it wouldn't let go of me.

The cell door wouldn't open. I tried to slide it, and it wouldn't move. I got my weight behind it and pushed, hard, but it wouldn't move. Of all the things that occurred to me might go wrong, I never once thought that the door wouldn't open.

I glanced at the clock. It was 4.03 a.m.

Kicked the door. It still wouldn't open.

I sat down on the bottom bunk, and felt the book beneath the sheets. All the air went out of me and I sat like that, my head down, for what seemed a long time. When I looked at the clock again, though, it said 4.07.

The rope, I thought. I had to get to the rope. Now, when the walls were thinnest. I reached out and put my palm to the wall between my cell and Stumpy's. It felt thick and solid and cold.

And then it came to me: it had to be mine. Whatever this was, whatever crazy game, it had to be my reason and my rope.

I closed my eyes and saw the park. A group of kids were playing Frisbee by the lake. The Frisbee span, too high, out over the water – and was snatched from the air by a young lad, who fell back to earth, laughing.

I opened my eyes and the rope was there. It hung in the middle of the floor, a strong, thick rope, in a little pool of spring light. I dropped to the floor and knelt by it, but I didn't touch it, not yet. I put my hand into that light, feeling it on my skin.

And then I saw my hand, really saw it, and drew in a sharp, hissing breath.

My thumb was gone. My left thumb. Not all of it, just the part from the middle knuckle to the tip.

I turned it in the light and it was a short, thick stump. Pulled it out and my hand was whole again. I grabbed the rope, pulled on it, and it held. It was a strong rope, a good rope. But there was a sour, sick taste in the back of my throat, and I wondered just how far away Stumpy was.

Dimensions, the book had said. Bending things with your mind, so that what is there is also here. What if Stumpy didn't fall, not really? What if he climbed until he found a door, only it didn't lead to a park, or a house, or a gazebo: it led to a place a little like this, and through the door was someone a little like him. And he bent things with his mind, and turned them, and he changed places.

Because at this time of night, at 4.00 a.m., it seemed the walls between were thin. I could feel it, like I could taste that sour taste in my mouth. They were thin, and in that moment, it didn't seem like Stumpy had gone very far at all.

I swallowed. Stumpy believed in payment. You always had to pay for things, even if it was just a story. It was what he saw as right, his way of slapping meaning on the world. What had he said? *"I always pay. I always pay and I always expect to be paid."*

Now I had to pay. I had Stumpy's book, after all. And I thought of his wife with the gardener, grinning, laughing, while Stumpy worked on her gazebo, making a love seat just big enough for two. I closed my eyes, and thought of hitting, and eyes, and grinding. And in the middle of it all, a rope.

I thought then how lucky it was that Stumpy had shown me that picture, the photograph of his wife; how lucky it was I knew what she looked like. Because I had a feeling I'd be paying her a visit real soon. And then we'd have a chat, a quiet little chat, me and Stumpy's wife. Payment.

I looked up, swallowed hard, trying to get rid of that taste, and I tried the rope once more. It was solid. So I took hold, and lifted my feet from the floor and wrapped them around it. I closed my eyes, then opened them again, but didn't look down. I saw only that park, the sunshine, felt the clean air in my lungs. I saw them, and held them in my mind, and I started to climb.

JOEL LANE
THE HOSTESS

Not long after I moved to Birmingham in the 1980s, a family feud led to one of the worst crimes in my experience. It happened in Digbeth, an old industrial district now taken over by warehouses and wholesale businesses. The narrow backstreets and rotting factories hid a multitude of stolen goods. But most of the actual crimes happened elsewhere. The Digbeth police station was busier with drunks fighting in the Barrel Organ and the Railway Tavern than with professional villains.

For two decades, the O'Kane family had been significant players in the black economy of Digbeth. They were a family of craftsmen: one could hide the pieces of a stolen car in another dozen vehicles, another could work stolen gold and silver into brand new jewellery. Three of them had done time, but they were a close family and we'd have needed something much nastier to put them out of business. I think the Digbeth team had a sneaking respect for their dedicated work on the wrong side of the disused tracks.

The Marin family were something else again. New money, well-spoken, an attitude you could break a glass on. The three brothers formed the core of an under-achieving but vicious gang that specialised in drugs and prostitutes. Its informal office was the back table of the Bar Selona, a dive frequented by people who'd been banned from the Little Moscow. There were some severe beatings around that time, of men we knew to be involved in similar business. But the victims weren't talking even when their mouths healed.

I saw the youngest Marin brother one night in the Railway Tavern, when I was relaxing off-duty at a rhythm and blues gig. The band finished late, and when I came out of the function room a lock-in was in progress. I might have been tempted to buy a drink, but just at that moment a thin-faced man in a suit entered the pub in the company of a young policewoman. Who wasn't, of course. It was some lad's birthday, and the girl put handcuffs on him before starting a striptease. I walked out, but the girl's minder shot me a look that could have frozen vodka.

We had an informer at that time who warned us that the Marin and O'Kane families were at odds. There was a fight outside a pub near the Parcel Force depot that resulted in a close ally of the O'Kanes being glassed: a classic 'Belfast kiss'. He lost an eye. Then the house of the elder Marin brother burned down when he and his wife were away for the weekend. We found the charred remnants of a petrol-soaked blanket inside a broken rear window. Just after that, something scared our informant so badly that he relocated to the Netherlands.

While we were struggling to get to grips with the situation, Theresa O'Kane went missing on her ninth birthday. She was the only daughter of one of the family's more law-abiding members. He and his wife didn't hesitate to call us. Theresa had been walking home from her school in Highgate with a friend when a car had stopped and two men had got out. One of them had hit the friend with a cosh, and she'd blacked out. When she'd recovered consciousness Theresa was gone.

That night, we put out an appeal on local TV and radio. Nothing. A day of frantic searching and questioning followed. The Marin brothers didn't have perfect alibis — that would have been too obvious — but we had nothing on them. Another night fell with Theresa's parents — both of whom were under thirty — in a state of numb desperation. Then another dark November day. Another night.

The call came at six in the morning. A homeless man, looking for a place to sleep, had wandered through the viaduct off Digbeth High Street after a troubled night. The mewing of seagulls had caught his attention. Behind one of the arches, near the porn cinema, he'd found a heap of dead rats and a few dying gulls. There was an acrid smell in the air. Using a stick, he'd pushed the rats aside — and then run to a phone box.

Theresa O'Kane had been garroted with wire. Her body cavity had been opened up, packed with rat poison and sewn shut again. Poison had also been forced into her mouth and throat. We were shown post-mortem photos. The body had only been under the viaduct a few hours, but our pathologist estimated the time of death as the evening of the abduction. She hadn't made it through her birthday.

Of course, the murder was in the papers for weeks – though we managed to keep the rat poison quiet. The O'Kane family had to go through the standard press cycle of bogus sympathy, suspicion, revelation, blame, abuse and final indifference. 28% of *Daily Mail* readers thought the O'Kanes were tragic victims, while 72% thought their criminal record was directly responsible for the child's death. It was business as usual: the memory of a dead child being falsified, mass-produced and put to work on the streets.

Small wonder that the O'Kane family sold their homes and were scattered overseas before the end of the year. The Marins continued their operations. We never managed to prove their connection to the murder, let alone the vicious symbolic gesture that followed it. But within a couple of years, we had some luck with their drugs racket and put the two elder brothers away. They weren't sufficiently big-time to own the police or local authorities. Then the youngest brother died of a septic ulcer, and the gang was finished. Other bastards replaced them, of course.

Years passed. I moved to the Acocks Green station and lost interest in Digbeth. The area slipped further into silence, with old houses and even churches being used as storage space for construction materials. As rents fell and concern for preservation became increasingly absurd, the ground was laid for the area's colonisation by offices – but that was still a decade off. Turf wars were still going on: pubs were set on fire, building projects were subject to overnight 'accidents'. The only people living in the district were in hostels or on the streets.

I'm not sure when it started. Some time in the early nineties. We thought it was one of the new gangs making its presence felt. An old man who'd been drinking in the Eagle and Tun was found dead in Lower Trinity Street, a few yards from one of the arches of the railway viaduct. Two days later, a homeless woman was seen dying in convulsions under the railway bridge by the Taboo cinema. Both deaths were the result of strychnine poisoning. Which could be rat poison, though we found no sign of it in the area.

A week after that, three children aged nine or so were found dead. They'd been playing with a ball in a disused car park near the Digbeth viaduct. Again, it was strychnine. Some of the powder was smeared on their mouths. The local police station went into overdrive, trying to find a drug dealer who might have sold them (or given them) a wrap of painful death. They arrested every addict they could find. It was late October. A few days before Theresa O'Kane's birthday.

Childhood memories are strange things. Who can predict when a buried memory will come to the surface and cause harm? It could be at puberty, or on leaving home, or after a broken marriage, or after the loss of a child. And when the trauma is profound enough to tear you out of the world...what then? I'm not de Richleau, I don't have those certainties. The best I can do is guesswork. There was no way I could banish Theresa, unless I could stop the ruthless from controlling others. But maybe I could make her back off.

We kept a police watch on the viaduct, and no-one was going there at night any more. At three a.m. we packed up and left the poorly-lit brickwork to whatever crept in the shadows, picking over scraps of litter. An hour later, I came back alone. Wearing a black tracksuit, surgical gloves and a scarf over my face. Under the scarf, I was wearing a flesh-toned latex mask I'd got from a Soho colleague with underground contacts. The eyes and mouth were narrow slits.

A half-moon was just visible through a skin of cloud. There was frost on the pavement. Miles away, fireworks were slamming doors in the night. I paused under the bridge where the homeless woman had died. Rain had drawn spikes of lime from the brickwork. Then I walked slowly on, past the private cinema to the viaduct.

From the pub in Lower Trinity Street, you can see three railway arches. I stood in one of them and lit a cigarette, then dropped it and stamped it out. A trace of smoke filtered through the cold air. The smell of rotting brick was overwhelming. About twenty yards away, against the wall, a Victorian iron urinal had been closed up for decades. She was standing there, watching me. Her face was slightly out of focus, as if one of us was shivering.

I waited under the viaduct, cupping my hands over my mouth to trap the warmth. She was hesitant, but determined. It was her birthday and no-one else had come. *Did they tell you it was a surprise party?* I thought. Her hair was dark and tangled. Her face was as white as the frost. Her school blouse and skirt were torn and smeared with oil or tarmac. As she moved towards me, looking sick, I held out my arms. Then I turned my face so her lips would touch my cheek.

Her small hand pressed into mine. I felt her grip more as a purpose than as a sensation, since her hand was as weak as fresh snow. Her mouth fastened on the slick non-flesh of the mask. Then she let go of me. Her face closed in on itself, flickered like old celluloid. I watched her turn and walk slowly away, back into the shadows of the industrial estate.

When there was no further sign of movement on the street, I peeled off the mask and gloves and slipped them carefully into a plastic bag. I'd dusted them with strychnine powder before putting them on. I wasn't sure if I'd told her a kind of lie or a kind of truth. Either way, she'd got the message.

There were no more unexplained deaths in the Digbeth area for a while. A few more children died from poisoning, but that was just a result of the amount of toxic waste in the ground. If police work teaches you anything, it's that gradual death is very rarely a crime.

LUKE SHOLER
WE ARE TWO LIONS

...danger knows full well
That Caesar is more dangerous than he:
We are two lions litter'd in one day,
And I the elder and more terrible
— *Julius Caesar*, **Act II, Scene II**

I guide the clipper up my skull, going against the grain. Hairs fall into the bathroom sink. Outside, a lean rain dusts the asphalt. People say you're on your way.

I let the blade-guard ride the contours of my head, imagining you're doing it, like you used to, your chest grazing my back. If it has to happen, I want it like that. Your lips and then the muzzle against my skull.

I've never done this before: stay in a hotel just two blocks from home. From the open window I can see the black iron balconies of my apartment building. So far, no lights have come on inside my flat. But maybe you've learned caution.

Tonight the neon letters atop this hotel seem to dye the whole sky indigo. In the mirror behind the television I catch a glimpse of my torso. It could be yours. We wore the same size suit.

It comes back so hard I have to shower to fight it. Bits of hair run down the drain. It reminds me of the sand running off your shins and feet, after the beach. The way it would glitter. The way the knife glittered in your hand, that first time.

People say you're back.

If only it wasn't true.

I dry off, then lay out the hardware.

*

Certain cities should change our faces, certain acts. Amsterdam, the month before we met. I wonder what it did to mine.

It didn't take a full week to verify the intelligence, but that's how long I spent.

The Dutchman owned a law firm specializing in trademarks. On Egelantiersgracht, just a few blocks from where Anne Frank had hid, stood his tall narrow canal house. White window frames set off the dark brick façade. A hoist beam stuck out from the ornamented gable.

I verified that the Dutchman smoked a pipe, that he worked only a few hours each morning, that he kept a half-Indonesian mistress in a flat near Waterlooplein. Every afternoon, he would descend the stoop in front of his house and sit reading on a bench along the canal. His large stomach suggested strength, breeding. Upstairs the curtains would shift, where his wife stood watching. Then, in the evenings, he took invigorating walks to Waterlooplein.

Back home, Singer didn't go into why. Motive's only important if it can affect the outcome.

I'd assumed it was his wife, then I knew it was. The sixth day, while the Dutchman read on his bench, she took the table beside mine at a nearby outdoor cafe. I was writing postcards that I would later drop unstamped and unaddressed in a trashcan at Schiphol airport. She said, "Do you have a light?"

I neared it to her mouth, my thumb on the spark wheel.

She inhaled. Then, with her chin, she meaningfully indicated her husband. "Thank you."

Which is why, when I approached his bench the next afternoon and asked directions to the Anne Frank house, I was so taken aback.

"Please stand blocking me," he said, "so she won't have to see."

Upstairs, the shifting curtain. I walked away, fast.

But it was too late to pull out.

Waterlooplein. In the black-and-white sunset, the wind carried the foretaste of rain. An ambulance glided by, lights spinning, siren mute. The Dutchman and his mistress strolled across a bridge and turned onto Verversstraat. I followed. Suddenly we were the only ones on the street. Halfway down it, a slide built to look like a yellow brontosaurus fed into a tiny sunken courtyard. She slid down into it. He lit his pipe, smiling. I put the silencer to his head.

Exit Amsterdam. The jet engines seemed to drag the girl's screams down the runway, up into the troposphere. In the end, only she had been surprised.

Back to Madrid and tobacco breakfasts, reckless traffic in the round-abouts. Below the city, immigrant construction workers and Spanish civil servants crammed together on the 7:30 a.m. trains, while above, daylight splintered over the cemetery of apartment towers.

I shaved meticulously, and went to see Singer.

Before he sat down, before we even shook hands, I said, "What the fuck was that?"

"What?" Then, to the barman, "Dos cafés con leche, largos de café."

Singer's hair was short, the color of pepper. A few months after I settled in Spain, my money ran out. I took stock of myself – no working papers and only one valuable skill – and reached out to a few Marines I knew from the Gulf War. On a three-way call, one introduced me to Singer, saying, "He acts as a broker. Clients have needs and he finds a contractor." A test project, then I was in. Now all my projects reached me through Singer, along with instructions, intelligence. It had always been good.

"I can think of a name for it," I said, "but I want you to tell me I'm wrong."

The barman set our coffees in front us.

"It was clean and well paid. Just your style."

"It was carrion. He sat there all week, waiting for it. His wife spectating."

"Has the second payment hit your account?"

"That's not the point."

"No?" Singer's mobile phone beeped. "It had metastasized," he said, reading the text message.

"What?"

"You ever see somebody die that way? It's like a tree falling and rotting, but all sped up. Like in those nature programs."

"The Dutchman?"

"By the time they diagnosed him the cancer was everywhere. He wanted to die standing in the forest. Not fallen, eaten by insects."

After that I was between projects.

Being a contractor is like being a professional soccer player, the time between games far longer than the games themselves. The trick is to structure the days, so time doesn't grow faster while you grow slower.

Each morning in the Parque del Oeste, I did my warm-up and stretches, followed by push-ups, crunches and pull-ups. Then I would begin my run, going up the Paseo del Pintor Rosales. The run branched out from there, sometimes taking me into the Universidad Complutense campus, where sleepy-faced girls smoked on the way to class; other times down Princesa, where shop assistants dressed mannequins in the plate-glass windows.

A walk to cool down, a shower back home, and then it was breakfast in Conde Duque, reading one of the store-copy newspapers, its pages creased and smudged from previous fingers. Afterwards I might buy lamb or veal at the Mercado de los Mostenses, dodging the young men pushing hand trucks. Or maybe I would go online and monitor my investments, authorize a trade. Other days I drove out to the storage unit where I kept my tools, cleaning and reassembling them while traffic coursed like a river down the nearby highway.

But the nights were harder to solve. The *versión original* cinemas sometimes, but after a week I had normally seen everything good and the employees started to recognize me. One night I Googled every family member and friend I could remember, finishing with my own name, zero search results, and proceeded to look at myself for so long in the bathroom mirror that my face became a stranger's.

Often I would drink in Chueca, my back and elbows resting on the bar. It was like tossing a coin: heads, I met someone and grappled and gasped with him until one or both of us came; tails, the faces retreated and blurred into a mural more and more impossible to work my way into.

Other nights, restless with a need I could not define, I would drive around the M-30 ring road, lap after lap, staring up at the illuminated honeycombs of the tower blocks, the hundreds of thousands of lives whose proof was before me and whose contents I could not imagine.

That's what it was like between projects.

That's what it was like before you.

I had been checking in with Singer about once a week, to see if he had anything. Not yet, had been his invariable reply.

Then he called, told me to meet him the next morning.

"Looks like I've got another project," he said, stirring the sugar into his coffee with a tiny spoon.

I waited.

"Nothing like Amsterdam. I'll confirm it soon."

That same day I met you.

At El Salmantino I stood eating a tortilla sandwich at the bar. You entered, and ordered a glass of beer in an accent that sounded French. The barman held it under the tap until it overflowed, edged the froth off with a foam scraper, and set it in front of you. In the mirror behind the bar, I watched you take off a large backpack with thick shoulder straps and dangling clips. Suddenly you turned. We were the same height.

"Can you watch my stuff for twenty seconds? I'm just going to use their bathroom." Pale blue eyes and pale brown hair. The oil in it told me it had been at least two days since your last shower. Even still you were striking.

On the bar you had left a lighter, a pack of cigarettes, and a mobile phone; on the floor, your backpack.

Your smile when you returned. Your lips were wet and full of blood, your teeth strong. Something happened in my stomach, like driving fast over a dip.

You offered me a cigarette, a gesture of thanks.

We were talking and I forget the words.

In the corner the slot machines lit up, dozens of lights blinking.

You were taking a year out before going to university. You pointed at your traveler's backpack. Unplanned summer, the labyrinth of Europe. If you liked a place, you stayed. If not, a bus, a train.

Another round of beers.

"Where are you from?"

You showed me a red passport with a white cross. "Switzerland. But my family is Croatian."

Everything in reverse order. I learned your name last.

"Stephane."

Three kisses on the cheek, the way it's done there.

"Hey. What are you up to? Right now."

Next bar, nightfall, and we started throwing darts. Right foot forward, three fingers on the barrel. I won the first game and was winning the second. Suddenly, before I could pluck my darts from the board, you began your turn.

The first dart struck mine in the triple 20 and both fell to the floor. The tip of your next dart smashed into the tail of mine and again both fell. The third you embedded in the outer bull, right alongside mine.

Stock-still facing each other.

Outside, a car alarm went off.

"Do you have a hotel?"

And then you were in my flat, our belt buckles clashing as we made out in the hallway, our voices husky and wordless as animals'.

The morning after, you took my lower lip between your teeth, let go, and said, "Do you trust me?"

I leaned back against the kitchen counter, eyes on yours.

"If you do, give me your keys."

I thought about your backpack spilling dirty clothes onto my bedroom floor, the bracelets and rings you'd left on my nightstand. "All right."

You went out.

Opening the burner valve of the stove, I clicked the lighter and the flame materialized like a blue upside-down spider. I set the coffee maker over it.

Out on the balcony, I had my first cigarette of the day. No sign of you on the street below, where people towed their own shadows and an old man dug through a dumpster containing broken bricks and clods of plaster.

The coffee maker started to gurgle. After turning off the flame, I smoked another cigarette, then a third. I started to think about the keys I'd given you. You knew where I'd parked. Sickeningly, it dawned on me: I had just traded my car for a backpack full of dirty clothes.

I was pulling open cabinets and drawers, searching for the spare set of keys. Before reporting it, I had to go down and check, but didn't want to get locked out.

Then the door swung in. You were panting. "Fourth story, no elevator. No wonder you're so fit." In your arms, paper bags full of fruit. You smiled. "No pets, no plants... You need something fresh in here."

I was standing behind you in the kitchen while you chopped a pineapple, its juices soaking the cutting board. I wanted to ask, demand: *what took you so long?* But instead, I slipped my hands under your armpits and across your chest.

"Why are all the drawers out?" you said.

"Thieves. How much longer till it's ready?"

You were yanking the green tufts off of strawberries, dividing them lengthwise. To your left the salad bowl was filling: slices of banana, kiwi, apple.

We had breakfast in the living room, while barking dogs and motorcycle engines came in through the open windows.

Afterwards, on my back, I brought my knees to my chest. You smeared a marble of lubricant over my anus, kissed me as you pushed in.

You brought fresh fruit the whole rest of that week. We woke up later and later, having spent the nights in restaurants and clubs, and I skipped exercising entirely. Then I got a text message from Singer: *Confirmed.* By the time I met him for the briefing, you'd already moved in.

"Where do you go, in the mornings? I wake up sometimes and you're not there."

"Shorter," I said. "Change the blade-guard."

"Any shorter and your scalp will show."

"Change it."

You did, and gave the side of my head another pass. Against the grain, like I'd told you.

"Aren't you going to answer my question?"

"Nowhere."

"For two and a half hours?"

We were standing shirtless in the bathroom, you behind me, both facing the mirror. Bits of hair lay on my shoulders and collarbones, on the rim and bowl of the sink.

"The park," I said.

"What for?"

"I've got a project coming up. I need to be in shape."

You switched the clipper off and knocked some of the hairs out.

"What exactly do you do, anyway?"

"Contract work. I told you."

"Yeah, but, what?"

"I deliver short-term, high-complexity projects. Data migration, mainly. Almost always in live environments."

"Computers," you said, skeptically.

I nodded. "And web-based applications."

A click and the clipper started humming again.

As you finished shaving my head, you said, "You know, it's funny. A friend of mine works in IT. His shelves, they're full of computer books. I haven't seen a single one in your entire flat."

"They're at my office," I lied. "I keep a small one on the other side of the city."

"So that's where you go in the mornings?"

"No. The park. I just told you."

Your brow wrinkled. You started to ask another question.

I checked it, the only way I could think: "You manage to get up early tomorrow, you can come with."

The alarm on my mobile phone rang and your legs were out of bed before I could turn it off. At the park, the grass bore dew from the night before. I knew if I pushed you hard enough the first time, there wouldn't be a second.

After the warm-up jog, I guided you through the stretches, forcing you to reach an inch past your limit and hold it. Then push-ups, one set of seventy with the hands close together, another with the hands far apart. During the crunches I made sure you kept your thighs perpendicular to the ground, your shins parallel to it. At the overhead bars, we hung for a moment, letting our arms and torsos loosen.

"Pull slow and smooth," I said. "Visualize your Adam's apple even with the bar. Don't stop until I do."

I expected you to get two or three. At nine, your arms gave out.

We jogged up the Paseo del Pintor Rosales, and from there I led you over concrete and asphalt, avoiding any grass, on a circuitous shade-free run that deposited us an hour and a half later beneath the two slanting towers at Plaza de Castilla. Our temples were pounding, our T-shirts wet with parabolas of sweat.

"Finish line," I coughed.

"So," you said, once you'd got your breath back. "We start the same time tomorrow?"

The next morning I made the run longer and faster. The one after, we pressed on even through an exhaustion that made us both stumble. On a sun-bleached sidewalk you suddenly bent forward and vomited something hot and clear as spa water. Trembling, you wiped your mouth with your shirt, and started running again.

I realized then I wasn't going to shake you off.

So you became my exercise partner. And soon I was training harder than I had since the Marines.

One morning our run ended in the Parque del Retiro. We were walking the paths to cool down. A runner was coming towards us. Beside him on a leash loped a Doberman pinscher, ears pointed, tail docked. To the right and behind, I heard a phlegmatic growl.

The pit bull must have slipped out of its collar.

The Doberman's black lips pulled back.

Barking, the two dogs lunged at each other with the unreal attraction of magnets. They fought, twisting and snarling, and as the pit bull moved in from underneath the Doberman bit it across the muzzle and a second bite just behind the ear was immediately broken by the pit bull's thrust in and up, and its jaws clamped around the Doberman's throat.

By then the owner of the pit bull had arrived, and grabbed his dog by the skin of its neck, trying to pull it off.

But the pit bull could not be dislodged. The Doberman began to slacken, as though falling asleep.

Suddenly the owner of the Doberman sunk his clenched hand into the pit bull's side and pulled out and blood came and he struck until the animal fell limp and the Doberman was released. He stood back up, folding the pocket knife; and then I saw the sprinting policemen.

"We're leaving," I said. "Now."

You didn't react. I had to push you into motion.

For a long time we just walked, numb and unconnected as sleepwalkers.

On the way out of the park, we finally spoke.

"It's not fair," you said.

"What?"

"The small one would have won."

"I need it," you said.

"What for?"

"To get around."

"Use public transportation."

"For work, too," you said.

"What do you mean?"

"I want a job. To do something, get money."

"What kind of job?"

"Well, I need to look. It will be a lot faster if I have it."

I drew a long breath and looked around the showroom.

"Besides," you said, "a lot of jobs require you to have your own vehicle."

You swung your leg over the leather seat of the motorcycle. Hands on the grips, you swiveled the front tire and it squeaked on the polished floor. You were making engine noises, grinning. I couldn't say no.

You were sloppy, careless. On the bathroom mirror there were water spots and gunk from where you'd styled your hair and flossed your teeth. After shaving, you never cleaned the stubble from the sink. I'd find the milk sitting out on the counter, bits of dried food on the dishes you'd washed. These things irritated me but I held my tongue, afraid you'd get defensive, afraid I'd seem petty.

The next project had been confirmed for nearly two weeks, but I was making no headway. Singer was asking for a status check. With you in the flat, I couldn't plan.

So after exercising one morning, I drove out to my storage unit, telling you I was going to the office. You said fine. You were going to ride around the city looking for work.

The storage unit was ten feet by fifteen, with three concrete walls and the fourth like a garage door. There, with a naked light bulb overhead, I laid blueprints, snapshots, maps and photocopies on the workbench and began to envision how I would do it.

The Bank of Spain, built of pale gray granite, occupies an entire city block. The Bank's Director General de Supervisión, known for his incorruptibility, had come across a lack of compliance in a certain credit institution. The sanctions would be crippling. The owners got in touch with people who knew people who knew Singer.

I spent a few more afternoons in the storage unit. I made notes, drew lines, calculated times and distances.

In the meeting, Singer gave me a deadline. "Some jobs don't require one," he said. "I leave it to providence. But the director is about to make a very unfavorable recommendation."

When I got home you were crying. Your backpack was already by the door.

"My father's had a stroke."

You had no money. I bought you a plane ticket to Geneva. From there you would take the train to La Chaux-de-Fonds, where your parents lived.

That night we did not make love and the next morning I gave you a short tight embrace and watched you go through passport control.

I called your mobile a day later. "How is he?"

"Not good."

"How are you?"

"I don't know."

"I miss you."

"Listen," you said. "It costs me a fortune to receive calls here. We can text."

I went to some of the stores I used to like. Looking through the CDs, books and garments, I felt a kind of ulcer that rendered everything valueless. I bumped into shoppers, had no voice to apologize.

The next afternoon, I entered the storage unit but something was wrong. Tools were missing, documents.

I sat down, dizzy, thinking about the implications, thinking about Singer's deadline.

The remaining documents I shoved into a black garbage bag. I put the rifles and pistols back in their cases. I gathered up scopes, magazines, bipods, silencers, gloves, cleaning rods, solvents, cotton patches, brushes. I filled the trunk of my car. I laid the rest in the back seat, and threw an open bedroll over it.

Accelerating, I merged onto the highway. I drove fast and then slow, studying the rear-view mirror.

Later I spotted another storage facility.

There was nothing to do but continue planning.

The day before you were due home, you sent a text saying *Looks like he'll pull through. Am staying an extra week to make sure.*

I tried to call but you didn't answer.

So I texted back. *Date and time of flight? Land line I can call you at?*

A day passed. All you wrote was *Don't worry. Will take metro home from airport.*

I forced myself not to respond.

His love of current events and his dislike of traffic jams had led the

Director General de Supervisión to take the metro to work. Each morning he would calmly read El País while his colleagues gritted their teeth in a fog of car horns and brake lights. Stepping off the train a few minutes before eight, he would push through the one-way exit gates, walk through the underpass beneath the Calle de Alcalá, and emerge at the tall wrought-iron doors of the Bank of Spain.

After a week of shadowing him, I went to the new storage unit for my gear.

I returned home. I was sitting in the dark at the living room table, rehearsing tomorrow morning in my head.

A key entered the lock.

You walked in, carrying more bags than you had left with. You stood at one end of the hallway; I stood at the other. You were pale, rigid. You set the bags down on the hardwood floor.

"You're back," I said.

You knelt to unzip a bag, hands shaking. You took some documents out and spread them on the floor. You lifted out a pistol and placed it on top of the documents, then did the same with a second one.

"I know what you do," you said.

We stood there, my stolen guns between us.

"I read about the men you killed."

I didn't react.

"At first I didn't know what to do."

I stepped towards you.

"But it's all I've been thinking about."

I took another step.

"I needed extra time to absorb it. To be sure."

I realized then you must have followed me out there on the motorcycle. "You didn't go to Switzerland. It was all an act."

"You were hiding something. I had to know what."

"Now you know."

"I could have left you."

I said nothing.

"I could have gone to the police."

I came closer.

You swallowed.

I stepped quick and stood directly above the guns. Our noses were almost touching.

"Why didn't you?"

You wouldn't meet my eyes.

"Why – didn't – you?"

"I want to do what you do."

"What?"

"I want you to teach me."

I walked you backwards, my fingertips stabbing your chest. The guns and documents were now behind me. I backed you up against the wall. I spun you around, frisked you. Nothing. I took my keys back. Opening the door to my flat, I pushed you out onto the landing.

"Goodbye, Stephane."

I shut the door, bolted it, and walked alone back down the hall.

That night I didn't eat, gliding the silencer back and forth across the table like a rolling pin. The deadline was still tomorrow.

I woke before the alarm clock went off, my nerves like electrical wires. A long jog and a long shower, then I inspected my tourist outfit in the mirror. I remembered fighting with you for space in that same mirror, nights we were going clubbing. The smell of two different colognes, just sprayed, tingling in our nostrils.

I was pretending to buy a metro ticket from the machine when the Director General de Supervisión came through the exit gates. He wore a charcoal suit and carried a briefcase. I stepped into stride behind him, entered the underpass.

Its pink textured walls were stained with layers and layers of urine. Graffiti wriggled across the diffusers of the white fluorescent lamps and traffic noise filtered through the low corrugated ceiling. Halfway through the underpass, eyes down, clothes loose and soiled, a kid stood begging for coins.

I unzipped my camera bag and took longer steps.

The director had been walking in a straight line, but deviated as the beggar placed himself in his path.

"Señor," said the kid, grabbing his arm, "una ayuda. Por favor."

My bottom three fingers wrapped around the grip, index slipping through the trigger guard.

"No llevo nada," the director said, and pulled away.

Then, just as I was drawing it out of the camera bag, something glittered in the kid's hand and he fell into the director as though pushed.

His arm jerked in and out and the two of them collapsed like fainting dancers among cigarette butts, dead leaves, and cellophane wrappers. I kept walking, unable to breathe, unable to think.

I walked until my legs and back ached, making eye contact with no one.

When I got to my building, I didn't know what time it was.

The light in the stairwell ran on a timer. I hit it, climbed. There, on the landing outside my door, you slept, loose and soiled clothes dark with blood.

You slept for twenty-four hours straight, like someone breaking a fever. By the time you awoke, I had already disintegrated your clothes in bleach, ground down the knife, and arranged to meet Singer for a debriefing.

He leaned in close, cupped the back of my neck with his hand. "Why didn't you use a bullet?"

I pushed the hip-fold leather wallet over to him.

Singer opened it. It contained 135 euros, along with the Director General de Supervisión's national ID card, his parents' names on back.

"What are the newspapers saying?" I asked.

"Mugging gone wrong."

"What are they not saying?"

His eyelids tensed.

"Assassination," I answered.

He pushed his chair back. He stood up and slammed the wallet in front of me, spilling my coffee. "I work with you because you're clean. Don't let that change."

Those first few days back you had very little appetite. Slow taut meals, your head down. No noise but the clink of silverware. We shared a secret now, that no one could ever know.

I told myself, *Just until I figure out what to do.*

But the only way I could protect you – from the police and from yourself – was by letting you stay. It was the only way not to lose you.

So I asked, "Do you still mean what you said?"

You met my eyes, the first time all day. From upstairs came long deep scrapes; the neighbors were moving furniture.

"About wanting to learn?" I said.

You gauged me. You nodded.

"You're sure?"

"Yes."

"Even after – ?"

"Yes."

"Then you need to accept three rules. One, training will go exactly how I say. Two, you won't kill again until I say you're ready. Three, if you break one of these rules, training stops and you're on the street."

Your jaw flared as you bit down on your molars.

"Yes or no," I said.

You were quiet.

"Yes or no?"

You nodded.

The mornings were almost like before. We would start in the Parque del Oeste, the dew on the grass darkening our running shoes. I expanded the physical training to include the daily dozens, same as in boot camp. Side-startle hops, bends and thrusts, leg lifts, trunk twisters, all of them. A long run followed, and when we jogged in sync down the Castellana, past hotels and ministries and stadium flags and double-long buses, I could almost forget how drastically the stakes had changed.

You had become a killer. And though I couldn't prevent it, I was a direct cause of it. Your survival, your development, were now my responsibility.

In the beginning, we didn't touch weapons at all. First you needed to become patient, disciplined, independent.

After instructing you on the difference between concealment from view and cover from fire, after teaching you how to stalk a target and estimate distance, after showing you how to select a firing position and ensure an egress route, I made the city our training ground. It was a variation of one of the stalking exercises I used to do in the Marines. One of us acted as sniper, the other as observer. The sniper had to get within 180 meters of the observer without being detected, at which point he would fire off one blank round. The observer would then raise a miscellaneous object. Still hidden, the sniper identified the object, proving he was close enough to have easily taken out the observer. You and I did it the same way, only with mobile phones and Bluetooth headsets, shorter distances. We practiced in financial districts, shopping centers, industrial estates, plazas, parks, suburbs.

Impatient, you asked when we'd move on to the shooting. "Marksmanship only makes up ten to twenty percent of it," I said. "The hardest part is stalking the enemy and going undetected."

You got into it then, displayed craft. One morning on the Gran Vía, I received an incoming call. Your blank round. I was standing in the shadow beneath a theater marquee. Without moving my head, I scanned a half circle. Scores of people, none of them you. I held up a folded copy of the Financial Times, black headlines on salmon paper. "Name it," I said into the headset. I could hear street noise, but not your voice. The call ended. As I started to walk away, an old bootblack signaled to me and I shook my head no. He was sitting on a small, padded wooden box, his brushes and disks of shoe polish arranged on the sidewalk. Something felt wrong. Later, at home, you showed me a picture you'd taken with your mobile phone. Me glancing at the bootblack. You'd been less than fifteen meters away.

For discipline, I signed you up at a tae kwon do dojo run by a small South Korean man who inspired amazing fear and loyalty in his students. I signed myself up, too. We went three nights a week, arriving early to get in time on the punching bags.

When we were testing for orange belt, they had us spar against each other. I came in with a front snap kick, which you blocked, exposing your midsection, and in the same movement I executed a mid-air turning kick to your side. You half stumbled, regained your fighting stance, and closed in. You threw a fake jab, and with the same arm landed a crushing back fist to my temple. We continued. I kept you at bay with crescent kicks, but you swept my supporting leg out from under me, and as I was getting back up your instep cracked down across my nose and blood spattered the floorboards and my dobok. The judges ended it there. The pride on your face was unmistakable.

In those months, I taught you everything you would need to know, not just for the profession, but for the life around it. How to drive a car – manual and automatic. How to manage a bank account, disguise the source of your income. How to wear a suit, iron a shirt, knot a tie. Just in case, I bought you two new identities – one Belgian, one Canadian. To neutralize your accent in English, I hired a private tutor from Ontario. I made you memorize facts about imaginary families, governments you had never lived under. You would become a chameleon, nationless.

The only property that I owned was a 110-acre finca in Extremadura. Two decrepit farmhouses, their stone walls over a foot thick, stood on the land, along with various outbuildings, a corral, two watering holes, and three wells. The finca was silent, surrounded by nothing but large grazing farms. I had purchased it as an investment, and as a place to disappear to, if it ever came to that. Which is why I blindfolded you the May night I drove you out there. And why in those weeks, I never took you into town. But you didn't complain. On the finca, you learned to use guns.

If I taught you more than I should have, if I was overgenerous, part of it was because I never intended to see the program through, never intended to allow you to kill again. The other part was that my life, with you in it, had become priceless. The days had never been so vivid, the sensations so crisp. I felt resurrected.

You. I have never had so much hunger for another person. Your long, nail-bitten fingers. In my mouth, they tasted of tobacco and coins. At the toilet you stood with your feet wide apart, one hand on the wall above the cistern. From the boutiques along Fuencarral you coveted jackets and shoes, and I took pleasure in buying them for you. You had this way about you when you entered a club or bar, like you knew a secret, like you didn't need to be there; it was thrilling to be at your side. More than once we fucked from the start of lunch till after the siesta, while in the flats around us people fried food, scrubbed plates, watched TV. Afternoons of saliva and sweat. I would nearly faint after coming, my forehead between your shoulder blades, nose against your spine.

After almost a year of training, we decided to summer on Mallorca. Our plane landed in Palma at night. The cathedral glowed above the masts in the marina.

July, August. I had taken a house on the north side of the island. At sunset, lone swimmers crawled out to the buoys and further. Every week, a different town would celebrate its fiesta, streamers and temporary stages enlivening the plazas. We found coves that only the islanders knew, where millionaires anchored their yachts for the afternoon before continuing on to the Port of Pollença or Formentera. You turned bronze. On your rented motor scooter you wore a black horse-riding hat, just like the local kids.

But you started to go quiet for long periods, look for excuses to do things on your own. On beaches and in restaurants, your eyes lingered on certain men.

In September we drove down to Palma to party in your favorite club, and found it closed, high season over. We tried a different one that played house music, but you didn't like it. You started complaining. I tried to cheer you up.

"Why the fuck are we even here?" you finally said.

"You're the one who wanted to go out."

"I mean Mallorca. This island's like a prison."

I walked off. When I came back, I found you sitting in the VIP section on a white leather sofa with a man in a navy blue polo shirt, his skin even tanner than yours.

Leaning over the waist-high wall, I called your name. Either you didn't hear me or you were ignoring me. A big man in a black suit and black shirt stood guard at the entrance. I tried to call your mobile. You didn't answer. I walked up to the big man and told him I was going to order a bottle at the VIP bar. He let me in. I talked to the barmaid until the big man stopped watching me.

"I just spotted a colleague," I told her. "I'll be right back."

"Stephane," I said, touching your neck. "It's time to go."

You looked up.

"He can stay," the man in the polo shirt said, rising, "as long as he likes."

I smiled. Wrapping my arm around his shoulders as if he were an old friend, I thrust my fist into his solar plexus. By the time the big man realized what had happened, I'd already led you out to the parking lot.

We were driving fast along the shore.

"Stop!" you screamed.

I didn't.

Russia in the nineties was known as the wild east. As the government transferred ownership of state-held enterprises to private individuals and groups, businessmen fought for the tremendous wealth and power at stake. Bypassing the ineffective legal system, they settled their disputes with hitmen.

One, who had done jobs for an oligarch and later relocated to London, was now talking to journalists on condition of anonymity. I guess he thought enough time had passed. The oligarch didn't.

It was the project Singer gave me after you and I returned to Madrid.

I told you nothing about it.

The deadline was tight. Two afternoons in the storage unit, then I caught a plane to Heathrow. I recognized the Russian coming out of the pub Singer had mentioned. Short military haircut, tattoos on his hands. I stalked him down Brick Lane, and through the East End. The steel skeleton of an unfinished office building rose high into the night, flanked by luffing jib cranes and absent stars. The Russian went into a fast-food shop run by a Muslim man with an untrimmed beard and a white knit cap. He came out with a doner kebab. I put two bullets in his back before he could eat it.

When I arrived home, you acknowledged me with a nod, nothing else. At dinner you answered my questions with single syllables.

Later that night I woke up covered in ash, the bedroom light still on. You weren't there. Rolling over, I saw the upside-down ashtray in the sheets, the scattered butts of the cigarettes you'd smoked after I'd fallen asleep.

Entering the dark living room, I stepped on chips of plaster that had fallen off the wall onto the hardwood floor.

You were smoking on the balcony, shirtless. Your hand was wrapped in gauze, brown ovals seeping through. Four stories below, a garbage truck progressed down the street, its crew slamming the trash cans empty and resonant back down on the sidewalk.

"Thanks for remembering to take the ashtray with you."

You remained in profile, the neon letters of the Hotel Meliá Madrid Princesa dyeing your face indigo. Suddenly I hated your beauty and the power it gave you over me. I wanted to strike you and hold you in the same instant. I said, "What happened to your hand?"

"I couldn't sleep."

"Well, you can sweep up the plaster tomorrow."

Somewhere, the metal shutter of a restaurant clattered down.

"Come on," I said. "Let's go inside. We need to get up early to train."

You snickered.

"What?"

You just shook your head.

"What?"

Below us, a car was parallel parking.

"Stephane."

You said something then, bitterly and to yourself. Something about time and flesh.

I started to go back inside.

"You want to know why I can't sleep? I saw something today, when I was out riding around."

I stopped.

"I parked near this statue, in Getafe. That's what the inscription said." You were shaking. "We are time wrapped in flesh. I'm ready. Every day I wait is wasted."

"That's enough."

"No. It's not. You fly away, do a job, leave me completely out. So why should I get up early and train? To never actually do it?"

"You accepted the rules."

"A fucking year has gone by!"

"You're not ready."

You fell quiet, and stood still for so long that time seemed to loop back on itself.

"Stephane."

You didn't react.

"Right now you think life is a hundred-meter dash. It's not. It's a marathon."

Televisions lit the walls inside the flats across the street. Above us, the stars and satellites glimmered indistinguishably. When I went back inside, you still didn't react, handsome and remote as a model in a photograph.

We reached a compromise. It wasn't what you wanted, but it was all I could allow: you would help plan the next project.

Weeks passed. Singer didn't have anything. To soothe your impatience, I took you out to the finca a few times. You could now disassemble and put together a gun as quickly as me. I hung targets in the olive grove, taught you to shoot with both hands.

Finally, in December, Singer sent a text message. He had a project.

OK, I responded. *Tomorrow at 11. I'm bringing someone.*

I pushed through the revolving door of the Café Comercial, you in the quadrant behind me. Singer stood as we reached his table. I shook his hand, then introduced you.

We laid our coats and scarves across the booth and sat down.

"Well," Singer said. "Are you going to explain this?"

"I'm training him."

"What are you talking about?"

"Certain projects, high-profile ones, are too complex for a single contractor."

Singer was looking from me to you.

"Right now, I'm not getting those projects. And I know you have them."

He rubbed his chin.

"I'm building a two-man team, to be able to take on those kinds of jobs."

"Do you have any references?" he asked you.

"No," I said.

Singer asked if he could talk to me alone for a minute.

You went outside to the news kiosk.

He was tapping his lighter on the table. Then he spoke. "You bring someone new into the relationship, he's your responsibility. Whatever happens."

The next target, Francisco Sancha, was a 52-year-old Spaniard who owned three different brothels in Alicante and Valencia. Pink and blue neon lights decorated the facades of the concrete buildings. Inside, Romanian girls in their late teens and early twenties lay down with customers on narrow beds in windowless rooms.

Recruited by fellow countrymen back in Romania, the girls had been lured to Spain with the promise of jobs as nannies or house cleaners. Once they arrived, their countrymen sold them to Francisco. The Romanians had revolvers and full details on the girls. If they refused to work, if they tried to escape, they would be killed, or their families back in Romania would.

Francisco had paid the Romanians less than agreed for the latest batch of girls; shrugged off their reminders. But the Romanians supplied other brothels in Spain. They couldn't let Francisco set precedent. So they met with someone who then met with Singer.

You and I planned it together. We drove down once, just to scout. We learned where he lived, what streets he drove, which brothel he spent the most time at.

Back in Madrid, I told you to sketch some scenarios. You came up with a fair number, but only one convinced me. Together we blueprinted it. He would die the second week of January.

We got separated on New Year's Eve.

In a club lit by red fluorescent tubes, you went to the men's room while I went for another round. Back where we'd split up, a drink in each hand. I tried to call you but your mobile phone was either off or without a signal. I searched the dance floor. Around me people swayed, wearing tinsel wigs, paper garlands, glow-in-the-dark eyeglasses. I entered the restrooms, nothing. One more tour of the dance floor, another call. I left.

On the balcony of my flat, drinking Scotch from the bottle. A police helicopter hovered like a dragonfly above the Gran Vía, where confetti speckled the sidewalks and gutters. The bottle slipped out of my hand and exploded on the curb below.

I tried your mobile again then fell asleep, thinking, *year that starts without you ends without you.*

I neither dreamed nor rested, and woke at dawn with dry eyelids.

A noise from the kitchen.

I walked barefoot, silent.

The refrigerator door was open and you stood drinking tropical juice straight from the carton. Head back, dark denim jeans low around your hips.

I embraced you from behind and you jumped in fright spilling juice down your chin and chest. *Putain!* you exclaimed, and I knew then – I could smell him on you – that you'd been with someone else. My legs were trembling and I shoved you against the refrigerator, slamming the door shut, bottles and jars crashing inside.

"Who?!" I shouted.

You spun around and tilted your chin up, defiant. I struck you across it with the heel of my hand, and your fist connected with my ear just before I pinned your shoulders against the refrigerator; magnets and papers fell.

Both of us panting.

Something red-black pulled me, heavier than gravity. I pressed my lips to yours and you bit and I tasted blood but continued kissing. No words. I forced you around, pulled your jeans down, and spat into my palm. Gray dawn, your face in profile. I ejaculated inside of you as pigeons clapped their wings in the interior patio.

Brief impersonal conversations the whole rest of the week, you not making eye contact.

When you finally did, it was to discuss your role in the project.

"Planning and observation," I said. "We already agreed that."

"I was just thinking – "

"The other option is you don't go at all."

Your lips were pursed. You nodded once, then again.

Francisco Sancha started work in the afternoon and always finished around five in the morning at the brothel called El Nenúfar.

It sat in the center of a large parking lot. Fields surrounded it on three sides. The fourth was a highway, where tractor-trailers and cars whooshed along the asphalt. An irrigation canal, lined with reeds and tall grass, ran through the fields.

We crawled in after midnight, faces painted the green and rust colors of the terrain. We took position, lying prone among the reeds. We were looking straight at the back door of El Nenúfar. In about ninety minutes, Francisco would emerge with his colleagues and walk to his car.

I handed you the rifle. Extra practice, a realistic simulation. "Imagine he's halfway between the back door and his car," I whispered. "Estimate the range."

You used the mil dot reticle on the scope, performed calculations in your head. "Four hundred meters."

"Good. Now dial in the scope."

You adjusted it.

"Let me check," I said.

"Hold on. I'm just – "

Suddenly the back door of the brothel opened and two men in their early thirties came out.

"Don't do anything," I whispered.

They smoked several cigarettes, the tips tracing orange lines in the night. Then they went over to a Seat car and raised the lid of the trunk.

"¡Oye!" called a man from the doorway. "¿Por qué tardáis tanto?" He stepped out into the parking lot. He was older than the other two. Without the scope, I couldn't be sure who it was.

The rifle shot cracked like brittle thunder and the older man fell spinning to the blacktop. The two others scrambled ducking behind the Seat. I covered your mouth, wrested the rifle from you. Francisco Sancha was dragging himself back towards the doorway. My shot bored through his cranium.

Half a dozen men ran shouting out the back door.

"Fall back!" I hissed.

We crawled along the irrigation canal, the reeds and high grass concealing us. Four men ran out into the fields, pistols drawn, while others started cars and swept the darkness with their headlights.

You were ahead of me, crawling too fast; your form broke from the grass and shadows.

"¡Está allí!" they shouted, believing you were alone, and dashed stumbling over the uneven earth towards you.

"Roll into the canal," I whispered. "Take it all the way back to the car."

In the dirt I flattened out on my stomach. Resting the fiberglass stock of the rifle on my bag, I looked through the scope. They were two hundred meters from the canal where you crawled unarmed. I waited, getting my heart rate down. Fifty meters. Twenty-five. I squeezed and the man closest to you fell straight backwards as though his throat had hit a wire, and I pulled the bolt back and forward before his body touched the ground.

"¡Joder! ¡Hay más de uno!" They crouched, and fired in a forty-five degree arc going from where you had entered the canal to where I lay in the dirt. One bullet came so close it flung soil across my arm.

I shot once, then again: one man covered his heart with his gun hand; the one beside him pitched forward clutching his abdomen.

The last man dropped to the earth and fired three shots in my direction, then stopped, cursing his empty clip. A jeep, high beams bouncing, was now racing through the field towards me. Four more men rode inside.

I started sprinting to where we had hidden the car.

The jeep must have been unable to cross the canal; the men were now running behind me, yelling and shooting.

Something flicked my knee and I plunged forward and down and dirt filled my mouth and dried my tongue and I was up again running with nothing but darkness in my ears, and you already had the car in motion when I opened the passenger door, which a bullet had perforated just a second before, and the windows burst into crushed ice that bounced off the upholstery and floor mats as our tires rolled on dirt and then asphalt, and behind us now in the vast dark field muzzle flashes continued to bloom like ghostly orange flowers.

You drove fast and in total silence. I was ripping shirts, bandaging my knee. Dark blotches moistened the passenger seat.

On the bare plateau of Castilla-La Mancha, I spotted a turn-off for a rest stop.

"Take that exit."

Under the white fluorescent lights of the men's restroom, I struck you open-handed across the face. At the metal sink, I made you scrub the camouflage paint off. "Stay here."

I limped to the car and limped back with your day bag. I dropped it at your feet.

You ran after me, apologizing, grabbing at my coat.

I did not turn around.

Later, in the January dawn, I pulled over. I screamed and screamed until my throat bled, and my skull rang, and I could no longer weep.

A sign with seven stars on a red square welcomed me to the Comunidad de Madrid. I called Singer.

"I want to tell you before you hear it from someone else. It wasn't clean."

"Hold on," he said. I heard a woman's voice in the background, a toaster popping. A few seconds later a door closed. "What the fuck are you talking about?"

"I need a doctor. And I need to get rid of a car."

When I came up from the anesthesia I was lying on a white-sheeted bed. It had four wheels, with lowered metal rails on each side. My leg was raised, wrapped in white bandages.

A dubbed-over TV show filtered through the wall. I fell back asleep.

"The doctor did a good job," the voice said. "But you're going to need months of physical therapy before you can run again."

The TV was still coming from the next room, and for a moment I wondered why it was in English.

"It must have been adrenaline alone that got you out of there."

My eyes were still closed.

"What happened?"

I turned my head away.

He clapped his hands twice. "I know you're awake."

I breathed in, then out. "I fucked up."

"That's clear." Singer rose from a chair in the corner. "But I asked what happened."

"I miscalculated the first shot. They saw the flash from the second."

"What about your pupil?"

"He wasn't there."

"No? I thought – "

"He left around New Year's. Decided it wasn't for him."

"The policía are in a frenzy. Sancha and the Romanians were part of a ten-month investigation. Now they've got a triple homicide. And your fucking rifle shell casings are sitting in their evidence room." Singer was standing above me. He held a medical record folder.

"They won't find prints on them."

"Maybe not. But they know they came from a third party."

The TV in the next room turned off. He leaned in, his face less than a foot from mine.

"It's messy. Clients will think it's not safe to bring their problems to me anymore."

I couldn't make eye contact.

"When you get out, we'll talk about indemnification." He tucked the sheet under my chin and slipped the folder under my pillow. "I'm leaving these papers with you. The physical therapists will want to see them."

From the doorway, almost as an afterthought, Singer said, "Where did you say your boy went?"

"Home."

He nodded, biting his lip. "That's funny. Because Sancha's men claim they saw two people in the field. And your blood was only on the passenger seat."

Singer refused to wire me the second payment, and made me refund the first to cover the medical expenses. The next project took more than six months to reach me. A man who moved cocaine in Vallecas.

"I want to make sure you understand," Singer said, extinguishing his cigarette in the glass ashtray. "No partners, no pupils."

Then he told me the contract value. It was one-fourth of what I was used to.

"Don't you have anything else?"

"You do dirty work. That's all I can give you."

The years without you passed faster and slower than I could have believed. I continued working with Singer, and even though the projects were small and infrequent, I carried them out more carefully than ever. I had to. I could no longer run.

The physical therapists insisted on the power of a positive attitude, and so I showed them the same optimistic face they showed me. But after six months of special stretches and exercises, my right knee still could not support my full body weight. I continued for another half year, then stopped. I limped; I wore a knee brace under my trousers. In the metro passageways, I was keenly aware of the currents of people overtaking me. On the stairs I climbed as slow as the old men.

I remember some things from the years that you were gone, but there are entire months I cannot account for.

I know that I did not change the sheets and pillowcases until they lost your scent completely, smelling finally of just my own sweat and aloneness. In supermarkets, night outside and the bright white lights inside, I wandered past Tetra Briks of orange juice and milk, past bags of frozen vegetables and paella, feeling like an organ had been scraped out of me, the in-store music making my eyes water.

When I saw men sleeping in ATM vestibules, their heads covered in stained cardboard boxes or sleeping bags, I thought of you. The lives you could have had. Night buses and night trains, you leaving nothing but the grease mark from your hair on the window, like the ghostly bodyprints left by birds when they fly into glass doors. Maybe you returned home, to go to university. But you were ambitious and impatient, gorgeous and young. You must have discovered how valuable you would be to certain men. The countries and oceans they would take you to. Silk bathrobes the color of dried blood, beds you could not touch the edges of. You burned to become something else though. And why you needed to become it, I could not explain. Whenever newspapers ran articles about contract killings, I looked for signs of you.

My income had diminished so much that I was forced to gradually sell off my stocks. The cash-flow problems persisted. In the end, I sold even the finca.

Instead of running, I now swam and did water exercises at a swim club in the Barrio de la Estrella. At night, I rode your motorcycle around the M-30 ring road, and unless I dismounted to buy fuel I would return home without having spoken to a single person. Sometimes, drinking in Chueca, I would meet men and have sex with them in the same night, never learning their last names or saving their phone numbers. There was no reason. And there was no reason to look for anything else. Just as one day in September we realize summer has irrevocably passed, I knew my time with love was over. I no longer had the courage, or the faith.

As a scout sniper in the Gulf War, I was teamed with a spotter who wanted to study astronomy. He pointed out constellations, explained the lifecycles of stars. There are old ones called white dwarfs that continue to give off light billions of years after their cores have collapsed. I had become one of those.

One morning, two years after I abandoned you, I stepped onto the metro. The train car was full of schoolchildren on a field trip. Teachers and monitors stood talking together. While the kids jumped and laughed and screamed and ate snacks and threw things, two boys sat calmly on seats, arms around each other. They were eight or nine years old. Each leaned his head on the other's.

I flew to Switzerland, certain I would find you. For a few days I watched your parents' apartment. Then I rang the buzzer. No one answered. I rang the neighbors'. Your parents had moved back to Croatia, where their Swiss francs could buy a better retirement. I asked about their son. "He left years ago. To study."

Back in Madrid I looked for photographs of you and me together. I realized we had never taken any.

Another year passed.

Yesterday Singer sent me a text message. All it said was: *we need to meet.*

"Your boy's in the city."

My cup clinked on the marble tabletop of the Café Gijón.

"What's he doing?"

"Looking for work."

"What are you talking about?"

"He has references now," Singer said, slipping me some newspaper clippings.

I read them. I swallowed my coffee, the aftertaste like acid. "How do you know? Have you seen him?"

"No."

"Then how do you know?"

"Listen – " his eyes sharpened focus " – I'm telling you as your friend."

"What?"

"You're living in that same flat, right?"

"Yeah."

"He's on his way."

Two hours later I vacated my flat. Carrying a suitcase and duffel bag, I limped down the stairs, pressed the square button to unlock the street door, and stepped onto the sidewalk.

Near my car, three kids were passing a semi-deflated soccer ball. As I was opening the trunk, the ball cannoned into a shop shutter with such a bang that I dropped my keys. The kids laughed. I looked quickly around, and got in.

For a long time I just drove, changing streets and highways at random.

I should have been planning the next move, but all I could think about was you. Your slender knees. The way you instinctively slouched in chairs. Or your hands, black with grease after tuning up your motorcycle. Our summer on Mallorca: eating snails, swimming in coves. In your sleep, you spoke French to ghosts.

And I thought about your kills, the one I saw and the others I read about. The owner of a construction company you visited at a Parisian hospital while recovering from surgery: you delivered balloons and flowers and four bullets to the head and chest. A well-known Athenian businessman: in a traffic jam you simply rolled up beside him on a motorcycle and placed a shopping bag full of explosives on the roof of his Audi. Or the associate-turned-accuser of a British property tycoon whose habitual gardener, ill, would be sending a substitute. Wearing a white boiler suit and latex-fingered gardening gloves, you rang the doorbell, asked a question about the yard, and stabbed him in the heart in front of his grandsons.

That was your style: unpredictable, devil-may-care. The very opposite of what I taught you. And what I was now up against.

Because I knew what you wanted. Cast out as an apprentice, you were coming back as a master. To prove you were better, to take my territory.

I checked into a hotel next to Barajas airport. Planes took off all night long, blinking white and red. All night long I considered boarding one.

The airport hotel. I took long showers, ordered room service. I sat at the glass-topped desk, turning the key card over and over. I knew: if I ran, I would run forever.

"You have to."

"I can't," Singer said, watching the cars pass on the Calle Costa Rica. "Even if I wanted to."

We were sitting in the shade under the maroon awning of a cafe called La Madrileña.

"You don't understand," I said. "The way he works. He's brilliant, a wild card."

"You don't understand. In this sector, word of mouth is everything."

"All you'd have to do is – "

"It's about reputation, trust. I'm neutral, no matter what. That can't change."

"This is different."

"This isn't even business. This is the two of you."

"Singer."

"I'm not getting involved," he said, leaving coins on the circular table and standing up. "You made him, you can unmake him."

I exited the highway and parked in front of my storage unit. I collected the tools I knew I would need, and a few more I hoped I wouldn't.

Back in the airport hotel, I stopped opening the curtains. I slept with the TV on.

"If you're here, that means you've changed your mind."

"I'm here because the game has changed." Singer handed me a copy of the day's paper. "Page sixteen."

We were in the Parque del Retiro, near the railing that enclosed the main pond. On the olive-green water couples floated in rowboats.

I read the article. A Spanish prosecutor and the man suspected of ordering his killing had been found dead within forty-eight hours of each other, each from a single bullet, identical entry points. The man's driver and bodyguard had also lost their lives.

"Your star pupil," Singer said.

"How do you know it was him?"

He slid a cigarette from the pack, lit it.

"It's not his style at all," I said. "Too professional."

"He's gotten better."

"How do you know?"

Singer looked away.

"How do you – "

"Look. Thanks to your boy, I'm in a world of shit."

"You gave him that project?"

He said nothing.

"You're fucking working with him?"

"We discussed the prosecutor."

"I don't – Why were you even talking to him?"

"He asked question after question. Not just about the job, about motives. Next we talked contract value. He walked out, telling me to call him when I had something bigger."

"Then what?"

"Then it made the papers."

"You never paid him?"

"He cut me and my contact out. Went direct to the client."

"How are we going to do this?" I said.

Singer and I were in my apartment. It was night. We stood in the living room in the dark.

He approached the balcony, opened the sliding glass door, and stepped out. The man-sized neon letters of the sign above the Hotel Meliá Madrid Princesa dyed his shirt indigo. For a while he stared at them. Then he lifted the lid off of an empty flower pot.

"Give me a spare set of keys to your flat," he said. "And move into that hotel."

The curtains are drawn in my new hotel room. I am screwing a suppressor onto the barrel of my rifle.

Night falls. I take position at the window. The Hotel Meliá Madrid Princesa looms like a marble matchbox over the Calle Princesa. Two hundred meters from the window I'm sitting at is the balcony of my flat. No lights inside.

Taxis and hatchbacks move down the rain-lacquered asphalt. Going from the hotel to my apartment building, a pedestrian would pass a puti club, a travel agency, a dry cleaner's, a bank, and a Chinese grocer's.

The feet of the bipod rest on the table that I've pushed to the open window. The city's bloodstream is regulated by the changing traffic lights. I look through the night scope.

You're out there somewhere, in that black-and-green maze.

You're coming home.

I make sure the DO NOT DISTURB sign still hangs from the outer door handle. In the bathroom mirror I examine my face. I am balding, in the back. The corners of my hairline have retreated.

I return to the window. The Torre de Madrid, crowned with antennas and satellite dishes, stands white against the dawn.

I fall asleep with my hands folded on my chest, like a person in a casket.

Rain falls across the city like static. In this dark hotel room, the carpet smells of solitude and anonymity. I'm staring through the night scope at the balcony of my apartment. The shot Singer promised I'd get. The shot I've been waiting two nights for.

At daybreak I shower and get into bed, seeds of water still on my skin. Soon, in nearby rooms, the housekeepers will be stripping beds, replacing towels.

As I'm falling asleep, an image enters my mind. You're walking towards me from the other side of a plaza. I'm sitting on a bench smiling. In your hand is a red apple.

South of my hotel rise the dome and bell towers of the Catedral de la Almudena. Searchlights stroke the undersides of the clouds. It will happen tonight. I know.

I put my head under the bathroom faucet. Cold water.

Back at the window, I stare through the night scope. Everything appears in shades of black and green. The centers of your eyes, if I could see them, would glow a demonic jade.

I have measured and re-measured the distance to my balcony. What I focus on now is my breathing. A 7.62-millimeter round rests in the chamber.

When I see the figure on the balcony, at first I don't believe it's you. You squat to lift the lid off the flowerpot. You reach in. Standing back up, you give me a perfect headshot.

All I want is to call it off.

You turn. I squeeze the trigger. You fall into the living room.

I vomit into a leather wastebasket. When I look again, only your feet and lower legs show.

I will have to enter to confirm it.

If I had not hesitated, it would have gone exactly how Singer had planned.

He had contacted you saying he understood what happened. Once the Spanish prosecutor was dead, the man who had ordered it decided to ensure his own safety by having you killed too. You were acting in self-defense.

Singer wanted to meet. He had a potential opportunity.

Leaning across the table, he gripped your forearm. "You pissed me right the fuck off with that stunt. You also impressed me."

You smiled, the pride uncontainable.

"I'm always on the lookout for high-performance contractors. But it's like I explained before. The projects you want all go to someone else. Your former instructor."

You nodded.

"He's reliable. But he can't think on his toes. Not like you."

"He's taking early retirement. I already told you that."

"The difference is, now I'm giving him to you. As a test."

Singer described how it needed to happen. "I've hidden a pistol in an empty flowerpot on his balcony. A Russian piece, untraceable. Use it."

"What if I can do it a better way?" you asked. "A silent way?"

"You want to work with me? Prove you can follow instructions."

In the stairwell I give Singer a missed call, so his team will set out. Then I put on a para-aramid fiber vest and ease open the door to my apartment. It is dark, soundless.

I step in, pistol drawn. In the small entryway, I lean against the wall before glancing around the corner.

Crouching, I move down the hallway.

I can see into part of the living room, but you're not there.

I wait. Nothing.

I adjust my grip, enter the living room.

Ambient light from the street. You are lying facedown. A dark streak leads from where you fell to where you dragged yourself against the wall farthest from the balcony.

I approach you, trembling, pistol aimed.

I wait.

I prod you with my toe.

No reaction.

I train the pistol on your head. You lived here once, and though you were the center of me, you were never mine.

A second before I squeeze the trigger you roll over but I have too much weight on my bad knee and can't jump back and you embed a knife in my groin, nicking the femoral artery. My shot goes wide, and plaster and brick explode around you. I double over and you slap my gun away and with your other hand fire Singer's Russian pistol. The bullet slams into my chest like a battering ram. I fall backwards. You spring on top of me and the pistol is there and the smell of gunpowder and brick dust and blood and I roll and smash your hand against the radiator and the gun clangs and goes skidding across the floor. We struggle weaponless, like serpents or wrestlers, and as the blood wets my leg and crotch something cool and white passes behind my eyes and somehow we end up in the hallway and you're on top of me strangling me and I extract the knife from my groin and work it around and jab it repeatedly into your side. Your hold loosens. You slump forward. Your lips press against my ear.

I drag myself into the living room. I'm reaching up, pulling drawers off their rails and onto the floor. Screws, nails, pliers, and a hammer spill out. I find the extension cord and wind it tightly around the very top of my leg. I tie a knot around the shaft of the hammer and turn that counter-clockwise, tightening more.

Singer's team is almost here. They will arrive in a delivery van, no windows on the sides or back.

I'm lying face-up on the living room floor, my leg elevated on a chair. Behind me, in the hallway, you lie crumpled and motionless. Two people's blood soaks my clothes.

An engine approaches and shuts off. Vehicle doors slam.

On Mallorca there was a cove that we found by accident. A cliff over-looked the transparent water. You climbed the path leading up to the diving point, while I stayed below on the beach. From the ledge you waved once and then dove, gleaming and symmetrical.

You were right. We are time wrapped in flesh. A life can be measured by years or by acts.

Feet collect on the landing. Singer's team will let themselves in. They will carry out the dead.

DAVE HOING
PLAINVIEW

PART TWO: THE BLOOD COOLS

Friday, July 3, 2009

Mike Alexander and his wife Beth joined in singing hymn number 474 from the old green Book of Worship as the Frischel girls followed the casket of their mother up the aisle and out of the church. The girls were hardly girls anymore – Lindsey, the youngest, must be nearing forty by now – but Saint Andrew's Lutheran Church hadn't changed a whit since Mike left town in 1976. In fact, the pew in front of him still bore the marks he'd carved into the wood on his last visit, the now immortalized initials of his special girlfriends at the time, VK72 + LF75 + ML76. Thirty-three years later, no one had replaced the pews, no one had sanded the old wood, and no one, as far as he knew, had taken much notice of his handiwork. All somebody had done was to apply layer after layer of varnish until the etchings were smooth and shallow indentations, barely visible except to those who knew where to look and what to look for.

But then, several of the pews in the back had graffiti of some kind. Kids like him, stupid kids.

When Matt Stigler, the pastor of Mike's youth, had been killed in a car crash two years ago, his daughter Evelyn had taken over his congregation. A female minister. Mike shook his head. Evelyn seemed sincere, but a minister? And so young. *Some* things had changed, and not for the better. The Reverend Evelyn Stigler marched solemnly behind the Frischel girls, fingers wrapped lovingly around her bible.

Beth nudged him while they waited for the usher to come and release their row. "Are we going to the cemetery?" she said.

"I think we should," Mike said. "Lots of old friends to catch up with afterward."

Beth glanced at her watch.

"Got somewhere you need to be?" Mike said.

"In this town?" she said.

Friday, July 3, 2009

Helen Frischel had been laid to rest next to her beloved husband Tom and daughter Leslie. The four surviving sisters had gathered in the old farmhouse, eight miles north of Plainview. Their husbands and kids were in the living room watching the Twins play the Tigers on TV. The suitcases were packed and arranged next to the kitchen door.

It was a cool evening, and Lara had the air off and the windows open. The stench of the Tanners' hog operation up the road drifted in on a light breeze.

"Jesus, how can you stand it?" Lisa said.

"Never used to bother you," Lara said, smiling.

Leigh closed the window. "Do you mind?" she said. "I sort of got un-used to it."

"Dad would have said that's the smell of money," Lara said.

"Maybe that's why I use credit cards," Lindsey said.

The women all laughed and sat down at the kitchen table. Lara brought them coffee. They looked at each other and didn't say anything for a while. The L Train was together again. For reasons never explained, Helen and Tom Frischel had given all five of their daughters names beginning with L. Just liked the sound of L, apparently.

Lara sipped her coffee. Like her, her sisters wore their hair short, as women seemed to do as they approached middle age. Leslie wouldn't have. She was so proud of her long, beautiful hair, that honey color somewhere between brown and blond. Had she lived, Leslie would have kept hers long. And been an artist. Or a singer. Or a CEO.

It was strange being forty-seven and having an older sister who never made it to twenty.

"You look like housewives," Lara said.

"What's your excuse?" Lisa said. She meant no offense by it, and none was taken. Lara had never married, choosing instead to care for their mother after their father's fatal stroke almost twenty years ago.

"Mom said that they would have gotten divorced if Dad hadn't died when he did."

"Those two?" Lindsey said. "Hell would have frozen over first."

Hell *did* freeze over, Lara thought. Leslie's murder had put a terrible strain on the marriage, a terrible strain. It wasn't until after their father's death that their mother had rekindled her love for him. Sadly, she found it easier to love the memory than the man. But in that the Good Lord was kind, for by the time He came for her, her mind was half gone, and she could no longer distinguish one from the other.

"We've talked," Leigh said.

"We're not going to fight you over the house," Lisa said.

"Mom wanted me to sell and split the money between us," Lara said.

"This is your home," Leigh said.

"Keep everything," Lindsey said. "You deserve it."

"All we'd like is a memento or two," Lisa said. "You know, of Mom and Dad."

"Take what you want," Lara said. "I've still got some of Leslie's stuff, too." She smiled wanly. Her sisters were still attractive women, kept their figures, wore their wrinkles well. Not too much makeup, no Botox or boob jobs.

This was probably the last time the L Train would all be together under one roof, until they had to start putting each other into boxes.

Saturday, July 4, 2009

Take away the new cars and modern fashions, and Plainview could be a Polaroid of 1962. Hell, the Motel 6 sign still boasted free color TV. Mike looked out the window of his room as the annual Independence Day parade crawled up Main Street. The high school marching band was wearing the same style of uniform he'd worn when he played trombone with them at halftime of football games in 1973 – and the uniforms even then had been fifteen years out of date. He'd heard that due to declining enrollment in the nineties Plainview High School had merged with Ridgemont's. The new blood certainly hadn't improved the musicians any. They were butchering the school fight song just as badly as the seventy-three band had.

The town may be the same, but the teenagers weren't. Crowds lined the sidewalks to watch the parade. Every boy under twenty had a baseball cap turned sideways on his head, an iPod in his ear, and camouflage pants two sizes too big pulled partway up so that his ass was hanging out. Mike couldn't hear what they were saying, but they probably flashed gang signs at each other and talked ghetto, stupid white kids pretending to be black in a town whose entire population wouldn't fill a Chicago block. Most had tattoos and, he imagined, piercings in places no sharp instrument should ever get near.

And then there were the girls…

Beth came out of the bathroom, topless. "Do my boobs sag?" she said.

Mike stepped away from the window and closed gap in the drapes. "Jesus, Beth," he said. "There are kids right outside."

"Well, do they?"

"You're fifty," he said.

"What's that supposed to mean?"

"It means you look fine, but you're fifty. Everything starts to sag. Who cares?"

Beth put her bra on. "Well, that cheered me right up. So what's so special about Helen Frischel?"

"As a person? Not one thing."

"Then why'd you drag me to the asshole of the universe for her funeral?"

Mike lit up a cigarette and sat on the edge of the bed. "Three girls were killed here in the seventies. Helen was the last of their parents to go, so I came to pay my respects. And while I'm here I thought I'd look up Al Grossman. He was the cop who worked the cases. He and I had some interesting times, I'll tell you. I think he's still alive."

"Killed? As in murdered?"

"Yeah."

"I figured someone running a red light would be big news here."

Mike drew in a long mouthful of smoke. "Used to be." Used to be *any* news was big news, yet in Plainview people barely reacted to Vicky Kajeski's death. Leslie Frischel raised a few eyebrows, but nothing more. It wasn't until Molly Lutz that there was any kind of general alarm, any real police involvement. Even then it wasn't long before Plainview was pretending nothing had happened. Crime might be the norm in big cities, but not here. Here it was an embarrassment. The sooner forgotten, the better.

Beth looked through her suitcase for a White Sox T-shirt. "Who did it?"

"Never caught him," Mike said.

"That's lame," Beth said.

"What do you expect? Grossman was no Sherlock Holmes – "

"I meant your reason for coming to the funeral. You just wanted an excuse to drink beer with your old poontang buddies."

Mike smiled. "I never need an excuse to drink beer."

Beth stood sideways in the bathroom door and evaluated herself in the mirror. She cupped her breasts and pushed them up a few inches. "How do I look?"

"You should probably put some pants on before we go out," Mike said.

Sunday, July 5, 2009

Lara poked her head into the sacristy after the service. Evelyn Stigler smiled at her, as she always did. Like her late father before her, Evelyn had time for everybody. "I see your sisters are still in town," she said.

"Leaving tomorrow," Lara said.

Evelyn hung up her robe, smoothing its wrinkles with the palm of her hand. She was wearing a plain white blouse and black skirt underneath. "What's on your mind?" she said.

"Trouble with God again?"

Lara always had trouble with God. She was a communion assistant who made herself say the right words and think the right thoughts, but there was a God-sized hole in her soul that no title or words or thoughts could fill. "No," she said. "Leslie."

"Ah, then it is about God."

It was true, in a just world no nineteen-year-old girl should die the way Leslie had, but that wasn't the problem today. "It's my sisters," Lara said.

"Your mother's will?"

"Nothing like that."

Evelyn removed the bookmarks from the passages she'd read in her sermon this morning. "Okay," she said, and sat down. "Tell me."

Lara remained standing. "They've never once mentioned Leslie since they got here. They talk about Mom, and some about Dad, and constantly about their husbands and kids, but not one word about Leslie."

"Your mother just died. Of course she would be on their minds." Evelyn patted the chair next to her. When Lara sat, the woman gently squeezed her hands. "Leslie's been gone a long time, Lara."

"But," Lara said, and for Christ's sake she was behaving as if Evelyn hadn't also lost someone, "they don't act as if she never died. They act as if she never lived."

Evelyn touched the sleeve of her blouse to Lara's cheek, drawing up her tears. "Is it so terrible that they left home?"

"I'm happy for them," Lara said. "I am, but..."

"But it never goes away," Evelyn said.

Sunday, July 5, 2009

Dozens of mourners had attended Helen Frischel's committal service on Friday, but today Mike was alone in the cemetery. The weather was finally starting to feel like summer, the temperature approaching ninety. A few people had been here after church, placing flowers on tombstones and talking to loved ones who could not answer, but the afternoon heat had driven them away. Not Mike. He liked hot weather.

Vicky Kajeski's grave was on the other side of the cemetery, but the Frischel and Lutz plots were within a few feet of one another. If he stood back he could see Leslie and Molly's graves at the same time.

Vicky had been his first, an experiment. Then Leslie, more confident but still feeling his way. But Molly, Molly had been perfection. Divine. Mike knelt before her marker. MOLLY LUTZ, NOVEMBER 11 1956—SEP-TEMBER 7 1976, BELOVED DAUGHTER. He ran his hand along the curved edge of the marble. The elements were already starting to take their toll in the form of little dirt-filled chips and cracks.

Mike closed his eyes and remembered, and as he remembered he felt that familiar sense of arousal. It was almost the same, almost. And yet now there was a numbness in him as well, a coldness that flowed through his veins. The sun beat down on his back and head. He caressed the marble, rubbed his face against it. Vicky and Leslie and Molly. Oh, if he could tear off his clothes and perch on the stone, if he could soak up its heat like a reptile, like a lizard, feeling it radiate through him, warming his blood, making him live again, bringing him back to life.

A woman's voice startled him from behind. "Mike Alexander?" she said.

He looked up from Molly's grave and saw Lara Frischel standing before Leslie's and Helen's and Tom's. He hadn't heard her approach. He was crying.

Lara smiled sympathetically. "She was your girlfriend back then, wasn't she?"

Monday, July 6, 2009

The old Holiday Station had been replaced by a Caseys, but the rest of Plainview looked the same, at least along the main drag. The town had no Walmart, no Target, no Wendy's, not even a McDonald's. Main Street was lined with bars, antique stores, and second-hand consignment shops. The Motel 6 stood across from Weissenfluh's Feed and Farm Implements. Just before the bridge crossing the Marengo River, John's Auto Body and Annie's Alterations faced the Emporium, a dilapidated dollar movie house that showed month-old films after they'd run their course in the bigger cities.

Mom's Diner, a fixture since before Mike was born, was as bland as ever on the outside, but its owners had remodeled the inside, adding a single flat screen TV at the front for locals to watch NASCAR or the farm report.

"Christ, they think they're a sports bar," Mike said.

Beth looked out the window and didn't speak. It was raining.

"Help you folks?" a waitress said. She was a doughy, middle-aged woman with bad teeth and reading glasses tucked over the top of her restaurant frock. Last time Mike had seen her she was a seventeen-year-old with a baby and no boyfriend in sight.

"Suzy?" Mike said.

"Just Sue now," she said. "Do I know you?"

Mike introduced himself and Beth.

"We live in Chicago," Beth said.

Sue put her glasses on and squinted at Mike, then shook her head. "If you say so. Remember the name, but..."

"How's your son?" Mike said.

"Which one? Oldest boy's shacked up with some gal over in Ridgemont. She don't want to get married. Youngest one comes and goes, I can't keep track. Kids, you know?"

"Whatever happened to Al Grossman?"

Sue's face brightened. "Chief? He's in a nursing home up in Lake Center. When Emmy passed, he sort of lost interest in police work. In everything, really. They never had no children to look in on him, so one day he just packs a bag and takes off. When I heard he ended up in the home, I started paying him a visit two, three times a year. Cantankerous old bastard still sings 'Suzie Q' every time he sees me. You remember that old song."

"'*I like-a way you walk*,'" Mike sang, playing an air guitar riff between lines, "'*I like-a way you talk* – '"

"Don't you start, too. Your husband's quite the character," she said to Beth.

Beth looked at Mike. She looked at Sue. She looked out the window.

"Think the Chief would mind if I stopped in?" Mike said.

"Can't promise he'll remember you any better than I did," Sue said.

"He at Windsor?"

"That's the only one up there."

"Ought to make it easy, then," Mike said. "You take credit cards?"

"We do, but our machine's broke. Let you write a check, though."

"Couple of burgers and Cokes to go, with fries?"

"*Diet* Coke," Beth said.

"Two number twos coming right up," Sue said, scribbling on her pad.

The drive to Lake Center took forty-five minutes. Beth ate her food and wouldn't speak. Mike tried to make conversation but quickly gave in to Beth's silence. The rain didn't stop. The wind was coming harder now. Thunder and small hail followed, *plink plink plink* on the glass and metal of their Explorer. Just inside the city limits Mike pulled up next to the entrance to the Pamida and gave Beth his Mastercard.

"Pamida?" she said. "*Pamida?*"

"It's like a Woolworth's, only moreso."

"What the hell would I want to buy in this godforsaken place?"

"You could come with me to see Grossman."

"What's he to you, anyway?" Beth snatched the credit card and an umbrella and got out of the SUV. "If you're not back in an hour," she said, "I'm going home with the first good-looking man I see."

"Knock yourself out."

Beth slammed the door and Mike headed back onto Highway 31. He'd been to Lake Center many times in his youth. Compared to Plainview, it was an exotic big city of almost six thousand. He used to sneak up here on weekends when he wanted to do some serious drinking or buy high quality weed he couldn't get from the pimply losers who sold the stuff in Plainview.

It was en route to here in 1972 that he'd picked up Vicky Kajeski hitch-hiking. He was seventeen, she fourteen, if he remembered right. She'd just had a fight with her father.

Windsor was only a few minutes away on Fourth Street Southwest. The building was immaculate, its bricks shiny with a fresh coat of white paint. The lawn surrounding it was a verdant green, but then, for reasons he never understood, grass always looked greener on cloudy, rainy days.

He parked in a spot marked Staff Only and went inside. The nursing station was only too happy to take him to Grossman's room. Other than Sue, Grossman never had visitors. A female orderly in a ridiculously short skirt led him down the hall. Mike was surprised she didn't give the old boys heart attacks wearing an outfit like that.

She knocked on the door to Room 14. "Mister Grossman, you decent?"

"Come look for yourself." The voice was older and thinner but unmistakably Grossman's.

"You have a visitor."

"'*Oh, Suzie Q,'*" he sang.

"Not this time," the girl said. She opened the door and nodded Mike in.

Grossman, clad in pajamas and a robe, was sitting in a wheelchair watching baseball on TV. "Who the hell are you?" he said. A two-hundred-fifty pounder when Mike knew him, Grossman was probably over three now. He still wore his familiar crew cut, but his jowls were more expansive and fixed, the color and texture of paraffin wax.

"You know me, Chief," Mike said. "Mike Alexander. I spent a lot of time in the back of your old Crown Vic."

Grossman stared at him, looked away, then stared again. His eyes hardened. He knew. He *knew*. "You should've done a damn sight more than that. We had your shoeprints on Frischel and blood type on Lutz."

"Yet you didn't arrest me."

"Prosecutor said no. If we'd had DNA then... And now the evidence is lost."

Mike leaned against the door frame and shoved his fists into his pants pockets. "The blood cools, Chief," he said unsteadily. He thought this would be easier. "I own my own construction business. I have a wife and a daughter. I'm a member of the PTA. I give to Saint Jude's. I volunteer at a homeless shelter. I got an award from Mayor Daley once." He looked down at his feet. "I just wanted you to know. The blood cools."

Grossman raised himself out of his chair. "And you think that's enough?"

"Don't you want to know why?"

"Don't talk to me about *why*. If I had my gun I'd shoot you where you stand."

Mike managed a smile. "Justice at last?"

"There isn't any *justice*, you sick fuck. You got to live your life and grow old. Those girls got to be teenagers, and that's it. No, I'd shoot you just because it felt good. But it wouldn't be justice."

Grossman pushed the button to summon an orderly. "What do you want from me?"

"I don't know," Mike said.

"Get out of here," Grossman said.

CRIMEWAVE ELEVEN : GHOSTS
CONTRIBUTORS

DAVE HOING lives with his wife Joni in Waterloo, Iowa. He is the co-author, with Roger Hileman, of historical novel *Hammon Falls*, which was published in June 2010. 'Plainview' is his first attempt at writing a mystery. He'd like to thank his friends Roger Hileman and Carol Kean for providing research and background information for this story.

Inspired by that old adage to write what you know, **NINA ALLAN** decided to do just that, and set 'Wilkolak' in the familiar but not always benign wilderness of South East London. Some readers may be familiar with Nina's short fiction through its appearances in *Crimewave*'s sister magazines *Interzone* and *Black Static*. In spite of a lifelong love and admiration for the work of such mistresses of the psychological thriller as Ruth Rendell and Patricia Highsmith, this is Nina's first ever crime story. As the old adage says, better late than never...

Not long after **CHRISTOPHER FOWLER** wrote 'The Conspirators' it virtually came true when a scandal involving a celebrity and a call-girl broke in Dubai. So much for dark fiction being far-fetched. Chris is the award-winning author of thirty novels and ten story collections, and creator of the popular Bryant & May mysteries. He worked in film for many years and has written for the BBC and various newspapers. He writes regular columns for the *Independent on Sunday*, the *FT*, and *Black Static*. He lives in King's Cross, London.

MIKAL TRIMM's short stories have appeared in numerous venues including *Realms of Fantasy*, *Postscripts*, the *Polyphony* series, and *Ellery*

Queen's Mystery Magazine. He currently wastes time in a small town outside of Austin, Texas. ("Pity, that," he says.)

RICHARD BUTNER writes short stories. He lives in Raleigh, North Carolina, in the United States.

CHERYL WOOD RUGGIERO writes in the Appalachian mountains of southwestern Virginia, USA. Her work has appeared in *The Three-Lobed Burning Eye, Abyss & Apex, AnotheRealm, CALYX, South Carolina Review, The Potomac, The 2River View, Pebble Lake Review,* and *Wolf Moon Journal,* among others, and is forthcoming in *The Dawntreader, Luna Station Quarterly, Cezanne's Carrot, Bewildering Stories,* and the anthology *Shelter of Daylight.* Her poetry chapbook *Old Woman at the Warm Spring* is due out from Finishing Line Press in February 2011.

ILSA J. BICK is a child psychiatrist and an award-winning, best-selling author of short stories and novels. She has published extensively in the *Star Trek, BattleTech* and *MechWarrior: Dark Age* universes, as well as original science fiction, fantasy and mystery. 'The Key', a supernatural murder-mystery about the Holocaust and reincarnation, was named "distinguished" in *The Best American Mystery Stories 2005* (edited by Joyce Carol Oates); a novelette-length sequel, 'Second Sight', has just been released in *Crime Spells* (edited by Martin H. Greenberg & Loren L. Coleman). Forthcoming are two young adult novels, in hardcover, from Carolrhoda Books: *The Draw,* a paranormal mystery which also made the semifinals of the 2009 Amazon Breakthrough Novel; and *The Sin Eater's Confession,* revolving around the murder of a gay high school student in a small Wisconsin town.

CODY GOODFELLOW's recent weird crime fiction has appeared in *Thuglit, Bare Bone* and *Creepy,* and the anthologies *Mighty Unclean, The Bleeding Edge* and *The Bizarro Starter Kit (Purple).* His latest novel, *Perfect Union,* and a collection of short fiction, *Silent Weapons For Quiet Wars,* are available now from Swallowdown Press. He lives in Los Angeles, which he says is a crime against nature.

O'NEIL DE NOUX has published seven novels, seven collections, and over two hundred short stories. After his home was seriously damaged by Hurricane Katrina, O'Neil and his wife resettled on the north shore of Lake Pontchartrain and he returned to law enforcement with the Southeastern Louisiana University Police Department. In September 2009, O'Neil received an Artist Services Career Advancement Award from the Louisiana Division of the Arts for work on his forthcoming historical novel set during The Battle of New Orleans.

STEVE RASNIC TEM's first two novels, *Excavation* and *The Book of Days*, have been re-released as ebooks from crossroadpress.com. His novella 'Among the Old' is a February release from Delirium Books. His stories have recently appeared in *Asimov's*, *Black Static*, *Postscripts*, *Visitations*, the *Black Book of Horror*, and *Null Immortalis*.

ALISON J. LITTLEWOOD lives in West Yorkshire, where she hoards books, dreams dreams and writes short fiction – mainly in the dark fantasy and horror genres. She is also currently working on a novel. Alison has contributed to *Black Static*, *Murky Depths*, *Dark Horizons*, *Not One Of Us* and the *Never Again* anthology, among other titles.

JOEL LANE's recent publications include a collection of short stories, *The Terrible Changes*; a novella, 'The Witnesses are Gone'; a chapbook, *Black Country*; and a collection of poems, *The Autumn Myth*. He recently co-edited (with Allyson Bird) an anthology of anti-fascist and anti-racist stories in the weird and speculative fiction genres, *Never Again*. 'The Hostess' is one of an ongoing series of weird crime stories that will be collected together in the near future.

LUKE SHOLER was nominated for the Edgar Allan Poe Award for his story 'Imitate the Sun', which first appeared in *Ellery Queen's Mystery Magazine* and was subsequently anthologised in the collection *The Adventure of the Missing Detective* and *19 of the Year's Finest Crime & Mystery Stories*. Other stories of his have also been published in *Eureka Literary Magazine* and *Crimewave*. In 2005 he won the literary contest at the University of Texas at Austin and was the featured poet of *Analecta*, their official literary and art journal. After earning a bachelor's degree in English Literature from the University of Arizona, he later took a master's in Marketing from the Universidad Complutense de Madrid. He has lived and worked in Spain since 2002.